TRIANGLE CLASSICS

ILLUMINATING THE GAY AND LESBIAN EXPERIENCE

And the Band Played On
by Randy Shilts

The Autobiography of Alice B. Toklas
by Gertrude Stein

The Beebo Brinker Chronicles
by Ann Bannon

Bertram Cope's Year
by Henry Blake Fuller

A Boy's Own Story/
The Beautiful Room Is Empty
by Edmund White

Brideshead Revisited
by Evelyn Waugh

The Celluloid Closet
by Vito Russo

City of Night
by John Rechy

Dancer from the Dance
by Andrew Holleran

Death in Venice
and Seven Other Stories
by Thomas Mann

Family Dancing
by David Leavitt

The Family of Max Desir
by Robert Ferro

Giovanni's Room
by James Baldwin

The Lure
by Felice Picano

The Naked Civil Servant/How to Become a Virgin/
Resident Alien
by Quentin Crisp

Nightwood/Ladies Almanack
by Djuna Barnes

Olivia
by Olivia

Oranges Are Not the Only Fruit
by Jeanette Winterson

Orlando
by Virginia Woolf

The Picture of Dorian Gray
by Oscar Wilde

The Price of Salt
by Patricia Highsmith

Rubyfruit Jungle
by Rita Mae Brown

A Single Man
by Christopher Isherwood

Skinflick/Gravedigger/Nightwork
by Joseph Hansen

The Sophie Horowitz Story/Girls, Visions and Everything/
After Dolores
by Sarah Schulman

Surpassing the Love of Men
by Lillian Faderman

The Well of Loneliness
by Radclyffe Hall

What Is Found There/An Atlas of the Difficult World/
The Fact of a Doorframe
by Adrienne Rich

Zami/Sister Outsider/Undersong
by Audre Lorde

SKINFLICK

GRAVEDIGGER

NIGHTWORK

SKINFLICK

GRAVEDIGGER

NIGHTWORK

JOSEPH HANSEN

QUALITY PAPERBACK BOOK CLUB
NEW YORK

SKINFLICK

*In memory of Doctor Dreadful
who left too soon*

He parked in sunglare on a steep narrow street whose cracked white cement was seamed with tar. The tar glistened and looked runny. He sat a minute longer in the icy draft from the dashboard vents. They'd been blowing since he got into the car twenty minutes ago, but the back of his shirt was soaked with sweat. And it was only ten in the morning. Los Angeles didn't get like this often. He hated it when it did. And this time it was holding on. It had been brutal at the cemetery three weeks ago. His father's nine widows had looked ready to drop. The savage light had leached the color from the flowers. The savage heat had got at the mound of earth from the grave even under its staring green blanket of fake grass. He'd stayed to watch the workmen fill the grave. The earth was dry. Even the sharp walls of the grave were dry. What the hell was he doing remembering that? He switched off the engine, grabbed his jacket, got out of the car.

The door fell shut behind him. In the oven air, he flapped into the jacket. He crossed the street. The house stared at him blind and sunstruck over oleanders. The curtains were drawn. The garage doors were down. The lots were hard to build on here. House front and garage front were only a step back from the street. On the short uptilt of driveway in front of the garage doors the tape the police had put down to mark where a dead body had lain had been pulled up. But adhesive from the tape had stayed on the cement, and summer dust and street grit had stuck to it and renewed the outline in grime. Tire tracks crossed it but there were no other stains. Gerald Ross Dawson hadn't bled. He'd died of a broken neck.

Cypresses crowded the front door, cobwebby, untrimmed. He groped behind them till his fingers found a bellpush. He pressed it and inside quiet chimes went off. Dave knew the four notes. Sometime in his early teens, without quite understanding why, he had dogged the steps of a handsome boy addicted to Pentecostal meetings. The Dawson doorbell chimes picked out the start of a gospel chorus, "Love Lifted Me." No one came to the door. He let the second hand go around the face of his watch once and pushed the button again. Again the notes played. Again no one came. He tilted his head. Did he smell smoke?

A path went along the front of the house, cement flagstones, the moss on them gone yellow and brittle in the heat. Arm raised to fend off overgrown oleanders, he followed the path. At the house corner, it turned into cement steps with ivy creeping across them. He climbed the steps, sure now that he did smell smoke. At the top of the steps, in a patio where azaleas grew in tubs and where redwood furniture held dead leaves, a dark, stocky boy of around eighteen was burning magazines in a brick barbecue. He wore Levi's and that was all. The iron grill was off the pit and leaned at the boy's bare feet. He acted impatient, jabbing with an iron poker at the glossy pages blackening and curling in flames the daylight made almost invisible.

He was half turned away from Dave. He was a furry kid, fur on his arms, even on his feet. A magazine was in his hand. He kept starting to toss it into the pit, then drawing it back. He wiped sweat

2

off his face with his arm and Dave saw the title of the magazine
—*Frisco Nymphets.* The color photo was of three little girls, aged
maybe ten, without any clothes on. The boy poked savagely at the
flames, making a small sound that reached Dave like whimpering.
The boy flapped the magazine in a kind of frantic indecision, then
dropped it into the flames. Dave could feel their heat from here.
He didn't want to go closer but he did.

"Good morning," he said.

The boy whirled, mouth open, eyes wide. The poker fell out of
his hand and clattered on the charred brick edge of the pit. Without
taking his scared gaze from Dave, he groped out behind him to try
to cover the magazines with his hands. That wasn't going to work.
He backed up and sat on the magazines. One slid away, off the
barbecue surround, onto the patio flags. *Six-to-Niners.* The naked
female children on this one held yellow ducklings. The boy
snatched it up and threw it into the fire. The flames choked out and
sour smoke billowed around them. Dave coughed, waved hands in
front of his face, and backed off, jarring a thigh against a redwood
table.

"Come over here," he said.

"What is it?" the boy gasped. "Who are you?"

"My name is Brandstetter." Dave handed the kid a card. "I'm
an insurance investigator. It's about Gerald Ross Dawson,
deceased. I came to see Mrs. Dawson."

"She's not here." The boy coughed and wiped his eyes with his
fingers. He frowned at the card in the smoke. His brows were thick
and black and grew straight across without a break. "She went to
the funeral home. Some women came from the church. They went
to see my dad."

"You're Gerald Dawson, Junior, then—right?"

"Bucky," he said. "Nobody calls me Gerald Dawson Junior."

"Were you cold?" Dave asked. "Did you run out of briquettes?"

"I don't understand you," Bucky said.

"That's funny fuel. Where did you get those?"

3

"I found them in—" But Bucky changed his mind about that answer. "They're mine. I'm ashamed of them. I wanted to get rid of them. Now was the first chance I had."

"Magazines like that cost a lot of money," Dave said. "How many were there—ten, a dozen? That's fifty, sixty dollars, maybe more. You were lucky to get that kind of allowance. Your father must have thought a lot of you."

"And look how I repaid him," Bucky said.

"You can only use so many Bibles," Dave said. "But shops that sell these don't cater to kids. It must have been hard to get them. Doesn't that count?"

"Not now." Bucky shook his head. "I hate them." Tears were in his eyes and not from the smoke this time. The smoke was trying to drift off. "He was so good. I'm such a sinner."

"Don't make too much of it," Dave said. "Everybody has to be eighteen sometime. When's your mother coming back?"

"Don't tell her I was doing this," Bucky said.

"I only ask questions," Dave said.

"The police already asked them all," Bucky said. "Why do you want to start it over again? It's too late. Everything's too late. They even kept his body downtown ten days." He turned sharply away, trying to hide that he was crying. He went back to the barbecue and poked blindly at the smoldering paper. Smoke huffed up again. He blew at it, making a wet sound because of the crying. Small flames licked up. "They're finally going to let us give him his funeral tomorrow. Can't you just leave us alone?"

"Where was he the night he was killed?" Dave asked.

"I don't deserve to be called by his name," Bucky said. "He never did anything dirty in his life. Look at these. I'm always dirty. I pray and pray"—he jabbed at the flaming magazines, outraged, despairing—"but I can't be clean. Look at me." He turned suddenly, flinging out his arms. Flakes of pale ash had caught in the black wool of his chest and belly. "Covered with hair. Anybody can see what I am. An animal."

4

"Genes," Dave said. "Did he often stay out all night?"

"What?" The boy blinked. His arms lowered slowly. It was as if Dave had wakened him from sleepwalking. "No. Never. Why would he? Sometimes he was late. But that was church work."

"Do you know what kind?" Dave said.

"This neighborhood"—Bucky began shredding up a magazine and wadding the shreds and throwing them hard into the flames —"isn't a fit place for Christians to live. It isn't a fit place to bring up children. Stuff goes on in that park there isn't even any name for. Have you seen those smut shops, those pervert bars, the movies they show? Filthy." He ripped at the magazine. "Filthy places, filthy people. Burn!" he yelled to the fire. "Burn, burn!"

"He was trying to clean it up?" Dave said.

Bucky went guarded and sulky. "I don't know. You know where he was. The police found stuff on his clothes. He'd been where there were horses. He'd made an enemy of Lon Tooker."

"Keyhole Bookshop," Dave said.

"Right. And he's got horses where he lives, in Topanga Canyon. That's why they arrested him. Don't you know anything?"

"I read the police report," Dave said. "That's why I'm here. It doesn't satisfy me."

"You? What difference does that make?"

"Fifty thousand dollars' difference," Dave said.

Under the soot that smeared his face, he turned a pasty color. "You mean you could hold back his life insurance? That's to put me through college. That's to keep my mom. She can't work. She's handicapped."

"I don't want to hold it back," Dave said, "but a couple of things are wrong and I have to find out why."

"The only thing that's wrong is he's dead," Bucky said. The tears came back. "How could God do that? He was God's servant. He was doing God's will."

"Lon Tooker was in his shop till midnight."

The fur boy scoffed. "The creep who works for him says. Any-

5

body who'd work in a place like that—what would they care about lying?"

"The shop hours are posted on the door," Dave said. "Noon till midnight weekdays. And if he kept those hours, then he couldn't have been home to his horses till two or after. Topanga's a long drive from here."

"What's that mean?" Bucky began shredding another magazine. "My mom didn't find my dad's body till she went out to get the *Times* in the morning."

"But the medical examiner says he died between ten P.M. and midnight."

"I got home at midnight," Bucky said, "from basketball practice at the church. He wasn't there. I would have seen him." Another wad of glossy paper went into the fire. For a second, a naked fifth-grader looked seductively over a skinny shoulder at Dave, then blackened and vanished. "Lieutenant Barker says the medical examiner could be wrong."

" 'Could be' doesn't mean 'is,' " Dave said.

"He got home, got out of the car to unlock the garage, and Lon Tooker jumped him," Bucky said. "The stuff from the horses rubbed off Tooker onto him."

"Nifty," Dave said. "Did you hear the struggle? Where do you sleep?"

Bucky jerked his head at corner windows. "There. I didn't hear anything. I was tired. I slept hard." He ripped at another set of pages. "Anyway, what kind of struggle do you think there was? Tooker got him from behind and snapped his neck. You learn how to do that in the Marines. Tooker was a Marine in World War II."

"It looks easy in the movies," Dave said.

"It happened," Bucky said.

"Tooker would have to be fifty-five," Dave said. "Your father was ten years younger."

"He didn't know anything about fighting," Bucky said. He poked at the burnt paper and big loose fragments sailed up through

6

the heat like sick bats. They settled up above on the ivy-covered slope. "He was a Christian."

"Not a soldier of the Lord?" Dave said.

"Are you laughing at him?" Bucky turned with the poker in his hand. "What are you? An atheist or a Jew or something? Is that why you don't want my mom and me to have his insurance money? Because we're born again?"

"If he was trying to open the garage door," Dave said, "where were his keys? They weren't in his pocket. They weren't on the ground."

"Tooker must have taken them," Bucky said.

"He was searched," Dave said. "So was his shop. His home. His car. They didn't find those keys."

Bucky shrugged and turned back to jab at the fire. "Tooker threw them away someplace. What good would they be to him?"

"Exactly," Dave said. "So why take them at all?"

"Why don't you get off my case?" Bucky said. "Don't you think we've got enough trouble, my mom and me, without you coming around and—" Down on the street, a car door slammed. The poker clanked again. Bucky turned pasty again. He stared alarm at Dave. "There's my mom, now. Oh, look, listen—don't tell her about the magazines. Please."

"Maybe you should quit for now," Dave said. "Put them away. Wait for another chance."

"If you don't say anything"—Bucky retrieved the poker—"it'll be okay. She won't come up here. It's too hard."

"Then I'll go down there," Dave said.

The smoke hung caustic in the slanting street. No wind stirred to take it away. It kept crawling down the hillside. It lodged in the shrubbery. A tall, wide-hipped woman came out of the garage where a tan Aspen showed an I FOUND IT bumper sticker. The woman dragged her right foot; a cane hung over her arm. She wore a new tan double-knit pantsuit over a new cocoa-color synthetic shirt. She'd had her hair done. It was iron gray. Effortfully she

7

stretched up for the garage door and dragged it down, clumsily shifting aside just in time for it to miss her. She turned toward Dave and stopped. An eyelid drooped. So did a corner of her mouth. But she got her words out sharply.

"Who are you? What do you want?"

He went to her, spoke his name, handed her his card. "When a policyholder dies by misadventure, we investigate."

"Where's my son?" She looked up. "What's that smoke?"

"He's burning trash," Dave said. "I've talked to him."

"He's only a child," she said. "You had no right."

"I'm not a police officer," Dave said.

"What did you talk to him about? What did he say?"

"That he thinks Lon Tooker killed his father," Dave said. Across the street, window-fastenings snapped. French doors opened beyond shaggy treetops. "Maybe it would be better if we talked inside."

"There's nothing to talk about," she said. "The police have arrested the man. I guess that means the district attorney must have been satisfied he was the right one. Why is it unusual that Bucky should think so?"

"It's not unusual," Dave said. She had to be close to sixty. It wasn't just that a stroke had left her half paralyzed. Flesh sagged loose beneath her jaw. Her skin was a web of wrinkles. There were liver spots on her hands. Gerald Dawson had married a woman almost old enough to be his mother. Bucky had been a last-chance baby. He said, "But it's too easy."

She gave her head a shake that made the loose lip quiver. "There's nothing easy about it. Everything about it is hard. Death is hard. Loss is hard. Even for Christians, Mr."—she glanced at the card—"Brandstetter. God sends these things to test us. But knowing that doesn't make the tests any easier to bear." She narrowed the eye whose lid she could control. "What are you doing here? You haven't brought a check from the insurance company. Have you brought another test?"

8

"Where was he that night, Mrs. Dawson?"

"On the Lord's business," she said. "I don't know the particulars."

"Who would know? Someone at the church?"

She started toward the door, using the cane, dragging the foot. "They've already said not. Maybe Reverend Shumate." Keys rattled in her free hand. She clutched at a cypress to haul herself up the short doorstep. She poked the key at the door. "It seems very hard that he should have been killed, going about his Father's business."

Dave said, "At the bank, his statements show he wrote a couple of large checks lately. Do you know why? Are his canceled checks here?"

"At his office," she said. "The girl there paid all the bills. It was simpler." The door swung inward. There was a breath of lemon-scented furniture polish.

Dave asked: "Why did he have birth-control pills in his pocket?"

She stopped moving, hand on the door latch. Slowly, painfully, she turned. She twisted her mouth in a wince of disbelief. "What? What did you say?"

"Among the items the police found in your husband's pockets —wallet, credit cards, the usual—was an envelope from a pharmacy on the Sunset Strip. And in the envelope was a folder of birth-control pills. The prescription was written to Mrs. Gerald Dawson. Would that be right?"

"The Sunset Strip." It was only six or eight miles west, across town. But she said it blankly, the way she might name someplace in Afghanistan. Then she didn't say anything more. She simply kept her gaze on Dave's face. She seemed stunned.

He said, "The doctor's name is Encey. Is he your doctor?"

Her face twitched. "What? Encey?" Then suddenly answers chattered out of her. "Dr. Encey." She nodded. "Yes, yes, of course he's my doctor. That's right. The pills," she said. "Yes, of course. Gerald promised to pick them up for me. I'd forgotten. In all the terrible things that happened, I'd forgotten about the pills."

"I can understand that," Dave said.

"I have a headache," she said. "It's this dreadful heat. Excuse me."

And the living half of her dragged the dead half inside and shut the door.

He dropped out of the expensive Hillcrest neighborhood down twisting streets past old apartment courts where doors were enameled bright colors and sported new brass knockers, where windbells hung in the trees, and where lissome young men in swim trunks clipped hedges or soaped down little sports cars at the curbs. Then, another level lower, he passed rickety wood-frame houses in need of paint, where radios blared mariachi music through rusty window screens, and little brown Mexican kids swarmed in yards where no grass grew.

He braked the Electra at Sunset for a red light. Across the broad curving stream of traffic lay the park with the little lake, the ducks in the rushes, the muggers in the bushes, the sunburned tourists rowing battered little skiffs and peering through Instamatics at the glass skyscrapers beyond the tops of palms. When the light turned green, he swung left, making for Bethel Evangelical Church. But he changed his mind because the door of Lon Tooker's shop hung open under a red-and-white tin sign, KEYHOLE BOOKS. It took a while to find a tilted street he could swing into and back up out of, but at least there was no parking problem. Except for a corner Mexican grocery, the rest of the flat-roof one-story brown-brick store buildings along this stretch held businesses that flourished only after dark.

The carpet inside Tooker's place was thick enough to make it dangerous for anybody with weak ankles. It was gold color. Flocked gold-color wallpaper rose above the bookshelves. Gold-color paint was new on a ceiling from which hung fake crystal chandeliers. Plastic-wrapped magazines lay back at forty-five-degree angles on low shelves. The color printing was sharp but the subjects were monotonous. Spread legs, lace underwear, girls lifting massive breasts while they leered and coaxed. Or youths displaying bulky penises. No little girls. But then, this wasn't all the stock. A few feet farther on, stairs carried the thick, gold carpet upward between frail wrought-iron railings. Thumps seemed to be coming from there. Dave went up.

Fake fur covered deep square chairs. On wood-grain Formica coffee tables glistened green bubble-glass ashtrays. Here the shelves were packed—except for those already stripped by the youngster with knobby elbows who was dumping magazines, big picture books, and paperbacks into cartons. He was sweating so hard his shoulder-length blond hair looked as if he'd just brought it out of a swimming pool. He didn't wear a shirt. Pimples the size of boils flamed across his coat-hanger shoulders. He winced at Dave for a second before turning away again for more books.

"Ah, Christ, did she leave that door open? Look, dad, we're closed."

"Forever?" Dave asked.

"You got it." The boy dumped a stack of magazines into a carton and worked at the carton flaps, tucking one under another, to keep it shut. "No more Keyhole Books."

"Not even a going-out-of-business sale?"

"Mort Weiskopf over on Western's taking the stock."

"What's the hurry?" Dave dropped into one of the fur chairs. "Money for lawyers?"

The skinny boy hitched at his pants. "What do you know about it? Where do you come from?"

"The company that insured Gerald Dawson's life."

"Yeah, the money's for lawyers. That son of a bitch goes right on making trouble even when he's dead. You know he came in here with a bunch of potbelly bastards from that church one night and tossed the place? Threw books all over. Dumped paint on the rugs."

"That was the time to get the lawyer," Dave said.

"We couldn't prove who it was. They wore masks. I mean, we knew but the lawyer said they had alibis—they got this club at the church, right? They were all there. On their fat knees. Praying. For us sinners."

"It could have been six other people," Dave said.

"Except Dawson was yapping orders," the kid said. "Quoting the Bible. Sodom and What's-its-name? All that shit. It had to be Dawson. Nobody else had a voice like that. High and gravelly, and cracking all the time."

"But the lawyer said you couldn't get him?"

"Dash, across the street, tried it." The kid grunted, squatting, heaping up magazines. "The guy who owns the Oh Boy! Lives halfway up the hill. Sees a funny light outside in the middle of the night. Comes out. His VW is on fire. Sitting there in his driveway. On fire all over. He knew it was Dawson and his vigilantes. But no, they were having a meeting, singing hymns. Shit." He heaved tottering to his feet under a load of coated paper and dropped the load into another carton. "And the cops don't care, you know? Fag-bar owner's car burns up. That's funny. To them that's funny, right?"

A young woman in a man's white shirt that she'd tied under her breasts, and in very small white shorts, stopped at the head of the stairs. She was honey color.

13

"We're closed for business," she said. She tried to lift the carton the kid had closed, squatting for it, trying to rise up. "Jesus. What's inside—bricks? We're not taking the building, are we?"

The skinny kid didn't look at her. "You want the cartons half full, say so."

"I don't want them at all," she said. "This is Lonny's idea. He gets so panicky."

"They lock you up for murder," the kid said, "it's probably hard to stay calm. Are you going to load the car or not? You want me to carry, you fill the cartons?"

She picked up the carton without seeming effort. Her thighs were boyish and hard-muscled. "If he didn't buy horses, he wouldn't need money." She turned with the carton and saw Dave again. "You look like you could afford a couple of overpriced palominos. How about half a dozen? Come on, beautiful. It's for a good cause."

"The seat's too high off the ground," Dave said. He got up. "Here. I'll carry that." She started to protest and he told her, "It's for a good cause, right?" Her car was two doors off in a weedy vacant lot between brick walls spray-painted with street-gang graffiti. The car was one of those eighteen-thousand-dollar Mercedes sports models with the roof that dips. The trunk space was limited. She was going to have to make a lot of trips to Western. "The kid says Dawson is the vigilante chief."

"We all say so," she said, "but we can't prove it. The straights went after the vigilantes when they ripped down the bushes in the park. Pensioners. Housewives with kiddies. They ruined their park to keep the fags out of the shrubbery at two in the morning. At two in the morning, who cares what's in the shrubbery? And they couldn't nail them. So what can us pre-verts and smut peddlers expect?" She slammed down the trunk lid.

"Did your friend Lonny take the short route?"

She stared. Her eyes were flecked with gold. "What does that mean?"

"Get fed up waiting for justice?" Dave said. "Eliminate Dawson before Dawson eliminated him? Replacing that kind of carpeting could run into money if you had to do it very often."

"You know what kind of a man Lonny Tooker is? The kind of a man that sets broken bird's wings."

"Hitler loved dogs and babies," Dave said.

"He's a big, strong guy. He could kill anything alive with his bare hands. A bull, an elephant."

Dave put a hand over her mouth. "You didn't say that."

Her eyes widened. "Oh God. No. I didn't say it. What I meant was—he's gentle. A big, soft gentle dreamer. A lover. He loves everything that moves and breathes. He's dumb as hell but he wouldn't hurt anybody, let alone kill." She looked at her watch. "Come on. I have to hurry."

Dave trotted after her. It was too hot for that but he did it anyway, shedding his jacket as he ran. At the top of the stairs, he asked the skinny kid, "Was Dawson in here the night he was killed?"

"Nobody was in. It was a dead night. About five stragglers. But nobody was here after ten. Just Lon and me. We played gin."

"Who won?" Dave laid his coat on the stair rail.

"I can answer that." The girl had another carton and was half-way down the steps with it. "Lon won. He wins any game you win by getting low points."

"She's right," the skinny kid said. He patted stacks of paperbacks inside a carton. He stood, and treated himself to a look at a magazine, flapping the sleek, flesh-tone pages over, but not, Dave thought, really seeing the tangles of bodies in the photographs. The kid slapped the magazine shut and tossed it into a carton at his feet. He reached for the cigarette Dave had lighted. Dave passed it to him. The kid blew the smoke out appreciatively. He took another deep inhalation and handed the cigarette back. "You know," he said, "those creeps are hypocrites, you know?" He tipped his head, frowning. "Is that the right word? Anyway—what I mean—they

15

cream themselves over this crap. They pretend it shocks them, but you can see from the way they lick their lips, they're practically coming in their pants."

"What kind of masks?" Dave asked.

"Ski masks. I kid you not. They were drooling. They want to look at this stuff like anybody. Only they didn't have the nerve to walk in and ask for it and pay for it and like that. Oh, no. They toss the place, wreck it, make out all they want is Lon to get out of the neighborhood, see?"

"I don't know," Dave said. "Do I?"

"Sure you do. We put the stock back on the shelves. And guess what? Some magazines are missing." The kid snorted a cynical little laugh and reached for Dave's cigarette again. "Somebody couldn't control theirself."

"Pictures of little girls," Dave said.

The kid squinted. "Yeah. How did you know?"

"Just a wild guess," Dave said.

"Not all real little," the kid said. "Up to about twelve or something. Creepy, though—right? I mean, acting like they're Mister Clean?" He looked at the cigarette. "You want the rest of this?" Dave shook his head. The kid sucked in smoke and let it out with a question. "What do they do—pass them around at those prayer meetings of theirs?"

"Did Lonny kill Dawson?" Dave asked.

"Over ten bucks' worth of magazines wholesale?" The kid bent and stubbed out the cigarette in an ashtray. "Forget it."

"Over trying to wreck his business," Dave said.

"You don't know Lon. All he wants is to play his guitar and ride his horses."

"Does he come to work in the clothes he rides in?"

"No way. Never. Always right out of the shower, always neat and, what do you say, crisp? You smell horse in here? Never. Look, he's stupid, but sweet stupid, okay? Not mean stupid. You should hear the songs he writes. They make 'Feelings' sound like a Nazi

16

march or something. And what he never wants is trouble. Not with anybody."

"He picked a troublesome business," Dave said.

"To help people feel good nobody cares about."

"A kindly philosopher," Dave said.

"Yeah, well, the money's not that bad. And Lon hates to worry about money. It gives him headaches."

The girl called from below, "Car's loaded. I'm off."

"Don't drive under any trucks," the kid called.

"Did Lon go home that night?" Dave asked.

"If you had something like her waiting for you"—the kid jerked his lank-haired head at the stairs—"where else would you go?"

"She wasn't there," Dave said. "According to the police report, Karen Shiflett didn't reach Tooker's Topanga Canyon place until morning. She'd been with a sick brother at a hospital all night."

"He's a hype. He tried to OD. Yeah."

"So there's no proof Lon didn't kill Dawson."

"He set himself up," the kid said glumly. "Asshole. He should never have called the cops after that raid and told them it was Dawson."

"He couldn't foresee Dawson would be murdered."

"He could stop believing in uniforms," the kid said.

3

Bethel Evangelical Church was a clumsy hulk on a backstreet corner. From outside, the stained-glass windows looked muddy. The structure was old frame, and the dazzling new white paint that covered the shiplap siding didn't hide that the lines were all off kilter. What didn't lean sagged, and what didn't sag bulged. Pigeons waddled in and out of latticework high on a bulky steeple. They made pigeon noises. Dave came down the off-line cement steps he'd climbed to a pair of brightly varnished doors that wouldn't open. He winced up at the pigeons. Then he walked a strip of new cement along a sun-hot side of the building to another set of steps that went up to a door.

It was marked OFFICE and he opened it and stepped into cool air that smelled of mice and mildew. The place had stood empty and neglected for too long, but now new paint was in here too, a sprayed fiber soundproof ceiling. The same sort of deep carpet covered this floor as the floor at Lon Tooker's sex shop, only here it was holy blue. Wood-grain Formica made the desk in front of him glossy. It held a white pushbutton phone. Beside the desk was a sleek electric typewriter. Slick-paper color pamphlets on alcoholism, abortion, divorce, narcotics, stood in a plastic rack.

Behind the desk, a closed door had a brown plastic tag on it incised in white, PASTOR'S STUDY. He knocked on the door. Silence. A third door faced the one he'd come in. He opened it and was on the platform of the church auditorium. There was a square pulpit. Back of a railing were blue-plush theater seats for the choir. Organ pipes went up, the new gilt on them looking crusty. On the carpeting, plastic buckets waited, filled with cut flowers. For the funeral tomorrow of Gerald Dawson? He turned around. Out in the stained-glass dimness, varnished pews ranked a half acre of newly carpeted flooring. The emptiness was big.

His father's widows would have liked it. The tiny, crowded mortuary chapel hadn't let them sit far enough apart in their gloves and veils. None of them had dared fail to show; attorneys, executors, were there as witnesses. Absence would have conveyed indifference to the millions in cash and shares Carl Brandstetter hadn't been able to take with him. To have claimed not to know of his death wouldn't have convinced anyone. A long obit had appeared with his Viking-handsome picture in a weekday *Times* business section, recounting his single-handed building of one of the nation's life-insurance giants, Medallion. A Sunday *Times* article had focused on his splashy not-so-private life. His death from a heart attack while driving his Bentley on a two A.M. freeway was on every TV newscast.

Dave pictured the widows scattered in the jammed pews. One had stood through the ceremony, at the rear, beside a fake twelfth-century baptismal font. Evelyn, if he remembered rightly. The stepmothers of his childhood were clear enough in his mind, whether he wanted them there or not. The later ones blurred. Most had been buxom blonds in their twenties who'd run to fat on their alimony payments, waiting for this funeral, when Dave had seen them together for the first and only time. But three or four, like the latest and last, Amanda, were dark. One of these, nineteen, his own age at the time, he'd almost fallen in love with. Lisa.

When she'd taken his hand in her small gloved one between flowering shrubs outside the mortuary doors, and turned up to him big doe eyes that didn't glow anymore, it was as if he saw her on old movie film, faded, scratchy. Her voice hardly reached him, and then it sounded ugly, guttural, all the long-ago romance of the foreign accent now scrap. Lines marred the beautiful bones and shadows of her face. She'd been slim and soft. She'd become scraggy. They'd tried reminiscing—this ballet with Eglevsky, that Heifetz concert at Hollywood Bowl—but not for long. His father's ashes weren't the only ones in that damp, fern-murky little chapel. Ah, the hell with it.

"Hello!" he shouted. To no one.

Outside, at the rear of the church, where the sun hammered an almost empty blacktop parking lot, he found a set of steps down into an areaway. The door at their foot opened into a hallway of small meeting rooms with steel folding chairs, now and then a piano, little red chairs, a hamster rustling in a box with a wired front. A sound reached him from double doors at the end of the hall. Loud slaps. They were swing doors. He pushed through them and was in a gymnasium where a tall man of maybe forty, jacket off but still wearing his tie, was dribbling a basketball, pivoting, shooting. Dark sweat patches were under his arms and down his spine. He saw Dave and let the ball ricochet off the backboard and bounce to the other end of the court where long church-supper tables with folded-up legs leaned against the wall. The man came at a lanky jog to shake Dave's hand. He panted. He mopped his face with a handkerchief.

"Tuesday morning ordinarily nobody comes," he said, "nobody phones. I sneak down here to see whether it's come back or not. I had it in high school. I got a college scholarship on it—Wheaton, Illinois. But by the time the term started in the fall, I'd lost it."

20

"You probably grew," Dave said. "It happens."

The tall man compressed his mouth and shook his head. "I don't know. Eye-hand coordination, whatever—it was gone, simply gone. I was frantic. I worked. I prayed. It never came back." He laughed at himself. "In my secret dreams, one of these days I'll come down here and it will be back the way it was." He raised a warning finger and his grin was a kid's. " 'Call no man a fool,' " he said.

"All right." Dave watched him pick up a seersucker jacket that matched his trousers. "My name's Brandstetter. I'm investigating the death of Gerald Dawson. For Sequoia Life and Indemnity." He almost said Medallion, a twenty-five-year habit. But the morning after his father's death, he'd cleared out his handsome office high up in Medallion's glass-and-steel tower on Wilshire. This was his first free-lance assignment. "The police don't seem sure of where he was the night he was murdered. That bothers me."

"I don't know, myself," the tall man said.

"You're the minister here?" Dave said.

"Lyle Shumate," the tall man said. Jacket over his arm, he headed for the double doors. "We're going to miss Jerry Dawson. A born leader. True Christian."

"He had a men's group." Dave followed the preacher. "They didn't meet that night?"

"Their meetings were frequent but not regular." Shumate went into the kindergarten room under pink and blue crepe-paper streamers and crouched to squint at the hamster. It came out of a heap of wood shavings and looked at him, bright-eyed. It was chewing. Shumate touched a bottle hung on the wire of the cage. There was water in it. "You're okay, my friend," he said, and stood.

"The Born-Again Men," Dave said.

"They'd get together by telephone," Shumate said, "and set a time." He pulled open the outside door. Heat and glare struck in. He let Dave go out before him and pulled the door shut. "But they

21

didn't meet that night." His soles went gritty up the steps. "Some of our kids have a gospel rock group. They used the Born-Again Men's room that night." He climbed to the door marked OFFICE and again motioned Dave through it ahead of him. "It must have been noisy in the basement that night."

"Basketball practice too," Dave said.

"You know about that?" Shumate said.

"But you weren't here," Dave said. "You can't tell me whether Bucky Dawson practiced with the team."

"If he says so, he did." Shumate went into PASTOR'S STUDY, sat behind a desk that didn't look busy, and waved Dave to a chair upholstered in nubby blue-and-orange tweed to match the curtains and carpet.

"It's a team that works hard," Dave said. "According to Bucky, they didn't quit till almost midnight."

"We lost the playoffs last year to the Nazarenes from Arcadia," Shumate said. "We don't want that to happen again. If Bucky told you they worked till midnight, they worked till midnight. He's the straightest boy I know. Intelligent, well-balanced, decent. We all look up to Bucky—youngsters and grownups alike."

"He acted troubled when I saw him," Dave said. "A lot of torment about sex."

"What?" Shumate stared, mouth working at a smile of disbelief. "We can't be talking about the same boy. I've heard Bucky on the subject—no one could be better informed and clearer headed. He talks to youth groups all the time. Sex, narcotics, abortion, alcoholism. All those matters the church used to stick its head in the sand about when you and I were kids. It's a different world. Those things have to be faced squarely and honestly today and dealt with."

"And Bucky Dawson faces them squarely and honestly and deals with them?" Dave said.

"And helps other youngsters to do so." Shumate nodded. Then

he frowned and sat forward. "You're not trying to say that Bucky was somehow mixed up in his father's murder."

"Not if he was here playing basketball," Dave said. "The medical examiner says his father was killed between ten and midnight. And I've got a problem with that. Bucky didn't find the body when he got home. His mother found it in the morning. Now, look, Reverend—"

"Call me Lyle," Shumate said.

"The police checked with the other men in Dawson's group, and they each told the same story. They didn't meet that night. They didn't go out on one of their vigilante forays—"

"Vigilante forays?" Shumate's face went stiff.

"You've heard about them. Harassing the customers going in and out of the massage parlors, the gay bars? Ripping out the shrubbery in the park? Setting fire to Dash Plummer's automobile? Throwing books around at Lon Tooker's place, pouring paint on the carpets?"

"There's no proof of any of that," Shumate said.

"No legal proof, no," Dave said. "But you're not a lawyer or a judge. You're a minister."

"The law has fallen into Godless hands in our country," Shumate said. "It protects evildoers. Decent people haven't a chance. I'm talking about human law. But there's a higher law—God's law."

"And Dawson and his raiders carried out that law—right? And they didn't see anything wrong with lying to the police about their activities, covering up for each other, because the police are trapped in a corrupt system, isn't that it?"

"I don't know about that," Shumate said stubbornly. "I never heard it from Jerry or any of his group or from anyone else in this church. Only from outsiders, barging in here with wild charges, people totally depraved, every one of them."

Dave gave him a one-cornered smile. "I didn't think See-No-

23

Evil, Hear-No-Evil, Speak-No-Evil were Christians," he said. "I thought they were monkeys."

"You and I both know where the evil is in this neighborhood," Shumate said, "and it's not in Bethel Church."

"Did Dawson have a high-pitched, gravelly voice?"

Shumate blinked. "You could describe it like that."

"Easy to mistake for anyone else's voice?" Dave asked.

"You couldn't miss it," Shumate admitted. "Why?"

"He captained the raid on Lon Tooker's shop," Dave said. "Six men. Masked. They all claimed afterward they were downstairs here, praying. Now—if they lied to the police that time, they could have lied to them about Dawson's whereabouts on the night he was killed. Now, I'm asking you—did they have some action planned for that night?"

"And I'm telling you," Shumate said, "I don't know. If Tooker believed Jerry Dawson raided his shop, then why doesn't that suggest to you what it suggests to the police—that Tooker killed him?"

"For one thing, the raid took place ten days before Dawson's death. Why would Tooker wait?"

"Maybe Jerry went there that night?"

"A witness says no. And Dawson didn't see relatives that night. He didn't see friends. He didn't come here to the church. He wasn't at his business. Where was he? Whom did he see and for what reason?"

"His life was an open book," Shumate said. "I knew the man almost as well as I know myself. He was uncomplicated, straightforward. He had a successful business, gave God the credit, contributed generously to this church—and not just in money; in works, good works of all kinds."

"He was around here a lot," Dave said. "All right, then tell me this—did you notice anything out of the ordinary about him before he was killed? Was there any change in him? Did he make any out-of-the-way remarks? Was he—?"

24

"Hold it." Shumate frowned, pressing his temples with his fingertips, eyes shut. "There was something. Yup. I'd forgotten about it." He gave Dave a look that was half smile, half frown. "You must get high marks in your job, Mr. Brandstetter."

"I've been at it a long time," Dave said. "You're about to break the Dawson case wide open, are you?"

Shumate laughed. "I don't think so. But it did seem a little odd at the time, a little out of character. It was after Sunday-morning service. In the parking lot. I went around there, wheeling an elderly parishioner in his chair. He only gets out on Sunday. It cheers him up to have a man to talk to for a few minutes. He's surrounded at home by a wife and three daughters. And after he was in the car and I was putting the wheelchair into the trunk, I noticed Jerry Dawson in a far corner of the lot talking to a big young fellow in a cowboy hat, cowboy boots."

"A stranger," Dave said.

"I'd never seen him before. He had been inside for the service, though, way up in the balcony at the back. He was noticeable because he has a beard." Shumate smiled faintly. "Like an Old Testament prophet. And bright blue eyes. Black beard, black brows, blue eyes."

"You didn't hear what they were talking about?"

"No, but I think they were quarreling. The boy swung away angrily. He slammed the door of his truck. It was one of those outsize pickup trucks, with big, thick tires. Some sort of machinery in the back. He burned rubber leaving that parking lot. But that wasn't all that was unusual. Jerry Dawson looked as if he'd seen a ghost. I waved to him, since he'd noticed me watching. But he didn't speak or wave back. He just walked off to his car."

"And he didn't bring the matter up to you later?"

"There was no later," Shumate said. "In two days' time, he was dead."

"No idea who the bearded kid was?"

"Dawson's business is renting and leasing film equipment. You know that, I suppose. Quite often Christian filmmakers come to him. He's known for giving them discounts. Since this young fellow sat through the service, I thought his connection to Jerry might be that. He could have been an actor." Shumate shrugged. "Director? I don't know. It's hard to judge people by their appearance anymore."

"His partner might know." Dave stood up. "Thanks for your time." Shumate rose and they shook hands. Dave went to the door, opened it, and turned back. "One more thing. Did he make any extra donations lately?"

"No." Shumate cocked an eyebrow. "Why do you ask?"

"In the last two months, his bank records show he wrote a check for seven hundred dollars and another for three hundred fifty. Not part of his banking pattern."

Shumate scratched an ear. "I don't know," he said.

4

Dave parked in a lot with the laughable name Security half a block below Hollywood Boulevard. Smells of onion, garlic, Parmesan, were thick in the hot air because the kitchen door of Romano's stood open. The old brick had been painted white. Iron barred the windows. He walked out the alley to the street front where the windows had cute green shutters and boxes of geraniums. He paused under a striped sidewalk canopy, thought about a drink, changed his mind. He passed a house-plant boutique, a jazz club with black shutters, a staircase door marked with the names of dentists, a place that hired out tuxedos, and came to the wide plate-glass front of SUPERSTAR RENTALS CINE & SOUND.

Inside, red camera cranes reached for a ceiling hung with spotlights large and small, round and square. Dollies squatted on thick wheels on a broad floor of vinyl tiles. Microphone booms glittered. There were movieolas, tape recorders, portable and immovable; there was equipment he couldn't put a name to. Cables and cords snaked underfoot. Long-haired youths in bib overalls and straggly moustaches explored the chrome-plated undergrowth. A pale girl in a wrinkled floor-length dress and sandals clutched a clipboard and checked items off a list with a felt pen. All of them whined and neffed at each other and at a resigned, rumpled, obliging bald man who led them to this corner and that, and kept rummaging out for them this scruffy substitute, that battered one. Dave asked him:

"Jack Fullbright?"

"Office," the bald man said, and jerked a thumb at a door beyond a glass counter filled with lenses and microphones on velvet. To reach the door, Dave had to step over a stack of empty thirty-five-millimeter reels. Then he was in a long room where more equipment stood around under weak fluorescent light gathering dust, or lay on steel shelves gathering dust. The aisle between the shelves was made narrow by strapped black wooden cases made for toting film onto and off of jets. Stickers on the boxes showed they'd been to Japan, India, and Beirut, to Spain and Iraq and Yugoslavia. Stacks of film cans also narrowed the aisle, and stacks of brown fiberboard boxes for mailing film reels.

At the end of the aisle a glass box of light was labeled OFFICE. He opened the door and typewriter chatter met him. A young woman who looked like most of the young women on the fronts of magazines these days stopped typing and gave him a smile that by the tiny lines it made in her sun-gilt skin said she wasn't going to be young a lot longer. The wrinkles in the J. C. Penney cheap-rack granny dress of the girl out front had come from sleeping in it. The wrinkles in the loose, unbleached cotton top this young woman wore had cost her the way the trendiest fashions always cost. Her hair was an artfully uncombed tumble of frizz. It was the color of the lenses of her big glasses—amber. Except that in the lenses, the amber turned smoky toward the top. Her voice was warm and jaunty.

"You don't want to rent anything," she said. "You've got everything—right?"

"I'm missing facts." Dave laid a card in front of her. "I need to see Jack Fullbright, please."

She read the card and her face straightened. She looked up gravely. "About poor Jerry? There's nothing wrong with his life insurance, is there? There couldn't be. I paid his premiums. The bills came here. I paid them with the rest."

"It's not that," Dave said. "It's his death that's got something wrong with it."

"Everything," she said. "He was a fine man."

"His personal accounts came here," Dave said. "You paid all his bills for him—household, and so on?"

"That's right." She tilted her head, frowning. "I don't understand, do I? I mean, it says here you're an investigator. Death claims. What does that mean?"

"Nothing, if you go out quietly in your bed," Dave said. "If you end up the way poor Jerry did, somebody like me comes around to look into why and how. Is Jack Fullbright in, please?"

"Oh, I'm sorry." She glanced at the telephone on her desk. "He's on overseas with London. A shipment got lost. A crew on their way to the north of Norway for a documentary about Lapps or reindeer or moss or something. What do you bet the equipment's in Rio? Luckily, we didn't ship it—they did. Now they want replacements by air freight—at no extra charge."

Dave looked at the glowing button on the phone. "How long can it take?"

"Till Jack wins," she said. "Look—the police already investigated. That lovely tough man with the big shoulders and the broken nose. Lieutenant what?"

"Barker," Dave said. "Ken Barker."

"He seemed to know his job," she said. "Do you always go around checking up on him?"

"He's overworked," Dave said. "He can give any one case only so much time. Los Angeles is big on people killing each other. Happens every day. Sometimes twice. He has to keep moving on to the next one. I don't." Dave glanced behind him. Against a wall of combed plywood, tacked with typed price lists and with calendars big on the phone numbers of sales representatives and freight haulers and small on dates, stood two chairs with split Naugahyde seats. They were heaped with *American Cinematographer* and *Stereo Review* magazines. "Which means I can wait." He set one of the stacks on the floor, sat down, lit a cigarette with a slim steel lighter, and smiled at her. "All right with you?"

"Maybe I can help," she said. "I hope I don't look it, but I'm the man of all work."

"I've been to his bank," Dave said. "The computer printouts puzzle me. I need to see his canceled checks."

"Oh." She gave a little doubtful shake to her head. "I guess I couldn't authorize that, could I?"

"Who is Mrs. Dawson's doctor?" Dave said.

"Dr. Spiegelberg. Irwin. Out near USC."

"She didn't change lately? To a Dr. Encey, out near UCLA?"

She blinked surprise. "Not that I know of. Maybe the bill just hasn't come yet. Did you ask her?"

"I don't believe her," Dave said.

"Oh, my!" Her eyebrows went up. "What kind of nasty, suspicious mind have we here? Not believe Mildred Dawson?"

Dave looked for an ashtray. "When she tells me he gave her a prescription for birth-control pills?"

"Ha!" She had a fine big laugh. "You're kidding. Just flick the ashes on the floor. It's fireproof."

"Where did he keep the girl friend?" Dave asked.

"Girl—" She looked genuinely shocked. "Oh, no, my dear, gorgeous Mr."—she peered through the amber lenses at his card— "Brandstetter, baby. Absolutely not. Never in a million years, love."

Dave shrugged. "His wife's half paralyzed. She's a lot older than he was."

"You don't know Jerry Dawson. There was an obsessively religious man. I'm not talking about Sunday. I'm talking about Monday, Tuesday, Wednesday, Thursday, Friday, Saturday, *and*

Sunday. You better believe it. As for sex—the subject just plain didn't exist." She gave a crooked little remembering smile. "I mean, there was a man who could genuinely blush when a woman said 'damn' in his presence. Definitely up-tight aw-shucks down-home." She gave a little ironic laugh. "A girl friend! Wonderful."

"Who?" A fortyish man who looked harried came out of an inner office. He baked himself a lot by swimming pools. His shirt was open to the navel on a body he plainly worked hard to keep looking young, flat-bellied, chisel-chested. He wore tight linen slacks. A little silver chain circled a throat not quite but almost stringy. He had a blond frontier moustache and blow-dryer hair that looked as if he'd been running his fingers through it. He came to a stop and looked at Dave through big silver-rim dark glasses. "Who are you? I'm Jack Fullbright." He came on, holding out a brown, long-fingered hand.

"Brandstetter." Dave got up and took the hand. It was sweaty but the grip was firm. Fullbright's smile showed big white teeth too even not to have been capped. "I'm an investigator for Gerald Dawson's insurance company. I've got a few questions. Can you give me a little time?"

"Sure, sure." Fullbright tilted his head at the office door. "Go right in. Pour yourself a drink. I'll be right there." He bent over the poodle-haired girl, spreading rumpled carbon copies of shipping manifests on her desk. "We'll split the air fare. This is what they need, absolute minimum. Get it off by Emery as soon as Rog can collect and pack it, right? I'll talk to him about the overtime —don't worry. Meantime, get SeaLanes to put out a tracer from San Pedro. They're already doing that from Southampton. Got it?"

"You're going to split the charges?"

"Not till SeaLanes makes it up to us. Good baby." He came into a room that didn't look as if it bore any relation to the girl's office. There was a lot of real paneling and genuine cowhide. Where there was no sense in there being a window, since outside were only trash cans and parking lots, stood an eighteenth-century Japanese folding screen—or a good reproduction. People in small boats admiring a moon above piny mountains. The bar that Fullbright went behind wasn't Formica—it was honest-to-God teak. "Hey, sorry to keep you waiting." He rattled Swedish crystal and a bottle of Schweppes from a refrigerator he had to stoop to. Ice cubes fell out of his hands into the glasses as in a conjuring trick. He waved a green bottle. Tanqueray. "Gin and tonic all right with you? I mean, I've got Heineken's here."

"Gin and tonic is fine," Dave said. "Thanks."

Fullbright poured. "What's wrong about Jerry? I thought the police had the case taped. He tried to put a local, friendly pornographer out of business, and the local friendly put him out of business instead. No?"

"You don't sound moved," Dave said.

"He knew this operation." Fullbright dropped sprigs of mint on top of the ice and bubbles in the glasses. "He handled money well." Fullbright came from behind the bar, handed a glass to Dave, and sat down at his desk. "But he was a sanctimonious pain in the ass."

"His wife and your secretary tell me his canceled checks are here," Dave said. "Can I see them? He wrote a couple in the last few weeks that need explaining."

"Why? To whom?" Fullbright looked wary.

"To me. Nobody knows where he was that night. That bothers me. I think something was going on in his life besides this business, that church, and his family."

"He was out with his 'Keep Our City Clean for Christ' squad." Fullbright shrugged disgust and drank. "Ripping up the seats of X-rated movie houses and castrating faggots. Saving our children, as the orange-juice lady says."

"I don't think so," Dave said. "The checks?"

"Have you got the right?" Fullbright set down his drink and reached for his phone. "I better check with our lawyer."

"As long as I go on thinking," Dave said, "that Lon Tooker

didn't kill Gerald Dawson but that maybe Mildred did, or Bucky, Sequoia Life and Indemnity is going to keep the fifty thousand dollars Dawson meant for them to have. Have you got something against them?"

Fullbright was staring. "Mildred? Bucky? You think they killed him?"

"For reasons that would make you laugh or cry if I named them to you," Dave said. "Let's clear up my sordid imaginings, shall we? Show me the checks."

Fullbright's hand was on the phone but his suntan had turned a little yellow. He let the phone go and stood up. "Come on," he said without expression, and went out of the office, across the plywood room where the secretary was pointing out things on the shipping manifests to the bald man, and into another office where a big film poster featuring a hilltop crucifixion against a stormy sky was framed above a desk coated with dust. Fullbright pulled open the top drawer of a green metal file cabinet. "In here." He gave Dave a sour glance and started out of the room. "Help yourself."

"Leave the door open," Dave said.

Fullbright left the door open. He didn't go back to his office. He went with the bald man into the storeroom.

The checks were in the envelopes the bank had mailed them in. The bundles for each month were wrapped in blue and white statement sheets. The one for seven hundred dollars and the one for three hundred fifty were both written to a Sylvia Katzman. The rubber stamps on the back in red said hers was a Proctor Bank account, Westwood branch. Dave put the checks back and shut the file drawer.

"Thanks," he said to the secretary.

She was talking into her phone. She waved a ball-point pen at him without looking up.

In the storeroom, the bald man was on his knees, working up a sweat, grappling with some heavy piece of equipment on a lower shelf. Fullbright stood over him, reading the crumpled manifest in his hand. Dave asked him:

"Did Dawson have a young customer with a black beard who drove a big pickup truck, machinery in the back?"

"If he did," Fullbright grunted, "I never saw him."

"Thanks," Dave said.

5

At the dark little bar, he used Max Romano's phone to reach Mel
Fleischer at Proctor Bank headquarters. And to find Amanda
where he feared he'd find her, moping around that big, beautiful,
blank house in Beverly Glen, needing somebody to get her off dead
center. He'd failed before. This time she said she'd come. She came.
She stood blinded in the shadowy restaurant after the savagery of
the street glare, swaying a little, afraid to take a step. She too wore
one of those wrinkled, blowsy, loose-woven cotton tops over knickers and knee boots. From her shoulder hung a straw bag that
matched the floppy sun hat on her dark, wing-smooth hair. Max,
bald and pudgy, arm loaded with menus, waddled to her and spoke
to her, probably gentle words about Carl Brandstetter's death. And
she saw Dave and came on, doing her best to smile. It was going
to take more practice. Dave got off his stool to move the next one
for her.

"You look great," he said.

"I feel forlorn," she said. "I hate it when people go away and
don't come back." The bartender raised eyebrows at her and she

nodded at Dave's drink. "But what right have I got to mourn to you? I have only a year's worth of memories to ache over. You've got a lifetime's."

"You couldn't help it," he said. "Nobody could. It was going to happen and it happened. You're young. Start over."

"I keep walking in circles," she said, "like something sad in a zoo. Only sadder."

"No. You've got the key. Open the cage. Go."

"Where?" Bleakly she rummaged in the straw bag. Cigarettes came out, the thin, long, brown kind. She set one in her mouth and pushed the pack at Dave. He took one and lit hers and his with the thin steel lighter. "At least when I'm home, I see him, I hear him. This room, that room, out by the pool. I hear that laugh of his. He makes a loud ghost."

"You can turn into a ghost yourself that way," Dave said. He watched the bartender set a glass in front of her. He took the ticket. "I know. I went through it a couple of years ago. Till I got out of the house we'd shared, I couldn't function. Even after I found somebody alive and he came in and rattled around in the kitchen and slept in the bed with me, it was no good."

"Doug?" she said. And answered her own question with a nod. "Yes, Doug. And now he never knows where you are when I ring you up." She tasted the drink.

"He never knew where I was before," Dave said.

"You're breaking up," she said. "And you're 'no longer with us' when I call your office at Medallion."

"I got out of there before they threw me out," he said. "With no time to spare. Walking through that tenth floor the day after he died was like swimming through a school of great white sharks. Vice presidents."

She peered at him. "You're joking. Aren't you? I mean, why? Why would they throw you out?"

"Bad employment risk." He tilted up his glass and let the ice rattle against his mouth. "Untrustworthy."

36

"But you were there for years!" she protested.

"Forever," he said. "Shall we eat?"

In drum chairs upholstered in black crushed velvet at a table where a candle flickered in a tubby amber chimney, she laid down the big, floppy menu. "Don't you own stock? I thought Carl said—"

"Enough so I won't starve," he said, "but not fifty-one percent." He put on shell-rim half-moon glasses to read the menu and wondered if the cold salmon was fresh. "Not enough to control policy. Carl had the fifty-one percent. But it won't stay in a block. Not now. The widows will get it. Sorry."

"Not this one," she said. "A house worth conservatively a quarter of a million dollars, and two expensive automobiles. One. The Bentley was totaled. He didn't leave them the shares."

"They'll get them in court," Dave said. "That's the kind of lady he married. Present company excepted. And Lisa, possibly. And probably Helena—she already owns two hundred racehorses and half Ventura County." He laid aside the menu, took off the reading glasses, and tucked them into his pocket. "The stuffed flounder is reliable."

"I'll have the stuffed flounder, then," she said. "You come here a lot, don't you?"

"Since Max had a full head of hair," Dave said. "Nineteen forty-eight. That would be well before you were born." He looked around. "Maybe I'll stop, now. One ghost too many, I think."

"We were here one night with that police lieutenant. Mr. Barker. He said you were the best in the business. How could they fire you?"

"He's a friend of mine," Dave said.

"Carl said so too." She swallowed some of her drink. "And I've read clippings. *Newsweek. The New York Times Magazine. People.*"

"Dear God," Dave said. "Did he keep clippings? The sentimental old bastard. I never knew that."

"He thought the world of you," she said.

"Please stop," he said. And Max touched his shoulder and set a French boudoir telephone on the table and crouched with a grunt to plug it in. Dave picked up the receiver, looking *excuse me* at Amanda. In his ear, Mel Fleischer said, "Sylvia Katzman lives in one of thirty-eight units she owns up above the Sunset Strip." He read off the address. "How's Doug? Gallery beginning to pay its way?" Doug sold pictures, sculpture, and pottery on Robertson where everyone else sold antiques. Mel Fleischer collected California painters of the twenties and thirties. He owned more Millard Sheets pictures than anyone else. Mel said, "Has he tracked down that Redmond for me, yet? It's a grisaille of eucalyptus trees by a pond. Some detective-story writer owned it who died. Is the will out of probate yet?"

"You've got me," Dave said. "Doug doesn't talk to me a whole hell of a lot. He talks French to a Polynesian princess called Christian Jacques who runs a restaurant across from the gallery. If you can't reach him at home, try the Bamboo Raft."

"Oh, is that how it is?" Mel said. "Listen, I was so sorry to hear about your father."

"Thanks," Dave said. "Look, I want to buy you dinner for this. Tonight? Tomorrow?"

"Tomorrow. And can it be for two?" Mel asked. "And Japanese? I mean, who can stand all that vinegar and raw fish? But there's this adorable boy who can't seem to stop creeping into my rickety old couch of pain. And wherever I go, I glance over my stooped and aged shoulder, and there he is, with longing in his almond eyes. Of course, I'm going to wake up and it will all be a dream. He's all of twenty-two. Can you feature it?"

"Bring him along," Dave said.

"He wears happy coats," Mel said. "You know, the short ones that come about to here? 'Happy' is hardly the word. Would you accept 'hysterical'?"

"In your case, yes," Dave said. "Make it Noguchi's on Sawtelle

Boulevard. That's just above Venice. About eight o'clock? And, hey—thanks for Sylvia Katzman."

"I have a feeling she won't thank me," Mel said.

"I won't mention your name," Dave said. "That way, she can't send you poison-pen letters from Tehachapi."

"Bless you," Mel said. "See you tomorrow night."

Dave hung up. He said to Amanda, "Clippings don't mean a damn to vice presidents. They can't read."

"What you're saying is," she said, "that they always wanted you out, but they couldn't do anything about it while Carl was alive."

"He warned me," Dave said. "There's an annual prize given to the biggest fag-haters. The front-runners are always the same—police departments large and small; governments federal, state, and local; the Florida orange-juice crowd; the army, navy, and marines; homosexuals themselves; and insurance companies. Only the last two are not sucker bets. And the insurance companies always win. Everything."

"Like the Las Vegas casinos?" she said.

"Penny-ante stuff," Dave said. "The casinos have to play fair. Who ever heard of an insurance company playing fair? When they don't like the odds, they cancel out."

"You're strange." She blinked through the cigarette smoke that curled lazily around the candle chimney. "Why did you stay in the business if you hate it so? Because of Carl? It was all right if it was him doing it?"

"My part was to play straight in a vicious game," he said. "I liked it. I still do. That's why I'm not quitting. I'm one of the lucky people getting paid to do what I love to do. Almost no one manages that in this life. Oh, I'd rather have written a good string quartet. I couldn't write even a bad string quartet."

A waiter in a black velvet jacket took their orders.

"I'm not good at anything," Amanda said.

"You decorated that house," Dave said. "They had it in *Home* magazine. Why don't you set up shop on Rodeo? Better still why don't you decorate my new place for me? As of day before yesterday, it's all mine, the bank says."

"You make me dizzy," she said.

"Not so dizzy as walking around in circles feeling sorry for yourself," Dave said. "We'll go there after lunch. All right? Get ready for a challenge."

"You're working," she said. "You mustn't feel you have to give me occupational therapy."

"Gerald Dawson isn't going to get any deader," Dave said. "And his wife and son aren't going to run away. If I were them I would but they won't."

"What kind of place have you found?" she asked.

"I think the former owner was a wolf in a grandmother's nightcap," Dave said.

He took three wrong turnings up shaggy Laurel Canyon before he found the right one. He'd only been twice before. And his mind was on Jack Fullbright. When Dave had gone back out to the sizzling parking lot, he'd seen Fullbright loading a cardboard carton full of files into the hatchback of a flame-painted Datsun 260Z. What for? Was it regular? Fullbright's clothes, suntan, manner, car, didn't belong to the image of a man who took the office home with him. Didn't the police case file on the Dawson murder say Fullbright lived on a power launch at the marina? But how had Dave put the wind up him? By asking to see into the files? Which meant to Fullbright he might ask again? So Fullbright removed what he didn't want seen? What? Why?

The road was called Horseshoe Canyon and it was steep and only one car wide, and the blacktop was gray with age and had potholes that were almost craters. The Electra lurched and scraped bottom, climbing. Back of him, he saw in his mirrors Amanda's Bugatti managing the climb nimbly as a spider. The Electra was so long it was hard to get it to turn in at the wrecked driveway that

40

dropped down to the house, which crouched, all weathered brown shingles, under ragged pines and eucalyptus. Actually it was three buildings joined by roofs. He got out of the Electra. Amanda got out of the Bugatti and said:

"Yes, well—you'll want gardeners right away, won't you?" She crunched across shed needles, leaves, peeled bark. "French doors all the way across. That's nice."

"You ain't seen nothin' yet," Dave said, and led her around to the courtyard, where a wide-spreading old live oak sheltered paving whose square red tiles had sunk and tilted and made treacherous footing. A broad, heavy door, squared off in glass panes, opened onto a single wood-walled room crossed by big beams under a pitched roof. "Thirty-six feet by twenty-two feet. How about that?"

"It's glorious," she said. But she frowned at the fieldstone fireplace at the end. "That's a bit stingy, isn't it? And the materials are wrong. And it's the wrong shape. What do you say to something about this wide"—she stretched her arms—"with a raised hearth? Secondhand brick, no?"

"I don't have to say anything," Dave said. "You say."

She cocked her head at him, and her little smile said she couldn't quite believe her luck. She shrugged, took off the hat, and pirouetted slowly, looking the room over. "It's so California," she said. She rubbed a circle in the dust of a windowpane to see out. She said, "You don't want to cut all those marvelous trees. They're so right for the place. It's John Muir, isn't it, John Burroughs, Joaquin Miller?"

"With smog," he said.

She ignored that, took steps backward, frowning up, nibbling her lip. "But they do make it dark. What do you say to clerestory windows above the French doors?"

"Raise the roof, kid," he said. "The shop on Rodeo was a good idea. You spend other people's money with grace and abandon. They'll love you in Beverly Hills."

41

She blinked at him. "Those tainted shares?"

"Hey," he said. "Do it. Start today. Only first, come look at the cookhouse."

But an engine roared outside. Amanda turned again to peer through the glass. "You've got visitors," she said.

They went back out to the cars. A tow truck tilted backward down off the potholed trail. A leathery man in greasy coveralls was squatting to fasten the winch hook under the back of the Electra. When he saw Dave, he took a folded paper out of his breast pocket and handed it to him. "Brandstetter?" he said.

"Right. But I didn't call you."

"It's Medallion Life Insurance." The voice belonged to a boy with yellow rag-doll hair in the cab of the wrecker. "It's a company car. You don't work for them anymore. They want their car back."

Amanda stared at Dave. He grinned.

"You're not going to believe this," he said, "but I honest to Christ forgot. This is the twelfth or thirteenth one. It got to be a habit. I haven't driven a car that belonged to me in my entire life." He laughed and lifted a hand to the tow-truck man. "Take her away, friend."

"You want to get anything out of it?" the man said.

"No, but you want the keys, right?" Dave handed them to him. "There's a ball-point pen and a pad of paper with nothing on it in the glove compartment. A rag to wipe the windshield. And an operator's manual. Medallion is welcome to them."

"But what will you do?" Amanda cried.

"Get you to drive me down out of here," Dave said. "Once you've got your list of things to do to the house ready. Then you can help me pick a car I can get into this driveway."

6

The Triumph kept trying to run out from under him. His foot was going to have to learn new gentleness or he would end up on the moon. He left it in a parking lot bulldozed out of hillside back of a row of stucco store buildings, record shops, places to eat and drink, second floors filled with talent agencies and ex-UCLA film students claiming to be producers. The parking lot was filled with vans and Porsches and Lotuses, paid for by dreary fathers in Des Moines and Kansas City with more love or desperation than common sense. It was a quiet, empty time on the sidewalk that passed the shops. A black youth sat on a curb, elbows on knees, hands clutching his head, talking softly to himself. A girl in a T-shirt stenciled COWGIRLS NEED LOVE TOO went past with a canvas guitar case. She wore denim short shorts and tooled boots. A trio of twelve-year-olds of one sex or another came out of a shop, each carrying a *Grease* album, and wobbled away down the sidewalk on ten-speed bicycles.

Nobody much was in the drugstore. There were long shiny aisles of toys and cosmetics, headache remedies and cold medicines, paperback books and bath towels, drinking glasses and electric can openers. A box of wax crayons lay in the aisle he took, broken open, strewn. With a red one a little fist had traced FUK on the glossy floor covering. Bernard Shaw would have liked the spelling. Dave crouched and dropped the crayons back into the box, shut the box, laid it back with the dozen yellow-orange boxes just like it.

The next section of the aisle was lined on one side with rakes, hoes, trowels, with flower pots plain and glazed, with bright little growing plants in green metal racks, and on the other with bags of plant food and fertilizer and peat moss. Motor-oil cans were stacked at the end of the aisle. And he was facing a white counter with a sign above it in gold cutout letters—PRESCRIPTIONS. A gray-haired man bent his head over something beyond glass panes. Dave tapped a bell on the counter and the man came out in a white jacket with a yellow SMILE button pinned to it. He was Japanese, with baggy eyes and horn-rim glasses. They were bifocals, and he tilted his head back to read the license Dave showed him.

Dave said, "I'm investigating the death of Gerald Dawson. For Sequoia, the company that insured his life. He picked up a prescription in here." Dave named the date.

"I can't reveal anything about prescriptions." The pharmacist handed back Dave's wallet. "You know that."

"You don't have to. It was for birth-control pills. Dawson picked it up for his wife. All I want to know is, did you ever see his wife?"

"Hundreds of people get prescriptions filled here," the pharmacist said. "You said he picked it up. You want to know what his wife looked like. Does that make sense to you? That doesn't make sense to me."

A young man who had to be the pharmacist's son came rattling down a set of steps at the back of the glassed-in room. He came out to the counter with a carton marked UPJOHN in his hands. "I remember him," he told Dave, "because the next morning they had it on TV he was murdered."

"I'm making up a prescription," his father said, and went back to bend his head over his work again.

"They had his picture." The boy worked the latch of a white gate that broke the counter and came out with the box. He set it on the floor, tore it open, began taking bottles out of it and arranging them on a low shelf. "It said he was a churchgoer, a pillar of his church, right?"

"That's the man," Dave said.

"Maybe," the boy said. "But not his wife. No way."

"A woman about sixty," Dave said. "Paralyzed on one side. Drags her foot."

"That's what's wrong," the pharmacist's son said. "She's about fifteen years old. And I mean, she is wild. Did you see the ice-cream counter? Up front by the check stands? You know what she made him do while he waited to get the prescription, right here where you're standing? She made him buy her three ice-cream cones. At once. And there's a record counter over there." He pointed. "There's nothing to play them on. I mean, they're junk. Boxcar-sale stuff. If you listened to them you wouldn't buy them, okay? So what does she do? She goes to the kiddies' toys. And there's these little ten-dollar players, plastic, made to look like bugs and panda bears and that. And she takes and finds a floor plug in the lamps and she sits down and plays the record. Loud? I mean, loud-loud! And the poor man is standing here turning redder and redder, right? And she's sitting there on the floor in her little shorts and tank top and licking first one flavor ice-cream cone and then another flavor and then another one and dripping it all over the rug, right? I remember her."

"Who's Doctor Encey?" Dave asked.

"One of the happiness boys," the pharmacist's son said. "The tall glass building two blocks thataway."

45

"You mean he sells prescriptions," Dave said.

"They're usually to put actors to sleep or to wake writers up or keep directors calm. Or people who call themselves those things. But they can be almost anything."

"You fill the prescriptions?" Dave asked.

"That's what we're here for," the boy said. He put the last bottle on the shelf, poked the flaps of the empty carton down into it, and stood up. "Encey's still got his license. It's no secret what he's doing. Nobody in charge seems to want to stop him. What did Dawson get that night? Birth-control pills? That's not such a big deal."

"You're sure the girl was with him?" Dave said.

"They were in together before. She points. 'Buy me this, buy me that.' He falls all over himself to buy it. She's not very bright. I mean"—he edged past Dave with the empty carton, back behind the counter, clicking the lock shut on the white gate—"she used poor English. I think she's a high-school dropout, one of those runaways. 'I'm going to be in the movies, I'm going to be on TV,' you know? Come to Hollywood. I don't know where a man like that found her. I mean—he looked like what they said he was on the news—somebody who passes the collection plate in church Sunday mornings. Typecasting."

"She impressed you," Dave said. "Is she pretty?"

"Too young. Flat-chested, hips like a Little League pitcher." He frowned to himself, blinking. "I don't know. There's hundreds of them along this street. But, yeah—she was different. They've all got Farrah Fawcett hair, you know? Looks like they borrowed it?"

"Blond and abundant," Dave said.

"Howard?" the gray-haired man called.

"Have you seen her in the last week?" Dave asked.

"I don't think so," the boy said. "Excuse me?"

Outside in the heat, the black boy had got up off the curb and was acting. He was waving clenched fists, popping his eyes, and mouthing angry words without sound. Two sweat-shiny college boys jogged past in red track shorts. They didn't even turn their heads. The black boy seemed to be looking at Dave but he wasn't. What he saw was inside his skull. A shiny green moped buzzed around the corner. A girl in a bikini rode it. Flat-chested. Quantities of yellow hair. Dark glasses. Had Jerry Dawson bought her a motorbike? It purred on past.

No one had slashed the cloth top of the Triumph. It whipped out of the parking lot. It seemed to have only two speeds—motionless and breakneck. As he steered it out Sunset, the speedometer kept jumping from zero to sixty. The street off the Strip where Sylvia Katzman's sand-color boxes of apartment units climbed the hill rose in sharp bends. The Triumph zipped up them with brisk little shrieks from the new tires. The address was in big wooden cutout numbers that stuck out on tin struts from the stucco. Dave ducked the car under the place and into a tenant's empty parking slot. The door at the top of inside stairs was locked. He went up the ramp to the sidewalk and climbed for the front doors among plantings. He'd warned her by phone from the expensive cowhide-smelling Jaguar-Triumph agency that he was coming, and she was waiting for him in the lobby in a green-and-yellow striped tank top and yellow shorts, harlequin glasses set with rhinestones, and yellow platform sandals. Her hair was brassy piled-up ringlets. She was five feet tall and twenty pounds overweight. She unlocked the glass door for him.

"I don't understand what it's about," she said. "Insurance, did you say? A tenant of mine?"

"Gerald Dawson. I don't know whether he was a tenant or not. I only know he made out two checks to you in the past eight weeks."

"He didn't live here," she said. "It was for his daughter. Charleen. She'd married somebody and they split up and her mother wouldn't have her back and her father felt different about it and he got this place for her. On the quiet, you understand. Is there something wrong or something?"

"He's dead," Dave said. "Is his daughter here?"

"Oh, dear," she said. "Oh, that's too bad. The poor man. He wasn't even old. What happened?"

"Somebody broke his neck on a dark street," Dave said. "Or that's how it looks."

"Listen," she said, "it happens every day. What do you think I pay for security for around here? I light the front of this place like a—you should excuse the expression—Christmas tree. Do you know what's down there? On that Sunset Strip? People out of a nightmare, that's what. I keep that garage lighted. I have a man down there at night in a uniform with a gun. He'd probably shoot himself in the foot if he had to use it, but maybe he'll scare the muggers and the rapists, you know? What can you do?"

"What about Dawson's daughter?" Dave asked.

"She must be on a trip," Sylvia Katzman said. "I haven't seen her for days."

"It's a big place," Dave said. "You could have missed her. You don't play *concierge*, do you?"

"I play pan," she said, "three nights a week. If you mean, do I watch the tenants going in and out—no, of course not. Everybody has their own life. They're entitled to be free. This isn't Europe, thank God. This isn't Russia. Where they go and when they come back is their business."

"What's her apartment number?" Dave asked.

"Thirty-six. On the third level. With a view."

"Who came to see her?" Dave asked. "Anybody besides Gerald Dawson? Part of your security system involves tenants having to come down here in person to let their visitors in, right?"

"Unless they lend their key," she said. "They're not supposed to, but who can predict what people will do? Could I see your identification?"

He let his wallet fall open so she could read his investigator's license. "She ought to be told her father is dead," he said. "The funeral is tomorrow. No one else in the family knew she was here."

"She won't go to the funeral," Sylvia Katzman said. "She won't even care that he's dead. Except he won't be here to pay her rent anymore. He was very good to her, and she treated him like dirt. Listen, mothers know girls. Fathers can be fooled. Her mother was right."

Somewhere distant a telephone rang. Sylvia Katzman waggled pudgy, ringed fingers toward carpeted stairs. "Go, maybe she's home." She hurried off in the direction of the ringing phone, buttocks wobbling inside the tight shorts. "You're a nice man to come and tell her. But you're wasting your—" A door closed, cutting off the last word. If with Sylvia Katzman there ever was a last word.

Dave climbed in air-conditioned silence to the third level and went along a gallery past five glass fronts to the glass front of thirty-six. She was right. The view was good. It would be better without the brown haze. But below, Los Angeles sloped off for miles toward the sea. On a clear night there would be a carpet of lights, on a clear day treetops. The curtains were drawn on thirty-six. He pressed a button. A buzzer went off inside but no one came to the door. Somebody had scraped with a thumbnail at a United Fund Drive sticker inside the glass. The traffic down on Sunset made surf noises. A blue jay squawked. Dave poked the buzzer again. Again no one came. He snapped open a leather key case and slipped a small blade into the lock. It turned.

The walls were bare and painted melon color. He stood on brown shag carpet. Brown velour couches made an open-sided square around a coffee table where flowers were dead in a brown pottery bowl. He smelled decayed food. Two TV dinners in aluminum trays lay on a brown Formica counter with melon-color stools. Mold grew on the food, and soft drinks evaporated in glasses. Beside an incongruously clean stainless steel sink were stacked unwashed dishes. When he opened doors under the sink, soft drink cans, Colonel Sanders boxes, taco wrappers tumbled onto a spotlessly clean, glossily waxed floor. Incongruous again. He opened the window over the sink to let the garbage smell out if it would go. Almost near enough the window to reach out and touch, an embankment, propped at its foot by cement blocks, rose very steeply twelve, fifteen feet to a curved street. On the near side of the street, a chain-link fence had been cut into at the bottom, the corners of the cut folded back. The refrigerator hummed.

In the bedroom, the piece of furniture meant to be slept on was round. The sheets were satin or some wonders-of-modern-science substitute. They were melon-color and half off the bed that looked as if wrestling had taken place there. A pillow half out of its melon satin cover lay in a corner. He opened closet doors that ran on rollers. Not much hung there, and what did smelled of stale sweat. Dresser drawers held blue jeans and T-shirts and pullover sweaters with the kind of turtleneck that droops. There were pantyhose, little clean underpants, little clean socks. He shut the drawers. In the bathroom, the medicine chest held aspirin, cold medicine, deodorant, toothpaste, toothbrush, disposable razor. Hair had been cut in here. Dark tufts lay in corners of the coral tile floor. It clogged the basin drain.

He went back into the bedroom and frowned around at it. What was missing was a jacket to keep her warm nights. The closet had showed him caps, hats, a couple of flimsy scarves and a tumble of shoes. He blinked. A poster was Scotch-taped to the wall over the bed. A naked young man knelt, face pressed into the belly of a standing girl whose head was thrown back, lips parted, eyes closed. She was naked too. His hands gripped her buttocks. The background was black. The lettering was red. ALL THE WAY DOWN. That was at the top. At the foot was A SPENCE ODUM PRODUCTION. The girl had big breasts and didn't appear to be blond.

Out in the room with the view, he looked again at the glasses on the breakfast bar. Each of the abandoned soft drinks had a plastic swizzle stick angling down into it. One was a sickly yellow, the other a sickly blue. He bent close but the light was bad. He found a switch and bulbs went on inside brown, hard-finish lamp shades over pottery bases around the room. They gave feeble light but it was enough. Lettering was stamped into the sticks. He put on his glasses and bent close again, trying not to breathe the stink of the decayed food. The lettering read THE STRIP JOINT and gave an address on Sunset.

He tucked his glasses away, rubbed at the aluminum plate around the door lock with a handkerchief, and rolled the door shut with the handkerchief covering his fingers. The lock clicked. He pushed the handkerchief away in a pocket and pressed the button at thirty-five. No one came. No one came when he pressed the other buttons down the line. All the units on this level watched the soiled and poisonous air blind, deaf, and lifeless. It didn't matter. He already had too many answers. What he needed now were the questions to go with them.

7

CINZANO was stenciled large on the red-and-blue umbrellas over the tables in front of the Strip Joint. At the tables, youngsters in bikinis and surfer trunks, ragged straw hats and armless shirts, breathed the exhaust fumes of the close-packed homebound traffic on the street, and washed down avocado-burgers with Cokes, Seven-Ups, Perrier water. Scuba-diving goggles set in black rubber rested on top of the long wet golden hair of a suntanned youth. Edging between the crowded tables, Dave stumbled over swim fins. There was the cocoa-butter smell of Skol.

Inside, the smell was of bourbon and smoke—not all of it tobacco smoke. The lights, if there were any, hadn't been turned on. If you wanted to see, you saw by what filtered in from the dying day outside through bamboo-blinded plate glass. The crowd in here appeared older, and Peter Frampton wasn't blaring from loudspeakers as he was outside. Dave sat on a bamboo stool beside a plump, chattering man in a checked linen jacket, and told a vague shape in skin-tight coveralls behind the bar that he wanted a gin and tonic. In the gloom at the room's end, a pair of angular lads in black, not-very-crisp shirts and jeans was puttering with microphones, amplifiers, speakers, on a small platform. Feedback screamed. Everyone looked at the corner. The feedback stopped. The bartender set the gin and tonic in front of Dave but didn't go away. He stood leaning with his hands on the bar.

"You want something else?"

"What more could I possibly want?"

"It's always something," the bartender said. "What is it this time? Who's supposed to be dealing in here now? Who's supposed to be snorting in the men's room?"

"I'm not a cop," Dave told him.

"You're something like that," the bartender said. He had a drooping, corn-color moustache and his hair was going thin, but his skin had a youthful sheen to it and his eyes were clear and healthy. They blinked, speculative. "Maybe you're a deprogrammer, except I can't smell greed on you. You can't be a private eye. They don't have those anymore. And when they had them, they didn't look like you."

"Insurance," Dave said. "Have you seen a thin girl child named Charleen? Blond, about five-four, no breasts to speak of, no hips to speak of, maybe in company with a small, dark, intense church-deacon type in his forties?"

"The kids can't come inside during the day," the bartender said, "and that's when I work so I wouldn't see a kid." He looked past Dave. He called, "Priss?"

The young woman who came wore the same sort of baby-blue bib coveralls as the bartender, except the legs of hers were cut very short and with little splits at the sides. She had loose poodle hair like the secretary at Superstar Rentals. Her smile was bright, brisk, professional. The bartender asked her about Charleen.

"She came here," Dave said. "She had swizzle sticks with the name of this place on them."

"Oh, honey." The girl laid a hand with open fingers on her forehead. "They come by the gross. Is that all you've got? Haven't you got a picture?"

"They were an odd couple," Dave said. He described Dawson again.

"What's odd?" Priss wagged her head with a wan smile. "Sweetheart, a girl could come here with a two-toed sloth and nobody would notice."

"The kids do come in here at night, right?" Dave said to the bartender. "You've got a band. Not for us tone-deaf old drunks, surely. So they must dance, no?"

"That wall slides back. On the other side. Soft drinks only. Eight-thirty. Also junk food, okay?"

"That all?" Priss wondered.

Dave lifted his glass to her. "Remember me to the two-toed sloths."

She went away. So did the bartender. Dave worked his way through clusters of balding men talking talent, talking albums, talking contracts, to the little platform. One of the angular youths had gone off. The other one sat at the keyboard, fiddling with switches, playing runs. Dave stepped up onto the platform. Drumsticks lay crossed on a snare. He picked one up and tapped a cymbal. The youth at the keyboard turned to him, flinching.

"Mustn't touch," he said.

Dave put the stick down carefully and told him about Charleen and Gerald Dawson.

"He's a bad dancer," the skinny youth said. "The worst she ever brought. But she only brought the other ones once. They liked it. He hated it. It figured she'd bring him back over and over."

"Sensitive to others, was she?" Dave said.

"He was a jerk. He deserved it. What did he need with her? She was like a ten-year-old. No boobs, no nothing. But he fell all over himself. She could make him do anything. And she wasn't even smart."

"You sound like you knew her," Dave said.

His hair was black and lank, lusterless, uncombed. It went inside the greasy collar of his shirt when he shook his head. He ran long, knuckly fingers under it to free it. "You sit up here and run through the same sets night after night it gets mechanical and boring," he said. "So I watch, you know? What you see isn't Aldrich or Coppola or Scorsese, and it's only clips, but I make up the rest of the script. She's this turkey-ranch hick, right? And she runs away from Gobbler Gulch to the bright lights, and the town preacher comes to fetch her and it's Sadie Thompson all over again. You know that old Joan Crawford flick? That was John Huston's father in that, did you know? John Huston is old as God himself. That was a long time ago, man."

"You made this up," Dave said. "But you never talked to her?"

"Did I say that?" The knuckly fingers played a phrase from "The Maid with the Flaxen Hair." The electronic sounds came out tinkling, silvery. "I talked to her. She was a talker. Anybody she could grab. She was going to get into films. She was peddling her scrawny little ass up and down the Strip all night. And the johns she got all told her the same thing. They were agents, directors, producers. They'd get her into films. And she believed them. They told her she had beautiful facial planes, all right?" Woodwinds faked themselves inside the circuitry. What came from under his fingers sounded tender, yearning. It contradicted the sourness of his words.

"What did you tell her?" Dave asked. "That you could get her a recording contract?"

"My sheets needed changing," he said. "My decor is piles of dirty laundry. She liked my cock very much but I don't think my life-style convinced her I had the clout to help her with her career." He snapped off a little what-the-hell laugh but the music kept on sounding sentimental.

"Dawson wasn't an agent, a director, a producer," Dave said. "He couldn't get her into pictures."

55

"I don't know." The shoulders went up and down without affecting the smooth work the fingers were doing. "He sure as hell didn't look it. Him I'd have figured to be paying the rent or something, you know? But about the time I saw him with her first, a little before, she said she'd made it. She had a part. A big part. She was going to be a movie star. She'd even met the producer."

"Did she name him?" Dave said.

"How could she name him? Somebody drives a new Seville along here waving an open door at the girls on the sidewalk—he's going to give his real name?" The Ravel piece came to an end. He looked at Dave. "Who are you and what do you want with her?"

"You said the man would do anything for her," Dave told him. "I think he died for her. He died, that's for sure. If I can find her, maybe she can tell me why."

"She hasn't been around," the musician said.

"For how long?" Dave said. He named the date of Gerald Dawson's death. "Would that be the last time?"

"You think she's dead?" His skin never saw sunlight. The darkness of his hair and moustache, the intensity of the little light glaring off the sheet music on the instrument, reflecting into his face, made it look like ivory. Now it turned to chalk. "Christ, she was only sixteen."

"Is the date right?" Dave said.

"Yeah. No. I don't know. Who reads calendars all the time? Every night is the same in here." His mouth trembled. He sounded as if he were going to cry. "Jesus. I guess that's right. Ten days ago, right? Yeah, it must have been about that long."

"She hasn't been back to her apartment," Dave said. "Where else would she go?"

"I don't know, man. She slept around, right? For bread. I mean, nobody's ever going to get her into that glass slipper. A pumpkin is always going to be a pumpkin for her. What a dumb, crazy little kid."

"Do you write your own lyrics?" Dave said.

He grinned wanly. "That's a quote from some flick." But the tune under his fingers now was "Pavanne for a Dead Princess," the celesta sound giving it a toy-shop aptness. "Who knows? You could check who's suddenly signed million-dollar contracts and moved into Beverly Hills mansions."

"Million-dollar contracts I don't think she'd get," Dave said. "Did you ever hear of a producer called Odum? Spence Odum?"

"They keep making those pictures about that Little League baseball team. The Bad News Bears. She could be in the next one. *The Bad News Bears Meet the Dirty Old Men?*"

"She didn't tell you this producer who signed her was named Spence Odum?"

"She didn't give me the name," he said. "She stuck out her tongue when I asked her. She flounced away, right? Grammarschool stuff. 'Ask me no questions, I'll tell you no lies.' " He made his voice simpering. His hand flipped switches. Debussy mourned. Then stopped. The cover came down over the keyboards. "I've got to eat."

Dave gave him a card. "If you remember anything about her that you haven't told me, call me, will you?"

The card went into a shirt pocket where there were ball-point pens and cigarettes. The skeletal thighs slid off the high bench. "Later," he said, and dropped off the platform and wove in and out through the knots of talkers, and after a pause to put on dark glasses, out into what was left of the daylight. Dave set down his unfinished drink and followed. Eating still went on. So did Peter Frampton. The temperature had cooled and shirts had come from nowhere to cover the suntan-oiled shoulders. Priss came at him, empty tray at her side.

"Charleen Sims," she said. "A big, dumb kid was here with a picture. Scrawny little blond. In a high-school yearbook from some tacky little town in the boonies. Showing her picture to everybody. Had anybody seen Charleen? I forgot before."

"Now is a good time," Dave said. "What did this big, dumb kid look like? Did he have a name? What was the name on the yearbook? What tacky little town in the boonies?"

"You know what you could take him for?" she asked.

"A two-toed sloth?" Dave said.

"Big Foot," she said. "The monster that's supposed to run the woods in Oregon or Washington or someplace? You've seen those fake movies, haven't you? Bad, grainy, eight-millimeter shots of some naked guy with a lot of hair and beard tromping through the underbrush? They don't have sound but you can hear the grunts?"

"He didn't grunt his name for you?"

"He was very paranoid. No names." She clasped the empty tray to her chest with crossed arms. "He hung onto that book like this, wouldn't let anybody see the cover, only her picture. He didn't want questions, just answers: where was she. A week later he was back. It was sad. He'd lost the book. It figured. Charleen was dumb but she'd wised up a little here. He was childish. Naturally somebody ripped him off. He was lucky they left him his undershorts. He cried about the book, really cried, like a little kid. It was the only picture of Charleen he owned." She looked past Dave, frowned and nodded. "I've got to pick up an order. Look, I'm sorry I forgot before."

"One more second," Dave said. "Have you seen him lately? Big Foot?"

"No, it's been, what, two weeks? He was frantic. About the book. Thought he might have left it here. He hadn't." She tried to go inside. Dave stepped between her and the door.

"You never saw her with him? He didn't find her?"

"There are nine million people in this town. How could he find her? He was lost, himself." She tried to edge around him. "Look, I have to—"

"What about Spence Odum? Did you see her with him?"

"What's a Spence Odum?"

"A movie producer. You get film people in here."

"Did he tell you he was a producer?" she said. "They lie a lot, you know."

"A poster told me," Dave said. "In Charleen's apartment. Over her bed. He makes the kind of movies she might just luck into."

"I don't get told people's names much." A shout came from the dusky sunset room. "Sorry—I have to go," she said, and this time he let her.

Kids with soft-drink cans sat on the hood and trunk of the Triumph where he'd left it, halfway up the hill. Skate boarders curvetted past him. He didn't speak to the kids. When he stopped and took out keys, they got off the car.

8

The sky still held leftover daylight but when he tilted the Triumph
up Horseshoe Canyon Trail the trees made it night. Big brown
supermarket sacks crowded the passenger seat. He had to juggle
with his knees to get a grip on them all. Slapped at by branches,
he blundered through the dark to the cookhouse. He had to set the
sacks down to unlock the door. Then it took him a while to find
the light switch. The bulb that answered it was weak. He brought
in the sacks and set them on a sink counter of cracked white tile
that Amanda had already condemned.

She'd condemned the cabinets too—of greasy, varnished pine,
none of the doors willing to stay shut. The stove and refrigerator,
chipped white enamel, were probably good for another ten years,
but she wanted him to have new ones. He wondered what color she
would choose—copper, cinnabar, heliotrope? He emptied the
sacks, stocked cupboards and refrigerator, where the bulb was out
but the air was cold. He'd bought a plastic bag of ice cubes. He
unwrapped a squat drink glass—he'd picked up six at the supermarket—dropped ice into it, and built a martini.

He left it to chill, crossed the uneven terra-cotta-tiled courtyard under beams from which vines hung in reaching tendrils, drooping big white trumpet flowers, to the third building, where fencing masks and foils rusted on knotty-pine walls. His stereo components sat on the dusty floor. He'd plugged them in and strung them together the day he hauled them up here from the rooms he'd shared with Doug above the gallery. Now he took the top album of the handiest stack and, without reading what it was, set the record on the turntable and started it going. The Mozart clarinet quintet. He turned up the volume, left the door open, and went back to the kitchen, the music trailing after him.

He'd forgotten to buy a can opener, but one hung off a divider between windows over the sink. Food from who knew what cans it had opened for how many years crusted the blade, but he overlooked that and cranked open a can of chili. He dumped the contents into one of his new supermarket aluminum saucepans and, while it heated, shredded lettuce with a dull, shiny supermarket knife onto a supermarket plate. He chopped up half an onion. There was no place to put the other half. He let it lie, shaved strings from a block of creamy Monterey jack cheese, then sat on the floor with his back against loose cabinet doors, drank the martini, listened to the music, and smelled the chili heating.

"You son of a bitch." Johnny Delgado stood in the doorway. He needed a shave. His clothes needed changing, had needed changing for some days. With a lot more gray in it than Dave remembered, his hair was shaggy and hung in his eyes. They glittered black in the bad light of the kitchen. He was unsteady on his feet. He hung onto the door frame and swayed. "You fucking vulture, perching in the trees, watching them tear me up, then coming down to feast off—feast off—the fucking carcass."

Dave got to his feet. "I can hardly find this place by daylight." The chili was bubbling. He set down his glass, turned the fire low, and gave the chili a stir with a shiny new perforated cooking spoon. "And sober. What kind of guidance system have you got?" He

61

cranked open coffee, rinsed out the sections of the drip maker he'd also brought from the supermarket, and used a yellow plastic scoop to put coffee into it. He filled a pan with water and set it on a burner. "They didn't tear you up, Johnny. You tore yourself up."

"You took my job," Delgado said.

"I didn't take it," Dave said. He got the lettuce out of the bin in the bottom of the fridge and shredded another plateful and put the lettuce back. "You gave it back to Sequoia and they didn't know what to do with it, so they're handing out pieces of it. The piece I got is what I'm told I do best—a murder case with everything wrong with it."

"They never tried to get me." Delgado found a kitchen stepstool and sat on it. "They've got my phone number."

"They had one." Dave poured the chili over the beds of lettuce. "You'd left that place. No forwarding address." He strewed handfuls of cheese shavings on the chili, where it started to melt right away. "You also hadn't paid your bill in a while." He sprinkled on the chopped onion. "They told Sequoia that." He stripped cellophane off a glossy box that held cheap stainless-steel knives, forks, spoons. Each was in its own soft plastic sheath. He tore the sheaths off two forks, laid one fork on a plate, and held the plate out to Delgado. "It made a poor impression. So did the news that you were drunk all the time."

Delgado made a face at the plate. "I don't want that. What're you trying to do? Man, that takes balls. Steal somebody's job, then offer to feed him."

"I offer to feed you," Dave said, "because you're a friend, you're a guest in my house, I've got the food, and you need something in your stomach besides bourbon. Eat it, Johnny, or I'll put it in your hair." He pushed the plate at Delgado and Delgado grunted sourly and took it. He fumbled with the fork.

"This is a crazy place," he said.

"And that fact got it through escrow very fast." Dave stood at the counter and ate.

"I went over there." Delgado tilted his head. "Where the music's coming from. What is that place?"

"A man taught fencing there," Dave said. "Eat."

"If I throw up," Delgado said, "you deserve it." He filled his mouth. It opened. Chili dribbled down his chin. His eyes got big. "Jesus! Hot!"

"Cold chili never did much for me," Dave said.

Tilting the plate dangerously, Delgado got off the stool, kicked it aside, tore open the refrigerator door. Bottles of Dos Equis glittered on one of the wire shelves. He reached. "Beer. Yeah."

"Beer. No." Dave shut the door. He kicked the stool against the door and pushed Delgado down on it. The man gave off a stink of neglect. Dave had never seen him in any shirt but the white, short-sleeved kind with a tie. The tie had vanished and the shirt collar was greasy. "You eat now. Here's water if you have to wash it down." He dumped out the last of his martini, rinsed the glass, filled it, pushed it at Delgado, who was staring at the bottles of bourbon, scotch, and gin on the counter. Dave passed the glass in front of Delgado's eyes. "Drink."

Delgado waved a hand. He ducked his head over the plate and began shoveling down the chili. "Take it the fuck away. I hate the goddamn stuff. I'll eat. How do I get into situations like this?"

"Running around trying to find people to blame for the shambles you're in," Dave said. "Nobody else wants the blame any more than you do."

"Marie," Delgado said, with his mouth full. "She gets the blame." He laughed harshly, spraying chili, onions, cheese. "Why not? She got everything else—house, car, bank account. Let her have the blame." He pawed at the food stains on his shirt, his trousers. "Christ, I look like a goddamn wino." He got off the stool and set the plate on the counter. Shakily, so that it rattled. It was still half full. He looked into Dave's eyes. "Don't shove food down me, okay? Just leave me the hell alone?"

"I didn't come to your house." The water in the pan bubbled.

Dave poured it steaming into the waiting pot. "You came to my house, remember? Sit down. No, you don't have to eat any more. You can drink, now. Coffee. A whole lot of strong, black coffee."

Delgado started out the door. Dave dropped the empty pan clattering into the sink, took two long steps, and caught his arm. Delgado tried to jerk away. There was petulance in the gesture but not much strength. Under the soiled suitcoat, his arm felt wasted, an old man's, and he wasn't even forty. Dave turned him around and set him on the stool again. Delgado glared at him.

"And then what?" he said. "You push me into the shower, right? And I'm still not sober enough to drive? So you put me to bed to sleep it off? Am I on track? Sure, I am. And sometime in the night, you're in the bed with me. Yeah, oh, yeah." He nodded, mouth twisted in a sneer. He rubbed the stubble on his chin. A scrap of beef came away in his fingers, he flicked it off. "You know what you are and so do I, and that's tonight's scenario, isn't it?"

"You wrote it," Dave said. "You tell me." The Mozart turned itself off. The only sound was the drip of water through the coffee grounds and the whirr of crickets out in the sweaty canyon darkness. "You need a shower. You need clean clothes. I can lend you a sweatshirt and a pair of jeans. You are too drunk to drive. That doesn't matter. I can drive you home. Where are you living?"

"Crappy motel in Santa Monica," Delgado mumbled. "If they haven't locked me out."

Dave studied him. "You want to stay here, don't you? That's why you came. Not to chew me out for taking your job. To have a place to stay." He unwrapped a supermarket coffee mug, rinsed it under the tap, filled it with coffee. "You are broke. You're lonely." He held the mug out to Delgado, who was watching him with nothing in his bloodshot eyes. "You're also horny. And you're offering yourself in payment for anything I can do for you, only what mainly interests you is getting your rocks off."

Delgado made a sound and knocked the cup across the room.

Coffee splashed the cabinets and ran down. The cup was tough. It didn't break. Delgado lurched off the stool and stumbled out the door. On hands and knees, he vomited. The sounds he made were loud and miserable. Dave stood in the doorway trying to see in the poor light from the kitchen and from the building across the way whether a garden hose was coiled somewhere among the broken hibachis, splintered surfboards, and bent lawn furniture beneath the hanging vines. Delgado's stomach spasms eased off. He wiped a sleeve across his mouth.

"I warned you," he groaned. "You had to feed me. You just had to feed me."

"Come get some coffee," Dave said.

"You think I'd take anything from you now?" Delgado staggered to his feet. He spat. "Knowing what you think?"

"Is what I think any uglier than what you think? Come on. Forget it." He led Delgado back into the kitchen. He stood him at the sink. "Wash your face." Delgado splashed water with hands that hadn't seen any for a long time. Dave handed him a supermarket dishtowel. He picked up the fallen mug and poured coffee into it again. "Drink this. Take the shower. Sleep it off."

Silently, sullenly, Delgado did as he was told. Dave led him across to the room with the fencing masks. He lifted folded jeans and the promised sweatshirt out of a carton on the floor. He steered Delgado to the bathroom where grit crunched on the white tiles. He shut the door on Delgado, and while the shower splashed, he set up the steel frame, lowered onto it the box spring that had been leaning against the wall, the mattress. He lifted sheets and blankets from other cartons and made up the bed. The shower ceased.

"Don't try to shave tonight," Dave said. "Tomorrow."

He took a blanket for himself, left the building, closed the door behind him. He unlocked the big front building, threw the blanket inside, clicked light switches until somewhere outdoors around a corner a glow came from untrimmed brush. He went out again. Someplace he'd seen a garden hose. He went toward the light, shoes crackling dried oak leaves and eucalyptus seed pods. The smell of the eucalyptus was strong in the night heat. He found the hose. He prowled for a connection. He screwed the hose to it and turned the tap handle and got a lot of hard spray in his face. He dragged the hose around the house corner and reached the mess Delgado had made and, using his thumb to increase the force of the water, washed the vomit off the tiles into the littered earth under the shrubs.

"The midnight gardener," somebody said.

Dave turned. He knew the figure—slight, trim, the overgrown grounds-light behind him haloing gray hair. It was Doug, whom he'd lived with for three years and didn't live with anymore. "Right around to your left," he said, "is the turn-off. Turn it off for me?"

Doug stepped into shadow. He gave a yelp that said the leaky connection had doused him. The hose quit running and Dave dropped it. Doug came to him. He wore a safari jacket of crash linen with the cuffs turned back. He was brushing water off it. Dave asked, "What brings you here? Did Christian fling himself into a volcano?"

"I wanted to see if you were all right," Doug said.

The door of the building where the fencing masks hung opened. Delgado stood there in the fresh clothes. The light behind him shone off his wet hair. "Listen," he said, "I want to thank you. I feel a hell of a lot better."

"You sound better," Dave said. "There's a carton of medicine-chest stuff on the bathroom floor. Take some aspirin. It might ward off a headache in the morning."

"I hate taking your bed." Delgado saw Doug and jerked. "Oh, hell. Who's that?"

"Never mind me," Doug said. "Just carry on as if I hadn't come. Obviously, I shouldn't have."

"Ah, Christ," Delgado said. "Dave, I'm sorry."

"Nothing to be sorry for," Dave said. "Sleep well."

Delgado hesitated, then turned, slump-shouldered, went back inside, and shut the door.

"You can still surprise me," Doug said.

"You want some coffee?" Dave said.

9

Tapping woke him. He flinched at the brightness of the big empty room and thought extra windows might be a mistake. Groaning, he rolled onto his back on the creaky chaise he'd dragged in from the courtyard—webbing slack on a frame of aluminum tubing, the stuffing lumpy in the gaudy flower-print plastic pallet. He clutched the blanket around his nakedness and sat up. *Tap-tap-tap.* He squinted at the French doors. Where Amanda had made the circle on the dusty pane yesterday, she was smiling in at him. He lifted to her a hand that felt as if it belonged to someone else. It was early to smile, but he worked at it.

"You'll have to clear out," she called. "All sorts of physical types are coming with crowbars."

He pointed to the door, tottered into pants, and went barefoot to let her in. He raked fingers through his hair. His mouth tasted sour. He and Doug had drunk Dos Equis and munched tortilla chips until late—how late he didn't know. The talk had been guarded, mannerly, but he hoped Doug wouldn't keep coming back. What you used to have was only that. And what they used to have was flawed from the start. He'd lost Rod to cancer, Doug had lost Jean-Paul in a car smash. They'd tried to make the losses up to each other. Life didn't work that way. Love didn't work that way—if love worked any way. What did they coat those tortilla chips with? Rust-color dust. Garlic was what he tasted. He ran his tongue over his teeth and opened the door to Amanda. Her T-shirt read HIS TOO. She was in ninety-dollar jeans. She was ready for work.

"Someone's in your kitchen," she said. "A lovely, haggard Mediterranean type with long black eyelashes. He offered me coffee in a sultry voice. I was cagey. It could be doped. I could end up in a brothel in Turin."

"Or a motel in Santa Monica," Dave said, "which is worse. Go help him with the bacon and eggs. If he makes any false moves, holler, and I'll come running. Soapy and stark naked but running."

"Promises," she said, and went to the cookhouse.

Dave hobbled and hopped to the fencing studio. Getting there barefoot was painful. A countertenor was having to do with Monteverdi when he switched on the radio. He rifled cartons for clothes and went into the bathroom. When he came out, showered and shaved, the music was piano and violin, something twentieth-century. Delgado and Amanda sat on the side of the bed and ate from plates on their knees. Mugs of coffee steamed at their feet. Delgado started to get up but Dave went to the cookhouse, got his own plate from the oven where it was keeping warm, poured himself a mug of coffee, and went back with them. He sat on the other side of the bed, drank some coffee to wash out the mint taste of the tooth powder, and swallowed some eggs.

"The car is full of catalogues for you to look at," Amanda said. "Sample books. Fabrics. Carpet. Furniture. I hope you haven't got a big day's work planned."

"I can work for him," Delgado said. He looked over his shoulder at Dave. "Who should I talk to?"

"Spence Odum. Maybe he knows where Charleen Sims is. Only

you have to find him first. I've checked the directories. He doesn't have a business address. He doesn't even have a home address. He makes skinflicks."

"I'll find him for you," Delgado said. "What do you want with Charleen what's-her-name?"

"I think it's possible she witnessed a murder."

Delgado was making Dave feel guilty about having checked the liquor bottles in the kitchen. He knew drunks. Delgado must have awakened feeling rotten. The remedy for that was to jolt down alcohol as soon as possible. To stop the shaking, the panic. The gin bottle was the only one Dave had opened himself. It didn't seem any emptier than when he'd made his martini. The seals on the Jack Daniels and the Glenlivet were intact. He said, "You don't have to do it."

"I'd like to," Delgado said. "Maybe if I do it right, you'll put in a word for me at Sequoia."

"You'll do it right," Dave said. "Maybe she didn't call herself Sims. Maybe it was Dawson. For what my advice is worth—I doubt that Odum belongs to any guilds. I doubt that he belongs to the Motion Picture Academy."

"I don't doubt that he drives a car," Delgado said.

"Two hundred a day and expenses," Dave said.

"No way." Delgado gulped the last of his coffee. "Twenty bucks for gas and lunch. And I wouldn't take that if I wasn't broke." He set the mug on the plate and stood. "I'll wash the dishes and get going."

"You're locked out of your motel," Dave reminded him.

"That's not your problem." Delgado took Amanda's mug and plate and started for the door. "Maybe I tried to make it your problem last night, but it's not."

"Don't worry about the dishes," Dave said. "You cooked the breakfast. My wallet's in the front building on the floor by the thing I slept on. Better take fifty. It gets expensive out there. You don't want to run short."

"Let me have those." Amanda took the plates out of Delgado's hands and went out into the leaf-speckled sunlight with them. Halfway across the courtyard she called back, "And good luck." She went into the cookhouse and water began splashing there.

Dave sat and finished his breakfast. He heard the door of the front building close and the crunch of Delgado's steps rounding the house and fading toward his car. But there was no noise of the car starting. Swallowing the last of his eggs, he got to his feet. He left the plate with Amanda at the sink and carried his coffee out to the front. Delgado leaned in under the raised hood of an old Pontiac with a smashed-out taillight. A pocketknife was in his hand. He was trying to make it serve as a screwdriver to fasten some wires. He saw Dave and straightened up, banging his head. He rubbed his head, wincing. But it didn't hide the guilt in his eyes.

"Relax," Dave said. "You fixed it so you could stamp off mad at me, or go off rejected and dejected, or however the scene played itself, and you wouldn't be able to get your car started. You'd have to stay. I've had it done to me before."

Delgado stared, making up his mind about whether or not to get sore. He bent back under the hood and worked with the wires again. "There's something you don't know about people," he said. "There has to be. It stands to reason." He grunted with the effort of what he was doing. "There." He got out from under the hood and slammed it shut. He folded up the jackknife and dropped it into the pocket of the jeans Dave had lent him.

Dave said, "When people run out of probable things to do, they do improbable things. That's all. Nothing so wonderful about that."

Delgado opened the door on the driver's side and got into the car. The door squeaked. Cotton wadding stuck out of a worn place in the seat. He started the engine and shut the door. "Only you don't get surprised," he said.

"Once or twice," Dave said. "It's dangerous. I don't like it. But

71

I know it's going to happen again. The odds are like that. I haven't met everybody in the world, yet. It only feels that way."

Delgado had made a bundle of his dirty clothes. It lay on the seat beside him. He must have put it there when he got up. He said, "I know what you mean."

"The trick is to remember that they only seem the same," Dave said. "They're not the same. And one of them is waiting to surprise the hell out of me."

"I hope it isn't me," Delgado said.

Dave slapped the window ledge and stepped back. "Good luck," he said. "Call me when you locate Spence Odum. Wait, I didn't give you my number."

Delgado grinned. "I swiped a card out of your wallet." He backed the car. Dust huffed from under the worn tires. The old engine rattled a lot at the effort it had to make getting up the rutted drive to the trail. Delgado raised a hand and let the Pontiac roll down the potholed blacktop. It backfired a couple of times. Dave didn't let himself think about how many drinks fifty dollars would buy. He went back to the cookhouse and helped Amanda with the dishes.

After that they sat cross-legged on the floor in the big room and looked at shiny pictures of objects to sit on and to eat off of, they ran their hands on carpet samples, fingered swatches of fabric meant to cover chairs and hang at windows. A gnarled man with one arm and two big, speechless sons arrived in a ranchero wagon and tramped around scowling at the work to be done. A lot of adding up took place on the backs of envelopes—brick, lumber, masonry, manhours, sheet metal, wiring, tile. A rattly pickup truck with board sides jolted into the yard and an old Japanese couple hauled gardening tools out of it. A chain saw began to snarl. When the brown old woman in man's hat and shoes shut it off for a minute, Dave heard the telephone. It was in the fencing room. He ran for it.

"This is Midnight," the voice at the other end said.

"Noon," Dave said. He glanced at his watch. "Ten minutes to one, as a matter of fact."

"No, man—Richie Midnight." Restaurant noises were behind the voice. "Back in Wisconsin it's still Mittelnacht, but how do you expect a deejay to pronounce that? How do you expect to put that on an album cover?"

"There's Engelbert Humperdinck," Dave said. "But let it pass. You found Charleen, right? What did she do, come in to dance again?"

"She didn't come in. I didn't find her. But I sure as hell went looking for her. She's dead, man. She's got to be. Disappeared when Dawson got killed, that joker she was with? Nobody's seen her. I mean, she was visible, audible, right? Everybody on the Strip knew her. Only way somebody like that could disappear is they're dead."

"Your friend Priss estimates LA at nine million souls," Dave said. "It's more likely she's just mislaid."

"That's not in very good taste," Mittelnacht said.

"Don't be so eager to cry," Dave said. "I don't know how much death you've seen, but it's not romantic."

"I was in Nam," Mittelnacht said.

"Did they teach you how to break necks?" Dave asked.

"They taught me how to mainline horse. And not to bitch at all the lousy pianos they gave me to play."

"None of this is what you called about," Dave said. "What did you call about?"

"There's this jock I ran into. He's around the Strip a lot. I mean, I don't know him. I know him. You know what I mean? He's not a close friend, just a dude. An actor. Only there's just one reason he ever gets cast. He's got this tremendous organ of procreation, right? And—"

"So he worked for Spence Odum," Dave said.

"You got it. And he knows where Odum's shooting."

"Tell me," Dave said.

10

The building with the number Mittelnacht had given him faced the Strip and looked all wrong. The facade was colonial—white pillars, green shutters. A sign claimed real estate was sold behind the green door with the shiny brass knocker. Dave waited for a break in traffic, then skidded the Triumph around a corner where the side street dropped sharply. There was an alley. He nipped into it. Spaces for cars backed on the rear walls of shops, trash barrels, broken crates. The barred, employees-only doors were mostly un-numbered. But a number matching that on the real-estate office was lettered in runny white paint on a plywood door where a tall girl in noticeable makeup and a costume of pink, red, and orange skirts, scarves, and sashes smoked a cigarette under a yellow turban with a cerise plume. He pulled the Triumph in beside a white van without lettering that somehow didn't look like anybody's vacation vehicle—it looked like business, anonymous business. The girl wore big fake-gold hoop earrings and had a husky voice. She looked Dave up and down hungrily and said with a regretful smile:

"Sorry. Nobody gets in."

The door opened. A college-age boy in glasses and with a prominent Adam's apple said, "Okay, he wants you."

"Excuse me," the tall girl said, "it's the big moment in the torture chamber." She dropped the cigarette, stepped on it with a gold sandal that showed toenails glued with glitter, and went inside. Dave went inside after her.

Before the door fell shut, daylight showed him washrooms littered with wigs, greasepaint tubes, boxes of tan powder, crumpled tissues stained with lipstick. NO SMOKING, a sign said. Then the door closed and the only light was out in a big brick room where it struck hard at a naked teenage girl struggling inside a gilt-and-crimson papier-mâché mummy case that stood upright. Shiny manacles held the girl's ankles and wrists, chains looping from them to cleats inside the case. The case had a split lid, the curved halves open. The tall girl stood to one side of the coffin, another dressed like her to the other side. Silhouetted against the light, a pair of men flanked a camera on a tripod. The only sound was the whirr of the camera motor. The girl screamed silently and writhed without conviction in the very loose chains, while the gaudy attendants slowly closed the lethal halves of the door. Thirty percent shut. Eighty percent.

"Freeze it there." The man who spoke had golliwog hair. He was big, barrel-shaped, soft. He moved out into the dazzling light— black suit, black cape, pasted-on mandarin moustache. He undid the manacles. The naked girl stepped out of the mummy case. Her hair was tawny, her skin tawny, flawless over a layer of puppy fat. She went away into the shadows. The gaudily rigged girls stood deathly still. The fuzzy-haired man returned to the camera. "All right." He ducked his head, did something to his face. "One second for makeup. Now! Camera? Action!" The motor whirred again. The gaudy girls went back to shutting the mummy case.

At the last moment, cape flying, a slouch hat hiding his mad hair, the man rushed into the light. He flung himself against the doors, jamming them shut. He swung to face the camera. He'd put

75

on a domino mask. He raised a fist at the camera, threw back his head and laughed in demented triumph. He'd fitted himself with joke-store Dracula teeth. He held the pose. He held the pose. Sweat trickled from under the mask. He held the pose. He broke the pose.

"Zoom, you asshole!" he shouted. "Zoom—remember?"

"Oh, shit, I'm sorry, Spence," the cameraman said.

Spence looked at the ceiling. "Herman, where are you when I need you?" He sighed, wiped his face. "Okay. Get it right this time." He turned back to the mummy case, leaned his hands against it, whirled, repeated the fist-shaking, the crazy laugh. He held the pose. The cameraman worked something on the camera. Spence held the pose. He broke it.

"Cut." He untied the cape and let it fall, made a face and took out the teeth. "That gets it." He dropped the teeth into a pocket. "Strike the mummy case."

"Don't you want the blood running out of it?" The boy with the Adam's apple came into the light holding a floppy script, blue covers, big brass brads. "That's the next shot you wrote down here."

"Not while I've got actors sitting around getting paid," Spence said.

Derisive laughter came from the dark.

"We haven't got ketchup right now, anyway," Spence said. "I'll smuggle a couple bottles out of Fatburger after supper."

"Cheap, cheap!" voices chanted from the dark.

Spence took off the domino. "Move it out," he said. "And let's have some worklights for a minute, okay?"

Someone warm, smooth, and naked brushed past Dave. Light switches clicked. The big brick room had walls of assorted colors. Against a red section, a dummy slouched in an antique barber chair. Above a wing collar, the dummy's plaster throat was cut. The head lolled back. Memory said something to Dave about a demon barber of Fleet Street. Manacles and chains draped a blue section of wall above a wood-frame torture device with ropes and a big wheel—a rack? A brazier with fake glowing goals had fake branding irons sticking out of it.

The switcher-on of lights brushed past Dave again. He was perhaps twenty, blond, smoothly muscled as a Roman marble. He wore his economical young flesh as unerotically as clothes. He went and sat on a butt-sprung daybed with a tattered spread of black velvet sewed with sequins. The girl from the mummy case sat there too, smoking a cigarette, legs crossed. The boy picked up a Coke can from the cement floor and drank from it. The boy with the Adam's apple, and another boy even younger and wearing earphones with the cord dangling, got the mummy case onto a two-wheeled dolly to cart it out of the way. Spence called to them:

"Easy. Don't bang it around. I want to use it in my next billion-dollar box-office smash. As a bathtub full of champagne."

"Ginger ale," one of the tall girls said.

"How about a sports car?" the naked boy said. "Paint on lights and a grill. Tack on some wheels. Let it roll off a cliff and catch fire. Just like TV. Sensational."

"Varoom!" Spence said, studying a script. He flapped over pages. "Okay, where's Inspector Hardcock of the CID?"

A middle-aged man said "Hah!" and came out of a corner where a brass bed glistened against purple-flocked wallpaper. He tucked his script under his arm, put a deerstalker cap on his bald head, set a meerschaum pipe in his teeth. He wore a moustache and a tweed suit, and he chuckled.

"This is fascinating," he said. "Why don't you film it in order?"

"I'll be lucky," Spence said, "if I can get it in order when I edit it. Where's the gun? I didn't give you the gun, did I?" He went past the couch where the naked youngsters sat and rummaged in a curve-topped trunk that had been gold-leafed and stuck all over with glass jewels. He came up with a tin pistol and tossed it to the middle-aged man. He went to a tall flat, painted to match the brick wall. The flat had a door in it. "You come in here. Bursting in, you know? Only be careful. It's only lath and cardboard." He squinted at a pair of heavy-headed lights on standards that flanked the door. He looked around. "Randy? Do me a favor, baby? Get these out of here. Out the back. I'm tired of moving them for every shot."

The girl who had let Dave in went and picked up the lamps. She was strong. She brought them past Dave. They creaked and squeaked and nodded. The girl widened her mascaraed eyes at him. She muttered, "How the fuck did you get in? You're going to be in trouble."

"It should happen to everybody once," Dave said, and pushed open the door for her. The sun was bright and hot out there. Clumsy in the skirts and scarves, she wrestled the lights outside. They clanked and clashed. Bright metal tags were riveted to them. The tags read SUPERSTAR RENTALS. Dave let the door fall shut. Spence was lecturing the middle-aged man in the deerstalker cap.

"You've discovered Doctor Dreadful's House of Horrors at last. You've been running all over Soho in the fog looking for it. You stare all around. You're appalled, right? We'll keep cutting in shots of the mummy case, the torture instruments, the dead dummy, all of it. So take your time. Then there they are—the kids you've been trying to protect. You gape at them. Really shocked, okay? You've come too late, all right?" He turned. "Junie? Harold?"

"Oh, shit, here it comes." Harold set down his Coke on the floor and pushed his beauty up off the couch. He looked abused and resentful. "This is where I have to carry her, isn't it?"

"That's rude." The girl called Junie uncrossed her legs, bent, and stubbed out her cigarette on the cement. "You know how I diet and diet." She got up, shaking back her hair.

Spence said, "You come in from over there by the washrooms, holding her in your arms. You walk into camera range right past here, got it? You stop where the tape is on the floor. Only don't look down for it, this time, okay? Feel it with your toes. You're stunned. No expression. That ought to be easy. Just stare at the Inspector. Junie, you've passed out from pain, remember? So let your head hang back, way back. Be dead weight in his arms, right?"

"Aw, Spence." The naked boy trudged back to Dave.

"It'll be over before you know it," Spence said.

"I hope you've got a truss in that trunk," Harold said.

"That would look fetching in the sex scenes," Spence said. "Bend your knees when you lift her. You'll be fine."

Junie grinned. "Be thankful he never makes retakes."

"Never use that word in my presence," Spence said.

"Do I have to pick her up now?" Harold said.

"Once for practice," Spence said. "You don't have to carry her till Hardcock comes in and starts looking around."

"Yeah, looking around *slowly*," Harold said. He blew air out through his nose. Disgustedly he got into a half crouch and held out his arms. "Come on, Pudgy."

But Junie saw Dave. "There's a strange man here."

"What?" Spence saw Dave too. He came over. "This is a closed set," he said. "What do you want?"

"To know where Charleen Sims is." Dave took out his wallet and showed Spence his license. "She told people she had a job in films. You're Spence Odum, right? She's got a poster from one of your productions on a wall over her bed. In an apartment she left hurriedly ten days ago and hasn't come back to. I don't suppose your posters get around much."

"We're very big in Possum Stew, Arkansas," Spence Odum said, "and Gopher Hole, Nebraska. But not in Ninevah and Tyre." He gave his wristwatch a pained look. "Listen, I'm on a very tight budget. I can't hang around talking. Who?"

"Charleen Sims," Dave said, "or maybe Charleen Dawson."

"Never heard of her," Spence Odum said.

"I'm suffocating back here." The middle-aged man opened the painted cardboard door in the painted cardboard flat. "If I have to turn this knob, I've got to use my right hand. The gun will have to be in my left hand."

"We'll run through it," Odum called without turning.

"Blond, small, slender," Dave said. "Possibly as old as sixteen but she looks twelve."

Odum clowned shock, eyes wide, fingers to mouth. "But—but," he stammered, "that's—why, that's—degenerate!" He held an open hand out to the naked young people who laughed. "Do I look like that sort of man?" He turned to the big brick room, holding out his arms. The cameraman was grinning. So were the boys stowing the mummy case in a corner. "Do you see anything decadent about this operation, anything depraved?" He turned back to Dave, taking off the slouch hat, clutching it to his breast. "I hope you won't spread that opinion around. It could ruin my future with Walt Disney Productions."

Junie giggled. Harold and the crew guffawed.

"It's Charleen's future that worries me," Dave said. "She's mixed up in murder. She may even have been murdered herself. Now, do you know anything about her?"

The laughter stopped. Odum looked sober. "No. I don't. I never met her, never heard of her. I don't know where she got the poster. Everybody rips everything off these days. You know that. I wouldn't use her. Too young. Truth." He turned away, turned back. "Why would somebody murder her?"

"Because she saw Gerald Dawson murdered," Dave said.

Odum moistened his lips. "Superstar Rentals?"

"The place you get your stuff from," Dave said.

"I don't know the girl," Odum said. "Believe me." He read his watch again. "Look, will you get out, now, please?"

"I'll be back," Dave said and left.

Blinded by sunlight, he was inside the Triumph before he noticed that Randy was in it ahead of him, in her hoop earrings and beaded false lashes. She gave off a powerful incense smell. "You want to buy me a drink?" she said in her husky voice. "Or do you want me to buy you a drink? Women's lib and all that. We could have dinner. It's not too early."

Dave still couldn't see so he reached out and laid fingers on her face. Under the heavy makeup was beard stubble. He laughed and turned the key in the ignition. The Triumph started with a splutter of loud little valves. He backed out of the shadow of the white van. "I have to see somebody at the marina," he said. "Do you like to eat at the marina?"

"I like to sit and drink mai tais at the Warehouse and watch the little boats sink in the west."

"It's those tiny parasols they attach to the mai tais." The Triumph raced down the alley and into the street. "Poor butterfly and all that, right?"

" 'Neath the blossoms waiting," Randy sighed.

The decor at the Warehouse was barrels and cargo nets. On the wooden decks big pots of flowers perched on tarry pier stakes. It was three. Most of the lunch tables stood empty. The tourists had gone away with their neck-strap Minoltas full of out-of-focus blue water and white boats. The boats tilting around the long, narrow bay had sails striped red and orange. The moored boats sported blue canvas covers. None of these was Fullbright's. Fullbright's was over yonder. He'd visit it next.

"No," Randy Van said, "Spence doesn't want to be fooled. He knows I'm a TV. Does he ever! If he could figure out how, TV's are all he'd use. But for obvious reasons, at least one girl has always got to be real." He twisted the dinky bamboo-and-tissue-paper parasol off his drink in fingers with scarlet nails. He'd abandoned the turban and most of the scarves in the Triumph out on the lot by the big wooden tanks of koi fish. He smiled at Dave. "Boo-hoo," he said. "Reality is always messing up my life."

"It can't be a career," Dave said. "He doesn't make any money. He couldn't pay union scale."

"Be serious." Randy sipped at the big drink that looked like laboratory blood. "He pays eighty a day, but even if he paid scale, he shoots in two days. Then he lays off for months. My career is running a double-needle sewing machine in a loft full of lady Mexican illegals. They think they're a persecuted minority. Hah!"

"He says he never used a skinny little tyke called Charleen. Blond? Hardly out of grammar school. Did he?"

"Never." Randy shook his head. It loosened his wig that was shiny black Medusa curls. He set it tight with both hands. "I've worked in every flick he's made, so I know. If he wanted to, he couldn't. The Iowa hicks that line up Saturday nights on main street would be outraged. Down Alabama way, they'd burn out the theater." Randy sipped his mai tai. A lot of lipstick had accumulated on the rim of the glass. "I mean, he wants me, but he sighs and hires big tits and lots of corn-fed ass. Like Junie."

"She looks like a college girl," Dave said.

"Pepperdine." Randy nodded. "She does it for laughs." He cocked an eyebrow. "You didn't think it was hard-core, did you? Oh, no. She and Harold will roll around naked on that brass bed and kiss and moan a lot, but that's all. The rednecks would burst a blood vessel if anything really happened. That's what skinflick means—what you see ain't what you think, but it makes you think it is."

"And he shoots them in two days?" Dave asked.

"On a lavish ten thousand bucks. Can I have a cigarette?" Dave pushed his pack across the shiny planks of the tabletop. He lighted cigarettes for both of them. "Thanks," Randy said. "Most of the budget goes on lights, equipment, studio rent. Music? He sneaks tape recorders into jazz clubs. Crew? College film students who want the experience and beg for the chance. Pay? What's pay?"

"Cameraman too?" Dave said.

"Now," Randy said. "Before, it was always Herman."

"Before what? Odum misses him. Where is he?"

"Dead. Herman Ludwig. Some kind of refugee from behind the Iron Curtain." Randy winced. "That expression always makes my teeth hurt. He was supposed to have been famous in Europe. Once upon a time." Randy gazed out at the curvetting boats, the gleaming water. He blew away smoke. "He was shot. On the parking lot in back of the studio. Late at night. Those two days usually stretch their full twenty-four hours. Spence was setting up. Herman went out to bring back coffee. And somebody blew his head off with a shotgun."

"Who?" Dave said. "When?"

"Nobody knows who. They just shot him and drove off. We didn't hear it. The place is soundproof. The sheriff found out later that neighbors heard it but nobody phoned in. I got sent out to find him when he didn't come back. I stumbled across him. Dear God." Unsteadily Randy gulped down all that remained of his mai tai. "Talk about your hair turning white in one night!"

"When?" Dave said again.

"Oh—what? Ten days ago? Spence really misses him."

Lieutenant Ken Barker of the LAPD said, "The Strip's not even city, you know that. It's county. You have to see the sheriff." He sat behind a green steel desk strewn with file folders, report forms, photographs. It was in a room partitioned off by glass and green steel from a wide glass-and-green-steel room where telephones jangled, typewriters rattled, men laughed, coughed, grumbled. Barker's nose was broken. His shoulders strained the seams of his shirt. His collar was open, tie dragged down, cuffs turned back. He was sweating. He drank from a waxed-paper cup printed with orange swirls. Shaved ice rattled in the cup. He set it down. "Christ, is this weather ever going to let up?"

"It's too much of a coincidence," Dave said.

"Two murders a night? It's damn near normal. You tell me how they could be more different—a broken neck in Hillcrest, a shotgun blast away out west in a parking lot."

"There's a connection," Dave said. "Spence Odum rents his lights and cameras and recorders from the company Dawson was a partner in."

"Don't a lot of people?" Barker said. "How many outfits like that are there? From what you tell me about Odum's operation, they sure as hell couldn't keep solvent if he was their only customer."

"He was their only customer who had a cameraman murdered the same night as Dawson," Dave said. "And that's not all. Dawson was sleeping with a teenage hooker called Charleen something, who told people on the Strip she was about to get into the movies, and who had a poster from a Spence Odum picture on her wall, and who disappeared the same night as Dawson and Ludwig died."

"They go off," Barker said. "The prowl cars see them every night, like matches in the dark. And then they don't see them anymore. Some middle-aged account executive with holes in his superego takes them on a expense-account jet ride to Vegas, some john, right? And strands them there. So they sit in some casino with a dead drink in one hand and a silver dollar in the other till the next john offers them twenty bucks, bed, and breakfast—and the next, and the next."

"Till they meet some crazy," Dave said, "who carves them up and puts them in a plastic bag with your name and address on it. I thought of that."

Barker's eyes were gunmetal color, about the same gray as his hair. They regarded Dave for a few seconds. "You are a terrible man," he said. "Did you know that?"

"You've got one now," Dave said.

Barker stood up, chair backing to deepen a dent in file cabinets behind him. "Skinny little blond. We've had her for a week. No ID."

The body didn't make much of a rise in the sheet that covered it. It didn't take up much room on the long steel slab the attendant in the green smock pulled on silent rollers out of a wall. Barker laid the sheet back. She had hardly any breasts at all. She was greenish pale except for the slash down her front made by the medical examiner and the cut where her scalp had been laid back and then replaced. The hair was the color of sun-bleached southwest hillside grass—between yellow and white. There were bruises on her throat, scratches.

"Strangled," Dave said.

Barker opened a file folder. "Right. Also skull fracture. Also raped. And"—he pulled the sheet all the way down—"she once had polio. One leg shorter than the other." Dave looked at it. It was sticklike, the knee a pitiful outsize knob. He took the edge of the sheet and covered the girl up again.

"I don't think it's her," he said. "Nobody mentioned any limp. One of my witnesses said she danced well. This one may have danced—I hope so—but it can't have been well." He called thanks to the attendant.

In the elevator, Barker said, "Did Odum tell you he hired your girl—Charleen?"

"He only got nervous," Dave said, "and pressed for time."

They got off the elevator. "Did you ask him about Ludwig?"

"I didn't know about Ludwig then," Dave said.

"You don't know about him now." Back at his desk, Barker emptied a heavy, sharp-cornered glass ashtray into a metal wastebasket. "He was in this country illegally. Ludwig wasn't even his name. He was scared to use it. He was scared to surface enough even to work where he might be noticed—Columbia, Paramount."

"He had a big reputation in Europe," Dave said.

"Oh, so you do know," Barker said.

"I know that," Dave said. "What else is there?"

"The Hungarian party had it in for him. His story was they were chasing him all over the world to kill him." The telephone on Barker's desk rang. He lifted the receiver, listened a minute, grunted "Thanks," and hung up. He looked at Dave. "And they found him. And they killed him, didn't they?"

"Why was he illegal? A prominent artist—they don't have trouble defecting. 'I lift my lamp beside the—' "

"It would make headlines. The baddies would get him."

"Sounds like paranoia to me," Dave said.

"The kind that gets you killed," Barker said.

"Maybe," Dave said. "It's neat but neatness isn't everything." He stood up. "So who do I see at the sheriff's department? You know all about it. So you looked into it. So you thought the way I think—that there might be some connection. Who do I talk to over there?"

"Salazar," Barker said. "But it's the way I told you. Ask Ludwig's widow if you want confirmation. Salazar will give you her address."

Dave picked up the receiver of Barker's phone. "How do I get an outside line?" he said.

The apartment was old tan brick, down a side street from Melrose in Hollywood. The windows were small. Cracked plaster Egyptian pillars flanked the door to a dark hallway that went straight to the back. At one side of the hallway, stairs went up. They were about to be boxed in by walls and a door. New fire regulations. The framework of two-by-fours was already in. The smell of fresh-sawn pine was pleasant, nearly covering the sad, sour smell of too many decades of living that seeped through the desperately fresh paper on the walls, the hopelessly fresh carpeting he walked on.

Number six was the last door in the downstairs hallway. After he pressed the buzzer he looked out the rear window. A pair of cats lay curled asleep in the sun on the green tin lid of a big trash module by a chain-link fence. Marigolds struggled in a strip of parched earth against the fence. He saw the stucco corner of a garage. A lock clicked inside the door. The varnish on the door was laid over fifty years of earlier varnish and was nearly black. The door opened four inches. The face that peered at him was bone white, almost fleshless, with fierce patches of rouge. Black lines had been drawn around eyes large, dark, but more annoyed than frightened.

"What do you want?" She had a thick accent and her voice was a gasp. "Who are you?"

"My name is Brandstetter." He held open his wallet so she could read the license. "I'm an insurance investigator."

"My husband did not have." She tried to close the door. He put his foot in it. "Please. I have no time."

"Another man was murdered on the same night as your husband," Dave told her. "It's about his death I want to talk to you. I think the two might be connected. Someone innocent is going to suffer if I can't clear the matter up."

Her laugh was harsh and turned into a hacking cough. "Someone innocent is going to suffer? That will be a novelty in this world." Her eyes went angry, her voice scornful. "The innocent are always the ones who suffer. What kind of man are you, not to know that?"

"I told you," Dave said. "The kind that wants to prevent it. If I can. You want to help me or not?"

She shut the door. A chain rattled. She opened the door. The rest of her was as wasted as her face. She clutched an armload of clothes to the flat bosom of a faded shirt. A green dish towel was tied over her hair. From what he could see of it, the hair was sparse. It started far back on her brow. She wore jeans that hung off skeletal hips. The jeans weren't roomy—she'd shrunk away inside them. He thought she was very sick and that she had once been very beautiful. She went and laid the armload of clothes in a big scuffed leather suitcase that lay open on a Danish couch with scratched woodwork and threadbare plaid cushions. A small suitcase lay on a chair. There was a brand-new, shiny red metal footlocker.

"Who was this other fortunate man?" she asked.

"Gerald Dawson. His business was renting film equipment. The camera your husband used. For Spence Odum."

"I do not know him." She lit a cigarette, the old-fashioned kind, short and thick, no tip. The first intake of smoke started her coughing. It wracked her, bent her over. It sounded like ripping canvas. The cigarette hanging in her garishly lipsticked mouth, she clung to the back of a chair till the coughs stopped shaking her. She whispered, "He never mentioned the name. Was he Hungarian? It sounds like not a Hungarian name. Dawson?"

"He was an American who went to church a lot."

Her wry smile showed teeth of surprising whiteness and evenness. He'd thought she was fifty. The teeth said thirty. "They would not be friends," she said. "My husband was an artist, an intellectual. He regarded religion as superstition." The cigarette bobbed as she spoke. Smoke from it trickled up into an eye. She squinted that eye. "He distrusted systems of thought. He felt they cramped the mind and made fools of people." She went into a farther room and came back with another armload of clothes. "He said religion only caused hatred and bloodshed. He was an intelligent man and a gifted one. You must not think he filmed only sex pictures for vermin like this Spence Odum."

"I don't," Dave said. "Why did he do it here?"

She knelt to lay the clothes in the footlocker. She looked up at Dave. "He had made enemies in Hungary. He would not keep quiet about the horrors of the regime. When they tried and jailed a friend who was a writer, he spoke out. If he had not fled, they would have killed him."

"But he never made any speeches in the West," Dave said. "He didn't come out as a dissident. He didn't lay charges about this writer."

"For my sake," she said. "For the sake of relatives left behind in Hungary."

"So he was out of the way and was no harm to them," Dave said. "Why would they come here and kill him?"

She shrugged and stood. Sick as she looked, she moved like a girl, a girl trained in grace. Maybe she'd been an actress. "He would not tell me what lay behind his fear. He wanted me to know nothing in case I should be caught and tortured."

"Did you ever think perhaps he imagined it?"

"He did not imagine his own death," she said. "That was quite a reality, was it not?"

89

"Yes, but the killer hasn't been caught," Dave said. "Maybe it wasn't someone from Hungary. Maybe instead it had to do with Gerald Dawson's murder."

"No." She shook her head. "They were following him. Always. He saw them in Portugal, and the same ones again in Brazil, and the same ones again in Canada."

"He saw them," Dave said. "Did you see them?"

"No, I did not, but that means nothing." She looked hard at Dave. "He was not mad. How can you think that when this has happened?"

"What about here?" Dave said. "Did he tell you he'd seen them here?"

"No. He told me we had escaped them at last." Bitterly she twisted out her cigarette in an ashtray on a cheap teak-veneer end table. A lamp whose tweedy white shade years and cigarette smoke had yellowed stood on the table. So did a five-by-seven photograph in a dime-store frame. She picked up the photograph and gazed at it. "And then, in a dark parking lot, seven thousand miles from Budapest, they killed him." With a sleeve of the old blouse she wiped the glass on the photograph and laid it on the folded clothes in the footlocker. She stood looking down at it, motionless. "And now, I can go home." She turned Dave the wry smile again. "I never said it to him, of course—but I was dying to go home." A bleak laugh rustled in her throat. "Now I am going home to die. Isn't it funny?"

Dave didn't answer. He had stepped over to the footlocker. He was looking down at the photograph. It was black-and-white. Against a background of river and bridge, a man and woman stood close. The woman was lovely. A breeze blew the picture hat she wore, fluttered the ribbons. She hung onto the hat and smiled at the camera. Her arm was around the waist of a big, grinning man, barrel-shaped, soft-looking. Frizzy fair hair stood out all over his head.

12

The sun bulged out as it got to ocean level. It was bloated and smoky red. He stood at the end of the long, white-painted pier and watched it go down. Sailing craft, power craft passed, headed for moorings. Sounds drifted to him from the boats, high children's voices, a man's laugh, someone having poor luck with a guitar. A crowd of heavy-bodied pelicans splashed down awkwardly into the red water. The wings of circling gulls were like porcelain, the red light shining through them. Nearby, ice cubes rattled in a martini pitcher. The tang of charcoal smoke reached him. He wanted a drink. He wanted to eat. He was tired. But when he'd been here earlier with Randy Van, the flame-color 260Z hadn't stood in the fenced and guarded parking lot belonging to this pier. Now the car was there. So he had to do this.

He clambered aboard a shiny white fiberglass cabin cruiser. It wasn't the biggest or showiest craft along here but it was big and showy enough, forty-five, fifty feet. The rear deck he stepped onto was glowing teak planks. Brass rails gleamed. He opened a pair of glossy hatch doors and a teak companionway took him down into a teak cabin with brass lanterns, buttoned cowhide couches, thick carpet. A stereo played softly. This, the car, the fact the cabin wasn't locked, all said he should be here. But he could be in a restaurant. That would be nice. Dave opened a door at the far end of the cabin. Beds were in the next cabin—not bunks, beds. He heard the splash of a shower.

Above the beds were cabinets. He stepped up on a bed and looked into the cabinets. Sheets, blankets, a life jacket, no carton. He stepped up on the other bed and the carton wasn't in those cabinets either. He got down and knelt and opened storage drawers under the beds. Clothes. Boat gear. He stood up, and one of the cabinet doors had swung open, and he rapped his skull on it. From beyond the door to the head, a male voice called, over the noise of the shower:

"Help yourself to a drink, baby. Fix me a G and T, will you? I'll be out in a minute."

Dave went into the forward cabin again and searched drawers under the cowhide couches. Cameras. Skin-diving stuff. No carton. He shut the drawers, looked around him, went behind a small bar. The carton stood on the floor. He picked it up, set it on the bar, put on his reading glasses. The flap corners of the carton had been tucked under each other to keep it closed. He tugged them up. Raw film was supposed to be in the box. It wasn't. A ledger lay there. He lifted it out and opened it. The entries went back more than five years. The handwriting was always the same though the pens used were different. The bookkeeping wasn't fancy—just amounts paid and by whom, never for what. The customer's names didn't tell him much—except Spence Odum's. The light wasn't good coming in through brass-bound portholes off the water. The music whispered. Small waves lisped against the hull. The boat very gently rocked. He laid the ledger on the bar.

Next in the box lay manila folders. In alphabetical order by customer name, the same names as those in the ledger. The folders held copies of invoices. Written by hand, not typed, by the same hand as had kept the ledger. The invoices weren't imprinted SUPER- STAR. They weren't imprinted at all, not even with an address. They were signed *Jack Fullbright*. They listed what Dave took to be photographic, lighting, recording equipment, each piece with a serial number. Charges were added up at the foot of a far-right column. All those he saw were scrawled *paid*. He chose a few invoices from different folders, creased them, and pushed them into a pocket.

"Who the hell are you?"

He turned around, taking off the glasses. A frail-looking girl in a bikini crouched halfway down the companionway with a thin hand on the brass rail. The dying light behind her said she was blond. There was a lot of hair and it shadowed her face. She took off big, round sunglasses and came down the last of the steps. Frowning.

"What are you doing? What's that stuff? Where's Jack?"

"In the shower," Dave said. "Are you Charleen Sims?"

She didn't answer. She ran past the bar into the cabin with the beds. "Jack," she said. "There's some dude out here, looking through your stuff."

"What!" A door slammed open. Fullbright appeared in the doorway to the front cabin. He was naked and wet. A white band around his pelvis interrupted the suntan. He stood still for a second, hands on the doorframe, staring at Dave, at the carton. Behind him, the girl looked scared. Then Fullbright charged. A swing of his arm sent carton, ledger book, files, flying. He lunged across the bar, grabbing for Dave. Dave stepped out from behind the bar. Fullbright's long reach knocked bottles off the shelf behind the bar. The bottles hit each other and shattered on the thick rug. Gin smells rose, whiskey smells. Dave pushed his glasses into a pocket.

"Take it easy," he said.

Fullbright didn't answer. He charged again. Dave sidestepped and put out a foot. Fullbright fell over it. His momentum pitched him into the companionway. He hit the steps hard. The crash was loud. For a few seconds, he lay face down and didn't move.

"Jack!" The girl ran to him, crouched by him, put her breakable-looking hands on him. "Jack? Are you all right?"

Fullbright moaned. Slowly he pushed himself up. He turned groggily on the steps. His look at Dave was savage. Blood ran out of his nose into his moustache, down his chin, into his chest hair. He put a hand over his nose.

"Oh, my God," the girl said.

"Why don't you get him a towel?" Dave said.

"He's bleeding to death," the girl said.

Dave took her skinny arm, pulled her to her feet. She was about as weightless as a bird. He swung her toward the sleep cabin. He slapped her butt. "Make it wet and cold."

She went, making whimpering noises. A cool, salty breath of air that said night was starting came down the companionway. Dave said to Fullbright:

"That was stupid. I'd already searched the box."

"Why?" It came muffled by the covering hand.

"It looked odd to me when you got it out of your office so fast after I'd been there. I thought you moved it on my account. Naturally that made me curious about what was in it. You run your own business on the side, no?"

Fullbright took away his hand to try to speak and blood ran down his front. "Ribbons, goddamn it!" He yelled this and blood sprayed fine in the bloody light.

"Coming!" She sounded panicked.

"Strictly porno and skinflick makers," Dave said.

Fullbright shut his eyes and nodded. He leaned against the wall. His chest moved as if he'd run a mile. His color was pasty. Ribbons came with a beach towel big as a blanket. It was heavy for her to lug. She held it against herself. Water drizzled out of it down her pretty legs. It soaked the papers scattered on the rug. She sat by him on the steps and began trying to mop the blood off him. He yanked a corner of the towel away from her and wadded it against his face, moaning again. He opened his eyes and glared at Dave. The towel muffled his words.

"You practically killed me," he said.

"You tripped," Dave said. "It's never safe to run on a boat." Watching Ribbons at her inept and tearful first aid, Dave found a cigarette and lit it. He told Fullbright, "I can understand your wanting to keep your little sideline secret from your partner. He was a religious fanatic. He wouldn't like it. He also was a business-man and wouldn't like your keeping all the profits for yourself." Fullbright began to shudder. Dave went into the cabin and stripped a blanket off one of the beds. He brought it back and pushed it at Ribbons. "He's chilling. Wrap him up."

"Why don't you get out of here?" she said. But she took the blanket and began getting it around Fullbright very clumsily. "Haven't you done enough?"

"I haven't found out enough." Dave said it from back of the bar, treading carefully in all the broken glass. He found a bottle of Courvoisier that Fullbright's hysteria had spared. Glasses hung upside down from racks over the bar. He took one down and half filled it. He went back to Fullbright, crouched in front of him, gently pulled away the hand clutching the wad of towel, tipped the brandy into his mouth. His eyes were closed again. He coughed, spluttered. Opened his eyes. He pushed feebly at the glass. "Take it," Dave said. "It'll make you feel better. Guarantee."

"He's dying," Ribbons whimpered.

"Nobody dies of a broken nose," Dave said. Fullbright had the glass in his hand now and worked on the brandy by himself. Dave stood up. "What I can't understand is why you'd bother to keep it a secret from me."

"The IRS," Fullbright said. "I never paid taxes on it."

"And you thought I'd run to the Feds," Dave said.

"Why not? I don't know you. I don't know what you're nosing around about. Yes, I was scared. I thought they had Jerry's murder all wrapped up. Then you walk in and it's a whole nother ballgame." He looked sourly at the strewn wreckage of his records. "I was going to take those out to sea tomorrow and dump them."

"So Dawson doesn't connect to Spence Odum," Dave said.

"Dawson connects to Old Rugged Cross Productions," Fullbright said. "Connected. To the Salvation Army, the Methodist Overseas Mission, the Baptist Synod, the Bringing in the Sheaves Women's Auxiliary."

An ashtray was on a coffee table in front of one of the buttoned couches. The ashtray was in the shape of a ship's helm, with a shallow bowl of amber glass set into it. Dave put ashes from his cigarette there. He looked at the weepy girl. "Your name isn't Ribbons. What is it really—Charleen?"

"I don't have to tell you anything." She looked at Fullbright. "Do I have to tell him anything?"

Dave said, "Only if your name is Charleen. And, if you'd really like to be helpful, where you come from."

"From Santa Monica." She jerked her head under all that heavy blond hair. "Two miles from here. All my life. And it's not Charleen." She made a face. "Yuck. It's not just Ribbons, either. It's —get ready for this—Scarlet Ribbons. From an old Harry Belafonte record my mom had when she was about ten or something. When she grew up she was going to have a little girl and call her Scarlet Ribbons. Believe it. Then she went and married a man named Schultz. And it didn't make any difference. Her name was Hathaway. Now that would have been almost all right, right? But Scarlet Ribbons Schultz? That's too much, isn't it?"

Dave smiled. "It's quite a bit." He asked Fullbright, "Feeling better?"

Fullbright pushed the towel into Ribbons's lap and stood up, hitching the blanket around him with one hand, the other one hanging onto the empty glass. "I felt fine until you showed up. I still would the fuck like to know what you want with me."

"Dawson was sleeping with a kid about like this one." Dave nodded at Ribbons. "In a top-level apartment above the Sunset Strip. She's not there anymore. I'm looking for someone to tell me where she is."

"Jerry? Sleeping with a teenage girl?" Fullbright laughed. "You have to be out of your mind."

"I don't believe he was murdered on his street," Dave said. "I believe he was murdered in that apartment and transported across town after he was dead and dumped there for his wife to stumble over in the morning. His wife and son."

"And you think Charleen—that's the girl, right? You expected me to have her here?" Fullbright took the brandy bottle off the bar and poured another shot into his glass. To do this he had to let the blanket fall but he didn't care. He drank from the glass before he picked the blanket up again. "I don't have her here. I never had her here. I never heard of her. If Jerry was really sleeping with her, you can bet he wouldn't tell anybody, least of all me. He had his moral superiority to maintain." He grinned. Very gingerly he touched his nose. Blood had stopped coming out of it but it was swelling. So was the flesh around his eyes. And turning dark red. "That's a wild idea. I mean, the wildest."

"Somebody's got her someplace," Dave said. "Unless she was killed the same night as Dawson, as Ludwig."

"Ludwig?" Fullbright's head came forward, scowling. "Herman Ludwig, the cameraman?"

"Shotgun," Dave said. "You didn't know?"

Fullbright looked stunned. He shook his head. "They got him, then—the commies?"

"That's what his wife thinks," Dave said.

"Jesus," Fullbright whispered and drank more brandy.

Ribbons took the wet and bloody towel back to the head.

97

"What about Spence Odum?" Dave said. "He never mentioned this Charleen child to you?"

"I haven't talked to Spence in—hell, how long? I find him when I want to get paid. That's about it."

"Take care of yourself," Dave said, and went up the companionway into what was left of daylight.

13

The headlights of the Triumph showed cut brush heaped high next to the driveway, almost covering the mailbox. The Triumph jolted down into the yard. Where limbs had been sawed off shrubs and trees, the wounds showed white. Under the naked-looking trees, sand was heaped, sacks of cement, stacked two-by-fours, bundles of wood shingles. The headlights shone back at him, multiplied in the panes of the French doors. He wanted the natural cover back.

He yanked the wheel of the Triumph to park it and the lights gleamed off a yellow motorbike. A youth sat with his back against it. He winced in the light and stood up. He seemed to unfold forever. He had to be seven feet tall. Reedy, all knuckles, wrists, joints, he came toward the car. Clean white Levi's, clean white T-shirt, clean fair hair cut short. Dave shut off the engine. Crickets. The boy leaned down to peer inside. He looked worried.

"Mr. Brandstetter? Can I talk to you, sir?"

"Not if you're selling magazines," Dave said.

"What?" The boy sounded ready to cry. "Oh, no. No, it's important. It's about—the case you're working on. Bucky Dawson's father? The one who was murdered, you know?"

"What's your name?" Dave pushed the door handle and the boy backed a step and Dave got out of the Triumph.

"Engstrom," the boy said, "Dwight." In the dark, his voice sounded too young for the size of him. "I saw you yesterday, when you came to see Bucky, and I heard you talking to his mom. I live across the street."

"In the house with the noisy window latches," Dave said. "Come on." He headed for the cookhouse. What he took to be bricks loomed in the courtyard under the oak. He said, "How did you find me?"

"I got worried. I asked Bucky. He said it was about the insurance and if you asked me I should just tell you the same thing I told the police."

Dave found the light switch this time without guessing. "You're on the basketball team at Bethel Church, right?" He opened the refrigerator and peered into the dark. "All I've got here that's nonalcoholic is milk." He looked up into the boy's scared blue eyes. "Will milk be all right?"

"Thank you. That's very kind." Engstrom stared around him. The kitchen was plainly stranger than he liked. It made him uneasy but he didn't run. "Yes, I'm on the team. I'm not a good athlete but I'm tall."

"I noticed." Dave unwrapped a glass, rinsed it at the tap, and filled it with milk. Engstrom took it, drank from it, and left a little-kid milk line on his upper lip.

He said, "Bucky said it was Sequoia Insurance, so I called them and they gave me this address. They gave me the phone too, but no one answered."

The plastic-bagged ice cubes in the freezer compartment had clumped. Dave took the bag out and banged it on the tile counter. He put the cubes that came loose into a glass and pushed the bag away again. "And what did you say to the police?" He measured gin over the ice cubes. He flavored the gin with vermouth. "That Bucky was with you in the church basement till eleven-thirty or twelve the night his father was killed?" He got olives from the refrigerator, dropped two into the drink, recapped the little bottle, shut it up in the dark again. Pushing the ice cubes clockwise with a finger, he turned to face the tall boy, eyebrows raised.

"Bucky said that was best. It wouldn't do any harm. They had the man that killed him. It would only confuse things and make a lot of useless trouble for his mother."

"But it wasn't true?" Dave tasted the drink. Warm.

"Reverend Shumate came down and said there was a phone call for him. Around nine. He went and didn't come back. I've been very—I felt bad about lying. Worried. Then when you came and started asking stuff, and Bucky was scared and begged me not to tell you anything different—well, I thought I better tell you the way it really was."

"Why not the police?" Dave lit a cigarette. "If you want to clear your conscience—they're the ones you lied to."

Dwight Engstrom's childlike face turned red. "Do I have to? I hate for them to know I lied before."

"It hardly ever works out," Dave said.

"I won't do it again," Engstrom said earnestly, "never in my life. I wouldn't have done it then for anybody else. But Bucky—I guess you don't know him too well. But Bucky would never do anything wrong."

"There aren't any human beings like that," Dave said.

"He just wanted to protect his mother," Engstrom said. "They had enough trouble already, didn't they?"

"How much is enough?" Dave said. "What did Bucky do with those three hours?"

"I don't know. I asked him. He said it didn't matter."

"It matters." Dave took jack cheese out of the fridge and cut squares off it. He held the small bright new cutting board out to the boy. "Eat. Did you get home at midnight?" Engstrom's big

101

clean hand fumbled little cheese cubes into his mouth. "Did you see Gerald Dawson, Senior, lying dead in front of his garage doors?"

Engstrom swallowed. "No, I came home the back way."

Dave took a bite of cheese. It had bits of *jalapeño* in it. Fiery. He nodded for the boy to eat some more. Engstrom shook his head. Dave set the board down and tried his drink again. It had chilled. He said, "But it was Shumate who came to get Bucky?"

"He was back in ten minutes. Reverend Shumate, I mean. That's why practice went on so late." Engstrom gave a wry little smile. "He's a basketball freak. He never wants to quit." He finished off the milk, set the glass down with a click on the counter tiles, and looked anxious. "It'll be all right, now, will it? You won't have to tell the police I lied, will you?"

"It won't be all right," Dave said, "you know that. But I thank you for coming and telling me. It will help. Not Bucky Dawson and his mother. It will help me." He put a hand in the middle of Engstrom's long bony back and steered him to the kitchen door. "Maybe I won't have to tell the police. But if I do, you won't feel too bad about it."

"Oh, yes, I will," Engstrom said, sounding again as if he might cry. He took three steps into the darkness and turned back. "Why won't I?"

"You'll be among friends," Dave said.

His legs ached, not from the climb but from sitting on the floor at Noguchi's. Also he was a little drunk from the flame-warmed sake. But the black-lacquer surroundings had been pleasant and the food had been all right. He'd kept away from vinegar and raw fish. Mel Fleischer had been amiable enough and his young friend Makoto had been good to look at. He hadn't worn a happy coat. He'd worn torn-off Levi's and a tank top printed with the USC Trojan helmet. In the candlelight, he'd looked carved out of some fine-grained brown wood rubbed to a flawless finish. He had a terrible accent but his smile made up for it. Dave hoped he'd understood as little English as he spoke, because most of Mel's talk had been about boys he'd had before Makoto. The stories were witty even if you'd already heard them, and Dave had. But he doubted they'd inspire fidelity.

He tried the buzzer at number thirty-six but no one came, and he worked the lock with the blade from his key case again. He rolled the glass door quietly aside and didn't turn on the lamps. He used the cord to pull the curtains across and went through the place with a small flashlight. Nobody'd been here. It was all the same as before. He checked the closet again, poked around among the little shoes. He didn't know why there should be so much grit under them. You didn't pick up dirt like this cruising sidewalks, sitting in the Strip Joint, doing the boogaloo. It wasn't sand from a beach. It was soil. It looked and crumbled between his fingers like crop-growing earth.

He went back into the main room and worked the cord so the drapes came open. Out there, Los Angeles sloped sparkling to the sea. The surf sound came again from the traffic along the Strip. And there was the sound of a stereo through a wall. More than simply the thud of bass. He could almost make out the tune. He stepped past the shadowy shapes of the velveteen couches and put his ear to the wall. It was that late Billie Holliday album, the one with too much orchestra. She'd had almost no voice left by then. *I'll hold out my hand, and my heart will be in it* . . .

He pressed the buzzer next door. The glass panel was open and the music came out clear and sad. A voice yelped over it. He thought what it meant was that he was supposed to come in so he went in. The unit was the same as thirty-six except for the bulky case of one of those television sets that projects its images on a wall, and modular shelves weighed down with sound equipment, amplifier, receiver, open-reel and cassette tape decks, record player, equalizer, all of it black-faced and very new. Big black waffle-front monitor speakers hung angled from the melon-color ceiling.

A young man's shaggy head appeared over the back of a couch. The face was familiar. From TV commercials—savings-and-loan, deodorant soap, dogfood. He had a wide mouth that curled up attractively at the corners. It didn't do that now. He frowned and stood up quickly. He was wearing a shower coat in narrow rainbow stripes. A fat paperback book was in his hand. He frowned and said something the music didn't let Dave hear. Dave looked blank. The young man went to the shelves. Billie Holliday sang *You brought me violets for my furs* . . . Then she wasn't singing anymore.

"That what you wanted? Too much noise?"

"It's not noise," Dave said, "and I didn't come to complain. I came to ask about the girl next door." He crossed the shag carpet to show his open wallet to the young man. "It's an insurance matter. Death claims."

"Is she dead? Is that what happened to her?"

"What makes you think something happened to her?"

The book was still in his hand. He took it to the coffee table where there was a stack of shiny books. He laid it on the stack and picked up a cigarette pack and a lighter. He offered Dave a cigarette and lit one for him and for himself. He shrugged. "She hasn't been around lately. And I always knew when she was around. Believe it."

"The walls are thin," Dave said.

"I'm not secretive and I like the view." He picked up an empty mug from the table. "She never complained about my stereo. I never complained about her tricks. A drink? Coffee? What?"

"Coffee's fine," Dave said, "if it's no trouble."

"Sit down." He went into a kitchen beyond a breakfast bar like Charleen's. Dave sat down and heard him pour coffee. "My name's Cowan, Russ Cowan." He came back with two mugs and set them down. The coffee in them steamed. "It must be interesting work." He didn't sit down.

"So must yours," Dave said.

Cowan grimaced. "Except I never know if there's going to be any more." He went back to the breakfast bar.

"I always know there'll be more," Dave said. "She brought pickups here?"

"You wouldn't think Sylvia would let her get away with that, would you?" Cowan poured brandy into a little globe glasses and came back with them. "But Sylvia concentrates on her cards. There's a lot she misses if it doesn't go on at an octagonal table." He handed Dave one of the little glasses, kept the other for himself, and sat down.

"Thank you." Dave passed the glass under his nose. It was Martel's. "Nice. When was the last time you saw the girl?"

Cowan squinched up his eyes and looked at the ceiling. "A week?" he asked himself. "No. It was longer than that." He snapped his fingers and grinned at Dave. "I know when it was." He named the date. "That's eleven days ago, right? The reason I remember is, my agent called. I had to buy him lunch at Scandia. He'd signed me for a big part in *Quincy.*"

"A good day for you." Dave set down the brandy glass and tried the coffee. It was rich and strong. "A bad day for Gerald Dawson. Somebody broke his neck."

"And that's what you're investigating?"

"He rented that unit for the girl. If Sylvia would have been upset about the tricks, think how he'd have felt. Did you ever meet him?"

"A little, dark, wiry guy in his forties? I never met him but he was in and out so much I figured he must be the one paying the bills. Who killed him? Why?"

"I was hoping you could tell me." Dave drank some more coffee and followed it with a taste of the brandy. "That's very nice. Was she noisy as usual that night? Or"—he glanced at the sound equipment—"were you listening to music?"

"I was sleeping. That was a long lunch. All afternoon. I was boozed stupid. I had a date for later." He wagged his head with a forlorn smile. "I wanted to wake up fresh and sober. Fat chance. My bedroom's next to her bedroom. All hell broke loose in there. Her yelling, him yelling, some old woman yelling."

"What time would this have been?" Dave asked.

"You bet I looked at the clock. Resentfully. You know how lousy you can feel when you wake up too soon after you pass out drunk? Early. What—eight, ten after?" He snorted a laugh, stubbed out his cigarette in a brown pottery ashtray. "I lay there thinking it was going to end soon. It didn't. So I got up and crawled into the shower. When I came out, I guess I heard the tag end of it."

"Could you make out any of the words?" Dave asked.

Cowan tilted his shaggy head, blinked thoughtfully, eyes twinkling. "Yeah, now that you mention it, I did. From the wedding service. 'For richer, for poorer, in sickness, in health.' Only not like at a wedding service. She was yelling it and she was broken up, you could tell, furious, desperate, everything." He raised his hands and wagged them.

"The girl? Charleen?"

"No, no. The old woman. Then it sounded like somebody fell down. I mean, this place is built very flimsily. I felt it in the floor under my feet. I thought I better go see. But I only got to the door there. And out this old woman comes. A big old woman, tall."

"Walking with a cane," Dave said, "dragging one foot."

"That one." Cowan nodded. "And then it settled down. I was clean but I still didn't feel good. I went back to bed. Maybe I got an hour's sleep, and then it started again. Only this time there were two men. It wasn't that loud. Except for Charleen screeching 'Get out of here and leave us alone,' I couldn't make out any words. The men didn't shout." Cowan took a cigarette from the pack Dave offered. Dave did the lighting up this time. Cowan said, "I guess I felt a little better by then. Anyway, I was curious. I heard her door slide and I went to see who this one was. A gangly dude in a suit that looked like J. C. Penney in Fresno."

106

"You didn't see his face?"

"I only see their backs. They have to go thataway to get to the stairs, remember?"

Dave worked on the coffee and brandy again. "What do you think was going on?"

Cowan shrugged. "She was Dawson's old lady, wasn't she? Man must've been her lawyer. Anyway, it wasn't over. Around nine-thirty, it started up again. Men shouting. I went to snoop and Dawson shoves this kid out. I mean hard. He hit that iron railing out there and I thought he'd go over it. But he didn't. Stocky kid, very black eyebrows. He was crying. He went and hammered on the door awhile but they didn't let him back in, and next time I looked, he was gone." Cowan nodded to himself, drank coffee, sipped brandy, blew out smoke. "Yeah, lively night."

"No developments beyond that?" Dave wondered. "Or did you lose interest?"

"I scrambled some eggs and watched some TV. I had a late date. My girl friend was house-sitting in Beverly Hills, kid-sitting, dog-sitting. The people were going to be home at midnight. We planned to hit the discos. So around eleven I started getting ready. And all hell broke loose next door again. I was shaving, so I didn't go look right away. But when I did, the kid was back. Charleen came running out on the gallery and he came out after her and dragged her back inside. She must have been drunk as hell. She was just barely able to stand up. He practically carried her."

"And Dawson?" Dave said. "Where was he?"

"I didn't see him," Cowan said.

14

Old nails shrieked, old lumber cracked. He lay face down, eyes shut tight, wanting to sleep again. He'd been too many places yesterday, all of them too far apart. The Triumph didn't ride easy. He felt bruised. That he could probably soak out in the shower. What wouldn't soak out were the faces, the voices, the sad facts. The trouble with life was, nobody ever got enough rehearsal. He groped out for the stereo and didn't find it. He turned his head and opened an eye. Knots in the pine wall stared at him. He pushed the power button. Harpsichord, Bach, Wanda Landowska. He blew out air, threw back the sweat-soaked sheet, sat up. He ran a hand down over his face, tottered to his feet, staggered to the bathroom.

"What a treat!" Amanda said when he came out.

He stepped back inside and took an old blue corduroy robe off a hook on the bathroom door. He put it on and tied the sash and came out again. He took the mug of coffee she offered and said, "The thing that is going to make you a success is that you get everything to happen right away. Nobody gets building materials delivered in two days. Nobody gets workmen on the job that fast."

He went out into the courtyard. The big speechless sons were on the roof of the front building ripping up shingles and kicking them off the eaves. Showers of dry leaves, seeds, dirt, fell with each kick. The one-armed father sat under the oak grouchily knocking old mortar off bricks with a trowel.

"Did you want it to happen later?" Amanda asked.

"Only if they invent a way to do it without sound."

"If they don't start early, they don't start." She studied him over the rim of her coffee mug. "Are you all right? I could send them away."

"No, I'm all right." From the cookhouse came the smell of bacon, the sound of bacon sizzling. He went that way. "It's the case that's all wrong. I said yesterday that if I were the man's wife and kid I'd run away."

"I remember," she said. "Have they?"

"I doubt it." Dave stopped at the cookhouse door. Delgado was in there. He looked rested and clean. He was turning bacon with a fork. Dave smelled coffee, heard the drip of it in the pot. Delgado smiled at him. It made Dave unhappy. Unhappier. He'd forgotten Delgado. He said to Amanda, "But now I *know* they should have."

She stared. "You don't mean they killed him."

"Respectability." Dave stepped into the cookhouse. "You remember respectability? No, you're too young. Everybody lived by it once. It never meant much, it hardly means anything anymore. It didn't bear any relation to reality. Today most people know that. But not everybody. Gerald Dawson found it out and it killed him. Now it's going to destroy his wife and son."

"Decency," Amanda began.

"Not decency. Respectability." Dave watched Delgado lay the bacon slices on paper toweling on the stove, watched him pour beaten eggs from a yellow bowl into a frying pan where butter sizzled. "What the neighbors think of you. Only there aren't any neighbors anymore. And if they think, they don't think about you, they think about themselves."

109

She gave him one of her long, thin brown cigarettes. The pack came out of a pocket in a chambray workshirt with pearl buttons. She lit it for him. "It's more widespread than you think," she said. "People pretend not, but it is."

Delgado said, "I located him for you." His glance at Dave was brief. He got busy laying toast on plates, bacon strips, spooning out the eggs. But the look was that of a kid wanting praise, needing praise, lots of it. "Nothing orthodox went far. Driver's license, I mean, that stuff." He turned and held out plates to Dave and Amanda. "But I thought about his business. And I started around places where they develop movies and record sound and that kind of thing. I didn't pick the big ones."

They went out into the heat and brightness of the morning. They trailed back across to the fencing room. They didn't sit on the bed today. They sat on the floor, backs against the wall, in a row, Amanda in the middle. Delgado looked past her, eager, pleased with himself. "I picked the little ones. And, sure enough, down Wilcox, across from the park, there's this dark little doorway kind of hidden next to one that opens into an honest-to-god shop— knitting? lamps? sandals? something. Anyway, behind the other door is a place where you can edit film and dub sound tracks and all that. Two, three rooms jammed with equipment, run by this little wall-eyed guy. And he wasn't going to give me shit." Delgado broke off, flushed, and said "Excuse me," to Amanda. He said to Dave, "Only there was this poster on the wall. A Spence Odum production, no less." Delgado washed down a big fast bite of toast with coffee.

"All the Way Down?" Dave asked.

"Sisters in Leather," Delgado said. "A lot of pudgy broads in nothing but crash helmets and boots on big black badass motorcycles. Dikey."

"Watch it," Dave said.

"So Odum's got this place he usually shoots," Delgado said. "He runs around to locations in a white van. He doesn't pay for permits.

110

He shoots and runs. But the thing he calls his studio is out on the Strip. Back of a real-estate office. One room. Some producer."

"You didn't go there," Dave said.

"I banged on the door," Delgado said. "Nobody came. In the real-estate office, they never heard of Spence Odum. Talk about respectable. It could have been a church." He poked into the pocket of a very crisp white short-sleeve shirt—he must have re-deemed a bundle of laundry someplace—and handed Dave a slip of paper. "There's the address."

"Thanks." Dave gave him a smile. "Well done."

"Anything else?" Delgado sounded eager.

Dave shook his head. "It's over. The son did it. Don't feel bad. You always have to chase a lot of wrong answers before you get the right one. You know that."

"Yeah," Delgado said but he sounded forlorn. "I know. What about the teenage girl—Charleen?"

"She was a witness," Dave said, "but we're not going to find her. The last time she was seen alive—if she was alive—was with Bucky."

"You said you liked it," Amanda said. "I think it's horrible. How can you go through it again and again?"

"It doesn't always turn out this depressing." Dave set his plate down, pushed to his feet, stepped over the plate, and went to where his slacks and jacket hung over a loudspeaker. He came back with his wallet and pushed into Delgado's shirt pocket a fold of fifty-dollar bills. "Pay off your motel so there'll be someplace I can get you when I need you—right?"

Delgado's face darkened. He handed back the money. "Stop acting guilty, will you? You didn't take my job. That wasn't me talking. That was Jim Beam."

Dave tucked the money into Delgado's pocket again. "I didn't say I was giving it to you. You'll earn it." He looked down at unhappy Amanda. "Forget it," he said. "I'm sorry for talking about it in front of you. Smile, okay? And go forth and destroy?"

"Just old two-by-fours," she said. "Not lives."

"Come on, now," he said. "It's not that simple."

"I'm sorry." Her smile was wan. "I didn't mean it."

He went to rummage in cartons for fresh clothes. "You meant it and it means you're a very nice lady, but I knew that anyway. I promise to wash the blood off my hands before I come back to you."

"Oh, Dave," she said. "I said I was sorry."

He headed for the bathroom to dress. Before he shut the door he said to Delgado, "Write down your address and phone number and leave it for me, okay?"

"A man's voice," Mildred Dawson said. She was no more than a tall, dim shape in the middle of a room darkened to keep out the sunlight, to keep out the heat. The room was hot and stuffy all the same. Dave wore a light knit soccer shirt, blue-and-white striped, and blue linen trousers, also light, but he was sweating. So was Bucky, sturdy and afraid in cutoff jeans, shirt open on his woolly chest. He kept sitting down and standing up again. Lyle Shumate kept murmuring to him. The woman, leaning crooked on her cane, said, "It sounded a little like Bucky. I asked who it was. He wouldn't say. All he would say was that my husband was at that apartment with that girl. Fornicating." She whispered the word.

Dave said, "Was that his expression?"

"Do you think I'd forget it?" she said. "He told me if I wanted to save him, I must come and take him away."

"Save him from what?" Dave looked at Bucky. "From death? Did he threaten to kill him?"

"From eternal damnation," she said.

"That means death, doesn't it, Reverend?" Dave peered through the shadows at the lanky man on the couch. "Didn't it occur to you that Gerald Dawson wasn't killed by Lon Tooker at all? That nobody jumped him out here on the street? That the voice on the phone belonged to his killer? That you were letting the wrong man suffer, possibly even die?"

"Any of us can buy eternal damnation any day," Shumate said. "Outside the redeeming grace of our Lord and Savior Jesus Christ, there is nothing but eternal damnation."

"That's not an answer," Dave said. "That's a sermon." He swung back to Mildred Dawson. "So you went. How?"

"I have my own car," she said. "You know that. It has automatic shift. I manage."

"How did you manage the main door at the apartment complex?" Dave asked. "It locks itself. Only tenants have keys. Was your husband waiting in the lobby to let you in?"

"No. I pushed the door and it opened."

"It was braced," Bucky said, "just a crack. With a brown rubber wedge. The kind made to put under doors, you know? Only it wasn't under this one. It was stuck in the crack. At the hinge side, where it wouldn't be noticed."

"But you noticed it," Dave said.

"I was noticing everything that night," Bucky said. "Nothing like this ever happened to me before."

"It isn't going to happen again," Dave said.

"Don't be abusive." Shumate put his arm around the boy's thick shoulders. "This boy has done nothing wrong."

"You've all done wrong and you know it. Or I hope you do. If you don't, that church of yours is in trouble." He turned back to Mildred Dawson. "He'd given you the apartment number, this anonymous man on the phone? You went there, right? Up all those stairs by yourself?"

"It was a struggle," she said, "but the Lord gave me the strength. Number thirty-six, yes."

"But they weren't fornicating when you got there," Dave said, "were they? They were eating supper."

"If you know, why do you ask?" she said.

"Habit," Dave said. "I sometimes get the truth. You asked him to come home, did you?"

"I don't believe you have any authority to question us," Shumate said. "I don't believe any of us is compelled by law to tell you anything."

"You might as well practice on me," Dave said. "It will get you used to the process. A detective lieutenant from the sheriff's office named Salazar will be repeating it soon."

"Gerald wouldn't come," Mildred Dawson said. "He'd found 'happiness' and he wasn't going to give it up. No matter what it cost. Him or me or Bucky or anyone. He was completely changed. I hardly knew him." She made a bitter, mocking sound. "A little stick of a thing, and she had him bewitched."

"Did he strike you?" Dave said. "Someone fell down. My witness heard it."

"He wouldn't," she said. "It was the girl."

"So you came home and called Shumate," Dave said.

Shumate said, "He wouldn't come for me, either."

"I didn't want Bucky to know," Mildred Dawson said. "I was so ashamed. But Gerald would come for Bucky. He loved Bucky and if Bucky asked him, he'd come home. So I told Reverend Lyle to send Bucky, and Bucky went."

Dave looked at the black-browed boy. "They weren't eating when I got there," Bucky said. "They forgot to lock the door. They were naked in bed together. And he hit me. Knocked me down, hard. He picked me up and threw me out. I banged on the door and cried. He wouldn't let me back in."

"But later he did," Dave said. "Around eleven."

"What!" Bucky stood up again.

"And you tried to take him by force and you broke his neck. My witness didn't see how you got his body out of there. But he did see Charleen try to run away. He saw you drag her back into the apartment."

"He's lying!" Bucky shouted. "I wasn't there then."

114

"He thought she was drunk because she staggered. But that wasn't it, was it? You were trying to kill her. She was half dead, wasn't she? Then, when you got her back inside, she was all the way dead—just like your father."

"No!" Bucky wailed. "I didn't kill anyone."

"You couldn't burn her up like your father's dirty magazines," Dave said. "What did you do with her, Bucky?"

"She was alive when I left there. My father was alive." Bucky choked on tears. He held out his hands, begging. "You have to believe me. Please! Please!"

"His father's car was here." Shumate stood and put an arm around Bucky. "Doesn't that convince you?"

"Not that he drove it," Dave said. "Anyway, it's Salazar you have to convince." He went to the door. Bucky ignored Shumate. He stared wide-eyed at Dave. Mildred Dawson stared. Dave opened the door and went out into the heat.

15

Piñatas hung from the old black rafters of a lean-to roof above Salazar's beautiful head. They seemed to float there like animals in a Chagall painting—papier-mâché goats, burros, chickens, furred and feathered in shredded tissue paper, colors bright and clashing, red, orange, green, blue, bubble-gum pink. With flat tissue-paper eyes, they watched Indianans in Bermuda shorts and sundresses inch their way along the narrow bricked lanes between the huarache booths, sombrero booths, serape booths, the cactus-candy and woven-basket booths of Olvera Street. Mariachi music twanged and tin-trumpeted from loudspeakers. The hot air was thick with chili smells from greasy taco stands. A quartet of rouged children with paper roses in their hair and spangles on ruffled skirts danced to the music.

Behind Salazar, strings of shiny painted gourds framed a dark restaurant doorway. He sat across from Dave at a gingham-covered table and ate enchiladas, as Dave did, washing them down, as Dave did, with orange soda from thick, lukewarm bottles. "I can't arrest him. How can I arrest him?" He wiped his chin with a paper napkin. He looked like a silent-movie idol—Gilbert Roland? "Ken Barker says he was murdered on his own street in LA. Ken Barker says this porno-shop owner killed him. Now I'm supposed to come barging in and say he was killed in some apartment on the Strip. His own kid killed him?"

"His own kid admits he was there," Dave said. "Cowan saw him there."

"Cowan didn't see any murder," Salazar said.

"But nobody saw Gerald Dawson alive after that. The Medical Examiner says he was killed between ten and midnight. And Bucky lied to Barker."

Salazar shook his head and moodily poked at his refritos with his fork. "It doesn't make a murder case," he said. "All it makes is a family fight."

"Come on, now," Dave said. "You don't believe that. What's the matter? Is it the car you're worried about? Why didn't the wife, the widow, think of it afterward, get into her own car with Bucky, drive back there, so Bucky could drive Dawson's car home while she followed in her own car?"

"People get hysterical, they forget details." Glumly Salazar drank orange soda. "Even details as big as a car."

"Alone, maybe," Dave said. "A kid, especially. But he wasn't alone. His mother helped. So did the preacher. They even remembered a detail as small as the keys."

Salazar's mouth was full of pink rice. He looked his question with big, smoldering brown eyes.

"If Dawson had driven himself home and was in the process of opening the garage, the keys would have been in his hand. They weren't. Or in his pocket. Or on the street. They weren't anywhere. Lon Tooker didn't have them. I suggest you search Bucky's room."

"You're kidding." Salazar paused with a forkful of enchilada halfway to his mouth. "Why hide the stupid keys?"

117

"Because two of them fitted the Strip apartment—the street door, the door to unit thirty-six."

"Why not get rid of them and leave the car keys?" Salazar put the forkful of food into his mouth.

"Because he didn't know which they were. There would have been keys to Superstar Rentals there too. Anyway, you mentioned hysteria."

Salazar washed the food down with orange soda. "And you mentioned presence of mind. You can't have it both ways, Brandstetter. If it was like you say, he could have stripped off all the keys but the ones for the car."

"Not without prompting a lot of questions," Dave said. "It was better to take the chance of the cops assuming the killer had taken the whole bunch and thrown them away."

"And why didn't he?" Salazar said.

"Because Bucky drove the car and he still has them."

Salazar cocked an eyebrow, pressed his mouth tight, shook his head. "Barker says you're very, very smart. But there are different kinds of smart, aren't there? What I hear in all this is the rattle of a cash register. You're trying to save that insurance company that hired you money. Tooker can't help you. But the widow and orphan can, right?"

"Tooker didn't have anything to do with this."

"What about the horse stuff on the deceased's clothes?"

"Check the closet in unit thirty-six," Dave said, "the shoes there, the dirt on the floor."

"Yeah, unit thirty-six." Salazar brushed a fly away from the guacamole bowl. "What did the widow and the kid care about unit thirty-six?"

"They didn't care about anything else," Dave said. "If you can't grasp that, no wonder you don't believe me. Let me explain it to you one more time. What they were trying to do by losing the keys to the place, bringing the body away from there, bringing the car away from there, wasn't just to avoid a charge of murder one. They wanted it to look as if Gerald R. Dawson had never set foot in that apartment, never touched that girl. To them, the Strip is Sodom and Gomorrah. Gerald R. Dawson was a saint."

Salazar didn't say anything. He only looked. He dipped a chip of fried tortilla into the guacamole, put it into his mouth, and munched. He licked his fingers.

Dave said, "They wanted the police, the *Times*, the *Examiner*, the 'Eyewitness News', everybody, the world, to think their beloved husband and father was, in death as in life, the same upright and unsullied crusader for Christ they'd always believed he was. Hell, Bucky showed me that the first morning I saw him. He claimed those porno magazines he was burning were his. They weren't. His father had ripped them off at Lon Tooker's shop. But Bucky didn't care about bringing what his unreal little world would call disgrace on himself. No matter what it cost him—he was going to protect his father's image."

"Even if he had to kill him to do it." Salazar picked up his orange-soda bottle and set it down again. He laughed. Not happily. Hopelessly. "Wow, that is weird, Brandstetter. You know that, don't you? Weird."

"If your lab people will take their little vacuum cleaners and go over that apartment," Dave said, "you'll see it's not all that weird. Mrs. Dawson wasn't able to save her husband from hellfire. Lyle Shumate was his minister and friend but he failed. Bucky failed, and he couldn't accept it. Maybe he talked it over with mama, maybe not. But he went back there and tried to use force and something went wrong. Bucky claimed his dad couldn't fight but he must have tried. Anyway, he ended up dead."

"Weird," Salazar said again, and stacked his dishes. "I mean, even if you accept it as accidental—it's still weird. And, anyway, what about the girl? You've been in that unit. Her body's not there. Where is she?"

"Damned if I know." Dave got off the creaky wooden chair. "I can't see Bucky killing her in cold blood." He picked up the check, took out his glasses, and read it. "But where did she go? I keep seeing twiggy little girls under haystacks of hair and hoping they're her. They never are." He tucked the glasses away. "I don't find Bucky easy to believe but I can't shake the feeling she's still alive."

"Not if he killed his old man." Salazar stood up and stretched. His fists struck the piñatas. They swung and jostled each other, rustling. "Not if she saw him do it." He steadied the piñatas.

Ducking under their trailing fringes, Dave went down through the dark doorway into the restaurant and paid the check. When he came back outside, Salazar was tossing dimes and quarters to the dancing children. Dave said to him:

"Check out that apartment, please?"

"Barker won't like it," Salazar said.

"It will be one less case for him to worry about."

Hot daylight came down through the roof into the big room. Sawdust drifted in the shafts. Above, the shadows of the speechless sons moved. Their shoes clunked and shuffled. Saws whined, hammers banged. Amanda stood looking up, shading her eyes with a hand and trying to talk over the racket. Beside her stood Ken Barker. He nodded. He pointed. His bulk made Amanda look very small and fragile. With *homo sapiens,* nature was still building experimental models. They could have represented different species. He crossed the sawdusty floor to stand beside them. Barker turned him a sour look. Through the carpentery noises he said:

"You're making yourself damned unpopular."

"I can't hear you," Dave lied. He kissed Amanda's forehead and led Barker out into the courtyard, where grouchy one-armed dad still sat in the speckled shade of the big oak, methodically clamping bricks between his knees and whacking mortar off them with his trowel. Amanda went to him and they conferred. Dave led Barker into the cookhouse, got beer from the refrigerator, pried off the caps, and handed a bottle to Barker. "Salazar drinks orange soda pop with his Mexican food. I thought I better have as clear a head as he had."

"Mrs. Dawson is getting out a restraining order against you," Barker said. "She told me and the DA you were harassing her and accusing her son of murder. I don't have to ask you if it's true. I know you."

Dave leaned against the sink counter and told him the whole long story. He was getting bored with it now. Also uneasy. There was a warped, pathetic kind of logic to Bucky's killing his father. An inevitability. Dawson had set standards he couldn't live by himself. His son was too young yet to have begun to doubt them. The thing had been building from the day Bucky was born. But not Charleen's death. They made an awkward match. He didn't put this into words for Barker. He finished his Dos Equis and his story. "There's no restraining order against you. Go through Bucky's room. You'll find those keys."

Barker dug into a pocket. He held up keys on a small bright ring that dangled off a stiff leather fob. Dave put out a hand for them. Barker dropped them into his hand. JESUS SAVES was stamped into the fob. There had been gilt in the letters once. It had almost all rubbed off.

"Where did you get them? Not from Tooker."

Barker's smile was ironic. "Bucky. This morning. After your visit, he thought it was time to tell the truth, the whole truth. He and his mother did go to the Strip to collect dad's car—but in the morning, after she found the body, before she phoned us."

"Meaning they didn't know he was dead till then?"

"You got it." Barker set his empty bottle down on the cold stove, opened the refrigerator, brought out two full bottles. He stretched an arm past Dave for the opener on the counter. The bottles went *fft!* when he uncapped them. He handed one to Dave and tilted one up himself.

"Why isn't that just another lie?" Dave said.

121

"Because Bucky remembered a witness. A black in a starchy security uniform who's too old to care about sleeping anymore and who looks after Sylvia Katzman's underground garage. He isn't too good at standing around these days." Barker reached into Dave's shirt pocket for a cigarette and let Dave light it for him. "So he parks his 1962 Corvair right next to the driveway on the street. And he sits in it. Until some tenant slopes in. Then he gets out and looks alert and protective with that big revolver on his hip until they leave the garage. Then he gets back into his car. He can see a lot from there. Not just who drives in, but anyone who walks up the stairs to the front door. He saw Mildred Dawson around eight, Lyle Shumate around nine, Bucky around ten. Come and go. He saw Bucky again when he came to fetch his father's car, a little after dawn next morning. They even exchanged some words about it."

"But he didn't see Bucky a second time the night of the murder?" Dave lit a cigarette for himself. "At eleven?"

"Negative," Barker said. "And never any Charleen—not at any time. Or any Gerald Dawson—dead or alive." Barker went and leaned in the doorway, gazing across the courtyard at the stolid sons on the front roof. He blew away tobacco smoke. It didn't drift much. The air was still. "Of course, he has to go to the toilet. The old prostate isn't what it once was. He could have missed Bucky coming back and carrying out two dead bodies. He doesn't think so. And neither do I."

"We know where Dawson's body went," Dave said. "but not Charleen's. It's not in her apartment—I've been there. But Cowan saw her try to run away and saw Bucky drag her back inside. And that's the last anyone ever saw of her." He frowned to himself. "She must have been hurt. She wasn't drunk. There were no liquor bottles in the place."

Barker turned and drank beer and studied him. "You know, you sound shaky. You're always on target. On this, you're missing all over the place. What is it? No ground under your feet? I knew you meant a lot to Medallion. I didn't think Medallion meant that much to you. You're all of a sudden insecure, right?"

"Forget it," Dave said disgustedly. "I make mistakes all the time. You know that. What did Salazar do—only tell me he'd look at that apartment?"

"He's got a team there," Barker said. "I happened to stumble across him. But Dawson wasn't killed there, and you know it." He cocked his head. "You've been through the place. You'd have found the signs, wouldn't you? He died of a broken neck. Broken neck, strangulation, suffocation—ninety-nine times out of a hundred, the muscles that control the bladder and bowels let go. They had let go, Dave."

"When you got to the body, yes," Dave said. "More than six hours afterward. In hot weather, that's normal. Ninety-nine times out of a hundred is a sloppy figure."

Amanda came to the door. "Ah-ha! Do I get beer too?"

"In judicial hangings, where the neck is broken," Barker said, "it's a hundred percent."

"In judicial hangings," Dave said, "there's anxiety beforehand, there are nerves at work. Dawson wasn't expecting his neck to be broken."

"Dear God." Amanda ducked in past Barker, peered into the dark refrigerator, and brought out the cardboard carton the Dos Equis had come in. It was empty. She said in a faint, wavery voice, trying to smile, "Time to go storeside."

"I'll go." Dave took a step.

"No, no. You two stay and have your cheerful little chat." She looked pale. "I think I'd like to miss it."

"I'm sorry all over again," Dave said.

Barker asked, "Did I say something wrong?"

Amanda gave her head a wan little shake. "It comes with the territory," she said, and fled. But she came running back, breathless, after a moment. "I forgot. Someone called Randy Van has been on the phone for you. Strange voice. Would it be a boy type or a girl type?"

"He hasn't made up his mind yet," Dave said. She looked blank and went away, and Dave told Barker, "Anyway, Tooker can go back to his horses."

"Not if Dawson was killed in front of his house," Barker said. "And I still think he was."

Dave shook his head. "That old black man was asleep."

16

The wig was different and so was the costume, if costume wasn't an unfair word. The wig was brown with sunny streaks in it, and the dress was shirtmaker, beige, twill, with agate-color buttons. The handbag lying on the bar matched. So did the big shoes, heels hooked over the braces of the bar stool. Nail polish and lipstick were red-orange this time. But nothing was different about the smile. It said Dave was welcome, more than welcome.

The sunlight was slivered by the bamboo blinds on the windows again. There were fewer agents and lawyers and clients in the room, and at the far end of it no one fiddled with the musical instruments on the bandstand. Dave took the stool next to Randy's and looked at the drink he was holding.

"Margarita," Randy said. "Will you?"

"Dos Equis," Dave told the coveralled bartender. He said to Randy, "So Odum lied. He does know Charleen."

"She never worked in any of his pictures," Randy said, "but she was going to."

125

" 'Was'?" Dave said. The bottle came and a cold, wet glass. "He changed his plans?"

" 'Is', then," Randy said. "I only meant it hasn't happened. He's writing a script for her. He showed me her photo. I said, 'Why, in God's name?' And he said it was a favor for a friend."

"Photo?" Dave said.

Randy upended the handsome purse. Out came cigarettes, lighter, lipstick, coins, a rattle of keys. The big male hand with the scrupulously female nails pushed a glossy snapshot along the bar at Dave. It looked as if it had been taken in a motel room. There was something wrong about the light—he wasn't sure what. She was naked and she really did look twelve years old. The obscene pose was pathetic. He raised eyebrows at Randy. "What friend?"

"Jack Fullbright," Randy said. "I think he took the picture."

"Odum parts easily with things to you," Dave said. "Things and information."

Randy licked salt off the edge of the margarita glass. "We've been close. We still are, every now and then. He likes boys who dress up in women's clothes. I told you that. He's warm and funny and kind."

"And not everybody likes boys who dress up in women's clothes," Dave said. "And all boys who dress up in women's clothes don't like fat, fiftyish pornographers."

"It's symbiosis," Randy said. He batted his false eyelashes at Dave and swallowed delicately from his drink. "Is that the right word? Or do I want 'exploitation'?"

"What's Fullbright doing for him?" Dave drank beer. He felt big, heavy, awkward. Every move he made seemed like an act, a fake. His voice sounded too deep. It couldn't be sad. He'd never wanted to wear a dress. It had to be funny. He bit his lip to keep from laughing. "Or had Fullbright already done this favor?"

"He's going to let Spence have all the equipment he needs free," Randy said. "What's funny?"

"You make me feel like Jack Youngblood," Dave said.

126

"And who might that be?" Randy tilted his head.

"A man who knocks people down on football fields."

Randy shrugged. "If you're butch, you're butch." He made his laugh giddy and patted his wig. "But football is not my kind of contact sport."

"When you were playing your kind with Odum," Dave said, "did he tell you why Fullbright wanted this favor?"

The margarita glass was empty. Randy pushed it to the back edge of the bar and lifted his chin to the bartender. "I suppose to keep the girl happy." Randy peered at the snapshot. He turned it toward himself. "Though I honestly can't think why."

"I can't, either," Dave said. "He's got a different little package of female bones now. Probably has twenty a year. I'd bet on it. What kind of script?"

"He's the one with the boat?" Randy's new drink came with a neat frosting of salt around its rim. He took a ladylike sip and chose a cigarette and pushed the pack at Dave. "Boats are sexy." Dave lit the cigarettes with his manly steel lighter, grinning again. Randy said, "The script? Something about a schoolgirl and her dikey gym teacher and the gym teacher's horny boyfriend. Who knows?"

"It sounds confused," Dave said.

"It'll be funny," Randy said. "That's why he can't make any money. The creeps that want to see sex movies don't want to laugh, and he keeps putting all these laughs in. It's the only way he can stand making the things. His problem is, he's got too many brains."

"It's not brainy to lie," Dave said. He watched a scarecrow youth at the end of the bar pull music sheets out of an attaché case and lay them in front of a plump man in a Cardin suit. "No, I wouldn't give you a dollar for his brains and Fullbright's in one package—one very small package." He looked at his watch. "How come you're not doing your Bertha-the-Sewing-Machine-Girl routine?"

"Because the immigration people are always rounding up the illegals and tossing them back over the fence, right? And it takes time for them to fix it up with the coyotes to get back in again, right? And Morry Steinberg's sweatshop gets very vacant during those periods. And however illegal Randy Van may be in however many ways, he, she, or it was born right here in the good old USA. Do you know Mitchell, South Dakota?"

"No, but don't hum a few bars for me," Dave said.

"Funny," Randy Van said. "Anyhow, when every other machine in the place is gathering dust, Randy's up there whipping out dem new blue jeans. So when I ask for time off, Morry never complains." He cocked a jaunty eyebrow at Dave and rocked his head. The hand that held the cigarette was bent far back at the wrist. "And today, I thought it would be fun to play Nora Charles, you know? Myrna Loy?"

"Odum is going to hate you," Dave said.

"Why? He didn't hurt anybody. And you're not going to hurt him." But the frivolity was gone. Randy looked at Dave anxiously. "You aren't, are you?"

"Earlier today, I'd have said no." Dave scowled at the brown bottle as he poured the last beer out of it. He shook his head, drank some of the beer. "Now I wonder." He looked gravely into the chorus-boy face with its thick coat of makeup. "That's what it means to be Nick Charles. A case makes perfect sense at noon. By one o'clock it makes no sense at all. But one thing I am sure of. This little girl"—he tapped the murky photograph—"was in the middle of it. And still is—alive or dead."

"Dead?" Randy forgot about his voice. It came out baritone. He cleared his throat and said, "Dead?" again, up an octave.

"Maybe, maybe not. You were in Spence Odum's living quarters, am I right? Any signs of her there?"

Randy laughed. "His living quarters are half wardrobe department, half prop room. Also carpenter shop. Also film-editing department. Also projection room. It's pure chaos. You could hide an elephant there. I didn't see any sign of her, no. I can't picture

Spence hiding a girl there, not a real, honest-to-God girl. Why would he?"

"Why would he lie to me and say he never heard of her?" Dave picked up the margarita glass and put it into Randy's hand. "Was he with you when Herman Ludwig was shot?"

"Of course. I told you—Spence was the one who sent me to find him." Randy gulped the rest of the margarita and set the glass down. "You don't think Spence killed him!" He began shoving the junk back into the handbag. "Spence couldn't step on a bug. He'd have nightmares of guilt, waking and sleeping. He wouldn't be able to eat, wouldn't be able to face people. You don't know him. He's very sensitive." Randy worked the catch on the handbag flap. "He can't even bear to hurt people's feelings. Pick up a gun and kill a human being? Even somebody he hated he couldn't do that to. And he was crazy about Herman."

"He's got a streak someplace that isn't nice," Dave said. "What about the man with his throat slit?"

"In the barber chair? That's a dummy, a joke."

"Somebody's hiding her." Dave got off the stool. "Let's go see whether he can tell the truth today."

"He's out in the van, doing location stuff," Randy said. "That's why I've got this time. I'm not in any outdoor shots. The makeup makes me sweat too much. My identity runs."

"He'll be back when it gets dark?"

Dave didn't hear Randy's answer because Mittelnacht came in at the sun-bright door. Outside it, the same suntanned youngsters were eating fancyburgers in the polluted heat. The same Peter Frampton record was yelling at them. Mittelnacht wore black glasses. A tank top dyed a dozen runny colors covered his skinny torso. The slept-in black jeans were the same. Today they were tucked into black cowboy boots. He headed for the black bandstand in the corner and Dave said to Randy, "Excuse me a minute," slid the photograph off the bar, and went after Mittelnacht. He caught up with him between empty tables. Mittelnacht took off the black glasses. His hair was lank. He smelled of baby-oil shampoo. "It's you," he said. "What's this?"

"You tell me," Dave said. "It's supposed to be Charleen."

"It is. Only where did you get it? Wow." His tone and the little brief smile that went with it were marveling. "What the fuck was she into? You know what this is, man?"

"I don't understand the question," Dave said.

"Some private eye," Mittelnacht said.

Dave took the photo back from him and studied it. "Infrared," he said. "Only to what point? Why would she pose in the dark? Was she shy?"

"Hell, she loved having her picture taken. It was a drag. Go to the beach, she'd spend twenty bucks and half a day in those take-your-own-portrait booths."

"Not this kind of portrait," Dave said.

"I've got some like that. On Polaroid. It's got a gizmo so we could appear together."

"Fully clothed, no doubt," Dave said.

Mittelnacht grinned. "Bare ass and banging."

"Somebody was with her," Dave said. "There have to be more of these pictures, a whole set, and in the rest, she's not alone. It was a setup. A dark motel room. Just her and some unsuspecting man. And a hidden photographer." He looked at Mittelnacht. "I hope you hung onto those Polaroids."

"Blackmail." Mittelnacht looked sober. "I'll get them back before I do a record that hits the charts. You bet your ass I will." His forehead wrinkled. "You didn't find her, yet? That Odum character didn't know where she was?"

"He didn't say so," Dave said. "But I'm going to ask him again tonight. If I find her, I'll try to get your pictures back for you."

"What's going on?" Randy came to them.

Mittelnacht looked him up and down doubtfully.

Dave said, "Mittelnacht, Randy Van."

They made indifferent noises. Mittelnacht said to Dave, "You really think she's alive?"

"Nobody's proved otherwise," Dave said, "and I need her to answer questions. If I can't find her, a boy that killed his own father is going to get away with it, and a man that never hurt anyone is going to end up on death row. So I have to believe she's alive, don't I?" He turned to Randy. "Do you like to ride horses?"

"Have they got sidesaddles?" Randy asked.

"Probably not. You can change. We'll stop by your place."

"I love the stopping-by-my-place idea," Randy said. "But not to change. I don't look right in britches."

"You never know till you try," Dave said. "Ah, the hell with it. We'll stop at a supermarket instead."

"What for?" Randy asked.

"Apples. If you won't exercise them, you can feed them, all right?" He lifted a hand to Mittelnacht. "Don't forget—if you see her, phone me."

Mittelnacht wasn't listening. He was staring hard at Randy. He said to Dave, "I don't think that's a girl."

"Ho-hum," Randy said.

17

It was up one of those narrow, crooked old Topanga roads that floods out in winter. Big sycamores dense with sunny green leafage leaned white trunks over a creek where the water ran summer-shallow among bleached boulders. The Triumph crossed a tough little new cement bridge. From mossy rocks beneath it, a fishing raccoon looked up. A plump gray quail led a crooked string of young across the road and into brush. Mule deer swiveled big ears at them from a clump of live oaks.

The human habitations here were mostly old and shacky. Rickety automobiles and dusty pickup trucks with camper shells waited beside them. Horses browsed by barbwire fences or found shade under corrugated plastic roofs held up by out-of-plumb four-by-fours. Their tails swished off flies. Dogs bolted into the road and chased the car, barking cheerfully. Dave kept reading tin mailboxes. The one that read TOOKER was neatly enameled white, a little housie, with the name punched out of metal along the roof peak and, topping it, a sheet-metal cutout of a bowlegged cowboy with Stetson and guitar. The old rail fence was fresh white.

The Triumph went up a drive of white gravel. The house was rickety bat-and-board but fresh white also. Fist-size rocks had been whitewashed and enclosed bright flowerbeds—nasturtiums, orange, yellow, Indian red. He parked between the Mercedes and a hard-used estate wagon, probably Tooker's. When he switched off the Triumph, he heard the slow tap of typewriter keys. At the side of the house, a deck was built around the trunk of an old pepper tree. Under the tree sat Karen Shiflett. A toy-red portable typewriter was in front of her on a TV eating table made of a wooden tray on tubular tin legs. At her bare feet were a box of envelopes and a stack of multigraphed letters. She bent close to the typewriter, peering nearsightedly. She poked the keys, studied an address book, poked the keys again. She didn't look up until Dave made a noise, setting down the carton of apples.

"Oh, hi! Where did you come from?"

Dave looked up the slope behind the house. Twenty yards off, half a dozen palominos fed on strewn hay in a white-railed paddock. Their coats shone golden, their manes and tails cream white. The paddock was half shadowed by a gaunt stable, open in front, sided and backed in vertical slats. Inside the stable moved the stick figure of the pimply kid from Keyhole Books. He looked healthier out here. When he stepped into the sunlight with a saddle blanket, his long yellow hair gleamed. He wore a green satin cowboy shirt, jeans, cowboy boots. Smoothing the blanket over the back of one of the horses, he stared down at Dave and Randy for a minute, then went back into the shadows of the barn.

"What happened to your horse sale?" Dave asked.

"Lon said no." She sighed and set aside the flimsy table that held the typewriter. She stood up and put out a hand to Randy. "Hi," she said. "I'm Karen Shiflett."

"Sorry," Dave said. "Randy Van."

"Nice to know you." Randy sounded faint and forlorn. Karen was wearing one of Lon Tooker's shirts again, knotted under her pert breasts again. Randy was eyeing those breasts. With thought-

133

ful sadness. Karen turned for the aluminum screen door that opened from the house to the deck. She wore drawstring trousers of thin Indian cotton. Her neat little butt moved saucily inside them. Dave heard Randy sigh.

"Beer?" Karen asked. "Or lemonade?"

"Maybe with tequila?" Randy asked.

"No problem." Karen raised eyebrows at Dave.

"Beer, thanks," he said.

"He didn't murder anybody," she said when she came out with a painted Mexican tray, glasses of lemonade, a tequila bottle, a can of Coors, and a basket of corn chips. "So he doesn't need any defense." She set the tray down on the redwood bench that edged the deck. "So it isn't going to cost him anything. So don't sell the horses." She put herself on the bench next to the tray and held out Dave's beer to him. She patted the bench on the other side of the tray and said to Randy, "I'll let you put in the fire-water, okay?"

"Lovely." Randy sat down, laid his handbag aside, took up the lemonade glass, and swallowed.from it deeply. He set the glass down, uncorked the tequila bottle, and laced the drink back up to the rim of the glass. Karen watched him interestedly, watched him recork the tequila, then looked up at Dave, squinting a little because of the sun through the pepper tree. "I told you Lon was a child."

"Maybe not." Dave took a blank envelope from the box and walked to the edge of the deck. He'd heard the paddock gate creak, the rattle of its latch. He heard the clop of hoofs. One of the palominos was coming downhill, the kid on its back, swaying in a tooled leather saddle. Dave vaulted the deck rail and climbed to the edge of the path. The kid reined in the horse. It looked at Dave with gentle eyes, blew softly through its big, velvety nostrils, turned its head away with a shake that rattled bit and bridle. "Do me a favor," Dave asked the kid. He held out the envelope to him. The kid swung down out of the saddle. "Scrape one of his feet a little," Dave said, "and put the scrapings into this for me."

"What for?" The kid took the envelope, blinked at it, fingered its smoothness, looked at Dave. "Some way it's going to help Lon?"

"If I hadn't thought so," Dave said, "would I have driven clear the hell out here?"

"I don't know why you want to help him," the kid said.

"He's taking up a jail cell," Dave said, "that rightfully belongs to the beneficiary of Gerald Dawson's insurance policy."

"You're trying to save your company money."

"You've got it," Dave said.

The kid shrugged. He let the horse's reins hang. It didn't offer to go anywhere. The kid put a shoulder against its glossy ribcage, bent, tapped the near fetlock. The horse lifted its foot. The kid used a twig to pry debris from the hoof. The horse put the hoof down again, took a step away and stopped. The kid picked up the debris from the path and tucked it into the envelope. He handed the envelope back to Dave. "I guess that's why they pay you," he said. "Hell, I could have thought of it and I didn't. It's going to show the horse stuff on Dawson's clothes didn't come from here, isn't it?"

"Hold the thought," Dave said, and put the envelope into a pocket. He turned back toward the house. "Thanks."

"You want to ride?" the kid said. "Your girl want to ride? They all need exercise. Karen's busy. And my ass is about worn out."

"Raincheck?" Dave said. "I want to get this to a lab."

"Don't wait too long." The kid swung back into the saddle. "They could starve to death."

"Not for apples," Dave said. "I brought a box."

"Beautiful," the kid said, and nudged the horse in the ribs with his heels. It ambled toward the road. "Lon better get his ass back here, that's all I know."

135

Dave returned to the deck. Karen and Randy weren't there. A breeze came from somewhere. Dry red berries pattered down from the pepper tree. The top sheets from the multigraphed stack slithered across the planks. He picked them up, glanced at them, laid them back on the stack and weighted the stack with a little green plastic pot that held a flowering cactus. He went into the house. The walls were paneled in fake birch. Paintings hung on them—little children with huge eyes, holding birds and small wild animals. A reel-to-reel tape recorder turned. A good-hearted, off-key bass voice, backed by instruction-book-one guitar chords, sang about saving the whales from the factory ships. Karen and Randy gazed at the pictures. Randy was cooing over them and downing lemonade. The tequila bottle was in his other hand. The cork was missing. He kept tilting the bottle over the ice cubes.

"We have to go," Dave said. Out on the deck again, he nodded at the multigraphed pages and the blank envelopes. "Trying to raise a defense fund?"

"Talk about hoping against hope!" Karen dropped dismally onto the bench again and wearily pulled the typewriter to her. "The creeps that came to that store wouldn't defend their own mothers —if they had mothers, which I seriously doubt. But"—she lifted her hands and let them fall—"it's the only mailing list I've got, that and a few Sierra Club buddies. I had to do something. He won't do anything." She looked up at Dave with tears in her eyes. "You saw his pictures. He painted those himself. I know they're lousy, but they're sweet. You heard that song. He's written a lot of songs like that. How could this thing happen to somebody like Lonny? How could he be so unlucky?"

"He's not so unlucky," Dave said. "He's got a friend."

In the Triumph, skidding and buzzing back down the canyon, beginning to meet upcoming cars now, people off work early, the start of the home-going rush, Randy sat silent, face turned away, gazing out the open window at the sunlight and shadows down the woodsy creekbed. The wind fluttered the neat, sun-streaked wig. He didn't seem to notice. Dave said, "Tequila got your tongue?"

Randy looked at him bleakly. "God, to have a body like that!"

"What's supposed to be wrong with the one you've got?" Dave asked. "It looks fine to me."

"It came from the wrong outfitter," Randy said.

18

The big brick room was blacked out again. This time, the lone shaft of light burned down on a sheeted body on a high table. Standing just inside the light were Spence Odum, wearing a false walrus moustache and a London bobby's outfit, and the man in tweeds with the deerstalker cap. The camera and the kid who operated it were silhouetted this side of the staring light. The camera whirred. Odum, hamming fear and trembling, slowly raised the sheet on the side away from the camera. He flinched at what he saw and turned his face aside. The man in the deerstalker cap opened his eyes wide and registered horror.

"Hold the expression," Odum said through unmoving lips. "Camera—zoom in on him tight and wait." The camera kept on whirring. "Okay," Odum said. "Cut. Turn on the lights."

The lights came on and the boy with the Adam's apple threw off the sheet and sat up. "I'm a star," he said, and jumped down off the table. He had on only jockey shorts. He kicked into jeans, flapped into a shirt.

"Quite fucked to death!" Odum laughed.

138

"What a way to go," the boy said.

"Where the hell have you been?" Odum sounded like an outraged parent. He was asking Randy, who stood with Dave just inside the door, next to the washrooms. "And what the hell do you want?" This he said to Dave. He came to them, walrus moustache bristling, billy club swinging at his belt. "I'm trying, for Chrissake, to get a cheap, trashy movie in the cans here." To Randy: "I needed you." To Dave: "You I didn't need."

"He doesn't take me to Fatburger," Randy said. "He takes me to places with tablecloths, where the waiters wear velvet jackets, and I can't pronounce the names on the menu, and the check is fifty dollars."

"Yes, but is it art?" Odum said. "I give you a chance to act, to express your deepest feelings. I offer you immortality. And you talk about food."

"I want to talk about murder," Dave said.

"Later." Odum swung away. "Harold? Junie? Bedtime." He went toward the corner with the shiny brass sleeping arrangement and the wallpaper. "Inspector Hardcock? You get outside the window, please."

The tweedy man, pipe in his teeth, leafed over a script. "Page forty? 'Registers shock, amazement, delight, pops eyes, licks lips'?"

"Did I write that?" Odum said. "Beautiful prose."

The naked boy and girl trudged to the bed. Junie reached for the gold velour coverlet.

"Don't touch that. Are you cold or something? You don't get under the covers, for Godsake. You're not doing this for love and human warmth. You're doing it for the camera. Anyway, there aren't any sheets on there."

"Cheap, cheap!" chanted the camera boy, the sound boy, the prop boy.

"Set the camera low so you can shoot over them while they writhe around erotically," Odum said, "and aim it at Hardcock's face in the window, okay?" He turned back suddenly and bumped into Dave, who had followed him. "What did you say you want?"

"First, you lied to me about Charleen Sims," Dave said. "You signed her for a picture. You're writing the script. You even have a photo of her. You know who she is and you knew it when I asked you before. Where is she?"

"I saw her once, yes," Odum said. "How important could that be? You looked like trouble. I don't need it."

"It was important to Gerald Dawson," Dave said. "The murdered man I mentioned? Why don't you tell me where exactly you fit in this?"

"I don't fit anywhere," Odum said. "I am completely out of it. The girl's gone? Great. I promised Jack Fullbright I'd star her in a picture. He promised he'd let me have raw film and equipment, no charge. He wanted her. I guess that was her price. I didn't object. I had this idea for a sexpot schoolgirl flick. They're doing good business in the cities these days. I'm sick of the farm-town mentality." He frowned under the little bill of the domed bobby's helmet. "Did you ask Fullbright where she is?"

"He claims he never saw her," Dave said, "never heard of her, never came near her."

"What? It was him who brought her here. What the hell does he mean?" Odum took a step backward. "Oh, now, wait. That son of a bitch. Did he send you here tonight?"

"You see?" Dave said. "You do fit into this, don't you? And tightly, too. Where is she, Odum?"

"No, I swear. Fullbright brought her in here and put his proposition to me and I said okay and I never saw her again. It didn't surprise me. I asked him for time. To raise the money. To write the script."

"She wasn't sleeping with Fullbright," Dave said. "She was sleeping with Dawson. She was with him when he was killed. Now, what do you know about Dawson?"

"He was a religious maniac," Odum said.

Junie and Harold were sitting side by side on the bed, like good

140

children waiting for their bath. Their nakedness made them look more innocent than children. Junie said, "Wasn't he the one that came in and ripped down the sets and threw stuff around?"

"When was this?" Dave asked.

"Who knows?" Odum shrugged big, soft, round shoulders inside the bulky bobby's jacket. "This was a sinkhole of vice and corruption."

"A stench in the nostrils of decent people." Harold went past them into a washroom and came out with two cans of Coke. "A plague spot of filth, an open sore."

"Jesus was coming," Junie said, "with a flaming sword."

"Not a spray can of Lysol?" Randy said. "When is he due? I'd like to look my best."

"The little man didn't give us a date," Junie said. Harold sat down beside her and handed her a Coke.

"Funny voice," Odum said. "He wanted to roar, but the madder he got, the more strangled he sounded."

"You couldn't stop him?" Dave asked.

"Spence ran and hid in the van," Harold said.

"I wanted a different perspective," Odum said. "He wasn't having his stuff used to make dirty movies. He hauled it all out of here —lights, cameras, the works. He was throwing it into the Superstar truck when Fullbright drove up. They had a big brawl, pushing, yelling, grabbing. Dawson threatened him all over the place. The police. The IRS. I don't know what all. Fullbright looked pretty sick. Dawson slammed the truck doors and took off."

"No words about Charleen?" Dave asked.

"You've got a one-track mind," Odum said. "Look, can I shoot my picture now, please?"

"Losing your sets must have slowed you down."

"Fullbright was back the next morning. With the equipment. He knocked the damages off the bill and he gave me cash to cover the extra day's studio rent. He apologized. I thought he meant it. Now suddenly he's trying to wreck me."

141

"He isn't," Dave said. "He never mentioned his deal with you. He claims he hasn't seen you in weeks."

"He hasn't," Odum said, "and neither has the girl. I wasn't mixed up with her. The only kind of girls I'm interested in turn out to be boys when they take their clothes off." Maybe it would have sounded funny anyway. It certainly sounded funny coming from a big, stolid symbol of British law and order. The only thing that saved it was that the uniform smelled of mothballs. "Fullbright was mixed up with her—that I can tell you. You can tell me Dawson was mixed up with her. I wasn't. I don't want any part of it."

"I don't know yet what Fullbright's part was," Dave said. "But Dawson's was to die. And so was yours."

"What?" Odum went pale. His big pudgy fingers shook as they worked loose the buckle on his chin strap. He took off the helmet. His hair sprang up frizzy again. He half turned away his head, watching Dave from the corners of his eyes. "What are you trying to say?"

"That Herman Ludwig was killed by mistake," Dave said. "Did you two ever stand and look into a mirror together? That parking lot out there is dark. Somebody was waiting in the dark with a shotgun. The same somebody who killed Gerald Dawson. On the same night. He saw a big, overweight, middle-aged man with thick hair standing up all over his head come out that door"—Dave pointed—"and he thought it was you, and he blew Herman Ludwig's brains out."

"No." Odum touched his lips with his tongue. He swallowed. His voice came hoarse, stammering. "It—it was the—the communists. From Hungary. He was always talking—talking about how they were following him, trying to kill him."

"The same night Dawson was killed? Dawson, who, like you, was a friend of Charleen Sims—if friend is the word? You see why I seem to have a one-track mind? You see why I have to find her?"

"If whoever it was tried to kill me for messing with her," Spence Odum said, "he had the wrong man. I swear to you I never saw her but that one time, that one time only." He looked away, was silent for a moment in a silence kept by everyone else in the big room. He gazed around at the room, the stretches of brick wall painted different colors, the torture instruments, the body in the barber chair, the glass-jeweled chest of costumes, the mummy case in a far corner. It was as if he were inventorying his life. He turned back to Dave. "Why not Fullbright, then?"

"I guess I'd better go ask him," Dave said.

19

The management didn't waste a lot of money lighting up the Sea Spray Motel at night. It was a bleak pair of oblong stucco boxes facing each other across a blacktop parking lot. The wooden stairs swayed as Dave climbed them. At the top, he squinted up at the white plastic circles set in the roof overhang. He gauged the power of the bulbs they hid to be twenty watts. The gallery he walked along sagged. The merry blue paint on the wooden railings was peeling. The varnish was scaling off the door of unit Twelve. Curtains were across the aluminum-framed window, blue-and-white weave with an anchor. Light was not leaking around the outside of the curtains. But Delgado's wreck of a car was parked below. Dave knocked. Someplace a small dog barked. No one stirred beyond the door. Dave knocked again louder. A door opened across the way. Television sounds came out. The door closed. Dave knocked again. And was rewarded by moans. He felt footsteps thud. The door jerked open.

"What the hell?" Delgado blinked. "Oh, shit. Dave?"

"I'm sorry." Dave looked at his watch. It was nine. "Were you asleep?"

"Yeah, well—informally." Delgado tried for a laugh. "I, uh, dozed off with the television on." He'd lost the crisp, clean look he'd had this morning. There was an orange stain on the front of the white shirt. Pizza sauce? The jeans Dave had lent him day before yesterday were crumpled. "Something on your mind? Something I can do?"

"You thought I didn't mean it," Dave said. Delgado stank of whiskey. The air that came out of the shut-up unit stank of whiskey. "You thought I'd paid your rent and thrown you away. What made you think that?"

"You said the case was over," Delgado said. "You've got your house to fix up. You've got Amanda. You don't have to work— only when you want. How did I know you'd ever have another case? I haven't got forever."

"It will seem like forever," Dave said, "on skid row, sleeping under newspapers in doorways."

"Yeah, well, I can take the stuff or leave it alone. What happened? The son didn't do it after all?"

"I don't know what he did. I need that girl to tell me. And I still can't find her. Odum doesn't know where she is. I'm going to see a man I think maybe does. The last time I saw him, he fell over my foot and broke his nose. I'm about to act very nasty to him. It came to me it might be a good idea to have someone along. Strange as it seems, I thought of you. Are you sober?"

Delgado half turned to peer back into the unit. For a clock? "I don't remember anything after the four-thirty news. That makes four hours. I must be sober, yeah." He looked down at himself. He brushed with a hand at the stain. "I need a shower and a change." His brown dog eyes begged Dave. "Can you wait?"

"You going to let me in?" Dave said.

"It's a mess," Delgado warned him, "a pigpen." But he turned

145

resignedly and Dave followed him inside. The bed was unmade. Soiled T-shirts, shorts, socks, were strewn around. The peeled-back lids of sardine tins glinted in the weak lamplight, the ragged lids of half-empty bean cans, soup cans, crowding a coffee table with merry blue legs and a glass top. A big pizza with one slice out of it drooped in its tin on the television set. A whiskey bottle rolled from under Dave's foot. Its label said it was a cheap supermarket house brand. It clinked against another bottle in the shadows. Delgado said, "I'll make it as fast as I can so you don't have to sit around looking at it." He rattled blue paper laundry bundles on a merry blue chest of drawers and went away into the bathroom.

In a cupboard in the kitchenette, Dave found a dusty box of trash bags. He flapped open one of the big green plastic things and went around the place with it, picking up greasy hamburger, hotdog, french-fry wrappers, fried chicken boxes, pizza tins, half-eaten candy bars, half-eaten slices of dried-out bread. There were two ashtrays. Both of them overflowed. He emptied them into the bag and with the edge of his hand scraped into the bag the butts and ashes strewn around them. More junk littered the kitchen, beside the sink, under the sink. He stuffed this into the bag too, twisted the neck of the bag, and looped it with the yellow plastic collar the bag-maker furnished. He set the bag on the gallery outside the door.

Food-crusty plates, cups of abandoned coffee, smeared glasses were heaped in the sink. He poked around till he found a bent box of elderly soap powder. Maybe he would startle Delgado in the shower when he ran hot water into the sink, but he took the chance. He didn't hear a yelp, so maybe Delgado was out of the shower by now. Or maybe the management of Sea Spray was more generous with hot water than with wattage. He had to explore again to find a rinse rack. A spider was living in it. He opened the window over the sink and let the spider go down outside on a strand of web. He splashed dust off the rinse rack, set it on the counter, and began drowning glasses in suds and steam. Delgado let out a long low whistle of surprise. He came fast into the kitchenette.

"Hey!" he said. "You didn't have to clean up for me. You don't have to wash my dishes. What is this?"

"You cooked my breakfast," Dave said. "Several times." He shook dust out of a blue dish towel and held it out. "You can dry, if it will make you feel better."

"I never played cleaning woman for you," Delgado said.

"I didn't need it." Dave began setting glasses in the rack. Delgado reached for a glass. Dave stopped him. "You don't know how to be a cleaning woman. Those have to be rinsed, first. Marie spoiled you. And your mother before her, I expect. Just wait a minute."

"Who is this guy we're going to see?"

Dave found a saucepan, ran hot water into it, poured the water over the glasses. "Now you can wipe," he said. He put the pan down and went back to washing dishes. "His name is Fullbright. He and Dawson were partners."

"Where do I put these?" Delgado said.

"On the shelf where you found them when you moved in," Dave said. Delgado looked helpless. Dave opened a cupboard. "There. That should put them in easy reach."

"You never give up," Delgado said, and set a shiny glass on the empty shelf. "Why did you break his nose?"

Dave told him about Fullbright.

Delgado said, "Maybe he owns a shotgun. You didn't go through every cupboard, every drawer. Dawson threatened to expose him for taking money out of the company, for not reporting his under-the-counter earnings to the IRS. Why didn't he break Dawson's neck to keep him from talking? Why didn't he try to wipe out Spence Odum when he realized Odum had heard the quarrel with Dawson?"

"Because it's been twelve days," Dave said.

"Maybe he doesn't look at the news," Delgado said. "He was

surprised when you told him it was Ludwig who was killed by the shotgun blast."

Dave set cups dripping with suds in the rack. "He'd have known the difference." He filled the pan again and sloshed steaming water over the cups to wash the suds off. "Odum's dark, Ludwig was fair. It would take somebody not sure, somebody who'd never seen them together, or never seen Ludwig at all, to mix them up."

"Did you ever think maybe Charleen had the shotgun?" Delgado touched a cup and drew his hand back sharply and shook it. "She'd only seen Odum once."

Dave loaded saucers and plates into the sink. "She couldn't break a man's neck."

"Fullbright could." Delgado picked up a cup using the towel to shield his fingers from the heat, dried the cup, hung it on a hook in the cupboard. "It wasn't just that Dawson was going to the IRS and the police or DA or whatever. You're forgetting—he had Charleen to start with, then Dawson had her."

"I'm not forgetting anything," Dave said. "I'm remembering too much. That's what's wrong."

"Aren't you supposed to do the silverware before the plates?" Delgado asked. "I seem to remember Marie saying—"

"Marie was right," Dave said, picked up handfuls of stainless-steel knives, forks, spoons, and dumped them into the soapy water. "He didn't have anything to do with horses. I don't think he took those records out of his office to keep me from running to the Feds about him. He had to have a likely reason. That was farfetched." There was a bin at the end of the dish rack for silver. He began putting it clean into this bin. The rattling punctuated what he said. "What he was afraid of was that I'd figure Dawson had learned he was cheating him and dealing in smut and had reacted as Dawson would naturally react and I'd figure this was a motive for Fullbright to kill Dawson." He splashed hot water over the shiny knives, forks, spoons. "Which doesn't mean he did kill him."

"Or that he didn't," Delgado said, finishing with the cups. "It could have been everything—fear of Dawson and hatred of Dawson for taking his girl—disgust with Dawson's holier-than-thou pose. I mean—things do add up." Delgado began to dry the stainless steel. "You can take this, you can take that." He opened a drawer and dropped the clean flatware into it. "But then comes the next thing. It's the total that gets you."

"Except—when it gets you, what do you do?" Dave set saucers in the rack, then swabbed off the plates and racked them to drain. He glanced at Delgado. "You give up and drink. Bucky loses control. What would Fullbright do?" He poured steaming tap water over the plates. He felt around in the greasy water that showed a lot of tomato sauce at its edges, found the rubber cover of the drain with his fingers, and pulled it away. He rinsed it off and laid it on the counter. The water went out of the sink with a sucking sound. He rinsed the sink. He took the towel away from Delgado and dried his hands on it. "I know better than to bet on human behavior, but I'm going to do it anyway." He hung up the towel. "Fullbright is in this up to his eyebrows, but he didn't murder anybody."

"You're on," Delgado said. He looked at the plates steaming in the rack. "Are we through here?"

"They'll drain dry," Dave said. "Come on."

20

Most of the boats rocking at the long white mooring were dark, asleep. Here and there, a light showed at a porthole and wavered in the black water beneath. But the lap of tide against hulls and pilings and the hollow knock of their heels on the planks were the only sounds there were until they neared the end of the pier. This was why Fullbright had no near live-aboard neighbors. The loud music from his big white power launch. Not the easy-listening kind that had whispered from the speakers when Dave was here last. This was some kind of rock. No lights showed. Shadowy figures sat around the sheltered afterdeck. The shifting colors of a television screen painted their half nakedness. Teenagers. They sat on the padded bench along the taffrail and giggled and murmured and passed from hand to hand a handmade cigarette. When Dave and Delgado stepped aboard, a blond boy stood up and came to them.

"No admittance," he said. "Private party." He had the bleached eyebrows, the deep tan, the muscles, that made him a lifeguard, a permanent surfer, a beach bum, or all three. The smell of sun came off him. He was taller and broader than Dave and had a wine bottle

150

in his hand. Baggy surfer trunks hung low off his hips and he wasn't steady on his feet. "Please leave," he said.

"This is urgent," Dave said. "Tell Jack Fullbright it's Dave Brandstetter. He'll want to talk to me."

"It's past business hours," the boy said.

"I didn't ask for the time," Dave said. "Go tell Jack Fullbright I'm here, please."

The boy half turned and set the wine bottle down on a low round table among other wine bottles, bowls of chips, bowls of ravaged sour-cream and cheese dips. "I can break your arms," the boy said.

"If you want cop-show dialogue," Dave said, "my friend here is wearing a gun, and if you try to get cute, he will shoot you in the kneecap."

The boy blinked white eyelashes at Delgado. Delgado glowered and put a hand inside his jacket over the rib cage. He told the blond boy, "He means it."

A girl wearing a white Levi's jacket over a bikini came around the table and took hold of the boy's arm. "Ricky, come on and sit down."

"Call him on the gun," a male voice said out of the dark. Another one said, "Yeah, let's see the gun."

Delgado took out the gun, held it up, put it back.

The boy said to Dave, "He told us not to let anybody down there. We can't go down there ourselves. If we have to pee, we pee over the side, right? He's got people down there. He's very busy and doesn't want to be disturbed."

Dave went to the companionway, laid back the hatch doors, pulled open the short, shiny, vertical doors. Light from the brass lanterns down in the cabin made a yellow sheen on the teakwood steps and sent streaks up the brass handrails.

"I really wish you wouldn't," the boy said. "He'll have my ass for this."

"He's probably had that already," Delgado told him.

"That's a sexist remark," Dave said. The children were picking up gear and starting to leave. "Don't go anywhere. He's your friend. He gives you booze and grass. Don't walk out on him when he needs you."

A girl and a boy went anyway. The others stood as they were, doubtful, looking at Dave and Delgado, then at each other. The boy named Ricky said, "Okay. What's it about? Who are you?"

"Private investigators," Dave said. "Working for the insurance company that Jack Fullbright's partner had a life policy with. He was murdered. It's serious, right? So you will wait, won't you?"

They murmured, took steps this way and that way, then one by one sat down. Dave went down the companionway. At the foot of it he stopped. Delgado bumped against him. "Sexist or not," he said, "I was right." He pointed.

The door in the bulkhead separating the cabin with the leather couches and bar and music system, from the cabin with the beds was open, and it showed Dave naked legs waving happily. Slim, shaved legs tangled with muscled, hairy legs. The music was very loud down here. Dave went and turned it off. In the sleeping cabin, a boy like Ricky, long blond hair in his eyes, tumbled onto the floor between the beds. He lay on his back, laughing. He was naked, and a naked girl fell on him. It was Ribbons. They started wrestling, or it might not have been wrestling. Then Jack Fullbright's voice said sharply:

"Wait a minute. Shut up, will you? Something's wrong."

He stepped over the suddenly stilled bodies on the floor and was framed in the doorway. He wasn't wearing anything, of course, except the little silver chain around his neck and a wide slice of adhesive tape holding thick folds of gauze over his nose. The tape went far out across his cheekbones. The flesh around his eyes that wasn't covered by the bandage was black and blue and swollen. He could only open his eyes as slits. They glittered.

"What the hell is this? What do you want?"

He reached around the door for a white terrycloth robe. Ribbons

152

stared amazed at Dave and Delgado between Fulbright's legs. So did the blond boy. He'd tilted his head far back. That it was upside-down made his alarm look comical. Fullbright stepped out of the sleeping cabin and shut the door. He flapped into the robe. It was floor-length and had a hood. He didn't put up the hood. Dave studied his motions. They were slow. He had to be full of painkillers. There was no way, without them, that Fullbright could have amused himself as he'd just been doing only a day after smashing his face on those steps. The pills would have hampered his capacities, but Dave suspected it had taken time and diplomacy and luck to set up this date. Fullbright wouldn't have canceled for anything less than a coma.

"Still the same thing," Dave said. "To know where Charleen is. You lied before. You knew her. You asked Spence Odum to put her in a film. It would cost you but you didn't seem to care. She meant something to you. So where is she, Fullbright?"

Beyond the door behind the man in the long white robe there was a rattling noise. Somebody stumbled on stairs. Dave looked a Delgado and Delgado pushed Fullbright aside, yanked open the door to the sleeping cabin, lunged through. Dave saw the boy's naked legs disappear at the top of a companionway at the far end of the cabin. Delgado had hold of Ribbons. She had on jeans now but no top as yet. She squirmed in Delgado's grip and let out little gasps with words muffled inside them of fear and outrage. She tried to hit Delgado with little thin blue-veined fists. Beyond the far companionway, there was a splash. The boy must have gone overboard forward.

"I'd like the truth this time," Dave said.

Fullbright didn't answer. He watched Delgado bring the struggling, whimpering Ribbons into the after cabin. Delgado set her down hard on the couch. She crossed her arms in front of her little breasts and glared up at Delgado through her tumbled hair. Her mouth pouted.

"I guess you're going to get it, aren't you?" Fullbright dropped disgustedly onto the couch opposite Ribbons. "Or you'll have the vice squad down on me."

"You're a poor judge of character," Dave said. He reached into a pocket and brought out the sheaf of invoices he'd gone off with the last time he left this boat. He flipped them at Fullbright. "I'm going to get it by offering you these back."

"Or you'll take them to the IRS." Fullbright nodded.

"And the police, and the district attorney, and any other agency I can think of that frowns on theft and cheating and embezzlement —to say nothing of murder."

Fullbright shut his eyes, shook his head, grunted, slouched down on the couch, hunching up his shoulders. "I didn't kill him. I felt like it, but I didn't. I figured out another way." A wise smile twisted his mouth at one corner.

"I'm cold," Ribbons said.

"To shut him up and back him off," Dave said, "after he discovered you were renting equipment to porno filmmakers and not even giving him a share of the take."

"It wasn't the money," Fullbright mumbled. "It was the sinfulness of it all. He was going to destroy me."

Dave stepped to him and shook his shoulder. "Don't go to sleep on me. Explain this." He held in front of Fullbright's face the fuzzy photo of wanton Charleen on the motel-room bed. The slits in the bruised swellings opened for a moment and closed again. "You took it, didn't you? Don't tell me why; let me guess. Dawson was with her."

Fullbright nodded slowly. His voice was almost inaudible now. "You know already. Why ask me?" He raised a very slow hand and very gingerly touched the bandage across his nose. "Leave me alone, all right?"

"I'm cold," Ribbons whined, and Delgado went into the sleeping cabin and brought back a white Irish hand-knitted sweater. She put it on. It must have belonged to the boy or to Fullbright. It was

154

much too big for her. She huddled down in it, glowering, sulking.

"You're welcome," Delgado said.

"I found him looking at magazines in his office one night when he thought I'd gone home, only I remembered something I needed and I came back." Fullbright blew out air wearily. "They had pictures of naked little girls in them." A sound came from Fullbright that was almost a laugh. "He put them away fast and I made believe I hadn't noticed. It really shocked me." He looked at Dave for a second and shut his eyes again. "I actually believed the son of a bitch was what he claimed to be. Until then."

"And he thought you still believed it," Dave said, "when he went over to Spence Odum's studio and tore it apart and snatched back all the stuff that belonged to Superstar Rentals. And threatened to wipe you out."

Fullbright nodded even more slowly this time.

Dave looked at Ribbons. "Take Mr. Delgado to the galley and come back with some coffee, please. On the double, as we say on shipboard."

Ribbons gave no sign of doing what he asked. Delgado pulled her to her feet. He pushed her ahead of him through the sleeping cabin.

Dave didn't watch where they went. He asked Fullbright: "You already had Charleen for a little playmate by that time, right? Where did you find her?"

"You wrecked my face," Fullbright said. "It hurt like hell. I'm full of dope. I can't go on with this. I can't figure out what the hell to say."

"Try the truth," Dave said.

Fullbright drew a deep breath and pushed himself a little more erect on the couch. He said loudly, "I found her in a place on Sunset called the Strip Joint, where kids dance and drink soda pop and hustle sex for bucks, for pot, for cocaine, for auditions, for whatever you promise them."

"And you rent stuff to filmmakers," Dave said. "So you have

155

connections with producers. She thought you could get her into the movies."

"Also I had a boat," Fullbright said. "She hadn't been on a boat before. She thought it was glamorous, only if I took it out she got seasick and if I didn't she got bored." His voice ran down. He blew out breath again and shook his head again. He was having trouble holding it up. "She was about to quit me. Then Jerry found my private records and ripped up Odum's studio and all that." Fullbright shut his eyes and shuddered, hunching down inside the big robe. He fumbled for the hood and pulled it crookedly over his rumpled hair. "Man, I have to sleep. I can't go on with this."

"They're bringing coffee," Dave said. "So you got Odum to promise to put her in a picture by offering him everything he needed free. And in return for that, you got Charleen to lead Dawson into temptation—remembering all those skinny girl children in the sex magazines that Dawson found so attractive, right? And you stationed yourself outside the motel room window and snapped photographs of Dawson he wouldn't like featured in his church bulletin." Dave bent to touch a drawer under the couch. "Using one of the cameras you keep here."

"Most people," Fullbright said drowsily, "don't realize they can have their picture taken in the dark." He smiled wanly to himself. "It shut him up. It backed him off." He whispered a laugh, opened his eyes to the extent that he could open them, and looked at Dave. "It also hooked him on Charleen. He couldn't get enough of her —even though he knew she'd agreed to frame him for me. Nothing mattered but sex with Charleen. He'd gone around all his life lusting in his heart after grammar-school girls—what's the word? —nymphets, right?"

"And keeping hands off," Dave said.

"Yeah, well—" Fullbright's eyes closed again and his chin rested on his chest. "He'd have broken sometime. He sure as hell broke completely when he broke."

Delgado came in with a big Japanese pottery mug of coffee. The hand that didn't hold the mug held Ribbons. Dave took the mug. Ribbons and Delgado sat on the couch again. Rick stood in the companionway. He didn't speak. He only looked. He appeared worried.

"Drink some of this," Dave told Fullbright. He seemed always to have to be doctoring the man. He put the mug at Fullbright's mouth. Fullbright jerked up his head. "I don't want it. There's nothing more to tell."

"Where did Charleen go after Dawson was killed?"

"I never saw her again." Fullbright, as if his hand weighed almost more than he could lift, tried to push the mug away. "I swear it. Think what you want, do what you want. I never saw her again."

"You were going to take those records out to sea and drown them. Is that what you did with Charleen? She was a witness to Dawson's murder, wasn't she? And you couldn't depend on her to keep quiet. You had to get rid of her."

"No. I didn't kill him." Fullbright rubbed his forehead. "What night was it?"

Dave named the date. "Between ten and midnight."

"I was here. I picked up a film from Cascade after I left work and brought it straight here. You can check their records." Fullbright numbly took the mug. He blew at the steam. He sucked up a little coffee and flinched. "Hot. It was *Deep Throat.*" He pointed overhead. A rolled-up movie screen was hooked to the ceiling inside its brown metal tube. "The projector sits over there." He looked at the companionway and saw Ricky. "What is it?"

"I was here that night," Ricky said. "Jude and Pepe were here." He turned and called up the companionway. "Hey! *Deep Throat.* You remember when Jack showed it?"

Jude was the girl in the Levi's jacket and not much else. Pepe was a brown boy a little bit overweight. He was chewing. A smear of white was at the corner of his mouth. Jude numbered the night when Gerald R. Dawson was killed. "It was a Monday," she said.

"I remember because that's my tennis night with my yuck little brother. Believe it, I canceled when I heard what was going down."

"Yeah." Pepe rubbed his crotch and grinned. "Going down. *Es verdad!*"

Jude looked at Dave with her eyes very wide open. "How does she *do* that?"

Ribbons, huddled down inside the big sweater on the couch, kept her sulky look. "Did you ever hear of special effects?" Then she giggled. "Trick photography?"

The children in the companionway laughed.

A car he didn't know was parked in the dark by the piled cement bags, the sand heap, the stacked lumber in front of the French doors. He went into the courtyard. The fencing room was lighted up. A stranger was in there. He sat on the bed, phone on the floor at his feet, receiver at his ear. The light in the room was overhead, two hundred watts, a naked bulb, bleak. Dave stood under the white flowers and trailing tendrils of the vine at the back of the courtyard and watched the man through the open door. He was half turned away but he looked young and spare. He wore a brown double-knit suit and shoes that gleamed. His brown hair was cut 1930s style, neat, the latest. He spoke into the phone and Dave thought he knew the voice. He went through the doorway and walked to the bed.

Randy Van looked up and smiled. He picked up the phone, rose, handed Dave the phone, handed Dave the receiver. Dave took them dumbly, staring. There wasn't a trace of makeup. There was no enamel on the nails. Dave said "Brandstetter" into the phone.

"The soil samples from the closet floor at unit number thirty-

159

six," Salazar said, "match the stuff from the clothes of the deceased, Gerald R. Dawson."

"Dandy," Dave said. "Anything else?"

"A lot of fingerprints. Who knows how long it will take to sort them out and get a line on them? Your witness, Cowan, told me she brought pickups there. She must have been busy. She sure as hell was too busy ever to clean the place. But he wasn't murdered there, anyway, Brandstetter. When the neck is broken—"

"The muscles that control bladder and bowels let go," Dave said. "I know that. I also know it doesn't always happen. Only almost always."

"Almost is good enough for me," Salazar said. "I don't want this case and I don't get this case."

"Don't hang up," Dave said, and put a hand over the mouthpiece. Randy was sorting through a stack of record albums on the floor. Dave asked him, "How long have you been here? Any other calls?"

"About an hour. Yes. A Lieutenant Barker of the LAPD. He got the report from the lab where we left that envelope of Karen's. They phoned him, like you asked."

"Did he tell you what they said?"

Randy nodded, studying a glossy color caricature of Mozart with a croquet mallet. "It's decomposed granite. It doesn't match. The other was alluvial." He looked up at Dave. "He's going to the district attorney about it."

"Thanks," Dave said. "You look very nice."

"I feel ridiculous in these clothes," Randy said. "Does that mean the one with the horses gets out of jail?"

"That's what it means," Dave said. "Why don't we drink to that? The cookhouse is over yonder."

Randy got to his feet, and put a kiss on Dave's mouth. "You're a nice man," he said, and went away. He didn't sway his hips.

Salazar whistled into the phone. Dave took his hand off the

mouthpiece. "Sorry," he said, and told Salazar about getting the soil sample from Tooker's place in Topanga and about what the lab had said and about Barker's reaction. "Now—I can ask him to do it or I can ask you to do it, but somebody has to do it," he said.

"What's that?" Salazar said.

"Test Bucky's shoes," Dave said.

"To see if what's on them matches what was in the closet?" Salazar asked. "You know, I don't see how just eating lunch with a guy could do this to somebody, but I'm starting to think like you. And it hasn't helped. I checked out the kid's shoes. Negative. I even showed the kid to Cowan. Cowan isn't so sure now. He says Bucky looks smaller. But maybe it was the light. It was dark before."

"It's still dark," Dave said. "I don't know. I just damn it don't know." He sat on the bed, scowling to himself, chewing his lower lip. Salazar asked him if he was still there. "I don't know where I am," Dave said. "Look, thanks very much. I'm sorry to have put you to all the trouble. I appreciate your cooperation, your help."

"Any time," Salazar said.

"Somebody killed that man," Dave said.

"Not the widow and orphan," Salazar said. "Write them their check and forget it."

"Sure," Dave said, but he wasn't listening. He was thinking about Bucky's size. He asked Salazar, "Are you going to be there for a while?"

"I'm already into my fifth hour of overtime," Salazar said. "I'm going home to bed."

"What about your stolen-property office? Can you leave word with them that I—"

"Nine to five, Brandstetter," Salazar said. "Somebody in this crazy place keeps normal hours."

"I'll see you in the morning," Dave said and hung up.

Randy came back carrying stubby glasses with what looked to

be scotch over ice cubes. He handed Dave one of the glasses. "Does that mean we've got all night?"

"I have something to do before sunrise," Dave said.

"You mean besides right here?" Randy said.

"After right here," Dave said. "You know, you should get dressed up funny more often."

It wasn't sunrise. It was after. But the old black man in the starchy tan uniform sat upright and wide-eyed in his faded blue Corvair next to the driveway ramp down into the garages under Sylvia Katzman's apartment complex. The street was steep and the worn right front tire of the car was turned hard against the curb. Dave put the Triumph into the lowest gear he could find with the stubby shift knob and climbed the hill. He got lost on twisting, narrow, shelflike streets but he found the place he wanted finally, and parked and got out. It was the place where the chain-link fence was cut at the bottom, the corners folded back. He looked down. There were the kitchen windows of the top row of apartments. The one on number thirty-six was still open the way he'd left it on his first visit. It was plain from here that climbing had taken place up the bank. The slant of the early sunlight, already promising heat again, showed up the marks of dug-in shoes or boots. And of something heavy having been dragged. He got back into the Triumph and lost his way again getting back down to the parked Corvair. The old man was drinking coffee out of a red plastic cup that was the cover of his Thermos bottle.

"Yes," he said, consideringly. "I saw a truck like that. Those big wheels that set it up high. Four-wheel drive, I expect. It rumbled. A lot of power."

"Machinery in the back?" Dave asked.

"Oh, yes." The old man nodded. He reached across to a glove compartment held shut by an arrangement of thick rubber bands. He worked these with arthritic fingers. "I have some cups in here."

The metal door of the glove compartment fell open. "Perhaps you'll share a little coffee? Tastes good first thing in the morning." He pulled a cup out of a nest of six and carefully filled it from the Thermos. His motions were slow and tidy. He handed the cup through the window to Dave. "It was posthole-drilling equipment." The old man recapped the Thermos. He put the cups back into the glove compartment and fixed it shut again with the rubber bands. "And on the front, there was an arrangement to attach something, probably a grader for laying down roads, you know?"

"The coffee's good," Dave said. "Thank you. When did you see the truck?"

"It was parked back up there." The old man raised a slow hand to point with a thumb over his shoulder. "I drive up there to turn around and come back down here to park in this space. This is a good old machine but it doesn't have much left in reverse. Two weeks ago?" He wrinkled an already deeply wrinkled forehead. "Not quite."

"It was here when you arrived?" Dave said. "That would be what—seven o'clock in the evening?"

"Right about then," the old man said. He drank coffee and stared thoughtfully through the windshield. He shook his head. "No, that wasn't the first time. First time was Sunday, the day before. Early. I was fixing to leave. Boy with a black beard got out of it. He couldn't get in the building. They have to know you are coming so they can come unlock the lobby door for you."

"Who came?" Dave asked. "Who let him in?"

"Maybe he never got in," the old man said. "He was still standing there when I left. He had on a cowboy hat." Now he looked hard at Dave. "Do you know," he asked, "the Monday when I saw the truck up there—that was the one they been asking me about. The police. The sheriff. Who came and went that night? Yes, sir! They been asking me about that night." A little weary smile

163

twitched his mouth. "But they never asked me one time about that truck. You the first one, the only one."

"But the boy with the beard wasn't in it when you saw it?" Dave asked.

"Nobody was in it. But later on there was. Must've been getting on for midnight by then. He come out and tramped up right here past me, so close I could have stretched out my hand and touched him. He unlocked the truck and climbed in and slammed the door and drove it right on up the street to the top, like you did just now."

"Alone," Dave said. "No skinny little blond teenage girl with him?"

"Alone," the old man said. He sipped coffee and thought again for a minute. "You want to know why I remember that? Why I paid special attention? Him getting in that truck and driving off?"

"Why was that?" Dave said.

"Because he didn't look the same without the beard."

"I'd bet on possibly a wallet," Dave said. "Almost certainly a duffel bag, maybe even Marine or Army issue. And clothes—work clothes, Levi's, chinos, work shoes, maybe cowboy boots. Underwear, probably dirty since he didn't know his way around."

The dark kid in uniform kept pulling cartons and parcels off steel shelving in the big room full of steel shelving. He and Dave looked into the cartons and parcels. When Dave shook his head, the kid pushed the cartons and parcels back in place. "You know," he said, "once I make detective, I'm going to quit and get into your line."

"I won't tell them you said that," Dave said. "You need time to think it over." He reckoned the child's age at about twenty. He was dark, with a rosy flush under smooth skin. "When you've had time, you'll change your mind." A date scrawled on a carton in felt pen made him stop. "Let's look in this one."

"I won't change my mind." The kid pulled the box off the shelf and held it for Dave. "I've read about you in the magazines. I saw you on the 'Tomorrow' show. What you do is what I want to do."

164

"Be in the magazines, you mean?" Dave said. "Be on television? It was twenty years before that happened to me. You know what it's a sign of?" He poked among soiled, crumpled T-shirts and boxer shorts in the carton. White boot socks stiff with sweat. There were no boots, no shoes. But there was a wallet, stitched with thongs around the edges, and tooled with a cross entwined by lilies. The wallet was empty. Dirt-crusty work pants had been folded to lie flat. He lifted them. "It's a sign your best days are behind you." Crushed khaki canvas. A knapsack. US ARMY. He lifted it out, laid back the flap. The book was there. He removed it. "Like the worn-out comedians on game shows."

"You don't look worn out," the kid said. "Is that what you wanted?"

Dave nodded. The kid put the box back on the shelf. Dave said, "Before you get into the magazines and on TV, most of what's cluttered up your life has been boring."

"You didn't make it sound like that," the kid said.

"The boring part you don't talk about," Dave said. The book was eight by ten, not thick but heavy. The cover was sleek stamped fabricoid, blue and gold, the gold partly rubbed off. ESTACA HIGH SCHOOL 1977. "Naturally," Dave said. "People watching the 'Tomorrow' show are sleepy. They only want to hear the exciting parts. Same for the magazine readers." He leafed over pages heavy with glossy coating. A girl's volleyball team under eucalyptus trees, mountains towering in the background. A football team, massive shoulder pads, gangly wrists. The a capella choir in pleated robes. Rows of little square photographs of faces, smiles, no smiles, impudence, dread, determination, defeat, dental braces, acne, eyeglasses, perfect beauty. FROSH. SOPH. JUNIORS. Charleen Sims looked at him. He checked inside the front cover. *Charleen Sims* in pale blue ballpoint, then *Charleen Tackaberry* in dark blue ballpoint, then *Mrs. Billy Jim Tackaberry, 456 Fourth St., Estaca, CA.* She dotted her i's with circles. Dave handed back the book. "Ever hear of Estaca? Know where it is?"

165

"It means 'stake' in Spanish." The kid pulled the carton out, dropped the book into it, pushed the carton back on the shelf. "So maybe it has something to do with vineyards, right? Wine country? San Joaquin Valley?"

"They should make you a detective pretty fast," Dave said.

"I might be wrong," the kid said.

22

He wasn't wrong. And that put it a long way off. It was nightfall by the time Dave found it, a wide main street with high curbs, most of the windows black in stores of cement block or gaunt old brick. Here and there a neon sign said HARDWARE in blue or JOHN DEERE in yellow or DRESSES in pink. There were three or four spaced-out streetlights on tall new silvery standards. A lone traffic light swung high in a wind that blew hot and probably would blow hot all night. The signal switched from red to green to amber and back to red again but there was no one to pay it any mind. Estaca, or most of it, was home for supper and television.

A young woman with lumpy hips stuffed into blue jeans and with a scarf tied over her hair came out the glass door of a store with bright windows. She opened the cab of a pickup truck, put into it a brown paper sack whose squared-off shape said it held a sixpack, and climbed in after it. PACKAGE STORE, the sign said, which meant that in Estaca you couldn't sit in a barroom and drink. If you wanted alcohol you bought it here and drank it where you could. The pickup rattled off up the block. Dave put the Triumph where it had been, on the bias, nosing the curb, struggled out of it stiffly, and stretched. It was no car to travel far in.

"Brand new, ain't she?" the man inside the liquor store said. He was fat. The T-shirt stretched over his immense belly was printed with a purple bunch of grapes and circling the grapes the fancily lettered words CALIFORNIA WINES. His hair was shaved halfway up the sides and crewcut on top. "Lots of pep, I guess."

"It's funny in wine-growing country," Dave said, "not to be able to go into a saloon." He eyed the bottles on the shelf back of the fat man. He wasn't going to find Glenlivet here. "What about restaurants? Are they exempt?"

"Wine only," the fat man said. "What kind is it? German? Italian? Japanese? No, it ain't Japanese. Funny, you think back. I was a kid, you couldn't kill enough of them. Now everybody buys their cars. People forget."

"Those that can," Dave said. "No—it's English."

"Guess you didn't forget," the man said. "They was our allies. You get there in the war?" He grinned lecherously with tobacco-stained teeth. "Boy, them blackouts was something. Anything could happen to you in them blackouts. Girls in every doorway, down every little alley. You didn't have to know where you was; wherever you was, all they had to hear was you talk American and they was unbuttoning your fly. You didn't get there, huh?"

There was a round wire rack of bottled cocktails. He took down two that alleged they were martinis. They were dusty. The line hadn't made the fat man any money in Estaca. "Just passing through," Dave said. "On the way to Germany." Beyond shelves of bread, crackers, potato chips, tall glass-doored refrigerators held cans and bottles of beer, waxed-paper cartons of milk, wrapped blocks of cheese. Ice cream and yogurt lurked in a frost-lined box with sliding glass tops. He located a plastic sack of ice cubes. "Now I'll be all set if you've got cups." He set the little bottles on the counter by the cash register and the wire rack of jerky beef and jolly, half-empty little yellow plastic packets of cheese sticks, corn chips, nuts. "Paper cups, plastic?"

"You figuring to have a party?" the fat man asked.

"All by myself," Dave said, and watched the fat man waddle off for a long transparent plastic sleeve of cups. "Do I have to take them all?"

"I guess not." The man untwisted the lashing on the end of the tube and took out half a dozen. "That okay? I want the count to come out." Dave nodded. The man began pushing buttons on a cash register. "Army, was it?"

"Intelligence," Dave said.

"Marines, myself," the fat man said. He named off the total and Dave paid him. The man laid the bills in gray metal trays. He handed Dave coins. "Maybe in thirty years they'll be buying Vietnam cars."

"Many boys around here fight there?" Dave pocketed the change and picked up the sack the man had put the ice and cups and bottles into.

"This isn't college-kid country," the man said.

"You know one by the name of Tackaberry, Billy Jim?"

"He wouldn't come in here," the fat man said. "Church would be where you'd find him." Little fat-pouched eyes of no special color looked Dave up and down. "He ain't done nothing, has he?"

"It's an insurance matter," Dave said. "Which way is Fourth Street?"

"I ain't seen him for a while," the fat man said. "Big black beard. Crazy eyes. Used to work for Lembke, farm machinery."

"Married, was he?" Dave said.

"Hell, I don't know. I just know Tackaberry's his name and what he looks like. You couldn't forget either one, could you? Fourth's the next after the traffic light."

"Thanks," Dave said and pushed out the glass door.

"Have a nice party," the fat man said.

The house sat back on a quarter-acre with four fruit trees in front of it. A five-foot-high chain-link fence closed the yard off. The windows of the house were alight. It might have started out clapboard or even stucco. What sided it now were asbestos shingles in a silvery green. A double gate opened to a driveway where a camper was mounted on a pickup-truck bed. There was a smaller gate for beings on foot to go through. He parked on the packed dirt in front of that, poked a hole in the bag of ice cubes, put cubes into one of the plastic glasses, and emptied half the contents of the martini jug over it. He set the glass on the dash and smoked a cigarette. He swallowed the martini, poured the rest of what was in the little jug over the ice, and set the glass on the dash again. He got out of the car, worked the latch on the gate, and went up a path of cement squares set in grass to a little plywood front stoop. He rapped on an aluminum screen door. A light went on over it. The inner door opened. A gnarled little man in his fifties squinted at him, didn't like what he saw, started to shut the door.

"Mr. Sims?" Dave said.

"I'm eating and I don't buy anything at the door."

"I don't sell anything," Dave said. "Your daughter, Charleen. Is she here?"

The man narrowed his eyes. "Who wants to know?"

Dave showed him the card in the wallet. "I'm investigating the death of a man whose life was insured by Sequoia. In Los Angeles. A man called Dawson. Your daughter knew him. I think she might be able to shed some light on what happened to him."

"In trouble," the man said. "In trouble, isn't she?" He unlatched the screen, pushed it for Dave to come in. The furniture was cheap and not new but it was clean. Everything stood on a floor of spotless vinyl tile exactly at right angles to everything else. There was fresh wallpaper printed with little pink rosebuds, but nothing hung on the walls. "How the hell did she get to Los Angeles?"

"I thought you could tell me," Dave said.

"Billy Jim sure as hell wouldn't take her there." Sims went into a kitchen where order books and catalogues with shiny color covers were stacked on the table. Also glittering bottles of cosmetics. There was exactly enough space to put a plate so the man could eat. A plate was there and he sat down to it. "I'm the Avon lady," he said without smiling.

"Why wouldn't he take her there?" Dave said.

Mouth full of mashed potato, Sims said, "Sit down if you want. Because he thinks it's wicked. Any big city. I warned her not to marry him. She wouldn't listen." He gulped down the food, Adam's apple moving in his scrawny throat. He nodded at the other straight wooden chair, and filled his mouth again. He talked with his mouth full. "He was all right before he went to Vietnam but he was crazy afterwards. She had her eye on him since she was twelve. He was older, of course. Guess all the girls thought he was something extra. Big and strong, and still he had a smooth way of talking, brighter than your average farm-town kid." Sims stopped, started to push back his chair. "Say, you hungry? You want to eat?"

But Dave had seen the dried-potato-flake box on the spotless kitchen counter, and the open can of Dinty Moore beef stew on the stove. "No, thanks," he said. "The US pulled out of Vietnam in 1973. What kept him?"

"Army hospital. Mental ward. Three years, that's right. And when he come back with that beard and that crazy look in his eyes, I said to her, 'Forget him. Pick somebody else. He's off his head.' But it had been 'Billy Jim' this and 'Billy Jim' that, all the while he was gone. She wrote to him damn near every day. He wrote to her too. Years, I'm talking about, you understand." Sims took his empty plate to a chipped sink with unplated steel faucets. He opened the door of a very old refrigerator. Notes on three-by-five cards were stuck to the door with transparent tape. They fluttered a little when he shut the door. "Ice cream?" he asked.

"No, thanks," Dave said again. He wanted to get back to the

171

martini chilling in the car. Martinis, plural. He was liking the sound of Billy Jim less and less. "I hoped she might be here."

"Hasn't set foot here since she married him," Sims said. He sat down and ate ice cream directly out of the carton with a spoon whose silver plating was almost gone. "No, that's not true. Jesus Christ!" He got up suddenly and turned away. He did something with his mouth. A glint of pink and white and gold wire rattled on the counter. "That ice cream hits that bridgework, makes you want to scream," Sims said, sat down again, took up the carton and spoon. "No, they lived here a little while. In her mother's old room and mine. Her mother's dead, you understand."

"I'm sorry," Dave said.

"She could handle Charleen. I never could," Sims said.

"Where did they go? Where do they live now?"

"Up the river valley back of nowhere. Had a baby." Sims licked the spoon. "Don't know why he picked her. He could have had his choice of girls." He sighed, closed the ice-cream carton, rose, and shut the carton up in the refrigerator. The spoon rattled in the sink. "Then again, maybe they saw he was mental, the war unhinged him. She didn't care. She was born without caution." He eyed Dave. "You're in a hurry, aren't you? I talk too much. Course, folks around here kind of like that. Nothing much to do. Passes the time. All right, let's see—they lived here till Billy Jim got some money from some aunt of his who died. He didn't like Lembke because Lembke uses foul language and doesn't go to church, and he didn't like me for the same reason. So he quit his job at the farm-machinery place and he quit this house, and I don't see them and I don't hear from them."

"Not even about the baby?" Dave said.

"Oh, about that, yes," Sims said. "What Billy Jim did was buy a mobile home and truck it up there and set it down in the middle of his ten acres of nowhere. He had it worked out in his head how it's developing up there, and maybe it is. And he put the money in machinery to dig postholes and dig wells and lay out roads and that kind of thing. Enough work to keep body and soul together. And he wanted to be away from people. He was forever over at the church before that money came, but after that he didn't seem to mind turning his back on the church folks like on everybody else. Just him and Charleen, that was how it was going to be."

"And the baby," Dave reminded him.

"No. Baby was killed. Windstorm, rain, all of that. Knocked that mobile home flat. He wasn't there, couldn't get there. Charleen was alone. Baby was dead in her arms when he came back and lifted the junk off her.

"Crazy thing to do," Sims said, "go way out there where there's nobody to help if you need help. Hell, everybody needs help in this life." He went back into the bare, rose-papered room. Dave went after him. Sims said, "When I had my heart attack, hadn't been for the folks next door I'd be dead. Heart attack's why I'm the Avon lady. Easy work. I don't need much income. Keeps me moving and gives me something to occupy my time." He pulled open the wooden front door. "No, she never had any caution. And now she's mixed up in some man dying in Los Angeles. How?"

"How did he die?" Dave said. "A broken neck. Someone attacked him and broke his neck."

Sims shook his head. "Maybe Billy Jim's got a point about the cities," he said.

"What's the address up there?" Dave said.

"It's not an address at all," Sims said. "I'll tell you how to get there."

"Did she write to you about the baby?" Dave said. "Telephone you? What?"

Sims peered past Dave out the screen door. "Billy Jim brought it here to be buried from the church. He's a religious fanatic. I didn't tell you that, did I? Not that wanting to bury your own child with a preacher in charge of things makes you a religious fanatic.

173

I don't mean that. I just mean I didn't tell you before. He's a religious fanatic. I don't hold with that. I don't hold with going to extremes. Take it easy, you live longer. What kind of car is that?"

"A Triumph," Dave said. "British make."

"About as big as a baby buggy," Sims said. "No, they don't have telephones up that way. Now, I have to tell you how to get there."

23

The mountains shouldered up black against the stars. Estaca seemed a long time ago. First the vineyards had stopped, then the sleeping cattle, the red steel fence posts, the barbwire. Now there was only the wind. There was only the worn strip of blacktop, only the little car hustling along it, whipped by the wind, chasing its pitiful outstretched lights. There was only him. It was big country. It was a big, empty night. He wondered if he'd understood Sims, if Sims had made a mistake. The martinis were putting him to sleep, the drone of the engine, the sameness of the rise and fall of the rock-strewn, parched-grass foothills. He switched on the radio. Gospel music twanged at him. He switched off the radio. He checked his watch and was surprised. It wasn't yet eight. He looked up.

And the headlights showed him a tin mailbox on a steel stake. TACKABERRY. He pressed the brakes but he'd been traveling fast and the Triumph went on by. He fought the unfamiliar shift knob, got the car into reverse, backed up to the mailbox. A little dirt trail cut off toward the mountains. He swung the Triumph into it. It ran

175

flat for a while, then started to climb. Chaparral and tumbles of rock showed themselves in the headlights when the track took twists. Dead windfall branches littered the ground under old live oaks. The road grew steeper. He shifted gears. The headlights shone at the sky. Then they tilted downward sharply. And out there, below, in the massive darkness, a tiny light showed.

He stopped the car, dry brush scraping its sides, switched off the headlights, got out and stood to let his eyes get used to the night. Wind blew his hair into them. He pushed it back. The light came from a window. Maybe he made out the shape of a house. It was so far off it was like a toy left by some lost child. He wished there were a moon. But even without its lights, the car would warn them he was coming. It was noisy. Noisier even than the wind where the wind had only scrub and rock to sound itself on. He got back into the Triumph, switched on the headlights again, and drove. *This is a mistake,* he thought.

Three old oaks sheltered the tin house. A tin porch ran along one side. On the other side, a lean-to roofed by stiff rippled plastic put in shadow a tractor and big sharp-edged shapes he couldn't name. He walked around the house in the wind. A generator hummed inside a corrugated iron pumpshack. There was no truck. That made him feel easier. He stepped up on the porch and banged the door. Just the wind—in the oaks, and making the house creak along its riveted seams. He banged again. Nothing. He tried the knob. The door was locked. The windows showed him blackness. He shouted, "Hello! Anybody here?" The wind took his voice out into the dark and lost it.

He stepped off the porch and walked around to the lighted window. It was set high and the glass was opaque. Under the lean-to he found an empty fuel drum and rolled it through the weeds until it stood under the window. He climbed up on it and tried to push the aluminum-clinched panel along in its aluminum groove. It wouldn't budge. He jumped down off the fuel drum and thought he heard a sound. But the wind was rattling the thick plastic roofing of the lean-to, and he couldn't be sure. He stood very still and strained his ears. There it was again. A cat? The sound was thin and plaintive. A hurt cat? Then the wind let up for a second and he heard the sound right and knew that it was human. It came from inside.

"Oh, help. Please? Help me?"

"Hold on," he called, and jumped up on the porch again. But this time the little blade from his key case was no use. It worked the lock in the brass-plated knob all right, but there was another keyhole in the door and nothing he had would even slide into it. When the wind let him, he kept hearing her crying and begging. He went back to the fuel drum, climbed up on it, rapped the glass. "I can't get in the door," he said. "Open the window."

It slid back. He was looking into a very small bathroom—toilet, shower stall, washbasin, mirror. She stood with her back against the door, staring at him, eyes large with fear. Her head was shaved. She was in dirty jeans and a dirty sweatshirt. He wondered only for a second, scared as she looked, why she didn't run. She was chained by the ankles. The ankles were thin, and the skin on them was rubbed raw. When he started to climb in she began to scream. He made a clumsy job of getting through the opening. He damn near fell on his head. And all the time she stood against the door and screamed. He twisted the cold tap handle of the washbasin, filled his hands with water, and threw it in her face. She stopped screaming.

For a few seconds she held her breath. Then she began to make the sick cat noise, a whimpering, keening sound. He knelt at her feet. What clamped her ankles were handcuffs from a dimestore play-detective kit. The chains attached were for holding dogs. They ran under the little veneered doors of the vanity that held the washbasin. He pulled open the doors. The chains were padlocked to the faucet pipes. He used the blade from the key case to unlock the handcuffs. He stood and pushed aside with his foot the chains and cuffs. He reached past her for the doorknob. She cringed away from him, both hands covering her mouth. He turned the knob but the door wouldn't open.

"He puts an iron pipe across it," she said. "I have to stay in here all the time he's gone."

"Billy Jim?" Dave said. "Where is he?"

"Off with the truck, working someplace. I don't too much care. When he's here all he does is read the Bible at me and pray at me." She sat on the closed toilet fixture and rubbed her ankles, wincing. "All that scares me, he could just forget me and never come back and I'd die in here. Or there could be a brush fire. It's dry and all this wind all the time. I'd shrivel up like bacon."

The wind made it hard to hear her. The sheet metal the place was built out of hummed. Dave said, "What right has he got to preach at you? You didn't break any necks. You didn't shoot anybody."

She looked up quickly. "Who are you?" Dave wet a washcloth in the basin and gently wiped the tears from her dirty face. He knelt and washed the sore ankles. She said, "You come from LA, don't you? You're a policeman."

"Gerald Dawson's insurance man," Dave said. "I've been hunting you for days. I almost thought you were dead."

"I been wishing I was dead," she said. "Him treating me like he does. Locking me up. Won't let me eat but once a day. Shaved off my hair. Threw out my makeup. Won't let me wear nothing nice. Not till I repent, he says." Through her tears she looked angry. "It's him needs to repent. All I done was go with men. I didn't kill nobody." She sniffed, unrolled toilet paper, and blew her nose. "And he keeps praying to God to forgive *me.*"

"Your father warned you against him," Dave said.

She shrugged. "I thought it was just he didn't want me to do something I wanted to do. That's how he was. Always at me not to do things. Turned out"—she made a wry face—"Billy Jim was no different. Men."

"Was that why you ran off to LA?" Dave asked.

She said, "We done fine right at the start, there. Lived in my daddy's house. Billy Jim worked at the farm-machinery place. He screamed in his sleep sometimes, and being around people made him sweat. He was always talking about how he wanted us to get out of Estaca, out in the country, alone by ourself. I thought it was the war and the hospital and he'd get over it, thought it was just talk, but it wasn't." She'd been staring at memories. Now she looked up at Dave. "Have you got a cigarette?"

Dave held out his pack to her. He'd crushed it, climbing through the window. The cigarettes were bent. He lit one for her, one for himself. "Go on," he said.

"Why did you want to find me?"

"Because you saw Billy Jim kill Gerald Dawson, didn't you? You have to tell the sheriff, the county attorney."

"How did you know to look for me here?"

He told her about the high-school annual.

"You're smart," she said, but she gave her head a worried shake. "Only you're not too young, and you don't look as strong as he is." She stood up on the toilet seat and gripped the windowframe. "We better get our ass out of here. He comes back and finds you"—she hiked herself up and started wriggling out into the night and the wind—"he'll kill us both."

"Can you make it?" Dave said. "There's a steel drum under the window."

"I see it." She wasn't just small and slim, she was limber and quick. She got out a lot more gracefully than he'd got in. He felt bulky and stiff climbing out after her and tried not to meet her eyes as he mismanaged elbows and knees. When he was on the ground, the wind whipping his hair, he told her, "Wait here," and went back under the rattling roof of the lean-to. He probed in the dark with his little flashlight and found a crowbar. He went back to her. She stood by the fuel drum, blinking against the wind, hands on her shaven skull. "What are you gonna do?"

"Break in," Dave said. "I want that shotgun."

The door was one of those with big diamond-shaped panes of amber pebbled plastic in its upper half. He smashed one of these with the crowbar, reached inside and worked the two locks, and turned the knob. He let her go in ahead of him and turn on a lamp beside a couch covered in hard-finish brown plaid. A chair matched it. So did the curtains. The floor was vinyl tile patterned to look like oak. A wooden television cabinet yawned empty of its works. A Bible lay on a coffee table.

"You look for the shotgun," she said. "I'll eat."

She went into a little kitchen and opened a refrigerator and took out a box of eggs.

"You don't know where it is?" Dave said.

"I don't want to. After I seen what it done to that man in that parking lot, I don't want to know. It was like his head exploded."

Dave slid back plastic veneered doors on a shallow storage closet. "You were bad luck for him. You were bad luck for Gerald Dawson. You were bad luck for yourself. Why did you go?"

"What would I stay here for? How would you like it? Ripped the insides out of the TV. Took the radio with him. Said I had to cleanse my soul of all that worldly trash."

Dave groped around on the overhead shelf.

She said, "He got to see the farmers he hired out to, but I didn't get to see nobody. No phone, so I couldn't talk to my school girl friends, not even to my daddy. Nothing to read except only the Bible."

Dave pawed aside hanging clothes to look in corners.

"He wouldn't let me have my movie magazines. Baby come and she was some kind of company when he'd be off in the truck. But then there blew up this big storm in March and caved this junky place right in on top of me and the baby died. I laid all night in the rain holding her, dead."

Dave crouched and beamed the flashlight over the floor. Shoe leather gleamed dully but there was no gleam of a gunstock or a gunbarrel either. He stood and rolled the slide door closed. She was frying eggs. In badly burned butter. He reached around her to shine the light into kitchen cabinets. Soap powders, bottled floor wax, pots and pans. Cans, cereal boxes, dried-soup packets. Mugs, plates. No gun.

"He never once took me into town. He had to go for groceries. He says it was bad for me. Guess he thought I'd make him let me see a movie. Never a week went by in my life I didn't see a movie. Till Billy Jim. I loved to read about the stars. I was pretty once, if you want to believe it." She ran a forlorn hand over her bald scalp. "I was a pom-pom girl. And a good dancer too."

Dave opened a door. A small bedroom was beyond it. There was another of the slide-door wall closets here. He searched it too, and the drawers under it. She said:

"What done it was, when the baby was dead, and he took her into Estaca to be buried, he wouldn't let me come along." From the corner of his eye he saw her empty a terrible brown mess from the pan onto a plate. "You want some of these scrambled eggs? You hungry?"

"No thanks." The shotgun could lie in sections in a dresser drawer. He tried that idea. She talked with her mouth full:

"I'm starved. Cornflakes and milk is what I get. Once a day. I told you that. He wouldn't keep the shotgun in there, not in the drawers." She stood in the doorway, shoveling in the food. "He'd think I'd find it and shoot him when he was sleeping. He don't believe how scared I am of that shotgun."

Dave kept going through the drawers, fumbling under clothes, slamming this one shut, yanking open the next one. He was sweating. He was doing this wrong. Everything about it he'd done wrong. It was stupid to have come here alone. He'd been lucky Billy Jim wasn't here when he drove up. She was right. He'd kill them both. Delgado had a gun. If he hadn't been bright enough to bring Delgado he should have brought Delgado's gun. He shut the last drawer.

"So I packed a suitcase and took all the money in the drawer and

181

got out on the road and put out my thumb. And in Fresno I caught a Greyhound. He never hid money from me. Why would he? No place for me to spend it, not way out here. But it wasn't much. I didn't care. I thought I'd get on television right away."

Dave stood on the bed and pushed a trapdoor in the ceiling. He set the little flashlight in his teeth and chinned himself. The metal joists creaked with his weight. He turned his head to make the flashlight beam scan. Dust was all there was. He dropped back onto the bed. The wind kept the house humming. It was like being inside a drum. He wished it would let up. He wouldn't hear the truck if it came. He pushed past her. He'd seen another trapdoor in the front room ceiling. She said:

"I didn't know how hard it would be. I didn't know much. But some girl I met says you could meet all kinds of show-business people on the Strip. You know where that is? And I did. And I was going to be in a picture, too—if Billy Jim hadn't come found me. I never thought he'd do that. He hated the city, any city. Scared him to death."

Dave chinned himself from the coffee table this time. But the little light didn't show him anything. He dropped.

"I know most of the story," he told her. "What I want to hear from you is how he killed Gerald Dawson."

"I had this apartment." She laid the plate in the sink and opened the refrigerator again and brought out a milk carton. From it she filled a glass. "Real beautiful."

"I saw it," Dave said. "Charleen, we can't stay here any longer. If that shotgun isn't here, then he's got it with him. And that could be very bad news."

Carrying the glass of milk, she went out the front door and stood on the long tin porch. "If he was coming, I'd see him. A long way. Clear to the top of the ridge." She stepped back inside. "You want the shotgun so you can take him back too—is that right? To keep him off you with his hands. To keep him from doing to you what he done to Jerry?"

182

"Where did it happen? In the bed?"

"In the kitchen." She went back on the porch. "Took hold of him, twisted his head somehow. You could hear the snap, and he was dead. I tried to run out of there." The wind was too loud for him to hear the next sentence. "Way he was hitting me, I thought he'd kill me too. I kicked him and ran out on the balcony but I was dizzy and my legs wouldn't hold me and he yanked me back inside."

Dave threw the cushions off the sofa. He groped inside for the mechanism that let it open into a bed. He found it and moved it. Sheets, blankets, two pillows. No shotgun. He looked around. "I went to that apartment. The sheriff's men went there. There was no sign of his having been murdered there. There should have been a mess."

"There was," she said. "I didn't know that happened to dead people. Billy Jim made me clean it up. It made me sick to my stomach. I kept having to run to the bathroom and throw up."

Dave went out past her. He stepped down off the porch, crouched, shone the little light under the porch.

She said, "But Billy Jim kept after me. Made me mop it twice and clean up all the signs where I washed the mop out, you know. Then he says, 'Now wax it.' And I laid wax on it while he was wrapping Jerry in a tarp from the truck and pulling and hauling his body out the kitchen window. Then I had to help him get it up the hill to the truck. He cut a hole in the fence so we could get through. To the street up above there." She said, "I don't know why. It's not cold. But I'm cold. I have to get a sweater."

There was nothing under the porch. Dave looked toward the dark ridge between this scoop of night valley and the highway. He went in after her. She wasn't getting a sweater. She was in the bathroom. She'd taken down the pipe that crossed the door and barred it when it hung in the bright brackets Billy Jim had screwed into the frame.

"What are you doing?" Dave said.

183

"I want to look nice," she said. Water splashed.

"Dear God," Dave said. "Charleen, come on. There's no more time."

"I'm coming," she snapped. "Just wait a minute."

"Why did he kill Dawson?"

"For corrupting me," she said through the door. "He warned him first, Sunday morning at the church. Jerry says get lost. So then the next day he phoned Mrs. Dawson what was going on with Jerry and me and for her to come get her husband. I didn't know that till afterwards, didn't know he was hid in my closet when they come—her, and the preacher, and Bucky boy. He was in there before Jerry and me got there. Must've killed him hearing me and Jerry in bed." Something happened to her diction. She was brushing her teeth and talking with the brush in her mouth. "My heart like to stopped when he jumped out of that closet after Bucky boy left. I didn't know him for a minute. He'd shaved off his beard."

"Yes, why did he do that?" Dave asked.

"To fool that old nigger-man guard," she said.

Dave tried the door. Locked. "Charleen, you're wasting time. We have to get out of here."

"Just one more minute," she said, and water ran hard.

"Why did Billy Jim stop at only two men? What about Full-bright? Wasn't he the one who started this whole thing?"

"Billy Jim never let me get to telling him about Jack. And when I seen what he done to Jerry and Mr. Odum, I wasn't about to tell him. That fancy boat, marijuana, cocaine, him taking them dirty pictures of me—he'd want to kill Jack Fullbright twice. I was so scared that night, I almost—"

She screamed. And it wasn't about memories. It was about now. Glass shattered. A male voice spoke words Dave couldn't make out. There was a heavier crash. He recognized that one. The top of the toilet tank. Billy Jim was dragging her out through the window. Dave ran across the meager living room and out at the door with the broken pane. The big, blocky pickup truck stood twenty steps off, engine rumbling, headlights dark. Of course. Billy Jim had seen the house lit up, seen the Triumph in the yard, known something was wrong. The trail down here wouldn't have been strange to him. He could drive without lights all the way from the ridge.

He appeared under his cowboy hat from around the corner of the wind-rattling house, dragging the kicking, screaming, stick-thin little girl toward the truck. Cowan was right. He was stocky like Bucky but bigger. Heels clattering, Dave ran along the porch. *You're not too young,* she said again inside his mind. And he launched himself at Billy Jim Tackaberry. Not bad for an old man. He got both legs just at the knees. The knees buckled. All three of them rolled in the dust. But Dave couldn't hold on. Tackaberry got a leg free and kicked Dave in the head. Hard. Dave didn't see anything or hear anything. Then he heard a gonging sound. Something had banged the body of the truck. He heard grunts, squeaky cries. His head hurt.

He groaned and moved. He got to his hands and knees and collapsed again. The truck door slammed. The big engine roared. Dave staggered to his feet. The truck came at him. He threw himself out of its way, tumbling among crackling brush. The truck hit the porch. A metal prop gave, the roof sagged with a shriek, the metal flooring buckled. The truck rocked. Its big gears clashed and ground together. The truck shot backward. The wide tires grabbed at the dirt. Dust kicked up and the wind ripped it away. Dave scrambled for the house, stumbling, falling, on his feet again. The truck skidded in a half-circle and chopped to a halt. Dave turned in the doorway. Light from the truck's instrument panel glinted along a shotgun barrel. Dave fell down, arms over his head. The explosion was big and bright. His sleeves shredded. His arms felt as if he'd stuck them into fire.

The truck roared off.

He tried to tell his father, "You can't criticize me. I only did the same thing you did." But his father was dead. And he couldn't form the words anyway. He heard the sounds he made. No more than mumbling. His father faded into the dark. Dave heard a squeak of rubber soles. A door clicked open. Light struck his eyelids and he opened his eyes. The light was hard, dazzling, painful. It glared off white walls. A big bottle hung above him with blood in it. A tube drooped down to him from the bottle. The bottle glittered. He shifted focus. A nurse, plump, middle-aged, no makeup, rimless glasses gleaming, looked at him from the foot of a white bed. Then another face came between him and her, a ginger-moustached young man in a tan uniform.

"Brandstetter? Who shot you?"

"Passed out and drove off the road, did I?" The words came out of him very faintly but his diction was back. "Tackaberry, Billy Jim."

186

"Loss of blood," the officer said. "Tore up your arms. What did you get blood all over your car for? That's a beautiful car, brand new. Why didn't you phone for help?"

Dave raised his arm to look at his watch. The arm was wrapped in white. The watch wasn't on it. "What time is it? Dear Christ, how long have I been here?" He tried to sit up. The nurse made a sound. The officer pushed him back on the pillows. "Where am I?" Dave said.

"Estaca," the officer said. He read his own watch. "How long —two hours, two and a half?"

"Ah, no," Dave said.

"The doctor had to sew up your arteries. That's why you have to lie still," the nurse said strictly. "You lost a great deal of blood."

"I need to phone," Dave said. A telephone crouched on the table next to the bed. His bundled forearms lay on the blanket. Only the fingers stuck out of the bandages. He worked them. That was all right. "Los Angeles. Lieutenant Jaime Salazar. LA County Sheriff's homicide bureau."

"You're in good hands here," the officer said.

"I believe it," Dave said. "But Tackaberry's going to kill somebody down there." He rolled on his side, started to reach for the phone. The nurse put his arm back. There was no pain. "They used locals," he said to her. "Was I that far out? What did I do, hit my head?"

"You should have worn your seat belt," she said.

"I'll phone for you," the young officer said.

"It's in the building on Temple Street," Dave said. "If he's not there, get them to patch you through to his home. Tell him—"

"You can tell him." The officer nodded at the bedside phone. "After I get him. Who's the target?"

"Jack Fullbright. He lives on a boat at the marina."

"Salazar?" the officer said. "I'll try." He went out of the room, and a tall child dressed like a doctor came in. He cocked an eyebrow, turned down the corners of his mouth approvingly. "You look okay for somebody who almost bled to death."

"Good. Then I can go. It's urgent." Dave tried to sit up again and was pushed back again. The doctor put the cold round circle of a stethoscope to Dave's chest. He shifted it. Again. He took the ends out of his ears. He pulled up the lid of Dave's left eye, right eye. Dave said, "It's a matter of life and death."

"You're a private investigator," the tall child said. "That's pretty romantic."

"It's life and death just the same," Dave said. "Two men are already dead because an Army hospital let a soldier out of the rubber room before he was ready. Tonight he tried to kill me. And he's on his way to—"

The door opened and the officer with the ginger moustache came in. "Salazar isn't at his desk. And your name isn't on the list of people they patch through to him at home. So who else?"

Dave told him about Ken Barker. "There's an address book with phone numbers in it in my jacket. Have you got my jacket?"

"What's left of it," the officer said.

"Well, if you can't reach Barker," Dave said, "please call John Delgado. He works with me."

The doctor took the telephone off the table and carried it to the windowsill and left it there. He said to the officer, "You do all the phoning—not him."

"I'm leaving," Dave said, "when that bottle's empty."

The doctor said, "You have a concussion. I'll want you here till Saturday."

"Splendid," Dave said. He looked at the ginger-moustached youth. "Okay. Please tell Barker to get down to the marina and arrest Jack Fullbright. He's got drugs on that boat. He's probably in bed with an underage kid. The idea is to get him into jail where Billy Jim Tackaberry can't get at him."

"Has this Tackaberry got a license number?"

"It was too dark," Dave said, "and I was busy. You can get the

188

number, can't you? And will you hurry and get Barker, please? LAPD. Homicide division."

"Right. We'll get the license number too. He tried to kill you, right? And you'll swear to that, right? So I'll put out an APB."

"Good," Dave said. "Only get Barker first, okay?"

But he couldn't get Barker. Barker had gone on a trip.

"So I tried your man Delgado. Nobody answers."

Dave looked at the bottle. The blood was dripping into him very slowly. The nurse touched the bottle. She touched the place where it was taped to the inside of his arm just above the bandages. Dave said to the officer, "There's another number in there. Amanda Brandstetter."

"That'd be your wife. You want me to tell her what happened to you? You want her to come and get you?"

"What's the matter?" Dave said. "Won't my car run?"

"It's all right," the officer said, "if you don't mind all the blood."

"Don't tell her what happened to me," Dave said. "Just tell her I got tied up here. Ask her to find Johnny Delgado and get him down to the marina. For the purpose I've already outlined, all right? To get Jack Fullbright off that boat and hidden someplace where Tackaberry can't blow him up with that shotgun. Tell her Johnny will be in a bar someplace near the Sea Spray Motel in Santa Monica."

"That doesn't sound like it would work very well," the boy with the ginger moustache said.

"Then you make an official connection to the LAPD," Dave said. "They'll act for you when they wouldn't for a PI—not even a PI who's been shot."

"You don't know Tackaberry's really going there." The boy looked uncomfortable. "I'd have to clear it with the chief. Tackaberry could be running for Mexico."

"Forget it," Dave said. "We wouldn't want to get the chief out of bed."

189

"If he got LA all upset and nothing happened, it could be embarrassing for me," the boy said.

"There's another number in my book. Randy Van. Tell him I got smashed up. He'll go down and warn Fullbright."

"Has somebody named Randy Van got muscles?"

"Enough to pick up the phone," Dave said.

"I did put out the bulletin," the boy apologized.

"It's all right," Dave said. "Just phone Van now."

The boy went and the doctor looked in. "Nurse? I want him to have something to make him sleep."

She left, rubber soles squeaking. Dave detached the tube from his arm. His watch, wallet, and keys were in the drawer of the table that had held the phone. His clothes weren't in the closet. He pulled back the loosely woven yellow-orange curtains at the window. Estaca looked as lively as when he'd come through earlier. Trees tossed shaggy in the wind, silhouetted against a streetlight. A step sounded in the hall. He went into the bathroom and turned the lock. Knuckles rapped. "Are you all right?"

"Fine," he said. "I'll be out in a minute."

And he was. Out the window. The short, starchy hospital garment tied in the back wasn't what he'd have chosen to travel in but it was all there was, and the citizens of Estaca weren't looking. By now they'd have switched off the TV and gone to bed. He rounded a sharp stucco corner of the one-story hospital, and there was the parking lot. In the moving shadow of a tree, the Triumph waited for him. The blood on the leather bucket seat had dried in the hot wind. It crackled when he sat on it. The carpet under his bare feet was spongy, sticky. Blood had splattered the instrument panel and the windshield. The steering wheel was crusty with it. He drove into the street. The swinging traffic light showed red but he ignored it.

The big waterside restaurants loomed up dark out of their spotlit landscaping, wide windows glossy black mirrors. The condomini-

190

ums stood up tall and black against the stars. His watch said it was almost three. He was dizzy and sick and his arms hurt. It was cold here and damp, and he shivered. He stopped the car at the gate to the parking lot where the live-aboard people left their cars. The candy-striped steel pole across the entry was snapped off. He looked at the little white gate house. He thought no one was in it and then he saw the big foot that stuck out the door. He left the Triumph. The guard's hat was over his face. He was folded awkwardly on the cramped floor. His hand was on the butt of his holstered revolver. A bloody hole was in his chest. Dave stood over him and used the telephone.

Then he ran across the parking lot. He ran out the pier. The tender soles of his feet kept picking up pebbles and making him limp. He kept brushing them off. The boats all slept dark on their tethers, lifting a little and falling a little with the lift and fall of the tide. It was deadly quiet. Light streamed up out of the companionway that opened from the deck of Fullbright's power boat. Dave swung aboard. He went down the companionway. No one was in the room with the couches and the bar. But the door in the bulkhead was open to the sleeping cabin. He saw the blood first and then Fullbright's body naked halfway into the washroom where no light burned. He touched the body. It was almost cold. He turned to get away from the blood smell, the slipperiness of the blood underfoot. And he heard splashing. He went up the companionway.

Below, over the side, someone feebly coughed. Someone retched seawater. Someone tried to call out. It came to Dave as a moan. He peered down into the water. Light fell from the portholes of the forward cabin but it only wavered in the water and showed him nothing. The weak splashing came from farther astern. He went back there. The light that reached out here from the parking lot was just bright enough to make the black water hard to see. He blinkered his eyes with his hands.

"Where are you?" he shouted.

"Help!" A white thing floated below. A rope lay on the polished planks. He lowered it. "Help!"

"Can you grab that?" He wound it around an upright and knotted it. "The rope. Grab it." But nothing was happening. Even the feeble splashing had stopped. He heard bubbles break. He went over the rail. The water was cold. The white thing drifted near him, sinking. He groped out for it. Cold human flesh. He grappled for a hold, found limp arms, a hard round skull. He needed to breathe and he let go and surfaced and heard far-off sirens. He smiled, filled his lungs, and went under again.

This time he got hold of the white figure and kicked and the two of them shot to the surface. His arms were around the ribcage from the back and there was no sign of breathing. Clumsily, one-armed, he pushed at the water, bumping the slippery curved hull of the boat, trying to reach the pier. The water deafened him. He heard the sirens. The water deafened him again. The water had soaked through the bandages. The pain from the salt was bright and fierce. He struck a piling with his head. He grabbed the piling and clung onto it.

He took a deep breath and shouted.

And he felt the pier shake with running feet.

It was Randy Van in a soaked white eyelet dress with a long smear of tar on it. He lay on the white pier planks and looked pale green and dead. Except for his legs. The flesh of his legs was lacerated and oozed blood. Paramedics worked over him in green coveralls, nightmare figures in the light from the open hatch of Fullbright's boat. One of the paramedics, a plump black with rolls of fat at the back of his neck, had his mouth over Randy's mouth. A white one in shell-rim glasses sat astride his hips, pressing hands to his lower chest. Somebody wrapped Dave in a blanket and asked him what was funny. Dave couldn't tell him how Randy would enjoy the situation if he knew about it. Dave's jaws seemed to be locked. It was cold. He was shivering so hard it felt as if his joints would come apart. He wished they had more blankets.

Randy made a sound. Water came out of his mouth. His eyelids fluttered. The torn legs kicked weakly. The black and the boy in glasses put him on a chrome-plated gurney and ran pushing it up the pier past staring people in bathrobes toward the parking lot where lights winked amber on and off atop police cars, and a light spun round and round atop an ambulance. The one in the green coverall who had put the blanket around him pushed him down. He was weak and he went down easily. He tried to say that he could walk but the shuddering wouldn't let him. He was pushed flat. His legs were hoisted. Then came another blanket and that was fine. He shut his eyes and the little wheels jarred over the planks. It went on so long it put him to sleep.

Amanda said, "My God, look at his arms! Dave!"

He opened his eyes. She was kneeling beside him. She had on a little pearl-gray derby. He said, "What the hell are you doing here? I only asked you—"

"To find me." Delgado swayed above her, unshaven, eyes bloodshot, shirttail out. His speech was thick. "To get me down here to rescue Fullbright. Only I couldn't find the fucking boat. All I did was get lost. I'm sorry, Dave."

"Not half so sorry as Fullbright," Dave said.

Ken Barker said, "They caught Billy Jim and Charleen in Chatsworth. It was the APB from Estaca that did it." He wore a sheepskin coat, leather side out. "I'm sorry they shunted your call off. I wasn't on any trip."

"I'm glad everybody's sorry," Dave said.

"Why didn't you say you were hurt?" Amanda said.

"I'm all right," Dave said. "It was two hundred miles from here. What could you do?" They were wheeling the gurney. Toward the gaping doors of the ambulance. The legs folded with a mild clacking sound and for a half second he was airborne. "Stop looking so scared," he called back to her.

"We'll follow you," she called.

The ambulance doors slammed shut. It was bright inside. The fat black paramedic hung up bottles of plasma. The siren moaned into life. The engine thrashed. The ambulance began to move. The black found a vein inside Randy's elbow and shoved a big, bright, hollow needle into it. He did the same to Dave. That place in Dave's arm was bruised and Dave passed out for a second. The tubes and bottles swung with the sway of the ambulance. Dave looked across at Randy. He wasn't corpse-green anymore. He smiled wanly at Dave.

"Thank you," he said. "Nice swim."

"I didn't plan for you to get shot up," Dave said.

"It was my own fault. I wasted time changing."

"Why a white eyelet dress?" Dave asked.

"I thought the sensible thing for him to do would be put out to sea. I mean, wasn't that logical? And, well, what else would you suggest a young lady wear for a cruise on a warm summer night?"

GRAVEDIGGER

For Bill Harding

1

When last he had noticed, nothing was out here but bare hills above an empty beach. He was jolted by how much time must have passed—not years but decades. Now expensive ranch houses of distressed brick sprawled under low shake roofs on wide lots back of white rail fences. Trees had grown tall, mostly lacy eucalyptus, but even an occasional wind-bent cypress. The streets curved with the curves of the hills. Sometimes he glimpsed the blue water of backyard swimming pools where no one swam because the wind off the sea was cold though the sun shone in a clear blue sky.

He got lost among the empty suburban morning streets but at last he found Sandpiper Lane and a mailbox with the number 171, and parked the Triumph by a little palm whose hairy fans rattled in the wind. He climbed out of the car and the wind blew in his ears. When it stopped for breath, he could hear the distant surf. He heard no nearby sounds, human sounds. Even if you lived out here, you had to go to work, to school. If a wife kept at home by young children sat drinking coffee and watching television in a kitchen, her windows were closed, the sound didn't reach the street.

The mailbox at 171 needed a new coat of black paint. Rust showed at the welds. Leaves and litter strewed the driveway that was a half-circle. They crunched under his soles. He stepped over newspapers, thick, held folded by loops of grubby cotton string, print faded by sunlight, paper turning color from the weather. SEARCH FIVE STATES FOR MASS MURDERER a headline read. AZRAEL REPORTED IN MEXICO, CANADA read another. He peered through small panes of dusty glass in garage doors. No cars were parked inside.

A dozen dry shades of red and brown, eucalyptus leaves lay heaped at the foot of the front door. The door was recessed, its yellow enamel cracked and, near the bottom, peeling, curling back on itself. The door must have looked cheerful once. It looked sad now. Dave pushed a bell button. Chimes went off inside the house. He waited but no one came. He rang the chimes again, inhaling the dark insistent eucalyptus smell. He rubbed his nose. He used a tarnished brass knocker at eye level in the middle of the door. Its rattle raised only echoes. Rubber squealed in the street. He turned. A new little red pickup truck swung in at the driveway of a house across the street. From the bed of the truck, a surfboard flashed signals at the sun.

The truck rocked to a halt in front of the door of the house and a boy jumped out of the cab and ran for the door. All of him but his face was covered by a black wetsuit, red and yellow stripes down arms and legs. He hopped on one foot while he jingled keys and tried to get one into the door. Dave ran down the driveway of 171,

2

holding up a hand, calling out to the boy to wait a minute. The boy flung a panicky look over his shoulder and disappeared into the house. The slam of the door was loud in the stillness of a moment's drop in the wind.

Dave trotted across the street, up the drive, dodged the little red truck, and rang another set of door chimes. He panted. He was getting old. Running wasn't natural to him anymore. From inside the house he heard a shout but couldn't make out the words. Were they "Go away!" or "Come in!"? He waited. The apple-green enamel on this door was fresh and dustless, as if it had been laid on yesterday. He regarded it for two or three minutes, whistling softly between his teeth. Then the door opened.

"Sorry," the boy said. He wore a red sweatshirt now and was tying the drawstring of a pair of red sweatpants. His hair was a blond mop. He was barefoot. "I had to get to the bathroom. You want them, across the street?"

"Westover," Dave said, "Charles. Any idea where he's gone? It looks as if it's been a while."

"What are you about?" the boy said. "All kinds of people keep coming. Once it was a marshal."

"I'm about insurance," Dave said. "Life insurance." He watched the boy start to shut the door and said, "No, I don't sell it. I investigate death claims." He took out his wallet and handed the boy a card. The boy read it and looked startled. "Brandstetter," he said, and smiled. "Hey, sure. I saw you on TV—Tom Snyder or somebody. You solve murders when the police can't do it."

"The police are busy," Dave said. "I'm not busy. How long has the Westover house been empty?"

"A week, ten days." He frowned. "Who's murdered?"

"Maybe no one," Dave said. "Maybe Serenity Westover."

"Oh, wow." Noon-blue sea light had been in the boy's eyes. It clouded over. He stared at Dave, at Dave's mouth, where the name had come from. He said numbly, "Serenity?"

"Do you know her?"

"We were in the same kindergarten, grade school, high school." The boy looked past Dave, maybe at the house across the street. "We had our first date together. Sixth grade." The wind blew cold, and that may have been what made him shiver. Or it may have been something else. "Jesus." He said it softly to himself, then backed inside and told Dave to come in. Dave stepped in and the boy shut the door. "I'm freezing," he said, and walked off. "You like some coffee? Some breakfast? I'm starved. I didn't eat before I left this morning. God, that water was cold." He was out of sight now, but Dave followed his voice. "There's a storm down off Baja, and the surf is way up, but you get so numb all you do is fall off. And after while, anyway, all you can think of is how badly you have to pee, and that's not easy in a wetsuit." Dave found him in a spacious kitchen of waxed wood cabinets and waxed red brick under sloping beams. "I should have gone to school. I knew how it would be. I've tried it before in weather like this. I don't learn very fast." A circle of flame burned high under a red-orange teakettle. The boy scooped coffee beans into a grinder of the same color. The grinder whirred and rattled while the boy held his hand on it. When the motor quit whining, he looked at Dave. "How do you mean, 'maybe'?"

"Her father claims she was one of the girls murdered at that ranch in the desert. The ones whose bodies they've been digging up. It's been in the news."

4

"Oh, wow," the boy said again. "What makes him think that?"

There was a breakfast bar with neat bentwood stools that had cushions of natural linen. Dave sat on one of the stools, took an envelope out of his jacket pocket, and slipped from the envelope a smaller envelope that was soiled, rumpled, and addressed in a childlike hand in blue ball-point ink. "You want to look at this for me?"

The boy came to the bar, carrying the clear plastic part of the coffee grinder that held the pulverized beans. He looked at the envelope without touching it. He looked at Dave. Stricken. With a finger, Dave pushed the envelope closer to him. He said:

"Is that her writing?"

The boy nodded. He gave a sad little smile. "It was always like that, never got any better. I've got a lot of her letters. I don't know why I keep them. She changed. She wasn't the same anymore. The way she was acting, I didn't want anything to do with her. She didn't want anything to do with me." He set down the container. The coffee smell that rose from it was dense and appetizing. He picked up the envelope and squinted at the blurry postmark. "Perez," he said, and stared at Dave again.

"Go ahead," Dave said, "open it. Take out what's inside." What was inside was a letter on dimestore writing paper in the same clumsy, childish hand, the same cheap ball point. Also a snapshot. The boy unfolded the letter and read aloud under his breath: "Dear Daddy. So you won't worry about me, I want you to know that I am very happy, now. I have found someplace where I can be at peace. . . ." He let the letter drop. He picked up the snapshot. "Oh, wow," he said again, and looked at Dave with tears in his eyes. "She was there. Look. That's her, standing right next to Azrael. Smiling. Oh, wow."

"You're sure?" Dave said.

"I saw her every day of my life almost," he said, "from the time when we were babies. Of course I'm sure."

"There are six girls in the photo," Dave said. "You mean the dark, roundfaced one with the long straight hair?"

"That's Serenity." The kettle began rattling. The boy picked up the container of ground coffee and went back to the counter beside the burner deck. He dumped the ground coffee into a glass coffee maker, fitted its sections together, picked up the kettle by its handsome bentwood handle, poured the boiling water in, set the kettle down.

"There wasn't much of a lens in that camera," Dave said. "The image isn't sharp. And she's not so different from a hundred thousand other girls her age."

The boy switched off the burner. "It's her." He got coffee mugs down from a cupboard, brought them to the breakfast bar, set them there. He picked up the grubby envelope again and peered at the postmark. "This was mailed almost two years ago. Just after she ran away."

"And in two years," Dave said, "she could have run away from Azrael, too, couldn't she? That's what makes Banner Insurance nervous about this claim. They're going to be even more nervous when I report that the man who filed the claim has also run away. Why did Serenity run away—can you tell me?"

The boy winced at him. "Is this how you do your job? I mean—don't you know anything about the Westovers?"

"That there were four of them, Charles, Anna, Serenity, and Lyle—father, mother, two children. I know their ages and that they live, or lived, across the street here. I have a telephone number that no one answers. I can't find an office, so I assume Charles Westover used his home. He's an attorney."

"Used to be," the boy said. "He got disbarred for bribing witnesses and went to jail for a year. That was when Serenity took off."

"Disappointed in her father?" Dave said.

The boy laid strips of bacon in a frying pan. "She could never be that. It was her mother. Her mother divorced him and Serenity couldn't forgive her for that and they fought all the time and finally Serenity left." The boy opened a big coppertone refrigerator and put the bacon package back and brought out eggs. "No—she and her father were crazy about each other. This thing about bribing the witnesses and all that took about a year or something, and he was in deep trouble, you know? And he didn't have time for her or anybody. He was trying to save himself, I suppose." The boy broke eggs into a terra-cotta-color mixing bowl and put the shells down a disposal that gulped and shuddered. "We didn't see him. He used to be friendly with my folks, he and Anna. But when this happened, he kept away. My dad didn't judge him. He was a friend, all right? But Chass was ashamed I guess, or afraid or something, and we hardly saw him at all. I mean, he'd speak if you said hi when he was coming out of his driveway or something, but he wouldn't drop over like before and he stopped going to the beach club and anything like that. Just holed up over there. And his wife was the same."

"And Serenity?"

"She went crazy, sort of. I mean, we were buddies—like

7

brother and sister, if you want to put it like that. We played together all the time when we were little and it was just"— he was beating the eggs with a fork and he moved his shoulders in a shrug—"a companionship that went on, all right? I used to wonder if we were in love, sometimes. I could never answer that." Butter sizzled in a frying pan, and he poured in the beaten eggs and set the bowl in the sink and stirred the eggs around over the burner-deck flame with the fork. "It just seemed like we'd always been together and so, maybe, we always would be. But then this rotten thing happened that her father did and she stopped coming around. I tried for a while to get her to. I mean, it was very"—he reached down plates from a cupboard—"I missed her, I was sad, I was lonesome, okay? But she began running around with beach bums and druggies from Venice, a whole crowd of freaks. She seemed to want to do every crazy thing they were doing. Drunk half the time, wandering around spaced out on God knows which kind of pills the rest of the time. Once, her mother went and found her living with some greasy weirdo that called himself a poet, in a ratty old dump, one room with a mattress on the floor. She wouldn't leave for her mother, and her mother asked me to go along to try to get her to come home. She was passed out on reds, and I just picked her up and carried her out to the car." He spooned the eggs out of the pan onto the waiting plates. He turned off the burners. He forked bacon onto the plates. He brought the plates to the breakfast bar and set them down. He gave a little bleak laugh at himself. "Hell, I forgot forks, I forgot napkins." He got these from drawers. The forks were good Danish steel. The napkins were linen that matched the seatcovers of the stools. He sat on the stool beside Dave, then got off it and went for coffee and sugar, spoons, and cream in a squat carton. He sat on the stool again. "Then the trial came and he went to jail."

"He didn't try to appeal?"

"No. Maybe he was tired of fighting. Maybe Anna saying she was through with him forever made him give up or something. That's what my father said. He's a psychiatrist." The boy began eating hungrily. "And that's when Serenity ran away." He cut at a bacon strip with the edge of his fork, stopped, looked at Dave. "You don't think he's right—Serenity wasn't one of those girls Azrael buried?"

"I don't know enough yet," Dave said, "to think anything. But for what it's worth, Banner Insurance is in doubt. Three of the recovered bodies have been identified and claimed. Three no one has come for. I guess they didn't send their parents letters and snapshots. One of them could have been Serenity. Blood type, hair color, height, and general skeletal conformation all match. But the girl in question was a perfect specimen—no dental work, never broke a bone."

"Serenity never broke a bone," the boy said. "Her teeth were perfect." The boy worked on the bacon and eggs for a minute. Then he said, "They take a baby footprint in the hospital when you're born."

"These bodies weren't in a condition to yield footprints or fingerprints," Dave said. "But I'm glad to know about Serenity's teeth and bones. That helps. Thank you. And to answer your question—yes, this is how I do my job. And now I do know something about the Westovers, don't I." He gave the boy a tight little smile. "I appreciate your help." He tasted the coffee. It was first-rate. "And I appreciate the breakfast."

"I don't know where Chass went," the boy said.

"What about his wife? Where is she now? Anna?"

"I think she runs a school for little kids, a playschool. Someplace in West L.A." He wrinked his forehead. "What does she call it? The Hobbit School. Yeah."

"Thanks. I'll look her up." Dave ate for a few minutes, drank some more coffee, lit a cigarette. "What about the son, what about Lyle? Does he go to college somewhere?"

"Juilliard in New York," the boy said. "Only not this year. He was around. I don't know, but I think he was working. Maybe to help his father out." The boy went away and came back with a brown pottery ashtray for Dave. He set it on the counter. "He's a musical genius." The boy got onto his stool again, sipped some coffee, laughed wryly. "All the kids thought he was a retard, a moron. He has this very bad speech defect, all right? And he wasn't any good at anything kids do—running, swimming, playing any kind of games. Very bad physical coordination, almost like a spastic, you know? And it turned out he's a musical genius. We treated him really badly, really mean. Nobody could stand him. He didn't do anything to deserve it. Kids are cruel, right?"

"But Lyle's not there now," Dave said. "And hasn't been there. Also for a week or ten days. Could he have gone away with his father?"

"I guess so. They never seemed to have anything to say to each other." The boy shook his head, frowning. "I don't see why he'd go. He had a lot of friends coming around all the time. Music coming out of the windows over there—sometimes till two in the morning."

"Did Serenity like him? Did he like her?"

"Not when we were really small," the boy said, "but when we all grew up a little, she got mad at us when we called him stupid and told him to get lost. Then, pretty soon, it wasn't a problem anymore. He got all wrapped up in music, practicing all day—only ten, eleven years old. Yes, sure, Serenity liked him—loved him, didn't she? Sure. I guess he loved her too. I never heard any different."

Dave checked his wristwatch, drank the last of the coffee from his mug, got off the stool. "I'd better find Anna West-over," he said. "You've got my card?" The boy nodded and got off his stool. Dave said, "If Westover or Lyle shows up over there, will you phone me? I'll be grateful. If I'm not there, leave your message on the tape, all right?" The boy said he would, and Dave looked around for the way out. The boy led him, opened the apple-green door. The sea wind crowded in. The sun hadn't warmed it. When Dave was halfway down the drive, the boy called:

"I wish it would be Serenity who shows up."

"So do I." Dave lifted a hand, walked on down the drive, crossed the street. He started to get into the Triumph and halted. He looked back. The green door was closed. He went to the 171 mailbox and opened it. It was jammed with envelopes. He shut the box, got into the Triumph, and drove away.

11

2

Anna Westover said, "Isn't it tiresome how right folk wisdom always turns out to be?" In an empty schoolroom strewn with naptime blankets, building blocks, toy xylophones, little red tables, little red chairs, she stood, small, thin, and brittle, facing a window where the clear morning light showed every line of worry and disappointment in her handsome face. She smiled wryly, and more lines appeared to frame her generous mouth. " 'As ye sow, so shall ye reap.' " She sighed, looked at Dave, straightened her shoulders. "How much I would have done differently, if only I hadn't been so sure of myself."

Outside the window, under old pepper trees, little kids in bright sweaters toddled and hopped, chirping and squeaking in a yard of grass-cracked blacktop, among gaudily painted swings, seesaws, jungle gyms. "It looks like a cheerful life," Dave said. "There have to be worse ways to earn your living."

"I agree," she said. "It's the loneliness I feel sorry about. I might have had my father and mother again, but a choice was given me a long time ago, and I chose my husband. Now I don't have him and I don't have them."

"People who make either/or propositions to their children can't be much of a loss," Dave said.

She had fine, clear, gray eyes, and they searched his face now skeptically. "Have you children, Mr. Brandstetter?"

He shook his head. "I was one once. Does that help?"

"Almost not at all," she said. She crossed her arms on her breast, clutching her arms. She walked around the room on legs that were good and straight and must have been beautiful before they became too thin. "What you want for your children is that they never stumble and fall and hurt themselves. Suddenly emotions take charge of you that you never knew you possessed. It's appalling how strong they are. Common sense hasn't a chance." She stopped and looked at him again. "But you mustn't think it's their fault—my parents, I mean. Of course they would be happy to have me back in the circle of their love again."

"Then, if you're lonely—" he began.

"I am also stubborn and ashamed. When I wanted to marry Chass, my father said he was no good, and that he would bring me sorrow and disgrace. He said he didn't have any moral fiber. He acknowledged that he was brilliant. He admitted that he had charm, grace, good looks, all of which would take him far in the law. But he saw into Chass as I couldn't see, and knew that intelligence, charm, grace, good looks don't add up to a man."

"What about ambition?" Dave said. "That's an expensive house out there at the beach. It takes hard work to earn a house like that. And he's only forty-five."

"Oh, yes." She nodded and smiled sadly with a corner of her mouth. "Ambition. Yes, indeed. The really dangerous ingredient for a no-good. That was what my father trusted least in Chass. Oh, yes." She laughed grimly. "Ambition he did have. I thought it was wonderful. It wasn't. It was a disease, a cancer."

A small oriental boy stumbled and fell in the yard. A mountainous black woman in a tent-size flowered smock swooped down, gathered him against her massive breasts, petted him, crooned to him. His cries from beyond the plate glass sounded like the reedy bleat of a squeeze toy.

"I was so in love with him, so proud of him, so sure of him. I begged my father to help him. He thought he could make me let Chass go by refusing. Instead, I quit school myself, went to work, and paid his way through law school. He came out at the top of his class. I was vain, and I rubbed my father's nose in it. Wrong, how wrong he'd been. Oh, was I vain and foolish." Laughing sourly at herself, she began gathering up the small blankets, folding them, stacking them on the lower shelves of bookcases full of rubber balls, dolls, mallets, teddy bears. "And fond and foolish was my father. I thought, and perhaps he thought so too, that he was acting on the strength of evidence. He was a lawyer, after all. He took Chass into his firm, made him a junior partner. But it wasn't the strength of the evidence, was it? It was guilt at having let me sacrifice my own education, my future—'sacrifice' would have been the word he used to himself—to put Chass through law school instead of helping him, as he could so easily have done, so easily. Guilt. And chagrin at having misjudged the man his daughter loved."

"He wasn't with your father's firm," Dave said, "when this witness-bribing thing happened?"

"Oh, no." She began picking up the scattered small chairs and arranging them neatly at the tables. "Chass

14

didn't stay more than a few years. He chafed. Things moved too slowly. Then the chance to handle a big criminal case came his way. He begged my father to let him handle it under the firm's umbrella. But it wasn't that kind of firm. It was corporate law, civil law, property management, that tame sort of thing. My father distrusted criminal law. He wouldn't hear of it. And Chass left the firm." She opened a door, switched on a light in a washroom, came back with a sponge and, crouching, began to wipe off the tabletops. A faint smell of orange juice reached Dave. "He did well on his own. I didn't much like the clients he sometimes brought to dinner. I didn't like them in the same house with my children. But that didn't often happen." She gave a little dry chuckle. "Just too often. But"—she sighed, rose, moved to the next table, crouched again, wiped again—"he was happy. Things were moving fast. He liked the courtroom, the confrontations, the reality—that was what he called it—the reality of it all. And, of course, he loved winning. And he always seemed to win."

"And the money?" Dave said.

"And the money." She wiped another table, rose and took the sponge into the washroom. Dave heard water splash. Over the sound of the water, she called, "That was when we bought that pretentious house, where the damned wind never stops blowing. Serenity was six."

"And Lyle?" Dave wondered.

She came out with the sponge. "Five. And a great worry. He couldn't speak, he could only make funny noises. It turned out that was his way of speaking. It still is."

"Did you take him to therapists?"

She was wiping tabletops again. "Oh, yes. I believe several of them went into other professions after encountering Lyle. At first, they insisted something was the matter with his brain." She found a spill spot on the asphalt tile floor and wiped the shiny surface clean. "He has the brain of an Einstein." She didn't sound pleased about Lyle. "If he wanted to speak, he'd speak. He simply can't be bothered."

"I'm told he's a fine musician," Dave said. "He was living with his father. Why was that?"

"It was his choice," she said briskly. "Ask him."

"Tell me where to find him and I will," Dave said.

"At Juilliard, in New York," she said.

"Not this winter," Dave said. "You mean you haven't seen him since he came home?"

"Is he home? I thought you said you couldn't find him."

"The boy across the street says he's been home, playing music at night, working during the day, to help his father out. The house is in poor shape. What happened to all that wonderful money? Did it go for his defense?"

"And he can't earn any more," she said. She stood in the washroom doorway, and smoked a cigarette. The motions she made were nervous. "He's disbarred. You knew that." She blinked. "The boy across the street? You mean little Scotty Dekker?" She laughed bleakly and shook her head. "How we misjudge children. I'd never have believed Scotty could understand a thing he saw or heard. A pretty little animal—that's what I always thought about Scotty."

"He's still pretty," Dave said, "and he's got eyes and ears, and maybe even a normal brain. But he evidently wasn't any closer to Lyle than you are. And he doesn't know where he's gone or why. Or his father, either. Where would they go, Mrs. Westover?"

"I don't know. And I don't know why it's so pressing.

16

What do you care? I suppose Chass finally ran from all the people he owes money to. The house is heavily mortgaged, for one thing. I presume he owes you money?"

"He doesn't," Dave said. "Do you hear from Serenity?"

Anna Westover stared. "Has something happened to her?"

"Do you know where she's been these past two years?"

"No. She never wrote, never telephoned. No."

"She wrote," Dave said, "to her father."

Anna Westover turned, threw away her cigarette. Dave heard the toilet flush. She came out of the washroom, came straight to him. "You have a way with you," she said, "like a good priest's, a father confessor's. But you aren't a father confessor, are you? You're something very different."

"Did your husband, ex-husband, come to you, or phone you for money at any time recently?"

"He would know better," she said. "After he got out of prison, he came once. But not for money. He wanted me to make love to him. I suppose he thought he could charm me back again, I don't know. He seemed very sad and shabby. I felt sorry for him, but I didn't let him do as he wanted. What is this about Serenity?"

Dave told her, showed her the letter, the snapshot.

"Dear God," she said, and sat down on one of the little round tables. "That swine. That son of a bitch." She was looking away. The window light was on her face again. Her face was taut. She turned it, lifted it to Dave. "You don't believe it, I hope. Because it isn't true, you know. It's simply a way for him to raise money. He saw the story about those poor, tragic girls on television, and he remembered he had that letter from Serenity, that photo. Oh, I know so well how his warped mind works. I can see him digging out

17

that insurance policy, rubbing his hands, sitting down at his desk to write that letter."

"Banner Insurance agrees with you," Dave said. "But how can you be sure? You say you haven't heard from her. The photo shows she was there. That is Serenity, isn't it? Scotty Dekker says it is."

"Why would she go there?" It was a cry of protest.

"She was on dope," Dave said. "She went some pretty low places, even before she ran away. Scotty told me about the room with the mattress and the rats in Venice."

"That was playacting," Anna Westover scoffed. "For my benefit. I was divorcing her cherished father. She was punishing me, trying to drive me back to him."

"And you weren't having any," Dave said.

"I knew him," she cried. "Serenity didn't. It wasn't reasonable. I'd forgiven him everything. There was a case where he won, and he was wild with elation—and the next day, the very next day, both principal witnesses were killed. Oh, certainly, by accident. Yes, of course. One drove off a cliff, the other set fire to his bed with a cigarette and immolated himself. I knew those weren't accidents. So did the district attorney. Those witnesses had been bought, hadn't they? And then killed to keep them from blackmailing Chass or his client later. They were not nice men."

"The district attorney couldn't make a case?"

"Not then," she said bitterly, "but he remembered and he waited and he made a case at last. Chass bought one too many witnesses for those gangsters who paid him so well. I knew. But what did Serenity know? How could I tell her?"

"You like folk wisdom," Dave said. "How about, 'The truth never hurt anybody'?"

"You never had children," she said angrily. "She was

18

fifteen years old. You can't reason with them at that age. The truth is the last thing they want to hear. He could do no wrong—don't you understand? So if I was divorcing him when he was in the deepest trouble of his life, who was wrong? Chass?" Her laugh despaired. "Forget it." She stood up. "And now you tell me she ran to that monster Azrael and he cut the living heart out of her and dumped her in a dirty hole in the desert. And that's my fault, too, isn't it?" She doubled her fists. "Oh, you are a horrible man. Get out. Get out of here."

"Just the messenger," Dave said. "I don't know that she is dead. No one knows. Why jump to conclusions?"

"Because that's she!" Anna Westover cried. "That's Serenity. Standing right next to him in that snapshot. That is my little girl, mister." And suddenly she was weeping. Hard and loud. She covered her face with her hands and ran stumbling into the washroom. She slammed the door and went on sobbing behind it. He went to the door and rapped gently. She quieted. He said:

"Don't cry. You could be right. He tried fraud, and when he didn't get the check, he figured someone like me would be coming around for the facts, and there weren't any facts, and anyhow what good was twenty-five thousand dollars going to do him? It wasn't enough to go to jail for. And that's why he disappeared. Where would he go, Mrs. Westover? Friends? His parents?"

"The only friends he had were vicious. He'd saved their rotten skins for them, but when he got into trouble, did any of them come to help him? Be serious." She opened the door, wiping her nose with tissues, wiping her reddened eyes. "He had no parents." Her laugh was brief and rueful. "That was part of his charm for me, wasn't it? An orphan.

19

The pathos of it." She touched Dave. "Find Serenity, Mr. Brandstetter." Her hand trembled against his chest. "He doesn't matter. Find her. Find her alive."

"Nothing would please me more," Dave said, "but I have to find her father too. It's my job. Where is he?"

"I don't know," she wailed. "How many times must I tell you that? Don't know, don't care. I'm nothing to him anymore, nothing to Lyle. They're nothing to me."

He didn't believe her. He changed the subject. He said, "Was there a woman?"

Her mouth opened in surprise. Then she laughed. Bleakly. "Sorry. He lied and cheated. But not that way."

"Sometimes the wife is the last to know."

"I'm not going to tell you how I know," she said, "but I do know—believe me."

"Right. Thank you." Dave crossed the shiny floor. When he reached for the doorknob, she caught up to him and gripped his arm. "Find Serenity," she begged again. "I don't want her to be one of those girls. That letter is old. She wouldn't stay with that monster. Why would she?"

"You tell me," Dave said.

"Don't believe Scotty." She shook her head, frantically. Tears were in her eyes again. "She wasn't bad. She just couldn't handle the breakup between Chass and me. That's all. She's a good child. Cheerful and bright."

"Try not to worry." Gently Dave pried her fingers from his sleeve. "He was betting on a long shot. There hasn't been a payoff. I don't think there ever will be. You keep remembering that."

And he stepped out into the cold noon sunshine.

3

"**S**o he's missing," Salazar said. He dealt with homicides for the L.A. county sheriff's office. Dark-haired, honey-color, handsome, he looked sick today, sallow. His steel desk was heaped with files and photographs and forms. The photographs had ugly subjects, what Dave could see of them. "Does his family want him back?"

"Nobody's worried about him but me," Dave said.

"Signs of foul play?" Salazar drank coffee that steamed in a styrofoam cup. It burned his beautiful mouth. He breathed a little puff of steam. "Jesus," he said, and pawed for a cigarette pack among the papers. It was empty and he crumpled it. Dave held out his pack and, when Salazar took a cigarette, lit it for him with a slim steel lighter. He lit a cigarette for himself. Salazar turned in his chair to look out at the cold blue sky. "You have any real reason to think he's dead inside the house?"

"He expected money," Dave said. "Go look and see."

"His car there?" Salazar tried the coffee again, cautiously this time, eyeing Dave over the rim. "Did you check the garage?"

"It's empty," Dave said. "The mailbox is full."

Down the hall a man began to curse in Spanish.

"So he went someplace," Salazar said, "and didn't come back." Salazar's office was one of a row of cubicles that looked through plate glass at a broad room where fluorescent light fell cold on desks where telephones kept ringing, and at some of which men typed, or leaned back in chairs, talking to other men who stood holding papers. Or the men at the desks talked into the insistent phones. They frowned and made notes on pads with pencils or ball-point pens. Now Salazar looked past Dave out into that room. A scuffle was going on out there. The Spanish curses were louder now, and there were shouts from the English-speakers. Furniture slammed. There was a crash. Dave turned to look. Far off across the big room, where everyone was now standing up to watch, two men in neat jackets and short haircuts were struggling with a fat, brown-skinned boy whose hair was long and held by a rolled bandanna. They all three fell to the floor and were hidden from view by desks. Some of the men from the desks headed for the fight. Salazar said to Dave, "I could check to see if he's turned up dead after an accident. What kind of car was it, do you know?" He reached for his telephone.

Dave shook his head. "Have you got a phone book that covers that area?" Salazar had the book. Stacked with others on the floor. He crouched for it, slipped it out of the stack, wiped dust off its slumped spine with his hand, laid it in front of Dave. Dave studied him. He was sweating and breathing hard. "You're sick," he said. "Should you even be here?"

Salazar sat down, making a face of disgust. "Fucking

flu," he said. "Had it since Christmas. Makes you weak. I'm all right." He wiped the film of sweat off his face with tissues from a torn, flower-patterned box almost empty. He nodded at the directory. "You going to call somebody?"

Dave flopped open the book. In the big outer room, the fat brown boy stopped cursing in Spanish and began snarling like an animal. Metal furniture crashed again. Dave turned to look. A file cabinet lay on its side, spewing paper. Six men loaded the brown boy out of the room like a captive beast. Dave blinked at Salazar.

"PCP," Salazar said. "It takes them that way."

Dave located the name Dekker and found a Dekker paired with Sandpiper Lane in a gray column on a gray page. He punched for an outside line. He punched the Dekker number. Scotty had not gone to school. He told Dave what Dave asked to know, Dave thanked him, hung up, and passed the phone to Salazar. "It's a Rolls, late sixties, a four-door hardtop, two-tone, brown and gold. Westover is five ten, hazel eyes, brown hair beginning to thin on top at the back, no extra weight on him, maybe one-forty. Lately, he didn't always remember to shave."

Salazar held the receiver to his ear. He punched the phone buttons with the rubber end of a yellow pencil. He asked Dave, "Marks or scars?"

"The tip of one ear is missing. The informant doesn't remember which ear. He's just a neighbor kid."

Salazar relayed Westover's description to someone in an office who had to do with keeping track of unidentified corpses. None of the unidentified corpses on hand fitted the description. Salazar tried another number and told someone about the Rolls. He waited a long time, receiver

23

trapped at his ear by his shoulder, drank coffee, finished his cigarette, snubbed out the cigarette in a square glass ashtray heaped with short, yellow-stained butts. He said "Yes" into the receiver, listened some more, grunted "Thanks" and replaced the receiver. "No abandoned or smashed-up Rollses, either," he said.

"Because it isn't in the garage," Dave said, "doesn't have to mean Westover drove it away. A car like that? Why didn't somebody steal it? The garage is padlocked, but that doesn't signify. He could be in the house tied up and gagged. He could be in there murdered. It's an expensive house in an expensive neighborhood. Why didn't somebody break in, kill him, plunder the place, and steal the car?"

"Because that's not the obvious explanation," Salazar said. "The obvious explanation is that the man has huge debts he can't pay. He was grabbing at straws, trying to defraud your insurance company. When it didn't pay off right away, he packed up and cleared out."

"His son disappeared at the same time," Dave said. "Eighteen, nineteen. Name of Lyle. Music student."

"What are you saying now?" Salazar asked. "That the son killed him and drove off with the family car?"

"Off the record," Dave said, "no. But if I said yes for the record, would you send a team out there?"

"Look at this mess." Salazar picked up and dropped the loose stack of files, papers, photographs, on his desk. One of the photographs slid to the floor on Dave's side. He bent and picked it up. A middle-aged black in a Hawaiian shirt lay in a leakage of blood by a back-alley trash module. Dave laid the photo on the desk. The black's bulging eyes

24

stared at him. He looked as if the last thing he could imagine was being dead. Salazar said, "We had one thousand five hundred and thirty-two homicides in this county in the last eight months." He tried to straighten the papers. "You haven't even got a crime. Why won't Westover be back tomorrow? Why won't the kid? Have you got another cigarette?"

Dave gave him another cigarette.

Romano's was crowded for lunch. It was dark after the sunglare of the street, and inside the door he blundered against backs and elbows. The bar at the front was small, couldn't hold a lot of patrons, and latecomers waiting for tables had to stand out here by the reservation desk with their drinks, if they'd been so lucky as to get drinks. Narrowing his eyes, trying to adjust them to the lack of light, Dave looked for Mel Fleischer. Mel was late too. Dave excused himself and edged between the drinkers, hoping Amanda had got here on time. Max Romano would have held the corner table for Dave forever, but Dave had finally talked him out of that. Dave's showing up was too often chancy. It wasn't fair to the hungry, it wasn't fair to Max. Today, everything was all right because Amanda was there, in a nubby natural-wool thing, bright blue scarf knotted at her throat, a puffed-up mockery of a 1920s boy's cap, oatmeal-color, tilted on her neat little skull. She had a tall margarita for herself and a smile for him. A young man sat with her—a stranger to Dave. Amanda seemed pleased with him.

She said, "Dave Brandstetter, Miles Edwards."

Edwards rose and was tall. He shook Dave's hand firmly,

smiled with handsome teeth, claimed it was nice to meet Dave, and sat down again. He wore a suit that looked expensive without making an issue of it. His dark hair and trim black beard and mustache, his long, dense, dark childlike lashes, contrasted with the pale gray of his eyes. He was tanned, except where dark glasses had kept the sun from his skin.

Amanda studied Dave. "You look tired and not happy."

The chairs were barrel-type in crushed black velvet. Dave sank into his with a sigh. "This case is not a case like any case I ever had before, and nobody is helping me—almost nobody."

"Take heart." Amanda offered him a cigarette, one of the long, slim, brown kind. "Remember the Little Red Hen." She lit the cigarette for him, then sat straight and waved into the candle shadows. "Glenlivet, please, a double, on the rocks?"

"And that car," Dave said. "You and I should never shop together. My tendency to impulse buying is bad enough without you backing me up. That car is a bone-cracker."

"What kind of car?" Edwards said.

"TR," Dave said. "It had to be small to get into my driveway." To Amanda: "Does he know about my driveway?"

"There's no way to describe it," she said. "Where have you been—a long way?"

"Up the coast beyond Zuma," Dave said, "back to a nursery school in West L.A., downtown to the sheriff's. Then out the freeway to Hollywood, and you. It's like riding in a dice cup."

"What car should we have gotten?" she said.

"That big brown Jaguar."

"But the driveway," she said.

"I'll hire a bulldozer. I'll change the driveway."

"Also you wanted to save gas," she said.

"Now I want to save me," he said. Max Romano himself, plump, his few remaining black curls plastered across his bald dome, brought the Glenlivet, squat glass, much whiskey, little ice, the way Dave liked it. "Thanks, Max."

"You look pale." Max handed menus to Amanda and Edwards. Dave waved his away. Max frowned. "Are you sick?"

"Not hungry," Dave said. Usually he liked the thick garlic-and-cheese smells of Romano's, but this noon, they made him feel a little queasy. "I'm all right, Max. Just bad-tempered. I got up too early. Ruins the whole day."

"Something light on the stomach," Max suggested. "A fluffy little omelet"—he wiggled fat fingers to indicate delicacy—"with mozzarella?"

Dave winced. "Maybe. Later. We'll see." Max went off shaking his head, face puckered with worry. Dave told Edwards, "One person you never miss around Max is your mother."

"You never had one," Amanda said.

"I had nine," Dave said, "in rapid succession. But you're the nicest."

"Known Max a long time?" Edwards said.

"Since before you were born," Dave said. He took in some whiskey and lit another of Amanda's cigarettes. "And while I was sitting here boozing with dead friends and lovers, what were you doing with those thirty-four years?"

27

Edwards grinned. "Only thirty," he said. "I'm a lawyer. Entertainment personalities, TV, pictures."

"Would you believe?" Amanda said.

She meant that he looked like a film star. That didn't surprise Dave. Carl Brandstetter had looked like a film star too. But Carl Brandstetter had been sixty-five when Amanda married him. So what surprised Dave was Edwards's youth. He was still older than Amanda but not much. It was only a surprise. It wasn't important. What was important was that he earned a living and probably a good one. He wasn't after Amanda for her money.

Dave wasn't only old enough to be Amanda's father—he worried about her like a father. The way she had moped around that big, empty Beverly Glen house after Carl Brandstetter's sudden death had troubled him, and he'd tried to take her mind off her loss by putting her to work, remodeling and decorating the ramshackle place he'd bought to live alone in up Horseshoe Canyon. When that was done, he'd talked her into opening a business, and in no time she'd got more clients than she could handle, and was too busy to mourn. But he was uneasy that she seemed to shun all men except him, an aging homosexual. Now here she came with a man, and Dave was jealous. Ridiculous. He laughed at himself.

"Dave?" Amanda's eyes were bright. "We've got something to tell you."

But Mel Fleischer arrived, tall, balding, patrician, in dark green tweed, lavender shirt, pale green tie. He was a heavy contributor to the philharmonic and the museum, collected California painters, and was a senior vice-president of Proctor Bank. He and Dave had been lovers—

28

though that was a flowery word for it—in high school, when the world was young. They had remained friends. Trailing Mel came Makoto, the Japanese college boy he slept with, stocky, broad-faced. A shiny red jacket was open over his muscular brown torso. He wore red jogging shorts, white gym socks with red trim, and no shoes. Roller skates dangled from his square, brown hand—white tops, red wheels. From across the room, Max watched Makoto with a sad shake of the head, mourning a restaurant dress code long defunct.

Dave made introductions. Makoto sat down, dropped the skates on the thick carpet, lounged in the chair. Mel sat straight, a Renaissance cardinal holding audience.

Amanda told Makoto, "Those are beautiful skates."

Makoto nodded a head of shaggy black hair and showed terrific teeth. He didn't talk much. Spoken English was not easy for him. Amanda handed him her menu. Edwards tried to give his to Mel. Mel smiled and shook his head.

"Scallops," he said. "They sauté them beautifully here, in brown butter." He passed Dave an envelope. "The sad story of Charles Westover—financial only, but I often think a good novelist could reconstruct a whole life from a study of a man's bank statements, don't you?"

"Balzac," Makoto said. He pronounced it Borzock. *"César Birotteau."* The last name was easy for him.

Dave put on glasses and peered at the pages from the envelope. "Credit check here, too. Thanks. I see he's keeping up the house payments. Jesus, a third mortgage!"

"He'd better. But, as you can see, his debts elsewhere are staggering. In round figures, two hundred thousand dollars. The house and car are all he has."

29

"Ahem!" Amanda said. Dave laid down the papers and took off the glasses. She was holding Edwards's hand on the table, and she was radiant. "I have an announcement, please. Miles and I are getting married."

"Ho!" Dave was startled. She'd never kept a secret before. "Wonderful. Congratulations." He kissed her cheek and shook the hand of Edwards, who grinned happily.

"Champagne!" Mel waved his arms. "Champagne!"

4

At two in the morning, the sprawling, low-roofed houses along Sandpiper Lane were dark. He stopped the Triumph by the little palm again, and got out into wind as relentless as yesterday morning's wind but colder. The little palm rattled its fans. Far down the road, around a bend, a solitary streetlamp shone. Here it was very dark. He looked up. No moon. Not even stars. He went up the driveway toward the black bulk of the house. Leaves and pods crackled under his feet when he stepped up into the front-door recess. The eucalyptus smell was musty.

From his key case he chose one slim shaft of metal after another. The third worked in the lock but the door wouldn't open. There must be a dead bolt. He found his way along the side of the house, feeling with his hands. The brick was rough. He shuffled and went slowly. Twice he stepped up into the spongy yield of mulch in planters to test windows. Both were fastened. At the rear of the house was a roofed, screened patio. Its door was locked, would have been easy to open, but he didn't open it, figuring the door into the house itself would be bolted.

He went around front again, to the garage door. The padlock gave easily. Holding its pitted coldness in his hand, he turned and looked up and down the street. No one. He dropped the padlock into the pocket of his sheepskin jacket, bent, and lifted the garage door just enough to be able to slip under it. Inside, in the smells of dusty tires, grease, gasoline, he let the door drop shut softly. He put his face close to the dusty little pane. No one. He risked probing the darkness for a second with the beam of a penlight. Nothing lay for him to stumble over on his way to the house door. He switched the light off and went to the door. It was not locked. He stepped up and into the house and closed the door behind him.

He stood braced for bad smells, death, decay. He didn't smell anything like that. The air was warm. Westover or Lyle had forgotten to turn off the thermostat. He went toward the front of the house. He felt rather than saw a large room open to his right. As if blind, he walked a slow step at a time, silent on carpet. He groped out with his hands. He bumped furniture. Something flimsy and metallic fell with a delicate clatter. He waited. No one had heard. His hands found curved, polished wood. A piano? What he wanted to find were curtains. He found them. Drawn across their windows. He thought he remembered that from yesterday morning.

He risked using the penlight again. The curtains were drawn on all the windows. What he had mistaken for a piano was a harpsichord. On its closed top lay a flute and an oboe. Dust muted the shine of their wood, their metal. What he had knocked over was a music rack. There were two more, each with music open on it. He righted the fallen rack. Printed on the cover of the music was *Anton*

Reicha: Strings, Woodwinds, Continuo. He set it on the rack, which trembled with its weight. He touched a key of the harpsichord. It sang sweetly. The harpsichord had two manuals.

He listened. He followed the penlight's thin beam into all the rooms, closing the curtains, switching on lights. No one—alive or dead. One room was a den, an office—desk, typewriter, files. He left that to look at bedrooms. There were four. In two, the beds were unmade. Over one hung framed photographs, eight-by-tens, six of them, in two rows. He recognized Wanda Landowska in beaky profile at a keyboard. He peered at the signature on another photograph. Igor Kipnis—another harpsichordist. Bookshelves stood in this room. On them, elaborate stereo equipment shouldered record albums, untidy heaps of music, books about music, composers, performers. Nothing distinguished the other bedroom. In both, clothes lay folded in the chests of drawers, clothes hung in closets. Shoes. Luggage.

There were three large bathrooms lined with mirrors, but only one had the look of having been in use. Pressure cans of shave cream, tooth powder, toothpaste, a pair of toothbrushes, two plastic-handled throwaway razors. Why won't Westover be back tomorrow? Why won't the kid? Something red sparked in the shag weave of a bathmat. He bent for it. A capsule. He checked druggist's amber plastic vials in the medicine chest. No Seconals. But he thought this was a Seconal. In the kitchen a few unwashed dishes were stacked on a sink counter. On a breakfast bar like the one at Scotty Dekker's across the street, slices of dark bread had slumped from a clear plastic wrapper and dried out. A quarter-inch of milk had soured in the bottom of a tall glass. Butter had puddled in its oblong dish. Cheese slices were growing green mold in their open packet. A half-empty jar of mayonnaise gaped, its lid beside it. A fly had died in the mayonnaise. Ferns hung in baskets over the breakfast bar. The fronds were drying out and turning brown. He rinsed the milk glass at the sink and watered the ferns.

Back in the den, he sat in the chair that had a tall padded leather back and padded leather arms and that swiveled, could turn to the desk, could turn to the typewriter table. Typed sheets lay stacked on the desk, facedown. A half-typed sheet was in the typewriter. It was a late-model electric typewriter. He switched on a desk lamp and peered at the typing. It didn't make a lot of sense. Something about making sure the mark didn't telephone the bank. He turned over the stack of pages. *"Confessions of a Con Man,"* the top page read, "by Howie O'Rourke, as told to Charles Westover." Dave put on his glasses and leafed through the pages. An introduction claimed that O'Rourke knew every swindle cunning and greed had devised since time began, had worked most of them, and had spent years in prison for getting caught at it. This book was going to tell all—no one who read it could ever be flimflammed out of his hard-earned money again. Dave checked the rest of the typescript, didn't find anything about insurance frauds, laid the sheets back together, tapped the edges on the dusty desk-top to straighten them, laid the stack on its face again, and rose to look into a brown steel file cabinet. In a folder labeled with the title of the book he found copies of query letters to twenty publishers. The letters asked for an advance of $200,000. Twelve publishers had replied. Negatively. None had even made a counteroffer.

Dave heard a noise. Not the wind. He slipped the folder back, quietly closed the file drawer, and switched off the desk lamp. Taking off his glasses, he moved in the dark to the door of the den and stood there listening, straining to hear. He had turned off the lights in each of the rooms as he left it. His eyes strained against the darkness. What had the noise been? The garage door. It went up and down on armatures and these were equipped with big springs which sang baritone when they stretched. That was what he had heard faintly. But the house was dead quiet, the night, the neighborhood, except for the snore of the wind under the eaves and, far off, the surf. He waited, heartbeats thudding in his ears. He thought he heard the soft click of a door latch. He didn't listen for footfalls. There was all that thick carpeting. Then a girl's voice, tentative, timid, called:

"Lyle? Are you here?"

Light glowed at the end of the hall. He went toward it. He said, "Lyle isn't here." He came out into the room with the harpsichord. Lamps glowed in the room, and a girl was standing on the far side of the room, a fat girl whose hips bulged in too-tight jeans. Her big shoulders and bulky bosom were covered by a hand-loomed Mexican pullover, red, yellow, orange, with its hood laid back. She wore wire-rimmed, round glasses, and her hair was long, straight, straw-color. She looked surprised but not scared. He said, "Who are you?"

She said, "Who are you?"

"I'm an insurance investigator," he said, "and my name is Dave Brandstetter. Now it's your turn."

"Where's Lyle?" she said. "I keep phoning and no one answers. I keep coming. I need my flute and my oboe. Nobody answers the doorbell. So today I tried getting in.

35

Somebody phoned the security patrol. Luckily I saw them coming and ran around back and climbed the wall. If they'd found me I'd probably be in jail now. For attempted burglary. Are you going to call the police on me?"

"It would be the sheriff," Dave said, "and I've talked to the sheriff, and he doesn't want to come here."

"Everything was locked up tight," she said. "I was going to break a window tonight. Then I saw the lock was off the garage door. First I thought they were back, but their cars weren't here. You got the lock off, right?"

Dave took it out of his pocket and held it up.

She blinked. "Did you break it?"

"I didn't have to," he said.

"Where's Mr. Westover?" She tilted her head, puzzled. "Insurance? Did something happen to him?"

"I don't know. No one seems to know. I'm here because he filed an insurance claim with a company called Banner, only when I came to see him about it, he was gone. Appears to have been gone for days. I don't see the sense of that. Except that he was in financial trouble. Maybe he couldn't wait for his claim to be settled. What kind of trouble was Lyle in?"

"He couldn't go back to school." She went to the circle of glittering music racks. She crouched and brought out from under the harpsichord two leather-covered instrument cases and laid them open on the polished wood of the harpsichord. One case was lined with dark blue plush, the other with maroon-color plush. "He was working." She pulled the flute to pieces and laid the parts in grooves in one of the cases. "In the studios, TV background scores, you know—and recording studios. To help his father out." She pulled the oboe to pieces and laid its parts in the sec-

36

ond case. "He joined the union long ago, he was one of the youngest members. And good harpsichordists who can play classical, pop, rock, on sight, and tune their own instrument besides—they're not common, okay?" She closed the cases. "That was the only 'trouble' he had—that he couldn't go to school. He's got a lot of studying to do yet—or that's how he feels." She snapped the catches closed on the cases. "Can I show you something?" she said.

Dave went to her.

She turned the cases and with plump, dimpled fingers touched little metal tags riveted into the hard leather. Dave put on his glasses and peered through them at the tags. Each tag read "T. Foley." " 'T' is for Trio," she said. She was a homely girl. Her nose was a knob with a pushed-up tip like a pig's. She was too old for pimples but she had them. Her cheeks were balloons. The lenses in those wire frames that made her little eyes seem to swim were thick because one of the eyes was crossed. Her voice was colorless. Her mouth turned down at the corners. But she had a beautiful smile. "With a name like Trio"—she groped in a crossways pouch pocket in the front of the Mexican pullover—"what could I be but a musician?" She brought out a wallet whose leather lacing had come loose. She showed Dave her automobile operator's license, covered in cracked plastic that had turned yellow. "Trio Foley" was the name on the license, and the color photo made her look fatter than she was. She put the wallet away. "I wanted you to know I wasn't stealing someone else's instruments. Can I go now?"

"You can go without asking me," Dave said, "but I wish you'd tell me first where you think Lyle has gone."

"He didn't say he was going anywhere," she said. "If he

had, I wouldn't have left my instruments here, would I? The others took theirs, violin, cello. I had a score-copying job that wouldn't leave me time to practice. We were set up to meet here again Friday. No one was home. We couldn't understand it. Lyle was the one who set it up."

"Would they know where he went—violin, cello?"

"I doubt it," she said. "They didn't say so. And they hadn't known him long. Not like I have."

"Would he have gone with his father?"

She made a face. "He was here because he has a very strong sense of responsibility, and he owed his father, or thought he did, for all his father had done for him financially to see that he got a first-class musical education and all that. But he was just being dutiful. He'd lost all respect for his father after his father . . ." She eyed Dave nearsightedly through the thick lenses. "You know what his father did? You know he went to prison?"

"I know," Dave said.

"I don't mean Lyle said anything. He wouldn't. But you could tell how he felt—he never smiled at his father, all he said was yes and no, okay? I guess he felt sorry for him, in a way, but he really didn't"—she moved those big, square shoulders inside the Mexican pullover—"well, have any use for him. He was in—despair over him, all right?"

"There has to be love behind that," Dave said.

"He was here, wasn't he?" she said. "But he wouldn't run away with him—from the man's honest debts? Nothing like that."

"Do you know Howie O'Rourke?" Dave said.

"That creep," she said. "He used to hang around in here at night, pretending to listen to us, smoking grass, drinking wine. Red hair, long sideburns, and this dead white skin, you know? Fish-belly white? He thought he was God's gift to women. He didn't want to hear us play. He just wanted to have sex. With Jennifer, or Kimberly—even with me." She smiled wryly. "Can you believe that? He'd sprawl there on the couch with his legs stretched out, feeling himself up and leering at us. Really. Leering. Finally, Lyle told his father to keep him out of here."

"They were writing a book together," Dave said.

"Mr. Westover was writing it. Howie couldn't write his own name. He was telling Mr. Westover all his garbage about being a con artist." She snorted contempt. "Howie couldn't be a con artist. Howie couldn't be anything. Oh, maybe a worm—if he practiced a lot." She lifted music from one of the racks, made a thick roll of it, stuck the roll into the pouch pocket, and picked up the instrument cases from the harpsichord. She started off, then turned back. "If they went together, why are both cars gone?" She shook her head hard, and with certainty. Strands of the straw-color hair fell across her face. "They wouldn't go together." She stuck out her lower lip and blew at the fallen hair. "No way would they go together."

"Take this." Dave held out a card. "And if you get any ideas about where Lyle might be, telephone me, will you? Maybe something he said will come back to you, or something Mr. Westover said. I'll be grateful."

She tucked the flute case under her arm, took the card, glanced at it, stashed it away with the music, the wallet. "You know what I never thought? When I telephoned, and rang the doorbell and all that, and no one answered? That they could be in trouble. I was the only one I thought

39

about—getting my instruments." The hair flopped across her face again when she shook her head in disgust at herself. "I wasn't even worried about them. I should have told the police or someone that something was wrong here." Her crossed, magnified eyes apologized to Dave. "I'm not much of a human being, am I?"

"If you weren't," Dave said, "you wouldn't be worried about it. Is Lyle a close friend?"

"I've been in love with him since the first time we met. At Buenos Vientos, right? The music camp? We both had scholarships. It's for gifted kids, master classes, a good conductor. Summers. He was all alone in this empty practice cabin—they're just boards and two-by-fours, no glass in the windows. He was playing the piano. The sun was shining on him. He's very beautiful."

"He has a speech defect," Dave said.

"You don't notice that," she said, "not after while. It doesn't matter."

"Does he know you're in love with him?"

"Do you know any geniuses? He wouldn't notice. All he notices is music." Her laugh was sad.

"Can you be insensitive and be a good musician?"

"I'm fat, cross-eyed, and I have a bad skin," she said. "He doesn't know how I feel because I haven't told him. What would it be—just embarrassing for both of us, wouldn't it? He's not insensitive—just the opposite. You'll see. He's not childish—he's very intelligent and complicated, but there's something about him like a little boy, vulnerable. As soon as you meet him, you start to worry about him, wanting to shelter him, you know? Not when he's playing—he's fine then, strong. But the rest of the time, you can see things hurt him, see the pain in his eyes. And you want to keep the pain away." She made a helpless little circle in the air with a plump hand. "I'm sorry. I can't explain it exactly. He looks so—fragile."

"Does he ever mention his sister?"

"Does he have a sister? Where is she?"

"Suppose he heard that she was dead, murdered," Dave said. "What would that do to him?"

She stared. She dropped the instrument cases on a long, low couch. They sank into deep brown velvet cushions. "Insurance," she said again. Her tongue touched her lips as if they were dry. "That's why you're here."

He told her what he knew. "What's your impression of Charles Westover?"

"Not that he'd do anything like that. He's like a ghost, gray, sad, kind of—shrunken. Oh, you can see just sometimes what he must have been like, charming, funny. But mostly—I don't know—like he was—well, beaten."

"Did he know Lyle was fragile? Would he have told him that he thought Azrael had killed his sister?"

As if her legs wouldn't hold her, Trio dropped onto the couch. The instrument cases clunked together against her porky thigh. She sat hunched up, knees tight together, hands clutched tight in her lap. She stared at nothing. She said, almost to herself, "If he did, that's why Lyle isn't here. He ran away once before. He told me. I'd forgotten. It was before I knew him. When his father got caught. Lyle just left, disappeared. His mother had the police searching for him. It was in the papers, on TV—'Teen-age musical genius vanishes.' Then he came back. One day his mother walked in the door here, and he was taking a shower, just as if he'd never been gone."

"Did he tell you where he'd been?"

"No. It's not that he's secretive. That sounds sly, you know, and he's not sly, he's open as a child, as a flower. I guess it's just that it's so hard for him to make himself understood that, after while, he decided trying wasn't worth it. Not if you can play."

"Maybe he's gone back to New York," Dave said. "I'll phone Juilliard in the morning. It's possible they'll know some friend he's staying with there."

"Maybe he could fly on credit cards." She didn't sound as if she believed it. "But he didn't have any money. He turned it all over to his father." She rose and picked up the cases again. "As fast as the union sent him his checks."

"What kind of car does he have?" Dave said. "Would it get him to New York?"

"It wouldn't get him to Nevada." She went through the lamp shadows toward the entryway. "It's a beat-up old Gremlin. Junk." She turned back one more time. "Serenity? That's his sister's name? Ironical, isn't it?"

" 'Trio' made you a musician," Dave said. "Maybe her name saved her. Serenity can survive a lot."

She winced a little smile and went away. He listened for the hum of the garage-door springs. When he heard it, he switched off the lamps in the harpsichord room and went back to see what else he could find in Charles Westover's den.

5

The Triumph jolted over the hump from Horseshoe Canyon Trail and dropped sharply down into the brick-paved yard of his house. Only the head lamps lighted the yard. Amanda had installed ground spots in the shrubbery, but the rains of February had brought rushing mudslides down from the hills behind the place. Mud two feet deep had uprooted the lights and swept them off down the canyon with other debris—brush, trees, automobiles, parts of houses. Dave had got off lightly—warped floors, waterlogged furniture, soaked and swollen books. And the ground lights. He'd ordered replacements, but the contractor's waiting list was long.

The lights of the Triumph jittered, reflected in the square panes of the french doors that crossed the front of the building. They also showed him a vehicle he did not know—a new custom van, glossily painted with rearward streaking flames. He wheeled the Triumph in beside it, checked his watch—it was four-forty in the morning—shut off the engine, and climbed wearily out of the car. Who did he have to meet now? He wanted to sleep. The van's license frame named a Sacramento dealer. With the pen-

43

light, Dave probed inside the van through the windows. Nothing showed who owned it. A new road map lay on the seat.

He switched off the penlight, dropped it into the pocket of the sheepskin coat, and walked around the end of the building into the bricked center court where a big old live-oak loomed up blacker than the surrounding blackness. A wooden bench had been built around the thick trunk of the tree. Plants stood on most of the bench, but there was space to sit down. The brickwork on which the bench was footed was uneven, and the props of the bench clunked when it was sat on or stood up from. The props clunked now. Dave halted and groped for the penlight again.

"I guess you don't need me," a voice said, "not staying out till practically sunrise. You been in some warm bed, and it wasn't mine."

Dave found the penlight and poked its narrow beam at the sound of the voice. The beam showed him a tall, skinny young black in a leather cap, corduroy car coat with wooden peg fastenings, driving gloves. His name was Cecil Harris, and he stood with shoulders hunched, looking cold. His eyes were large in his thin face, and they expressed reproach.

Dave said, "I haven't been in a warm bed. I've been working. You know the kind of hours I have to keep." He put away the light, crossed the uneven bricks, took the boy in his arms and kissed him. They stood holding each other tight. "It's good to see you. How did you ever find me?"

"If you were on the moon," the boy said, "I would find you. You know that. Don't you know that?"

"I know it now." In Dave's arms, the boy shivered.

44

"Let's get you inside. How long have you been waiting? Why didn't you telephone?"

"I wanted to surprise you." Cecil chuckled though his teeth were chattering. "You know me and surprises."

"The last time"—Dave took his arm and walked him away from the tree—"you were also waiting in the dark. In my motel room at La Caleta. I thought you were a mugger. Nearly broke your arm with a wine bottle. Only that time you were naked."

Cecil shuddered audibly. "No way am I going to get naked in this weather. Not out here."

Dave unlocked a door—not to the front building, the one with the row of french windows. To a back building. This property was odd. Two stables it may have been once, each a single enormous room, and over yonder a cookshack. Amanda had redesigned them all, building here a roomy loft for sleeping, unfinished pine to match the original walls. Dave reached inside for a switch that lit a pair of lamps. The big room was chilly and still held a faint smell of damp and mud. Dave crouched to light, with a gas pilot jet, kindling and logs in a wide, used-brick fireplace, another of Amanda's improvements. When he rose, Cecil had not moved from inside the door. Dave said, "You're old enough so your brother couldn't stop you coming to me, so that means you're old enough for a drink. Brandy is warming. Would you like some brandy?"

Pulling off the driving gloves, Cecil came to the fireplace. He held his hands out to the logs that as yet were doing less flaming than smoking. "I was thinking," he said, "of another way to get warm. It's in the Boy Scout manual, you know? Rub two bodies together till you get a spark?"

He raised his eyes to the shadowed loft under its canted rafters. "That where the bed is?"

"It won't go away," Dave said. "I need a brandy, if you don't. It will make everything go better."

"No way we could go better," Cecil said. "We go the very best. I never forgot. I think about it every day, every night. Especially every night. I thought those eighteen months would never go by." A couch, pine frame, corduroy cushions, faced the fireplace. He dropped lankily onto it. "I went to your old digs, on Robertston, above the art gallery. This is strange, but that was stranger. You know how strange it was—all those big empty rooms?"

"Emptier than you think," Dave said.

"Christian was there, looking like he'd just barbecued Captain Cook. He wanted me out of my bulky winter clothes and into his hammock under the banyan tree."

"Where was Doug?" Dave said. He meant Doug Sawyer, with whom he had lived for a few years before the advent of Christian. Doug was a painter, but made his living from the gallery he owned. Christian ran a Polynesian restaurant across the street, the Bamboo Raft.

"Luckily, he came up the stairs before my virtue got violated. That is one big tropical fruit, that Christian. And Doug—he told me about this place. It took some finding. Hey, thank you." Dave had put into his long fingers a glass globe with two inches of Courvoisier in the bottom. The firelight glinted red in the brandy. Cecil studied it. "Pretty," he said, and tasted it. "Whoo-ee." He grinned up at Dave. "I see what you mean."

"What have you been doing?" Dave dropped onto the couch beside him, tasted his own brandy, lit a cigarette.

46

"You got into television, right?" When Dave had met him, Cecil was a trainee from a local college, getting on-the-job experience at a mountaintop station above a small city up the coast. "That's a nifty van. The pay must be good."

"Not in back of the camera," Cecil said. "Up Sacramento way. I wanted to come here, but you know my big brother, the jailer, who thinks gayness is something you outgrow. Shit, if I grow anymore, the basketball scouts won't leave me alone. No, the pay for behind the camera—typing up your tapes of highway-commission meetings—is not like the pay for looking pretty and mispronouncing words in front of the camera. No, I was gifted with some bread on my twenty-first birthday. That is how I come to have the van. I bought it yesterday." He checked a new watch studded with stops on his lean wrist. "Excuse me—day before yesterday."

"Happy birthday." Dave kissed his neat little ear.

"And I drove it straight to you. Well, maybe 'straight' is not the word I want. Maybe I mean, I drove it gaily to you, all right?" He laughed, sipped his brandy, grew solemn. His eyes were big and reproachful again. "Shit, I was scared when you didn't come. You don't know all the thoughts I had out under that tree. I was colder inside than I was outside. What if you forgot all about me? What if you didn't care anymore?"

"You didn't write," Dave said.

"I wrote," Cecil said, "I just never mailed what I wrote. It wasn't what you'd call decent, you know? I was writing with my cock. What good would that do you—what good did it do me?"

Dave snubbed out his cigarette. He stood and shed the

sheepskin coat. "It will be warm up in the loft now," he said. He picked up his glass, cigarettes, lighter, went into the shadows for the brandy bottle, went to the foot of the stairs. "You want to see how warm it is?"

Cecil unfolded his long bones from the couch, tossed the leather cap on the couch, dropped his car coat there. He came to Dave. "You could put it like that," he said.

The Juilliard School of Music had not Lyle Westover seen since nearly a year. That was how the young woman with the German accent who answered the telephone there put it. She was a student. It was not her job, answering this telephone. She had answered it because the office staff had left for the day. But she did know Lyle, and he had not last fall returned to Juilliard his classes to resume. She did not know whether he was with friends in New York staying, but she could not names of his friends give to strangers on the telephone. She did remember that he had a student instructorship been awarded for last summer at Buenos Vientos—that was in California. She hoped nothing bad to Lyle had happened.

"If he shows up," Dave said, "will you let me know, please?" He gave her his number, thanked her, hung the yellow receiver of the cookshack phone back in its place on the endboard of a knotty-pine cupboard. Corn bread was baking in the oven of the stately old steel-and-porcelain country kitchen stove Amanda had had refitted to run on gas. Heat leaked from the oven and made the cookshack pleasantly warm. He glanced out the window. Cecil came out of the rear building in a starchy new white robe with deep kimono sleeves. He was scrubbing his hair with a big white bath towel. He stepped from the shadow of the live-oak into sunlight, turned his face up to the sun, blinking, feeling for warmth. Dave felt a sweet ache in his chest and turned away. It had been a long time since he had reacted to anyone this way. It was dangerous. Too many years separated them, decades. He was being a fool. He filled two yellow mugs with coffee and set them steaming on the country kitchen table Amanda had found in some junk-shop and stripped down to its original yellow pine. There were country kitchen chairs to match. The works of the refrigerator were new, but concealed in a gigantic old oak icebox of many doors.

"Thank God it's warm someplace." Cecil came in and shut the door. "This is southern California, man. Supposed to be desert. Keeps on like this, I will turn into a licorice Popsicle." He hung the towel over a chairback and sat down. "Ah, hot coffee." He took the mug in both hands. "Did you get New York? Something sure smells good."

"Corn bread," Dave said. "If you want to phone New York, you don't wait until two-thirty in the afternoon, Pacific standard time. You get out of bed like ordinary people."

"I liked it in bed," Cecil said.

"So did I," Dave said. The grille was ready, the eggs were beaten, the jack cheese was shredded, the avocado cut up. He made omelets. "I got somebody on the phone. I don't think Lyle is in New York." He bent and got the corn bread out of the oven. He lifted a corner of an omelet with a spatula. It was golden brown on the bottom. He folded both omelets. Burning his fingers, he cut generous slabs of the corn bread and let thick pats of butter melt into them.

He laid them in a basket with a yellow napkin over them and set the basket on the table. He slid the omelets onto plates, set the plates on the table. "To give you back your strength." He sat down across from Cecil. "Salt, pepper?"

"Look at that," Cecil said, and poked at the omelet with his fork. "What is *in* there, man?"

"Avocado," Dave said. "Cheese."

"Oh, wow." Cecil took a mouthful. His eyes widened. He opened his mouth and panted. "Hot!" he gasped.

"You wouldn't like it cold," Dave said. He pushed the basket of corn bread at him. "You want to play detective with me today? Or have you things to do?"

"Only thing I have to do is you," Cecil said. "Forever. From now on. All right?"

"All right." Dave smiled. "But I won't hold you to it."

"Hold me," Cecil said, "any way you want. Only the last time I played detective with you, you nearly got killed. That big dude with the beard on the smuggling boat?"

"There's no way you can take the blame for that," Dave said. "That was my own mistake."

"I shouldn't have left you by yourself," Cecil said. "I won't ever leave you by yourself again. This is better corn bread than Mama used to make."

"Ground the dried corn herself, did she?" Dave said. "Down on the old plantation?"

"Up in old Detroit," Cecil said. "Got it out of a ready-mix box from the supermarket. You add milk and an egg. No—she didn't have time to cook much. Always working. Working till it killed her. To turn my holy brother into a dentist, to buy me that van when I got to be twenty-one. What kind of case are you working on that kept you out till five in the morning?"

Dave told him. By the time he had finished, the plates were empty, the breadbasket was empty, they were drinking second mugs of coffee and smoking cigarettes. Dave took from a pocket of his blue wool shirt a flimsy pink form, rumpled, a carbon copy, smudged. He unfolded it and pushed it across the table to Cecil. "That was what I found—not in the files, on the desk. Westover rented a truck. If I'm right—on the very day he disappeared."

"If he took his Rolls-Royce"—the cigarette hung in a corner of Cecil's mouth, tough-detective style; he narrowed his eyes against the smoke while he read the form, and he used a Bogart voice—"what did he want with the truck?"

"Get dressed," Dave said, "and we'll try to find out."

Cecil got up. "Come with me while I dress."

"If I did, we'd never get out of here," Dave said.

The man behind the counter was a woman old and gray. The lines of the nonsense rhyme jumped into his mind and he had to suppress a grin in the storefront office of Momentum Truck Rentals in Santa Monica, where the walls were woodgrain plastic, and the plants that hung in baskets or crouched in corners were plastic. The woman in charge was a caricature little old lady, frail, in a doubleknit lavender pants suit stiff as cardboard. But he had no right to grin. He was gray himself and, if not as old as she was, still old. Cecil was making him forget that, making him remember that silly verse from his childhood. He showed the woman the pink flimsy.

"He didn't bring it back." She piped, she quavered.

"You mean he owes you money on it?"

"I mean he abandoned it," she said. "If you *read* this"— she tapped the flimsy with a bony finger—"you'll see he

51

said he was going to return it the next day. Well, he didn't return it the next day. He never returned it, just climbed out of it and left it."

"You know that?" Dave said. "How do you know that?"

"Because we notified the police, sheriff, highway patrol. A prowl car spotted it, notified us, and we had it back here, noon the following day."

"Did he come in alone?" Dave said. "Were you on duty?"

"He had a boy with him." The twang of guitars crashed from a loudspeaker in a corner over a pair of chairs and a plastic veneered table. She looked up at the speaker. She trembled back to a woodgrain plastic door, yanked it open, and shrilled into a room where a long-haired youth in a ten-gallon hat sat with his feet on a desk, munching a hamburger, "Turn that racket down. I have people out here." She slammed the door and came back. The guitars faded to a whisper. "Skinny, curly-headed boy," she went on, as if nothing had happened. "Man's son, I guess. Looked like him, a little. Had something wrong with him. Couldn't talk right."

"Why did he talk at all?" Dave said.

"I don't think he wanted the man to rent the truck," she said. "Hard to understand him, mouth full of marbles. I did catch one thing, though. Says, 'If you do this, you're no better than O'Rourke.' Reason I remember the name, my first husband was an O'Rourke. Dead now." She frowned, folded the pink slip, handed it back to Dave. "No, the boy was angry, nervous. While I made up the papers, he kept walking out like he was going to leave, just have nothing to do with it—but he always came back in after a minute."

"Did Westover pay in cash?" Dave asked.

52

"Most people use credit cards," she said, "but he had cash."

"Did you notice what kind of car he came here in?"

"Couldn't help it, could I?" she said. "Rolls-Royce, vintage. Now, you see your share of Rollses, especially if you drive through Beverly Hills, which I do, coming in to work every day from the Valley. But they don't often show up here. People like that don't rent trucks. They get their furniture hauled by moving companies."

"Did he say he was moving?" Dave asked.

"He didn't say what he was doing," she said. "It's none of my business. I wondered, of course. Guess I wondered out loud, but he didn't say. Not that I remember. He made the boy drive the truck, he followed in the Rolls."

"Where did they abandon the truck?" Dave said.

She turned to a computer keyboard and punched up the information. It came in cross-stitch letters on a television screen encased in grubby white plastic. "El Segundo." She read off a street address. She smiled at Cecil. She had pearly little false teeth. "What are you so happy about? I swear, you're grinning all over yourself."

"Just married," Cecil said, and bent double, and spun around, laughing. When he recovered himself, she made him a present, a tiny toy truck with MOMENTUM printed on its side.

The address was off the San Diego freeway in an area of lonely warehouses, abandoned rows of shops, weedy vacant lots strewn with automobile carcasses. Now and then an oil pump cast a nodding shadow in the long, late afternoon winter sunlight. Where people lived, existed, were clutches of shacks, broken-windowed, porches falling off, roof gaps showing fishbones of gray rafter. Black children in gaudy rags ran the cracked sidewalks, sick old black people hobbled, sick dogs dodged and slunk. In patches of shade among the rotting cars, tattered men sprawled, snoring openmouthed, clutching empty wine bottles.

"Soweto," Cecil said.

"You can't see this from the freeway," Dave said.

"They landscape that, don't they?" Cecil said. "Shit, you're driving through the real America, and you don't even know it. Green groundcover, flowering bushes, lacy trees. Fucking paradise. Here's the street." He steered the van away from the shacks, the blacks. Not a sound here. Grass sprouting through the asphalt. Bleak storage buildings—some of them cinderblock, the paint of sign lettering flaking, fading; some of them corrugated iron, the bolts weeping rust. It was one of these he stopped at. "This is it."

They climbed down out of the van. Shadows of gulls flickered over them. In the distance a ship's whistle sounded hoarsely. Again. They stared at the building. It had a loading dock and broad doors hung by wheels to a rusty rail. No one had used the loading dock or the doors in a very long time. Seasons of bramble crops had grown and withered in front of the dock. They crackled through the dead brambles and climbed plank stairs. At the far end of the doors was a window. They went to it and tried to see inside. The window was crusted with salt from the sea air. Dave spat on his fingers and rubbed some of the crust away. He put his face to the glass. Cobwebs that had trapped only dust were thick on the inside of the window. He wasn't sure of what he saw but it looked like emptiness.

"We could break it," Cecil said. "Nobody would know."

Dave went to examine the place where the doors came together. Hasps held padlocks, corroded, one at waist level, one at shoe-top level. "Tire iron?" he asked Cecil. Cecil fetched a brand-new tire iron. Dave pried the hasps loose on the top lock. Cecil wedged the iron under the other hasp, yanked, and it came loose too. Dave gripped the edge of the right-hand door and pulled. There were rusty squeaks up on the roller rail but the door didn't budge. Cecil took hold of the door with him and they hauled at it together. It didn't yield.

"I'm going to smash out that window," Cecil said.

"I think I saw a door along the side," Dave said.

They trudged through weeds—last year's tall, brown, brittle; this year's short, feebly green; trash in the weeds, beer cans, dusty wine bottles—between this building and the next. The passageway was cold, as if the sun never reached it. Dave climbed plank steps to a rickety stoop that trembled under him. The door was thin, an ordinary room door, old. He tried the gritty knob. The door was locked. He stepped back and aimed a kick with his heel just below the knob. The door didn't fly open. Instead, one of its panels fell out with a clatter that echoed. He knelt.

"Don't go in there," Cecil said. "Let me do that."

Dave poked his head inside. The light was poor but there was enough to show him the place was empty. He withdrew his head. "Never mind," he said. He got to his feet and descended the steps, brushing dirt off his hands, off the knees of his pipestem corduroys. "There's nothing in there—not even a broken crate."

"What did they bring that truck here for?" Cecil said.

Dave headed for the sundown street. Cecil followed. Dave said, "Lyle can tell us."

"You said you don't know where he is."

Dave opened the van door. "I've changed my mind," he said. "Tomorrow, we'll go ask him."

Cecil slouched in a deep chair alone in a far corner of the room and watched the news on television. At this end of the room were laughter, the tinkle of ice in glasses, the munching of *dim sum*. Amanda and Miles Edwards had brought the food, warm in foil, and had unwrapped it in the cookshack. It was being consumed in the long front building of Dave's place, which Amanda had made interesting by raising and lowering floor levels, expanding the fireplace, and adding clerestory windows so daylight could get in, because Dave refused to cut the trees that surrounded the place. It was past seven, yellow lamplight bloomed softly in the room, there were bays of velvety shadow, and the trees couldn't be seen now through the french windows.

What could be seen, reflected in the small square panes, were strangers who belonged to Edwards and Amanda— young fair faces, middle-aged glossy faces, vaguely familiar from television shows that depended for laughs on pratfalls and odd costumes—and friends who belonged to Dave. Mel and Makoto. Ray Lollard, plump and matronly, a telephone-company executive who sometimes helped Dave out with numbers hard to get, had brought Kovaks in clay-stained workclothes and two days' beard stubble. Kovaks was a potter who had set up shop in a stable back of Lollard's expensively restored 1890s mansion on West

Adams, and who seemed to make Lollard happy. A lean, dark, intense man talked with Amanda. He was Tom Owens, an architect Dave had narrowly saved from being murdered a few years back. Doug Sawyer, neat and slight, chatted with a pair of young actors. Happily, Christian hadn't come. Madge Dunstan stood with Dave—bony, freckled, her honest laughter showing long, horsey teeth. She was a very old friend, a successful designer of fabrics and wallpapers, an unsuccessful lover of beautiful young women whom she never could hold on to for long. Tonight's was tall, blond, boyish, famous from television commercials for a shampoo.

Dave hadn't caught her name. Nor was he listening to her while she talked at him. He was pretending to listen. He was watching the back of Cecil's skull, which he could just see above the chairback far away in shadow, the TV tube a bright kaleidoscope beyond him. He wondered if Cecil was sulking, and if so why. He had been merry fifteen, twenty minutes ago, enjoying everybody, everybody enjoying him. He had spent some minutes by the fireplace talking to Edwards. Dave had been occupied with mixing and handing out drinks and hadn't paid attention. But he remembered that they hadn't smiled, that they'd seemed earnest. Now Edwards was laughing, arm around Amanda, who was laughing with him. They looked fine together—handsome, happy, young. He wasn't worried about Amanda anymore.

But he didn't understand Cecil. Yes, television news enchanted him. Before he had met Dave, he wanted to be part of it. Dave went down two waxed pine steps, crossed Navajo rugs, went up pine steps. A glass hung in Cecil's long fingers, but he hadn't touched the drink in it. On the television screen was film from a handheld camera that bobbed, panning the stumbling progress of a young man in yellow coveralls, handcuffs, chains on his ankles, being led past a gray wall by uniformed officers. His hair was long and yellow and needed combing. He had a tangled yellow beard and blue eyes that glared savagely at the camera lens. Dave sat down in the chair beside Cecil, took the drink from his hand, sipped at it, and bent forward to hear the voice of the talking head that had replaced the jittery film. The sound was low. . . . "was released by Tucson authorities late this afternoon, when his real identity was established. . . ." Dave switched off the set.

Cecil looked at him, as if only now realizing he was there. He said, "They thought they had Azrael for sure. Looks just like him. Wrong man." He shivered. "Those eyes, though. This one's got to be crazy too."

"There are different kinds of crazy," Dave said. "Happily most of them don't murder girls and bury them in the backyard."

"This one's never even heard of Azrael." Cecil shook his head in wonder and disgust. "He never sees the news, never reads. He watches the clouds and the birds, the little streams rippling over the pretty rocks, right? He listens to the wind in the trees, and watches the sunrise."

"They'll get him for that eventually," Dave said. He handed Cecil back his glass. "Are you all right?"

"I can't go with you tomorrow." Cecil didn't look at him. He talked to the blank television screen. "I've got an appointment. For a job." He took a quick gulp of whiskey.

Dave blinked and felt bleak. "When did all this happen?

You were going to work with me, you were never going to leave me by myself again. Isn't that what you said? This is pretty sudden, isn't it? What do you need with a job?"

"You don't want a kept boy," Cecil said.

"Will you look at me, please? What the hell are you talking about? You'll earn your keep."

Cecil shook his head impatiently. "You don't need my help. You don't need anybody's help. Got along fine on your own all this time. Kept boy, that's what I'd be." He jerked his head to indicate the laughing people at the other end of the room. He pitched his voice up, pursed his mouth, fluttered his lashes. " 'What do you do, young Cecil? Do you act, do you interior decorate, do you style women's hair?' " He changed voices. " 'No, ma'am—ah jus' sleeps with Mistuh Brandstettuh.' "

"Edwards put this idea into your head," Dave said.

"He just figured I'd be wanting a job, and he's fixing it for me. A good job. Field reporter. On camera."

"You didn't want that anymore," Dave said.

"It will keep me honest." Cecil was big-eyed, imploring. "It won't change anything between us. Just, I can't be with you all the time. Don't they say that's best?"

"I don't know who they are," Dave said, "but Edwards is an interfering bastard." He stood up, turned, and Edwards was watching from across the room. Dave couldn't read his expression. Not smug. What the hell was it? Anxious?

Cecil tugged Dave's wrist. "Don't spoil it. It will be a good job, the pay will be great, it will make me feel righteous, like I was somebody fit for you to love."

"You were that before," Dave said.

"If you care how I feel," Cecil said, "you will sit down.

If all you care about is knocking Edwards upside his head, go on."

Dave sat down. "I care how you feel," he grumbled.

"I couldn't just live off you," Cecil said gently. "You know that wouldn't be right."

"I wish they'd go the hell home," Dave said, "so I could get you to bed and talk some sense into you."

6

It was lonely country, lifting gently toward ragged mountains through low hills velvet with new green from winter rains, hills strewn with white rocks and clumps of brush, and slashed here and there by ravines dark with big live-oaks. An eight-lane freeway had brought him into the hills from the seacoast, forty clean, sleek miles of new cement leading God knew where, nobody driving it but him, under low-hanging clouds, dark and tattered, spattering the windshield with squalls of rain one minute, the next minute letting shafts of sunlight through.

He began to pass vineyards that striped the hills, then shaggy groves of avocado, leaves and limbs drooping from the heaviness of the rain. He rolled down the window of the Triumph to breathe the clean air, the smell of rain on soil. Rain touched his face. A meadowlark sang. He wished that Cecil were with him. Then here was the green-and-white road sign warning him that Buenos Vientos could be reached by taking the next off-ramp. The off-ramp was a graceful, broad curve, but it brought him to a meager strip of worn and winding blacktop.

This climbed out of the groves, the vineyards, into the first and least of the mountains. Patches of snow began to show under clumps of brush and to the lee sides of rock outcrops. The sky darkened and the good winds for which the place was named turned mean, buffeting the little car, chilling him. He rolled up the window. After a while, he came among pines, scrubby at first, scattered, twisted by winds—then growing closer together, straighter, taller. They sheltered the little town. A clutch of shake-sided houses, a fieldstone filling station, a raw plank stable that rented out horses, a general store and post office with a long wooden covered porch, a bat-and-board café, BEER in small red neon in a window. From between the pumps of the filling station, a white-eyed husky barked at the Triumph as it passed.

The music camp was five miles farther on, a loose collection of raw pine buildings in a meadow. One of the buildings was large, two-storied, with glass in its windows —probably the dormitory and mess hall. The rest were one- or two-room practice sheds. Downhill beyond a screen of pines could be seen the lofting wooden arc of an orchestra shell. A faded, dented Gremlin stood under a big ponderosa pine beside the farthest of the practice sheds. Snow lay under the car. Dave pulled the Triumph up behind it and got out stiffly into the cold air.

He looked through the doorway into the little building. No piano, not now. A sleeping bag in a far corner, propped beside it a duffel bag, flap open. He turned and looked all around the little meadow. No sign of anyone. He called Lyle Westover's name. It came back to him in echoes from the silent slopes. He poked his head into the other practice sheds. Empty. His heels knocked hollowly when he climbed to the log-railed porch of the main building. From their solidity when he pounded on the plank double doors, he judged they were barred. Vacant rooms sent back the noise of his fists.

The car was unlocked. Nothing unexpected, nothing that gave answers. In the shed, he rummaged through the duffel bag—underwear, sweaters, wool shirts, corduroys. Also cans—baked beans, beef stew, Spam, a jar of instant coffee, crackers, a roll of toilet paper. Fifty feet behind the shed, charred sticks lay on a circle of blackened stones. The bottom of the gray enamel coffee pot was smoky. Pine needles floated in an inch of coffee in a gray enamel cup. In an unwashed steel skillet lay an unwashed steel fork. Downhill, a patch of duff had been scraped away. He dug there with a fallen pine branch. The hole held empty cans, labels still fresh. Snow began to fall on them. He covered them and went back to the shed. The sleeping bag was heavy when he picked it up. When he shook it, a pair of boots fell out. Dave scowled. Where the hell could he have gone in his stocking feet?

He stepped down out of the shed. The snow was falling harder now. "Lyle!" he shouted, "Lyle!" and headed for the orchestra shell. He turned up the sheepskin collar, hunched his shoulders, jammed his hands into the jacket pockets. He went down the center aisle, looking along the rows of pine-log benches. He hiked himself up on the stage, the cement cold to his hands. Doors—to storage rooms, dressing-rooms?—opened at either side of the shell, but they were padlocked. He used the shell to amplify his voice and shouted Lyle's name out into the snowfall. It

63

sounded very loud in his ears, but no answer came. His ears were so cold they ached. He covered his ears with his hands and climbed back up the aisle. At the top, he shouted the boy's name again, once to each point of the compass. He thought of following his voice out among the big pines. But the snow fell in dense earnest now. It was hard to see through. One man didn't make a search party anyway—not in country this big and empty. One man could get lost and freeze to death. He went back to his car.

In the little town, the windows of the café smiled yellow through the snowfall. It was only noon, but the snowfall made it dark. He parked beside a battered pickup truck and entered the café through a door hung with little bells that jingled. The air inside was warm, steamy, and smelled of cooking. A pair of leathery men, one old, one young, both in cowboy hats and quilted khaki jackets, sat at a counter shoveling down meatloaf, mashed potatoes, gravy, green peas. Thick white mugs of coffee steamed in front of them. They glanced at Dave and away again, seeing he was a stranger.

A plump, motherly-looking woman in a starchy print dress, new cardigan sweater, patched white apron, chatted through a service window with someone unseen in the kitchen. She looked at Dave with more interest than the customers had done. Dave laid a bill on the counter. "Can I have a cup of coffee and change, please, for the telephone?" It was screwed, black and battered, to the wall at the far end of the room. The woman took the bill and jangled open the cash register. She laid coins in his hand. She gave him a lovely false-teeth smile.

"You look half frozen," she said. "You drove through only an hour ago. I thought then you'd be cold. It's that cloth top. That's a cute little car, but you can't expect to keep warm in it. Not in Buenos Vientos in the winter."

"The coffee?" Dave begged.

"Coming right up."

The directory that hung on a chain off the phone was tattered, dog-eared, food-stained, but he found the San Diego county offices section and a number that looked as if it might be the right one. The motherly woman brought a mug of coffee to the end of the counter and set it there for him. She didn't go away. She stood watching him with open curiosity. The phone kept ringing at the far end, and Dave stretched to try to reach the coffee mug. She picked it up and handed it to him. He burned his mouth on the coffee. It had come out of an ordinary café glass pot but it tasted like farmhouse coffee. The heat of it made him shiver. He was colder than he'd realized. At last a voice came on the line.

"Sheriff station, Guzman speaking."

Dave gave his name, said he was an insurance investigator, and wanted to report a missing person. "From the music camp at Buenos Vientos." Yes, he knew it was closed, but this boy had been holed up in one of the sheds. "His gear is all there—clothes, even boots—and his car is there, but he's nowhere around. It's snowing hard up here. Somebody ought to try to find him. The name? Lyle Westover, age about nineteen, slight build. He—" A hand tugged Dave's shoulder and he turned. The motherly woman was shaking her head.

"Don't bother them," she said.

65

"Sir?" the voice on the line said. "Are you there?"

"Yes, just a second." Dave covered the mouthpiece. He asked the woman what she meant.

"Isn't he the little one that can't talk right?" she asked. Dave nodded. She said, "I thought so. You get to know them all here in the summer."

"You know where he is—is that what you're saying?"

"In the hospital at Cascada," she said.

Dave said into the telephone, "I'm sorry. False alarm. I'm at the café here in town. They've located him for me. Excuse the trouble."

"No problem, sir." The line went dead. Dave hung up.

"At least," the woman said, "I guess that fat girl took him to the hospital. She come running in here, asking where the nearest one was. I know her too. Trio, they call her." She laughed. "I guess because she's bigger than any three of the rest of them."

"When was this?" Dave said.

"Said she had somebody in the car very sick, and she had to get them to a hospital right away. Last night, around six. Busy in here. But she was scared, plain to see that. I told her the way to Cascada. She was so jittery, I wasn't sure she took in what I said. She was out that door before the words were hardly out of my mouth. I ran after her to yell the directions to her all over again, and that was when I saw who it was that was sick. Passed out cold, head over against the window glass. Oh, he was pale, white as a ghost, blue around the mouth. Frail little thing, anyway, you know."

Dave drank more of the scalding coffee, set the mug down. "She hasn't come back, of course?"

66

"She went up first in the morning. I saw her pass, saw her come down too, not more than an hour after. She tore right on through, lickety-split. I guess I was busy when she drove up there the second time. Never saw her. Then, of course, here she came, barging in wild-eyed, out of breath. Quick—where was the nearest hospital?"

"Thanks," Dave said. "Where is it?"

Cascada huddled dreary in cold rain. Its Main street storefronts were red brick, brown brick. Feed and grain, hardware, drugstore. Modern crisp-lettered white plastic signs gleamed, so did the windows at McDonald's and the Pizza Hut, but no one was around, and the effect was sad. He found the hospital at the end of Main street, where the motherly woman had told him it would be—a new, sand-color stucco building with a white rock roof, one story, maybe twenty rooms. The lawn around it was bright with new grass, the plantings of eucalyptus trees young and lacy. He left the Triumph on the new blacktop of a parking lot almost empty, glossy with rain. Plate-glass doors led him into a shiny little reception area. An elderly nurse pointed him down a hallway. In the hallway, he found Anna Westover, seated on a stiff, minimally upholstered armchair, and looking drawn and bitter.

"What are you doing here?" she said.

"I told you I was looking for him," Dave said.

"He's in a coma," she said. "He tried to kill himself with sleeping pills. God, that child, that child." Her voice shook. On the big, soft leather bag in her lap, her thin hands clutched each other so tightly the knuckles shone white. She was angry—at Lyle, or at herself? "What in the world is the use?" It was a cry from the heart. She looked up at Dave with tears in her eyes. "You struggle to raise them, to understand them, to make life easy for them, to train them not to make the stupid mistakes you've made. And what in the world is the use?"

"If you did all that," Dave said, "you don't have anything to reproach yourself for. He's a big boy now." He sat down on another of the stingy chairs. A low table was between the chairs, on it a jug-shape terra-cotta lamp, old copies of *Westways* and *Sunset* magazines, a terra-cotta ashtray glazed blue inside. "What does the doctor say?"

"That he'll probably be all right." She muttered it, rummaging in the big bag for tissues, wiping her eyes, blowing her nose. "But what's to stop him trying it again? If life is so terrible for him?" A squeaky sob jerked out of her. She drew breath sharply, bit her lip, shook her head, squared her shoulders. "Did you find his father?"

"No. I hoped Lyle could tell me where to do that." Down the hallway, crockery and metal clashed. A bald, red-faced orderly in rumpled white brought trays out of rooms and dumped them into rubber bins on a trolley. Dave lit a cigarette. "Trio Foley brought him here. Where is she?"

"Eating," Anna Westover said flatly. "Every hour on the hour. It comforts her, I suppose. She feels terribly guilty, poor thing. She blames herself."

He had been mistaken in thinking the Pizza Hut was empty. She sat at a rear table whose shiny orange top, reflecting into her face, made the pimples stand out. A wheel of pizza lay in front of her, heaped with, as the white plastic letters of the sign over the counter put it, EVERY-

68

THING. Three wedges of the pizza were already gone and she was choking down a fourth. Dave sat across from her.

"Oh, God." Her eyes opened behind the thick glasses. "I thought you were going to telephone me."

She gulped the mouthful of dough and sauce, cheese, sausage, anchovies. She drank from a big wax-paper cup of cola. Tomato sauce smeared her mouth and chin. She wiped them with a wadded fistful of paper napkins. She said, "I was afraid you'd frighten him."

"Why? I didn't frighten you."

Her dimpled fingers fumbled loose another slice of pizza. She lifted it toward her mouth. He caught her wrist.

"Wait a minute with the eating, please? Tell me what happened. He'd been living up there at the camp, cooking and eating and getting along. Then you showed up, and he swallowed Seconals. Now, what's it all about, Trio?"

"I told him." Her cry ricocheted off the shiny glass and plastic of the empty place. The blond boy and girl in uniform behind the counter stopped chatting and stared. "I went to make him leave there before you could find him but he didn't want to. Then I did just what I was afraid you'd do. I didn't mean to, but one thing led to another. Why had I come, and who were you, and what were you doing at the house, and why were you an insurance investigator, and—and—it all just came out, you know? About his father and his sister and the insurance and—" She couldn't go on. She picked up the pizza wedge and stuffed her face with it and sat there with tears streaming down her face, chewing, chewing.

"And then you ran away," Dave said, "leaving him all by himself with the knowledge that either his sister had been horribly murdered, or his father was so rotten that he had tried to defraud the insurance people by pretending he believed that had happened. Good Christ, girl, you were the one who said he was fragile, who wanted to protect him."

"Stop it!" She clapped her hands to her ears. "Stop it!" She had to wriggle mightily to free her bulk from the cramped space between table and banquette, but she did it with surprising quickness, and was on her feet and running for the door, all jiggling two hundred pounds of her, wailing like a siren. Dave sighed, got up, walked after her.

"Hey, mister, wait a minute." It was the blond boy behind the counter, rosy-cheeked, maybe seventeen but brave. "What happened? What did you do to her?"

"Gave her bad news," Dave said, "not gently enough."

The boy looked doubtful. He glanced at the blond girl. She nodded toward an orange telephone gleaming on a kitchen wall. Dave didn't wait for them to call the police. He pushed out into the rain and trudged after the wide, wobbling figure of Trio running away from him down the sad, empty street. When he caught up to her, she was hunched in a hospital hallway chair, trying to stop crying, Anna Westover bending over her, murmuring comfort. The woman glared at Dave.

"You bring joy wherever you go," she said.

"Trio," Dave said, "you saved his life. The mistake doesn't count. You fixed it. He's going to be all right."

She looked up at him, reproachful, face sleek with tears, glasses smeared with tears. She hiccuped. "I'm still hungry," she said, and burst out crying again.

He did look fragile, as if the least little tap would shatter him. Against the hospital pillows, his thin face was sickly pale, with a stubble of dark beard. His hair curled, soft as a child's, on his elegant skull. His eyes were large, brown, sorrowful. As Trio had said, he was beautiful, and looking at him made you want to shelter him. Yet his wide, mobile mouth was able to smile. The smile was sheepish for the trouble he'd caused, but it was real.

Dave was alone with him now. He had left the hospital at midnight, checked into a motel, tried to telephone Cecil and got no answer, had slept hard anyway. He'd headed back here through gray drizzle at seven. Passing the steamy plate glass of bright McDonald's, he had glimpsed Trio stowing away scrambled eggs and muffins. He'd met Anna Westover wearily crossing the hospital parking lot to her car, on her way back to L.A. to look after other people's children. She told him Lyle was awake, out of danger, calm, apologetic, and able to talk—if that was the word for it.

From the look of the tray beside Lyle's bed, he'd been able to eat. His talk came out mostly vowels. Dave looked around for paper and pencil so the boy could write his answers. Pencil and paper were there none. So he strained to understand, and before long, he didn't have to ask Lyle to repeat—at least not everything.

"The cap came off, and they spilled all over the bathroom," he was saying now. "I was in a hurry to get out of there, away from him. I almost left the pills. But I felt like dying. I was so ashamed. And I knew him. He'd do something even worse next time. I didn't want to know about it. So I picked them up and put them in my pocket."

"But you changed your mind at the camp."

"It's beautiful there, and far away, and quiet. I could think. Why should I take them? Whatever I did, he'd go on

71

trying to save himself any dirty way he could. I wouldn't change him by dying. I was getting ready to go home. Then Trio showed up, and told me this thing he'd done about Serenity, and I got hysterical again, and she got scared and ran, and I took the pills. I began to get very cold, and I crawled into the sleeping bag, and I was drifting off, and I realized I still had my boots on. It seemed very important to get those boots off. And that's the last I remember." He tried to smile at himself.

"You got them off," Dave said. "Tell me—what had your father done to make you so ashamed? You and he rented a truck that night. Was that part of it?"

Lyle said two words. Dave couldn't make them out. He must have looked blank, because Lyle repeated them, slowly, working his beautiful mouth, frowning with the effort. "Howie O'Rourke. You know about him?"

"He and your father were writing a book," Dave said.

"Publishers kept turning it down," Lyle said. "It wasn't going to get him the money he wanted."

"You were giving him money," Dave said.

Lyle made a face. "After the house payments we were lucky to have anything left over for food. He had to have two hundred thousand dollars. Thought he had to."

"To clear the title to the house," Dave said, "so he could sell it and get out from under. Explain the truck."

"Howie found a way to get the money. Crooked, of course. He'd run into a man he'd known in prison, who had a truckload of hijacked stereo equipment he couldn't sell himself because the police were watching him."

"Excuse me," Dave said. "A truckload of what?"

It took a minute, but Lyle made him understand.

"There was two hundred thousand dollars worth of it, hidden in an old warehouse. The man only wanted twenty thousand for it."

"Only? Did your father have that kind of money?"

"No." Lyle looked at the rainy window. Tears started down his face. "That was what made me want to die. He got it from Don Gaillard." He drew a long, wobbly breath.

"I don't know who that is," Dave said.

"The nicest man that ever walked," Lyle said. "My father's oldest friend. When I was little, I thought he was my uncle. He wasn't. They were just very close—in high school, college, law school." Lyle's hands lay on the coverlet, which was threadbare, bleached from too many washings. The beautiful thin fingers moved, running silent scales. He watched them for a moment, then gave Dave a wan smile. "I wasn't too happy when I was small. My father was very busy making money. And my mother never forgave me for not being able to talk right. Oh, she tried not to let it show, but I knew. I was really surprised to see her here."

"She wants you to live, she wants you to be happy."

"That's not easy, is it?" Lyle said.

"Not for her," Dave said, "not when you act this way."

"I didn't think. It was my father who was on my mind. Did you admire your father?" When Dave nodded, Lyle said wryly, "So did I. Then there wasn't anything to admire anymore." He drew another shaky breath. "Anyway, I loved Don. He had time for us. We loved having Don come over."

"So he was almost a member of the family," Dave said. "Why shouldn't your father go to him for a loan? Isn't that what friends are for, to be there when we need them?"

"Only they hadn't been friends—not for years and years. The break was sudden. Serenity and I couldn't understand. Where was Uncle Don? And they told us to forget Uncle Don, never mention Uncle Don again. I was too young to understand, but I figured out after while that Don must have told my father he didn't like the way he was going—criminal law, all that. He got out of law himself, began building furniture in his basement. Which made him poor, too, didn't it? At least not like the crowd my parents were in, the beach club, all that. Big cars. The best of everything. Old Don just didn't belong, did he?"

"They hadn't spoken in years?"

"That's it." Lyle nodded disgust. "I couldn't believe my father would be so creepy. Don isn't rich. He works hard for his money, works with his hands."

"But he had it," Dave said, "and he gave it?"

"Gladly. He'd give my father anything. That's how Don is. The kindest man, the kindest man. It probably was every cent he'd saved in his life."

"So you went to the warehouse with the truck and Don Gaillard's twenty thousand dollars to pick up the loot."

"Not the money. My father had already passed that to Howie to pay his jailbird friend. Howie was supposed to meet us at the warehouse."

"Why us? Why did your father take you?"

"To help with the loading. Someone he could trust. I said he was doing wrong. He'd be caught and go back to prison. It was a stupid risk. He wouldn't listen. I had to go, didn't I? I couldn't let him go alone."

"And Howie wasn't there, was he? And the warehouse was empty. It was a con game, wasn't it? How could your father have fallen for it, knowing Howie the way he did?"

"He couldn't believe Howie would do it to him. We sat out there in the dark waiting and waiting. Howie was sure to show up. Hell, hadn't he taken my father around and introduced him to the man that was going to fence the stuff? I was sick. Don's money—gone with that creep Howie."

"Maybe that was why your father filed that insurance claim. To get Gaillard his money back."

"Maybe. But that was even worse, don't you see? That was what had happened to my father. Anything for money."

"You don't know where he's gone?" Dave said.

"Maybe he told me. He was trying to talk to me, get me to forgive him. He was crying. I wouldn't listen. I was throwing my stuff in that duffel bag. All I wanted was out. He was crying outside the bathroom door while I was picking up those stupid pills. If he said, I didn't hear."

"But he was still home when you left?" Dave said. And when Lyle nodded, he said, "Report him missing as soon as you get home. Sheriff? Missing persons? It could help."

"All right, sure." Lyle looked at the door. It had opened. Trio filled the frame in her bulging jeans and striped Mexican pullover. Lyle smiled at her. She lifted her flute. It glinted in the pale, rainy light.

"Music?" she said.

7

It wasn't yet two in the afternoon, but Horseshoe Canyon was gloomy with the threat of rain when he passed the woman with the dog and swung the Triumph into the brick yard. He ached from the long, cold drive in the cramped little car back up the coast. It was stiff work getting out of the car. The woman came down the steep tilt of the drive toward him, looking worried. The dog was small and ragged and brown. Its hair fell into its eyes. The leash which it kept taut, darting this way and that, was red. Dave stretched and gave the woman a small enquiring smile.

"Mr. Brandstetter, isn't it?" she asked. He nodded, and she said, "I'm Hilda Vosper. I live just up the road." A triangle of plastic was tied over her gray hair. She wore a raincoat cinched tight at the waist. Jeans showed under the raincoat. Plastic covered her shoes. She wasn't young but she was handsome. Her blue eyes took in the front building. "Haven't you made this place attractive? Really rustic instead of just shacky the way it was before."

He didn't say he had liked it well enough the way it was before. "What can I do for you, Mrs. Vosper?"

"You're in insurance," she said, "somebody told me. I've been wondering why the checks haven't come for the mudslide damage. Did you get yours?"

"Yes. You mean you haven't received any checks?"

"The first ones, yes. But there should be others."

"All I know about insurance is death claims," Dave said. "I'm sorry. I'd like to help, but I can't."

"Yes, well, I just thought I'd ask," she said bleakly. "They don't answer letters. No one on the telephone knows anything." The dog had wrapped the leash around her legs. "Thank you," she said, turning to unwind the leash.

"Nice to meet you," Dave said.

The big wooden rear building was cold, no fire in the grate, and he kept the sheepskin coat on while he rang Salazar to tell him about Howie O'Rourke. Salazar's flu sounded worse. Dave splashed brandy into a snifter, tasted it, shed the coat, and headed for the bathroom. He cranked the Hot tap in the shower stall and, when steam began to billow out, shed his clothes. He swallowed brandy again, used the Cold tap to tame the heat of the spray, and was about to step under the spray when Cecil put his head in at the bathroom door.

"Where were you last night?" Dave said. "I phoned at midnight."

"They put me right to work." Cecil wore the big stiff white robe. He came into the steam and shut the door. "Night shift. I go in at four-thirty, get off at midnight. I was here by twelve-thirty." He dropped the robe. "No way for me to let you know, was there?" He drank some of the brandy. "Mmm-mmm! I could easily get hooked on that stuff." He raised his eyebrows and nodded at the shower.

"Are we going to get in there? Or let all that gorgeous hot water run down to the sea?"

"Come on," Dave said. It was a big enough shower. For almost anything. Almost anything was what they did. They even got clean. They rubbed each other dry with tent-size towels. Dave said, "I'd rather have you around nights. What about dinners by candlelight? What about plays and operas and ballets? Even movies? Even, God save us all, television?"

"You can applaud me"—Cecil flapped into the robe again—"on the eleven o'clock news." He opened the door, gasped, shuddered. "Shit, man, we're on a fucking ice floe. I got to put on clothes." His feet thumped on the stairs up to the loft. Dave put on his own bathrobe and followed. Rain pattered steadily now on the slope of roof just above them. Quivering with cold, Cecil whipped into undershorts, T-shirt, bulky white sweater, warm wool pants. He sat on the broad, unmade bed, to pull on thick white socks. "Maybe I won't have that shift too long. If I'm as dazzling as I think I am." He bent to tie his shoes.

"I hope you're right." Dave opened drawers and got out clothes for himself. "Damn Edwards, anyway."

"You're not thinking," Cecil said. "How many plays, operas, and ballets did you see last night? You were working, right? And the night before? Working." He jumped up from the bed and ran downstairs. "I am going to start a fire, warm this place up."

Dave dressed, listening to the rattle of kindling in the fireplace grate, the whoosh of the gas jet, the snap and crackle of green wood. He smelled the smoke. He went down the stairs. "My days begin early too," he said, and stood and watched the flames curl around the sticks, hungry to grow. "Cecil, we'll almost never see each other—not this way. Forget this kept-boy nonsense, and go with me where I go and when I go, and stay with me when I stay."

Cecil had been kneeling. He got to his feet, brushed his hands, set the fire screen in place. "Let's try it for a while," he said. "For my sake. Make me feel decent, okay?" He laid his hands on Dave's shoulders and put a kiss on Dave's mouth. "I want to be with you just as much as you want to be with me." He managed a wan little smile, and a little rise of his wide, bony shoulders. "Who knows how long I can stand it? Did you think of that?"

"No, but now that you've said it, I'll probably bring it up fairly often." Dave smiled. "All right. No dinners by candlelight. How about lunches? Starting today, now."

Cecil looked at that daunting watch. "Too late. All the chairs will be up on the tables by now. Waiters shooing out the last expense-accounters." He went to the door. "What we are going to do is open cans. I've checked out your cupboards. Mrs. Snow's clam chowder, with an extra can of clams, cream, butter, white pepper." He turned at the door. "Did you find him?" He opened the door.

"He doesn't have the answer." Dave stepped out and Cecil shut the door. They trotted, heads down under the heavy drops that fell from the matted brown vine on the arbor, across to the cookshack. "If we make this quick"— Dave lifted down a deep saucepan—"you can go with me to see a man who may have the answer."

Dave had been here before, years ago, with Rod Fleming, a decorator he'd lived with for twenty years, until Rod had died of cancer. But if Dave had heard Don Gaillard's name at that time, he'd long since forgotten. The shop was not, as Lyle Westover remembered it, in a basement, but on a side street just off La Cienega. Two-story, living quarters up an outside staircase, the building was grubby white stucco. Rain made runnels in the dirt on the plate glass, through which gleamed faintly the pale curves of carved chair arms and sofa backs, awaiting stain and varnish. A mahogany table glowed dark red.

The street door stuck at the bottom and had to be kicked to make it open. There were fresh-cut wood smells inside, smells of hot animal glue, the ether smell of shellac. No one was among the unfinished pieces in the front room, but a power-saw snarled in the back of the shop, beyond a plywood partition in which a doorway showed light. And when Dave looked through the doorway, he remembered Don Gaillard's round, snub-nosed face. The hair above it had been dark and thick when he'd last seen it. Now it was gray and thin on a pink scalp. But the man still had boyishly rosy cheeks and blue eyes that were a little too gentle. He switched off the saw when he noticed Dave and Cecil, and came through a snowfall of sawdust toward them. His eyes flicked quickly over Cecil, obviously pleased with what they saw. He held out his hand. Its grip was firm.

"It's not about furniture." Dave handed over his card. "It's about Charles Westover."

"Insurance?" Gaillard looked puzzled.

Dave explained about the claim on Serenity's policy.

"Oh, no!" Gaillard was shaken and the color left his face. "Surely not. She was such a lovely little girl. Oh dear, oh dear."

"The insurance people aren't sure it's true," Dave said. "Charles Westover is in big financial trouble, and they think this was a try at getting a little money."

"No." Gaillard tried to look and sound firm. "Charles would never do a thing like that."

"You know he served a term in prison?" Dave asked.

Gaillard snorted. "The kind of scum involved in that case always arrange for someone else to take the punishment."

"He didn't bribe witnesses?" Dave said. "He didn't stand by while men were murdered?"

Gaillard said impatiently, "Just why are you here?"

"Westover's disappeared. I'm trying to find him. He borrowed twenty thousand dollars from you the day before he vanished. I thought you might know where he is."

A door at the back of the shop opened. Damp air came in, the rattle of rain outside on trash barrels in an alley. The rosy, snub-nosed woman who entered was in her sixties, damp scarf over her hair, old raincoat, scuffed shoes. From under her coat she took a brown paper sack. "Soup," she said. "Eat it while it's hot." She set the bag on a workbench, turned, and was startled to see Dave and Cecil. "Oh, I'm sorry," she said.

Gaillard stood as rigid as something he'd put together out of wood with pegs and glue. He didn't look at her. He didn't make introductions. Between clenched teeth, he said, "Good-bye, mother." When she had gone back into the dismal alley and pulled shut the heavy, metal-covered door after her, Gaillard glanced over his shoulder at it, then asked Dave in an indignant whisper, "Who says I lent him twenty thousand dollars?"

"Lyle," Dave said. "You remember Lyle?"

Gaillard's testiness melted in a sentimental smile. "When he and Serenity were young, we had wonderful times together—Disneyland, Sea World, *The Sound of Music.*" He shook his head fondly and laughed. His teeth needed looking after. "I loved being with those children. I guess I never grew up, myself." He sobered. "I miss them."

"They miss you," Dave said. "Lyle does. He never understood why you stopped coming around. What happened?"

Gaillard looked away. "It's not relevant."

Cecil said, "His parents found out you were gay—right?"

"What?" Gaillard grew red in the face. "What did you say?" His eyes narrowed. "How dare you come into my shop and say such things to me." He closed big fists and took a step. "Get out of here."

Cecil backed, hands up, laughing shakily. "Hey, man, it was a friendly question."

Dave caught Gaillard's arm. "Easy. Think. How would he guess that? How would I?"

Gaillard blinked, dropped his arms, stared at the two of them for a second, smiled a sickly little smile. "Oh," he said. "I see."

"But there's more, isn't there? The reason you gave Westover that money when he turned up after ten long years was that you were in love with him, and you never stopped loving him, not when he got married, not when he finally told you to go away."

"He never did!" Gaillard cried. "It was Anna—that wife of his. She was the one who forced him to stop seeing me." Tears blurred his eyes, his voice broke. "What harm were we doing her? What harm? For ten years, she never knew, and then she stumbled on us together, and her life was ruined. Ridiculous." His mouth twisted in contempt. "It had never made the slightest difference between them. She hadn't the vaguest. He was a loving husband and a wonderful provider. We saw each other alone once a week—oh, sometimes twice. She never guessed." His thick fingers wiped at his tears. He took a deep breath. "All right. He was in trouble, and I helped him. He'd have done it for me."

"You really believe that?" Dave said.

Gaillard swelled up. "Absolutely. I know him better than anyone in this world."

"Then you won't be surprised to learn what happened to the money you lent him." Dave told the story as Lyle had told it to him. Gaillard sagged a little, but he kept a straight face. No surprise showed, no disappointment. When Dave stopped talking, what showed was charity:

"Poor Chass. What rotten luck. On top of all his other troubles. And Lyle left him alone? At a time like that? I'm surprised. He always seemed so sensitive."

"He still is," Dave said. "He tried to kill himself. Luckily, there weren't enough pills."

"Kill himself!" Gaillard's hand splayed open against his big chest. "Whatever for?"

"Out of shame for how his father used you."

"But—I was happy to have the chance to help Chass. Surely Lyle must have known that."

"He knew," Dave said. "That only made his father's taking advantage of you more humiliating. Charles didn't come back here afterward and apologize, now, did he?"

"Doesn't Anna know where he is?"

"I asked her for the names of friends he might have gone to. She didn't mention yours."

Gaillard's laugh was brief and sour. "No, I imagine not." He looked straight and deliberately into Dave's eyes. "I haven't any idea where he's gone. But I'm sorry that he didn't feel he could come back to me."

"You're not sorry about the twenty thousand dollars?"

"I'm sorry that it didn't save him," Gaillard said.

"Call me if you hear from him, will you?" Dave said.

"You're mistaken if you think he tried to cheat your insurance company," Gaillard said. "He's not like that."

"He's changed," Dave said. "You didn't notice?"

"He will always be the same to me," Gaillard said.

Outside, angling their long legs into the Triumph and out of the rain, slamming the doors, Dave starting the engine, Cecil lighting cigarettes for them both, they looked at each other. Cecil passed Dave a cigarette.

"He's lying about something," he said.

Dave let the handbrake go, and rolled the little car to the corner to wait for a speeding stream of rain-glazed cars to splash past. On that long midnight drive back from El Segundo in the Rolls, had Lyle, without guessing it, actually managed to make his father see himself for what he had become? "You think Westover came back here, begging forgiveness for wasting Gaillard's money, and Gaillard smashed his skull in with a Queen Anne leg?"

"Why wasn't it his life savings?" Cecil said. "No way did he want his mama to know about it. And he was not telling us everything, man. Something he knows we aren't ever going to know, you know? And maybe that was it."

"Uncle Don." Dave jammed the stubby shift stick into

low, and the Triumph shot across La Cienega, on its way to the television studios, where Cecil had to be at work in twenty minutes. "Lyle called him 'the kindest man.' "

"He was about to saw me up on that table," Cecil said.

"Like Pearl White?" Dave said.

"Pearl?" Cecil said. "White? Will you be serious?"

But both of them were laughing too hard.

A voice said, "I thought I'd find you here."

Romano's was quiet in its aromatic shadows, white napery and candlelight. It was early for dinner. Silver and glassware glinted on empty tables. Dave had come straight here from dropping off Cecil. He would pick him up at midnight. It was going to be a long evening. He had begun killing it with double Scotches. Then there'd been a simple little salad, fresh-baked salt bread, sweet butter. Now there was *ris de veau à la crème et aux champignons,* and a bottle of Sunny Ridge *pinot blanc* 1975. He was trying to keep from feeling sorry for himself. He looked up.

Miles Edwards looked elegant in handloomed tweed. His smile was tentative. He held a manila envelope. "All right if I join you?" Dave lowered his head and went on eating. Edwards sat down. He laid the envelope beside his place setting. "I'm not here to apologize," he said.

Dave tore off a chunk of bread and buttered it. He didn't look at Edwards. "I'm pleased about you and Amanda. Delighted. I thought I'd made that clear."

"About Cecil," Edwards said. "I'm here to explain."

"If I wanted an explanation," Dave said, "I'd have asked for it. An explanation isn't going to undo the mischief you've made. Suppose we forget it."

Edwards tugged at the snowy cuffs of his linen shirt so

85

that they showed an inch below his jacket cuffs. "He's very young," he said.

"So are you," Dave said, "or you wouldn't be trying this." He looked around the hushed restaurant. "Where's Amanda?"

"Dining with clients. In Malibu." A waiter came in a black velvet jacket with gold trim, and Edwards asked for Wild Turkey. Conspicuous consumption, 110 proof. "I could have tagged along, but I thought we ought to have this talk."

"Some people"—Dave laid his fork in his plate and faced Edwards squarely—"don't mind being manipulated. Some are too stupid to notice. Some can't live without it. I don't like it. Don't try it again. Not now. Not ever."

"You're good at what you do," Edwards said. "You're a superstar. You didn't get that way with a closed mind. You're acting emotional. Why can't you be fair with me?"

Dave laughed, shook his head, picked up his fork again, and went to work on the creamy sweetbreads and mushrooms. He drank some of the crisp wine. He touched his mouth with his napkin and laughed again. "Emotional," he said. "Why in the world would I be emotional?"

Edwards said, "Because you love that boy, or think you do. What about him? What about his future?"

"He wants to be a death-claims investigator," Dave said. "He helped me out on a case, year before last, and decided it beat running around rainy airports shoving microphones in the faces of politicians. He still thought so, until you took it upon yourself to tell him he wouldn't be a death-claims investigator—that he'd only be a dirty old man's fancy boy." Dave picked up his fork and laid it down again. " 'Be fair'? What was fair about that?"

"It was important." Edwards's mouth tightened inside its neat frame of black beard. "It was my duty."

"Jesus." Dave sighed, picked up his fork, and ate the rest of what was on his plate. He drank wine again, and refilled his glass. "You're a prig, aren't you?" he said. "I didn't think they cropped up in your line of work."

"By 'be fair,' " Edwards said, "I meant, do me the courtesy of letting me explain. I meant, make an effort to understand. I had a reason." The waiter brought his drink and a menu and went away. Without looking at it, Edwards laid the menu on the manila envelope. "I meant, why won't you listen to me?"

"If he wasn't a male," Dave said, "we wouldn't be having this cozy chat, now, would we?" He lit a cigarette and raised a hand to bring the waiter back. The odds were awful, but he still wanted to enjoy this. He would have coffee and brandy. Maybe he would act like Trio Foley and devour one of Max's giant chocolate mousses. "If he was one of those jiggly young women you brought around—the ones who throw pies on television? You're worse than a prig—you're a bigot."

"Wrong." Edwards shook his head emphatically. "No way. Why not give your paranoia a rest for a minute and just listen to me?" He was showing anger now, and that pleased Dave. He watched the boy's sun-browned hand shake as he picked up his stubby glass and drank. "I went through what you're about to put Cecil through." He set the glass down, slid the envelope from under the menu, and pushed it at Dave. "Look inside."

Dave blinked at him, shrugged, opened the flap, and slid from the envelope eight-by-ten glossy photographs. They were of a naked young man. The top one was. He was slender, his skin was dark, his hair very long, he had no beard or mustache, but it was Miles Edwards. If nothing else showed that, those pale gray eyes did. The waiter came back and looked over Dave's shoulder. Dave glanced at Edwards, who looked pained if not panicked. Dave slid the first photograph off the stack. The second one involved Edwards with a long-haired blond boy. Naked, and at play on a beach. Not volleyball. Dave looked up at the waiter, young, stocky, his crinkly black hairline low on his forehead. His name was Avram, and he grinned.

"Don't stop now," he said.

Dave smiled and obliged, turning the photographs over slowly. Some involved two youths, some three, but all featured Edwards. In some, he was alone, but even in these he was sexually active. Dave slid the photographs back into the envelope.

"Nice prints," the waiter said. "Good lab work." Sweat moistened his upper lip. His eyes were large and dark and they pleaded with Edwards.

"Coffee, please," Dave said, "and Courvoisier."

"And you, sir?" the waiter asked Edwards.

Edwards was surly, growled, "Wild Turkey," and handed over his glass. The waiter almost dropped it. He went off, and Edwards said, "I got lost in that world. The man who took those pictures picked me up from a high-school playground. He made me feel special. I lived like a little god. Nothing I could think up he wouldn't give me, no place in the world he wouldn't take me—cars, watches, clothes, Jamaica, St. Tropez, Paris, Rome, Tokyo."

"If he could just peddle your pictures, right?"

"It didn't seem much to ask. He didn't need the money.

He had independent means. Photography was just a hobby. Or maybe not. Maybe only beautiful boys. Anyway, one night when I was asleep, a beautiful boy killed him. On the docks at Marseilles. And there I was, without even a ticket back to the States. I sold the Rolex he'd given me, the camera. I peddled my ass in New York till I nearly froze. Then it was San Francisco, and three successive cases of the clap, and getting locked out of the last ratty room I could get. Then I went back to my family. I was damned lucky they forgave me."

"I don't pick up sailors," Dave said.

"But you're going to die," Edwards said, "long before he does. You know that. What kind of lies are you telling yourself?"

"I've listened to you," Dave said. "I don't want to listen to you anymore, all right?"

Edwards stood up. "Where's the men's room?"

Dave pointed. "On the way to the kitchen."

Edwards went that way. The waiter brought Dave's coffee and brandy and Edwards's whiskey. He gazed at Edwards's empty chair as if his heart would break. Dave told him, "Forget it. He's going to marry a pretty lady."

The waiter's shoulders slumped. He went away. Dave smoked, finished his coffee, his brandy. Edwards hadn't come back. Dave checked the men's room. Empty. He pushed the kitchen swing door. He asked the tall, sunken-cheeked chef named Alex. Edwards had left by the alley door. Back at his table, Dave frowned at the manila envelope. Edwards had forgotten his pictures.

8

Perez didn't appear to have any point, unless it was the wild flowers—lupines, poppies—blue and gold, that carpeted the desert for miles around in all directions these few weeks in February. A road sliced through the town, kept minimally paved, probably for the sake of those same few weeks. Perez had a gas station for wild-flower viewers. It had what a faded signboard boasted was a DESERT MUSEUM & GIFT SHOP, where a two-headed rattlesnake could be seen, and where maps were sold of abandoned mines and ghost towns. A board structure with a high false front claimed to be an EATERY. A tired wild-flower viewer could even sleep in Perez, at the ROAD RUNNER MOTEL, six scaly stucco units, each with a weedy patch of cactus garden. VACANCY—naturally. On the bone-gray wooden side of the grocery store, the paint faded on a sign for OLD GOLD cigarettes. Wax shone on ten dented wrecks in the dirt lot of JAY'S GOOD USED CARS. The tavern was called LUCKY'S STRIKE. From at least one window of every structure in sight hung a rusty air-conditioning unit.

Dave had already seen Azrael's ranch, three sad shacks

painted blue, doors and windows lately broken out, the wind moving through them, through the littered rooms, stirring cheap Indian cotton hangings in the doorways, shifting pathetic scraps of clothing, tufts of mattress stuffing, feathers from ripped pillows across cracked linoleum. Death and desertion. Behind the buildings, in what had been a sometime attempt at a vegetable garden, the wind had begun filling in the holes from which, two weeks ago, had been dug up the rotted bodies of Azrael's pitiful young disciples. Serenity among them? Each corpse had a gap in its chest. None had a heart. At Azrael's ranch there had been nothing to see, nothing to remember. So why did Dave know that he was never going to forget it?

A pair of big, dusty motorcycles stood in front of Lucky's Strike. The place inside was cavernous and dim. Country-western music twanged from a jukebox. At the far end of the room, beyond a sleeping pool table, the riders of the motorcycles—boots, filthy Levis, scabby insignia on jacket backs—operated electronic games that knocked and beeped and winked. The barkeep—Lucky?—appeared to have been beaten about the head a good many times in the remote past. His nose and ears were crumpled, scar tissue jutted above his eyes. He set the beer Dave had asked for in front of him, blinked at Dave's P.I. license, and looked obediently at the snapshot of Serenity standing at the ranch with the blond, bearded, mad-eyed Azrael and the other smiling girls.

"I seen her with him. They wouldn't come in here: he didn't believe in booze, you know. But I seen them in town, when he come in, in that van of his, to pick up supplies for his place. Yeah, I seen her."

"The important thing," Dave said, "is when. Was she with him any time close to the end, when he killed the sheriff's men and cleared out?"

"They was friends of mine," Lucky said. "You know why they was there? Sanitation. To serve a paper. Some preacher wanted him and his girls out of there. Sex cult, he says." Lucky laughed grimly. "Worse than that, wasn't it? Only nobody knew it then. We was all on their side. Hippies, forty miles from noplace—nobody to see them but lizards and kangaroo rats. If they wanted to do it on the roof, who cared? But this preacher couldn't rest. He must have watched them through a spyglass. Claimed the place was filthy, a pigpen, not fit. Raised hell with the department of health and sanitation. County. They wrote up the paper just to get the son of a bitch off their back. And Lon and Red drove out there to serve it. Marked car, of course, uniforms, revolvers on their hip, of course. And they park the car and start for the door, and this Azrael's there with a shotgun. Didn't wait to hear what they was there for. Thought they'd found out he murdered all them girls, didn't he? Blew their heads off, just like that."

The door opened and let in sunlight for a moment, along with three youngsters swinging crash helmets—more motorcyclists? No. Two of them were girls in very short shorts, kneepads, high-top shoes, padded vests over T-shirts stenciled Sand Hoppers in a circle surrounding a drawing of a dune buggy. Lucky served them, and the squat, black-bearded youth with them, Coors in cans, which they carried along to the electronic games. Lucky returned to Dave. "I can't say for sure how long before that I seen her." He pushed the snapshot away from him. "Why do you want to know?"

"It's an old picture," Dave said. "The last her family heard from her out here was two years ago."

"That a fact?" Lucky drew the picture toward him and squinted at it again. He shook his head. "No, that's her. She was usually the one who come into Perez with him. Always wore one of them, whatyacallit, dashikis? Nothing under it. Sun in the street, you could see her naked right through it." He handed the picture to Dave. "No, I'd say no more than a month, six weeks ago." He watched Dave slide the picture into his jacket pocket. His mouth was grim. "Guess that means she was the last one he killed, don't it? Who the hell do you suppose he fed the heart to?"

Dave stared. "What did you say?"

"After he killed one, he made the other ones eat their heart. Didn't know that, did you?" He looked smug.

"Am I supposed to believe it?" Dave said.

"Lon and Red wasn't my only friends in the sheriff's office. There's this diary this Azrael left behind. They ain't saying nothing to the TV people and the newspaper writers about it. District attorney's got it under lock and key for the trial."

"Names," Dave said. "The names of the girls?"

"If they was in there, you wouldn't be here, would you? The D.A. wouldn't have kept the names back—parents all over the country wondering if that's their little girl that ran off? Nope. Come to writing about them girls, he'd draw a little flower, or a moon, or a star, or a cloud—I don't re-member what-all. No names. Oh, yeah, one was a bird, too—that's it, a little drawing of a bird."

"Dear God," Dave said.

"But let one of them do anything he didn't like—talk back, disobey some crazy rule he made—he killed her, cut her heart out, roasted it, made the other ones eat it so they'd remember to do like he told them. Lot of other stuff in there, too, stuff you wouldn't believe. He was a mad dog. You know what Azrael means? Angel of death. Another beer?"

"That's enough," Dave said.

"Then it's over?" Cecil asked. "Tomorrow you write up your report, and Banner sends him his twenty-five thousand dollars?" It was one in the morning, rain on the roof. They sat watching the fire, sat on the couch under the looming rafter shadows of the big rear building, and ate wedges of warm quiche, and drank cold white wine. "Only where do they address the envelope? That's not your problem, right?"

"Tomorrow I do not write my report," Dave said.

"But now you know she was there to the end."

"Alive," Dave said. "Lucky saw her alive. Banner wants proof she's dead. They want to know that unclaimed corpse in the San Diego County coroner's refrigerator is Serenity Westover's. I can't prove that."

"Perfect teeth, perfect bones, dark hair." Cecil stood up, holding his own empty plate, and reached for Dave's. "Same size, same age. Don't you think it's her?"

"Just leave those till morning," Dave said.

Cecil looked doubtful. "Draw ants," he said.

"Too cold and wet for ants," Dave said. "Sit down." Cecil set the plates on the hearth, picked up his glass from the pine couch arm, grinned, and sat down. Dave put an arm around his bony shoulders. "I'm nearer to thinking it's her now. I was sure it wasn't when I was down there to talk

94

to the medical examiner the other day. That's why I didn't go to Perez then, didn't even think of it. The postmark was old. These kids go to a place like that, get restless, wander off to some other place they're not going to like any better."

"Unless it's Guyana," Cecil said. "They didn't wander off from there, did they? And they didn't wander off from Azrael's ranch, either, look like. Blue paint?"

"Sky blue," Dave said.

Cecil said, "If you couldn't get proof for them, how do they think they are ever going to get it?"

"When someone catches him," Dave said.

Cecil shivered. "Would you want to catch him, touch him, even look at him? Would you want to hear what comes out of his mouth?"

"I don't want to think about it anymore today, all right?" Dave turned Cecil's face from the firelight and kissed his mouth. "What are we sitting here for? It's late. Why aren't we in bed?"

"I been wondering that, myself." Cecil tossed off the last of his wine. But halfway up the steps to the loft, Dave following him, hands on his narrow hips, Cecil stopped. "I forgot. There's a message on your answering machine. I was here. I answered the phone, but I couldn't understand him."

"Lyle Westover," Dave said.

"Finally, I apologized all over the place, and said why didn't he call back, and I wouldn't answer, and he could put the message on the tape, and maybe you'd understand it."

Dave sighed, let go Cecil's hips, and went back down the

stairs. "It could be important," he grumbled, and punched keys on the machine. He had to listen three times, but at last he puzzled out the message. Lyle was back in the house on Sandpiper Lane. Checks should have been waiting for him from the musicians' union. They weren't. The mailbox was empty except for a gas bill, new. Did Dave think Lyle's father was picking up the mail? Dave hoped so. He lifted down the sheepskin jacket from a big brass hook beside the door. He called, "I have to go out. See you for breakfast."

"What!" The bedframe jounced. Heels thumped the loft planks. Cecil scowled down at him over the railing. He was naked, the firelight glancing off his blackness. "You going out? You leaving this?" He showed Dave what he meant. "What am I supposed to do with it here all by myself all night long?"

"You can bring it with you." Dave shrugged into the coat. "If you don't mind missing your sleep."

"Sleep would not be what I missed." Cecil vanished from view. "Wait for me. I'll be right there."

Cecil's head lay on Dave's shoulder. The boy was asleep, his breathing soft, slow, regular. They sat in the Triumph on Sandpiper Lane in the dark and the cold rain that the sea wind kept catching and rattling like grains of sand against the window glass. The wind, the rain, smelled of the sea. Dave stared at the heavy-headed silhouette of the iron mailbox down the street at 171. He checked his watch. Not that there was any point to that. Westover might come for his mail at any hour, so long as darkness held. It was twenty minutes past three.

Moving carefully so as not to disturb Cecil, Dave shifted

his position an inch or two on the grudging bucket seat. Painfully he drew up one cold-stiffened leg until the knee touched the little leather-wrapped steering wheel. He straightened the other leg, the knee joint snapping. He tugged up the woolly collar of his coat and huddled down into the coat a little farther, seeking warmth. Cecil murmured but did not waken. Dave fell asleep.

What woke him he did not know, but he sat up fast and straight. Cecil mumbled "What?" and rubbed a hand down over his face. "It's him," Dave said, and with a sleep-numb hand fumbled for the key in the dash. Through the drizzled windshield he watched a figure yank open the mailbox at 171, grope inside it, shut it again, and, hunched up against the rain, scurry across the black glossy pavement to a big dark car that waited with glowing taillights.

Dave's fingers found the cold little key and twisted it. The motor stuttered, coughed, quit. Cold. Dave twisted the key again. The starter mechanism gave its singsong whine. The big car moved away up the street. The Triumph's motor caught, Dave pedaled the accelerator. The motor choked and quit again. "Shit!" Cecil's hands gripped the dash, he bounced in his seat. "Come on, baby, come on. We gonna lose him, for sure." The red lights of the big car disappeared around the bend where the lonely streetlamp glowed sallow in the rain. The Triumph's motor caught, sputtered, smoothed out. Dave pawed for the leather-covered knob of the gearshift, moved it, remembered just in time to release the handbrake, eased down on the gas pedal, and they were moving.

Dave didn't waste time with the tangle of curved streets. He headed for the beach, the coast road. At the top of a hill, they saw the big lonely car below just as it swung onto the coast road, heading north. Skidding on the curves, they followed. Dave kept distance between them. There was no traffic, nothing but occasional massive eighteen-wheelers hulking along at seventy and eighty miles an hour, their turbulence knocking the Triumph almost out of control as they roared past. Not the big dark car. It held a steady pace on a steady course.

"He doesn't know we're tailing him," Cecil said.

The harsh lights of another semi glared in Dave's eyes from the rearview mirror. He edged the Triumph to the road shoulder. The truck hurtled past, huge wheels churning loops of water over the Triumph. Muddy water. It took the wipers a moment to clear the windshield. The high, square-cornered shape of the truck with its points of warning light diminished ahead of them. Under a high black bluff, it turned from sight. But down the clear highway the dark car was nowhere to be seen.

"We lost him," Cecil said.

"He turned up a canyon," Dave said.

Yucca Canyon, it was called. The road was narrow and crooked and steep. The little wheels of the Triumph hammered in potholes. Water dashed against the underside of the car. Big rock outcrops loomed in the headlights. Old oaks bent crooked limbs over the road. They didn't sight the dark car again. Maybe this hadn't been Westover's turnoff after all. Maybe Dave had guessed wrong. If Westover had realized he was being followed, all he'd have had to do was switch off his lights for a minute and crawl, say, into the shadow of that bluff to be out of sight. Visibility was that bad. Dave was ready to turn back, but then there the big car was again, a hundred yards on up the winding road, rounding a bend, yellow headlights raking brush and rock sparkling with rain. Dave pressed the gas pedal hard, and the Triumph began skidding on turns. The canyon yawned deep and dark below them, and Cecil's eyes grew big and he sat very still.

The pitch of the road turned downward, and soon they sped past a crossroads where a filling station slept, a building-supply yard behind hurricane fencing, a frame building that was a grocery store. Weak, watery night lights lit them dimly. The big car was out of sight again, but in a moment it would reappear up ahead. It had done that twenty times in ten miles. But now they drove fast and for a long time and didn't see it again. Dave pulled the Triumph up under a clump of dripping manzanita. He backed it, swung it around, and headed it down the way they'd come. At the crossroads, he took the turnoff he should have taken first. They crawled along twisting, climbing roads quick with flowing water, for half an hour, peering through the blackness. Dave braked the car again and looked at Cecil.

"Are you cold and miserable?"

Cecil nodded, cold and miserable.

"Let's go home and get warm," Dave said.

Yucca Canyon was even wilder and more empty than he had thought last night. At first, the road wound up from the coast among broad, low foothills, then entered a narrow pass, where it edged an arroyo overhung with the leafless, white, and twisting arms of big sycamores. Rain runoff plunged down the arroyo, foaming muddily, tumbling

99

boulders with its force. As the bent road climbed, the arroyo widened, dropped below road level deeper, full of oaks, and the mountains reared higher, rockier. Sometimes the road was a narrow shelf cut into cliff faces almost straight up and down. The drop from the road edge was steep and far to the bottom. That was what Cecil had been able to see or sense last night from the passenger seat while Dave had skidded the car around these crimps of ragged blacktop, what had made him silent.

He slept now, lean, long, naked, sprawled facedown in the broad bed on the loft, warm under blankets, unaware, Dave hoped, that he was alone. Dave had kept waking up, wondering if it was time yet to come back here. At dawn he had crept quietly into clothes, shaved, fixed coffee in the cookshack and heated a Danish and eaten it. He'd put on the sheepskin coat and started the Triumph, worrying at the protests of the noisy little valves, afraid they would waken the boy. They hadn't. Now he checked the time on his wrist. Eight-thirty. He wasn't going to be too early. In fact, was he ever going to encounter human life?

It was miles before he saw the first sign of it—a shacky ranch, board buildings under massive eucalyptus trees, bark hanging in brown rags, leafage shaggy dark reds, three rough-coated horses nodding in the morning sun in a muddy paddock fenced with splintery rails. Then no more signs of life for miles. Then leaf-strewn, night-damp rooftops below road level, sets of wooden stairs leading downward from clumps of tin mailboxes. Then nothing again for miles. He wanted that crossroads. Did it really exist? Now trails began breaking off the main road. Through the trees he glimpsed here a flash of window glass in sunlight,

100

there a chimney with a wisp of smoke rising from it. A car passed him, heading down the canyon. A rooster crowed.

And then the road dropped sharply, and he remembered that, and at the bottom of the long drop he found the fenced building-supply yard, the frame grocery store, the filling station. A wash of mud filmed the blacktop around the gas pumps and a boy in a blue coverall was washing the mud into the road with a garden hose. He had long straw-color hair and a big frontier mustache. Dave hated to sully the asphalt he'd only just purified. He ran the Triumph up beside the pumps anyway. The boy turned off the hose around a corner of the station office, then came at a bowlegged jog to see what Dave wanted. From under the long, mud-stained legs of the coverall the scuffed points of cowboy boots showed. They were worn down at the heel.

"Fill her up, please," Dave told him, and got out of the little car and stretched. The boy reached for the gas hose, said "Shit," and jogged into the office for keys. He unlocked the pump and took down the hose and stuck the nozzle into the Triumph. The pump began to whirr and ping. Dave said, "You worked here long?"

"All my life," the boy said without joy. "My old man owns it. Why?"

"Then you must know most of your customers," Dave said. "The people that live in the canyon?"

"Yeah, I guess so," the boy said. And again, "Why?"

"I'm a private investigator." Dave showed the boy the license in his wallet. "I'm looking for a man named Charles Westover."

"I don't know him." The boy pulled the nozzle out of the tank. "You didn't need much gas."

"Maybe I need some oil," Dave said. "Would you like to check it? And the water?"

"It's my job." The boy hung the gas hose back on the pump and worked the hood of the Triumph. "No Westover. Not unless he pays cash. Nobody pays cash for gas." He bent in under the hood, pulled out the oil stick, and wiped it with a blue rag from a hip pocket. He stuck it back in place and pulled it out again. "You don't need any oil." He replaced the stick, turned, stooped for the water hose. "You get to know their names from their credit cards. Everybody uses stinking credit cards. Country's going to hell."

"He drives a Rolls-Royce, two-tone, brown and gold," Dave said, "about fifteen years old. It's not the kind of car you'd forget."

The boy twisted off the radiator cap and fed a few jets of water in. The water overflowed. He dropped the hose, which snaked itself back across the wet tarmac and into its hole. The boy screwed the cap back on and slammed down the hood. "I remember it. Only been in one time, but I remember it. Sure."

"Westover is about forty-five, slight build, the tip of one ear is missing."

"It wasn't him." The boy wiped his hands on the rag and stuffed the rag back into its pocket. "It was a girl. Maybe a teen-ager, maybe older, twenty or so?"

"Brown eyes?" Dave's heart thumped. "Dark hair?"

"Blond," the boy said. "I couldn't see her eyes. She wore dark glasses."

Dave took the snapshot from inside the sheepskin jacket and handed it to the boy. "The girl in front?"

The boy shook his head. "Too fat," he said. "This one was skinny, sick-looking, kind of, pale." He handed back the snapshot. "Tacky, too. Ragged old sweater, dirty jeans, barefoot. I wouldn't have remembered, except what was somebody like that doing driving a Rolls?" He watched Dave put the snapshot away. "Is that Azrael?"

"That's who it is." Dave read the meter on the gas pump, dug out his wallet, handed the boy a twenty-dollar bill. "Keep the change. And tack this up somewhere, so it doesn't get lost." It was his card. "And call me if that Rolls comes in again, will you, please?"

"You think the girl in that picture is still alive?"

"It's not getting any easier." Dave got into the Triumph and rolled down the window. "You only saw it that one time?"

"Yeah." The boy read the card. "I'll call you."

"Thanks," Dave said.

Until two in the afternoon, doggedly, not missing a turn-off, he prowled the mud-slick back trails of the canyon, going slowly, searching with his eyes every foot of every crooked mile, for the Rolls—in a yard, a carport, hidden in brush. He didn't find it. He drove back down to the coast road and, with the sea glittering cold and blue in the sunlight to his right, headed home to Cecil.

9

By four o'clock, when Cecil scrambled lankily into the van to start for work, Dave standing shivering in a bathrobe in the damp, bricked yard, the sky had clouded over. The wind blew soft and damp from the southeast. It was going to rain again. Dave had promised to sleep until Cecil returned. But while Dave had been up in Yucca Canyon this morning, the telephone had wakened Cecil, half wakened him. Thelma Gaillard had left her number.

Now, at four-thirty, CLOSED hung from a grubby string inside the dirty glass pane of Gaillard's shop door, and the shop was without lights. Dave climbed the outside stairs and rapped the wooden frame of a loose screen door at the top. To the south, above rooftops, treetops, the sky was dark as a bruise, threatening. The door opened.

"Oh." She was startled. She touched her gray hair, smoothed her old brown cardigan. Her bluejeans were faded, shapeless, her tennis shoes worn. Her cheeks weren't rosy today. "I thought you'd telephone."

"I was in the neighborhood." Not true, but he liked to go, instead of phoning, to watch faces when they spoke, to look into eyes and rooms. Surprise was sometimes useful, let him see and hear what strangers weren't always meant to see or hear. "What was it you called me about?"

"Don. I don't know where he is. Come in." She unhooked the screen door and pushed it open. She glanced at the sky. He stepped inside. "Excuse how things look." She hooked the screen again, and shut the wooden door. "I'm so upset, I guess I'm just letting things go." It needed paint, but it was a neat kitchen, except for a few unwashed dishes beside the sink, an unwashed pan on a twenty-year-old stove. She led him down a narrow, dark hallway past the half-open doors of dim bedrooms, one of the beds unmade, to a living room with tired wallpaper and threadbare furniture—none of Don Gaillard's handiwork here—where a television set with bent antennae flickered and spoke. She said, "I thought you might know where he went," and moved to switch off the set.

Dave said, "Wait a minute, please."

It was a news broadcast. The pictures were of a van lying on its side in a stony ravine. The van was blue and painted with chalky-looking flowers, birds, stars, moons. The artwork was clumsy, amateurish. Men in suntan uniforms moved around the van. Desert stretched beyond. Mountains formed a ragged blue line far off. The newscaster's voiceover said ". . . definitely the vehicle known to have been driven by the missing California sex-cult guru and suspected murderer of two sheriff's deputies and at least six young women. Nevada authorities say their search will now be intensified, with—" Dave switched off the set.

"He probably wandered off out there and died," Thelma Gaillard said. "Deserts are terrible places, hot all day, freezing at night, no water. I used to worry so when Don and Chass went to the desert. Would you like some coffee? Tea?" She looked around, doubtfully. "Don may have some whiskey. It's so cold."

"I'm all right," Dave said. It wasn't cold in here. A gas heater hissed in a corner. "I'm not sure I understand. I don't know your son at all well. How would I know where he's gone?" He shed the sheepskin jacket. "How did you come to telephone me?" He sat down.

"I found your card in Don's workclothes," she said. Knitting lay on a couch that faced the television set. She sat beside it and picked it up. She only glanced at it for a second, then turned her blue eyes on Dave, but the needles began clicking in her fingers. "You see—just after you left the other day he came tearing up here in a state, changed his clothes, and rushed out. Without a word of explanation. I could see something had upset him terribly. I said, 'Tell me what's the matter,' but he just pushed me out of his way. All he said when he ran down the stairs was, 'I'll be back.' But he hasn't come back. He hasn't even called. And it's been two nights, now. And that's not like him. He never stays away nights without phoning me."

"But he does sometimes stay away?" Dave said.

"Yes, but he never breaks right into a working day, locks up the shop, runs off. He has orders to fill. He puts in sixteen hours a day down in that shop. Sometimes he won't even rest on Sunday. And why didn't he pack a suitcase? He didn't even take a shaving kit."

"He had no reason to run from me," Dave said. "Maybe somebody telephoned him."

"No. The phone up here is an extension. I always hear

106

the bell. No one phoned, Mr. Brandstetter. And it was right after you and that colored boy drove off that this happened. What did you say to him?"

"I came looking for Charles Westover," Dave said.

Her mouth fell open. The needles went silent. "Chass? But"—she gave a bewildered little laugh—"he hasn't seen Chass in years. Ten years, at least."

"You're wrong about that," Dave said. "Chass came to see him two weeks ago."

"Oh, no." She was positive. The needles dug into the yarn again, twisting, clicking. "You must have misunderstood. If Chass had come, Don would have brought him up here to see me. Chass was an orphan, you know. He always said I was better to him than any mother could have been." She gazed at the gray front windows, mourning a lost past, and her smile was sentimental. "I loved that boy and he loved me. He wouldn't have come without running up here to give me a hug and a kiss."

"Maybe you were out," Dave said, "at the supermarket or someplace. He came, Mrs. Gaillard. Don told me. Lyle Westover told me."

"After all this time?" She wasn't letting go her stubborn disbelief. She scoffed. "What for?"

Dave didn't want to be the one who told her about the loan. "I don't know. What I do know is that just afterward, Westover disappeared. I have to locate him. It's about an insurance claim. When I learned he and Don Gaillard were old friends, I came to ask Don if he knew where Westover was. He said he didn't."

"Don is always truthful," she said primly.

"But Westover meant a lot to him—isn't that right?"

"They were as close as any two boys I ever saw—men. After they broke up"—she quit working the needles and lifted the droop of blue knitting to study her progress—"Don wasn't the same person." She smoothed the knitting on her knees. "He's never gotten over it."

"So it's just possible, isn't it," Dave said, "that he shaded the truth to me, and went to help his friend?"

"How?" Her laugh was helpless, impatient. "I don't really understand what you're saying. Help him, how? What is this about insurance?"

"The Banner company thinks Chass may have filed a false claim. But he has worse troubles than that. Don didn't know how bad things had gotten for Chass until I came and told him."

"But if Chass isn't at home," she said, "how could Don go to him? Where?" Her look rested on Dave in mild reproach. "It was I who phoned you to find out where Don is—remember?"

"You said they used to go to the desert," Dave said.

She gave a nod and began knitting again. "They spent every weekend of their lives together, even after Chass was married. The desert, the mountains, the beach. I don't remember the names of the places, if they ever told me."

"Not Yucca Canyon?" Dave said.

Her look was blank. Plainly she'd never heard of it. "Is it so far away he couldn't get home in two days?"

"It's just up the coast." Dave stood and picked up his jacket. "What kind of car does Don drive?"

"A panel truck," she said, "dove-gray, with Don's name on the side, and 'Hand Crafted Furniture.' In yellow. Of course, it's old, and the paint's all faded now." She frowned. "What kind of troubles were these Chass had?"

Dave was back in Yucca Canyon, driving those twisty little trails, looking at cars in shrubby yards where rain sparkled on leaves in morning sunshine. No panel trucks—dove-gray or any other color. "Money troubles," he said.

"Money? Hah." Her mouth tightened at one corner. The needles clicked, bad-tempered. "Don is no fancy lawyer. You see how we live. No—if it was money, there's no way in the world Don Gaillard could help Charles Westover."

"Thank you." Dave moved to leave. "If Don comes home, will you have him phone me, please?"

"What if he doesn't come home?" She put the knitting aside, got quickly to her feet, reached out to him. "What if something's happened to him? I'm frightened." Her mouth trembled, there were tears in her eyes. "The streets get so slick in the rain. Maybe he's lying in a hospital someplace, unconscious, hurt, helpless."

"If he carried identification," Dave said, "you'd have been notified. Have you called his friends?"

She turned her eyes away uneasily. "He doesn't like me prying into his private life. He gets very angry. He has that right, I know." She sounded as if she didn't really think so. "He's a grown man, after all. But I was frantic." She looked up at Dave as if he could give her absolution. "I felt guilty even going into his room. But I went, and I found his little address book, and phoned some of them. No one's seen him. Most of them hardly seemed to know who I was talking about. Nothing but first names in that book—Pete, John, Ralph. They weren't any help."

"You don't know any of them?"

"He never brings them here," she said. "Maybe he's ashamed of me. That's how he acts, sometimes."

"I'm sure that's not true." Dave patted her shoulder. She was like a lost little girl of five who needed her tears dried. "Where's your telephone?"

She took him back to the kitchen. It was on a wall. He dialed Salazar. The deputy looking after his desk said Salazar was home with the flu. Dave doubted there was anything in Salazar's files he could refer the deputy to. He'd wanted Salazar to look for Gaillard. That might lead them both to Westover. He wasn't going to get that help. Still, the deputy surprised him. Salazar had located Howie O'Rourke. In the L.A. county jail. For breaking parole—drunk, disorderly, consorting with known criminals.

"Did he have twenty thousand dollars on him?"

"He lost it on the horses at Santa Anita."

Dave thanked the deputy and hung up. He told Thelma Gaillard, "I'm going now, but I want you to promise me something. To get on this phone as soon as I've gone and call the police, missing persons. Tell them about Don."

"Oh, no." She looked shocked. "Don hates the police. He'd never forgive me." She begged Dave with her eyes. Her cheeks were flaming red. "It's not that he's ever committed a crime. It's just little, well, indiscretions, boyish things. He gets tired and overwrought. He works so *very* hard. What harm does it do? But the police have been very nasty to him."

"He won't hate them," Dave said, "if he needs them and they help." He pulled open the door. Rain had begun to fall. The breath of the rain came cold through the screen door. "And if they find him, you let me know right away, will you? I'll appreciate it."

She stared at the phone, face pinched with dread. She

plucked nervously at her lower lip. She turned to Dave. "Isn't there anything you can do? You're a private investigator. It says so on your card."

"There's only one of me," Dave said. "There's a lot of them. Now, they'll ask you for a list of places he goes, people he sees—"

"He'd hate that," she said. "I don't know, anyway. He never tells me anything. I don't dare ask him."

"Mention Yucca Canyon to them."

"But I—" she started to protest.

"As a favor to me," Dave said, and went out and pulled the door shut after him.

He ran across the uneven bricks through the rain to the cookshack and built a double martini before he even took off his coat. While the martini chilled, he sliced tomato and avocado and laid the slices on lettuce on a plate. He tasted the martini, sighed, smiled, and switched on the radio. Brahms's *Liebeslieder* waltzes in the version for voices and piano. He sang along while he mixed a dressing of home-made mayonnaise, tarragon vinegar, sugar, Worcestershire sauce, seasoned salt. He lit the grille, tasted the martini again, and mixed a batter in a thick bowl. He dumped into the batter a half-pint of cooked shrimp that he'd stopped for on the way home from Gaillard's, spooned the batter onto the grille, pulled a slim green bottle of white wine from the refrigerator, and uncorked it. He turned over the fritters, which were a nice toasted color. He poured a tall glass of the wine and set it on the table. He transferred the fritters onto the plate, poured the dressing over the tomato and avocado, finished off the martini, set the plate on the table, and sat down to eat. But he had only swallowed a forkful of the salad, a gulp of wine, a bite of the fritters, when he remembered, and lifted down the telephone.

Lyle Westover said, "You just caught me going out the door." The syllables were mashed and jumbled, but Dave understood. "I'm flying to Nashville. A recording gig."

"I asked you to report your father missing," Dave said. "Did you do that?"

"Right away, to the sheriff, like you said. But they just wrote it down and stuck it in a file, I think. They never checked back with me. Did you find out whether it's my father who's been taking the mail?"

"It was dark, and I couldn't see him well," Dave said. "But I think so. The car was right. I'll watch for him again tonight. Look, I don't want to hold you up, but I need the answer to one question."

"I hope nobody finds out," Lyle said. "Country-western music. I'm not going to let them list my name in the album credits."

"Good thinking," Dave said. "Yucca Canyon. What would your father be doing in Yucca Canyon? Does he know someone who lives up there? Friend? Client?"

"Not that I ever heard of."

"There's an address book on his desk in the den," Dave said. "Have you got time to check through it, or will you miss your flight?"

"Trio's driving me," Lyle said, "and she goes very slowly when it rains. Rain scares her to death. She didn't get here as soon as she promised. I better go."

"Just get the address book," Dave said, "and put it in the mailbox. I'll pick it up tonight."

"All right. The union canceled those checks and made me out a new one so that's okay," Lyle said.

"Glad to hear it," Dave said. "When will you be back?"

"Three or four days," Lyle said, "unless something else comes up, unless I get more work."

"Good luck," Dave told him, and hung up. Now he could finish his meal. But he wasn't on the chair again before the phone rang. He sighed and lifted down the receiver. "Hello—Brandstetter."

"I'm in the Valley," Cecil said. "You wouldn't believe how wet it is out here." A siren moaned behind his voice. "I'm on this assignment. It's a hostage situation. This crazy brother is in this supermarket with thirty customers and clerks and one of those little machine guns made in Israel, and nobody knows when it will be over. One thing is clear to me. If only one reporter from channel three stays, that reporter is going to be me. So when I see you will be when I see you, right?"

"Better sooner than later," Dave said. "Try not to get shot, all right? I'll be staking out Westover's place again—unless there's a Yucca Canyon street number in his address book. Lyle's leaving his address book for me. So it looks like a late night for both of us."

"Not together," Cecil said.

"Whose fault is that?" Dave said.

"Don't start on me," Cecil said. "I'm already feeling bad enough." A voice roared through a bullhorn. Dave didn't catch the words. Cecil said, "I mean, it is going to be Noah's ark or nothing before this night is done."

"Try to keep dry," Dave said. "Thanks for calling."

"I don't think you should follow him alone."

113

"It's a hard rain," Dave said. "Maybe he won't show."

He finished his supper, poured another glass of wine, recorked the bottle, and stowed it away. He drank the wine while he washed the dishes and cleaned up the grille. He wanted that address book now, but he was too tired. He needed sleep. The book would be there at midnight. A few more hours wouldn't matter. He'd be a menace on the road, the way he felt. Stunned was the word for it. He ached with weariness.

He picked up the sheepskin coat, switched off the cookshack light, and ran across the courtyard to the back building, key in hand. He went through the high-raftered dark of the place without bothering to turn on a light. It was cold and damp but he couldn't be bothered to clean the grate and build a fire. He dropped the coat on a chair and climbed the stairs to the loft and the wide bed. In bed, he'd get warm. To ensure that, he kept his sweater on. He shed the rest of his clothes, slid between the sheets, and touched someone.

A voice said, "Welcome. I thought you'd never get here." A naked arm pinned him down, a naked leg. A naked body crowded against him, a mouth covered his, a bearded mouth. He jerked his head away, freed an arm, groped out in the cold for the lamp and missed. He tried to get out of bed, but arms held him. The owner of the arms was laughing. Dave's hand met the lamp and switched it on. Miles Edwards sat up in the bed, brushing hair out of his eyes and grinning. "The pictures didn't seem to do it," he said. "I decided on a personal appearance."

Dave was on his feet, kicking into his corduroys. "Get the hell out of that bed and put your clothes on."

"You're joking." Edwards threw back the sheets and blankets. He sat cross-legged. He was more beautiful now than he'd been in his teens when those pictures were taken. Still lean, but with better definition, harder. He held his hands open. "You don't want this?"

"Whether I want it or not is beside the point. You are, for Christ sake, marrying Amanda. And whether you give a damn about her or not, I do. How the hell could you imagine I'd do this to her?"

"What's Amanda got to do with it? Amanda and I are all right, we're fine. This is something separate and apart. Good God, you're old enough to know that."

"It's not a matter of age," Dave said, "it's a matter of cynicism. Obviously. But even if I did 'know that'—I don't think Amanda does know it. And I don't want her to have to learn. Not from you and me."

"She wouldn't. What would be the point? Oh, come on." Edwards got to his knees. Scoffing, but anxious. "You're not going to tell her? What for, for Christ sake?"

Dave turned away, found cigarettes on the stand under the lamp, lit one. "There's not going to be anything to tell." He leaned on the loft rail, gazing down into the dark. "We are going to forget it. And you are just very quietly going to slide out of her life, doing your best not even to leave a ripple of regret."

"Why? Because I go both ways? What do you expect me to do—change how I am? Can you?" The bed moved. Under his feet Dave felt the loft planks tremble. Edwards's arms came around him again. Edwards pressed against his back. "Come on," he pleaded. "You know you want to. I've been dying for you. I thought if you saw those pictures—"

Dave shrugged him off. "I don't think you're right in the head." Edwards's clothes lay on a chair at the far side of the bed. "If you want somebody, you don't aggravate him by everything you do." He grabbed up Edwards's briefs and held them out to him. "I haven't liked five minutes of the time I've spent with you, and I never will. Put these on, God damn it." He pushed the briefs into Edwards's hands. "And get your ass out of here. How the hell did you get in, in the first place?"

"You don't really want me to go." Edwards drew the little white knit shorts up his dark legs but not all the way. "You don't really want me to cover this up." Dave leaned on the rail and looked down into the dark again. Edwards said, "Amanda has keys, remember?"

"Jesus," Dave said. He turned. Edwards was sulkily flapping into his shirt. Dave said, "What about Cecil? I doubt that someone with your moral capacity can understand this, but what I wouldn't do to Amanda, I wouldn't do to Cecil, either."

Shaking his head in disgusted disbelief, Edwards sat on the bed and pulled on his socks. "I know how old you are," he said, "but you don't have to act like it. I never thought you would." He stood, and his glance pitied Dave. "True love?" he sneered, kicking into his pants. "Two hearts that beat as one?" He zipped up the pants, reached for his vest, his tie. "Please. That is not how human life is lived." He didn't button the vest. He draped the tie loose around his neck. He got into his jacket. "You deal with people all the time. You know that's all bullshit. People do what they want, they do what they have to." He remembered his shoes, and sat down again to put them on and tie them. "We all do."

116

"All right," Dave said. "What I have to do is throw you out of here, because what I want is not you. What I want is Cecil. And what I also want is for you not to give Amanda pain. She's had enough of that."

Edwards brushed past him without looking at him. He rattled down the stairs. Below, a ghost shape flapped white in the shadows. He'd brought a raincoat, of course. His heels tapped away. "Believe me," he shouted, "we're fine. We'll stay fine because she'll never know. Not from me." The door opened. Rain pattered outside in puddles on the bricks. "So, if you don't want her to have any pain, you just keep out of it, old man." The door slammed.

Dave went downstairs and bolted it.

10

Two steps from where Dave sat in the Triumph, a cliff dropped to the beach. He couldn't see the ocean. It was midnight and the rain still fell. But he could feel it thud against the cliff, and hear it hiss among rocks when it pulled back to strike again. The rain rustled on the car's cloth top and sifted against the glass. Charles Westover's five-by-eight address book Dave held propped open on the steering wheel. He read it by the beam of the penlight. He had passed the letter *M* and still found no mention of Yucca Canyon.

He had left the little car's parking lights on, its taillights, in case one of those juggernaut trucks decided to lay by on this patch of ground. Now headlights glared in the door mirror to his left. But what rolled up beside him was small and toy fire-engine red. A pickup truck. He had a blank second, then remembered. The door of the pickup slammed. Around its front, through the stab of its headlights, Scotty Dekker came at a jog, the rain turning his hair to taffy strings. He bent at Dave's window. Dave rolled the glass down.

"Are you all right?" Scotty shouted it so as to be heard

above the crashing of the surf. "I recognized your car." He peered. "You aren't sick or anything?"

"Just old," Dave said with a smile. He took off his glasses. "I've been reading. What have you been doing? Surfing?"

Scotty laughed, looked up at the rain. "Even I'm not that crazy. No, I've been up at my aunt's in Pismo. I'm just getting home. Good surf up there."

"That's why you didn't call to tell me about Lyle."

"Did he come back?" Scotty looked stricken. "Oh, wow. I'm sorry, Mr. Brandstetter." He wiped rain off his face with a square clean hand. "Is he all right?"

"He's all right," Dave said, "but he doesn't know what's happened to his father." He reached across to open the door on the passenger side. "If we're going to talk, you better get in out of the rain."

"I have to go. My folks were expecting me at six. They'll be worried."

"It's a bit after six," Dave said, and shut the door again. "Just one question. Did you ever hear Charles Westover mention Yucca Canyon—anybody he knew up there, any time he spent up there, anything at all?"

Scotty ran hands over his wet hair and shook his hands and made a face. "No. No, I don't think so. No, I'm pretty sure not. Yucca Canyon? What would somebody like Mr. Westover want up there? I mean, that's pretty raunchy, shacks and hippies and grow-your-own marijuana. It's all weirdos up there. Isn't it?"

"I'll take your word for it," Dave said. "Thanks, Scotty. You better go before it gets any later."

"Right." Scotty smiled, slapped the window ledge, straightened. He said, "I just wanted to be sure you were

119

okay." He bent again, blinking. "Reading? It's a funny place to read."

"It's an interesting book." Dave put his glasses on again.

"I guess so." Scotty stood erect again, looked around at the night, the windblown rain, peered in the direction of the pounding surf. He raised baffled eyebrows at Dave. Dave kept a straight face. Scotty gave a little wondering shake to his head, shrugged, said, "Okay, so long," and ran back through the headlight beams and climbed into the truck. The door slammed again. The horn beeped. The truck rolled away.

Dave grinned and went on checking addresses.

Yucca Canyon didn't appear in the book, and Dave drove back to Sandpiper Lane. The Rolls arrived earlier this morning. The rain had quit, the cloud cover was breaking up. He sighted stars through the windshield. The wind grew colder. He checked his watch. Two-ten. And the big, dark car slid past, showing nothing but its taillights. It halted at the curb in front of the dark Dekker house. The same slight man got out of it who had got out of it yesterday morning. Dave worked the lever of his door. The door opened three inches and struck the curb. He cursed. He ought to have known better than to park on the wrong side of the street. He shouted, "Charles Westover? Hold it, please."

The face that jerked in his direction was no more than a pale, featureless blur. The man turned, slipped on the wet paving, came down on one hand, one knee, regained his footing, and lunged inside the Rolls. The next second, it was on its way up the street. Dave yanked his own door shut, started the Triumph, and went after the Rolls. The big car skidded on the street bends. Over the noise of the Triumph's little engine, Dave could hear the squeal of the big tires. The Triumph hugged the curves, so that he gained on the Rolls, until it reached the straight strip of road that sloped down to the coast, when the Rolls pulled away.

It didn't stop, didn't even slow, when it reached the highway. It swung onto the highway in a wide arc, tires throwing fans of water. The turn took it clear across the far traffic lane. It looked as if it almost scraped the crash rail there. It lurched and swerved for a few seconds on the slick paving, then straightened out and settled down to gain speed. Dave checked his own meter. The needle jiggled past seventy, to seventy-five. The red taillights of the Rolls still pulled away. Dave argued the Triumph up to eighty, eighty-five. The Rolls must have been cruising at a hundred. Searching ahead for other traffic, scared that one of those giant trucks would appear, he noticed in the rearview mirror a pair of headlights behind him.

The canyon road was no good for speed, too many jogs, too many potholes, bigger tonight from the work of the new rains than they'd been last night, deeper, more of them. A good many times, the wheels of the Triumph jounced so hard in them he feared he'd break an axle. The bottom of the car scraped the paving. He was keeping the Rolls in sight, when trees, curves, thrusts of rock didn't interfere, but he judged the Rolls was going to lose him. Then he saw the headlights back of him again, and felt cold in the pit of his stomach. They were dogging him. They were following with intent. No one simply driving home would keep the speed he and the Rolls were keeping, not on roads like this, not when those roads were wet.

He wanted to get out of the way but he was on a long stretch here without the option of turnoffs, one of those places where the road had been cut into a cliff that rose sheer on the left and where the canyon yawned black and deep on the right. He risked a little more speed, but had to brake right away. There were too many bends. The lights behind him drew closer, shone harshly in the rearview mirror. For a second, he had the crazy thought that it must be Cecil. But the set of the lights was wrong for a van. Then the lights were upon him. There was a jar that snapped his head back, a crunch of metal, the shattering of glass. The Triumph leaped ahead. He pressed the throttle because there seemed nothing to do but try to get away. He didn't get away. The car following him swerved to the left, came alongside, veered into him. The lights of the Triumph streaked out over treetops shiny with rain. Dave yanked the door lever. The Triumph soared off the road. Dave threw himself into space.

"Flames like that?" Cecil said. "No way I could have missed it."

The hospital room was sunny. The wall he faced had cheerful paper on it. He had a separated shoulder, some broken ribs, and assorted cuts, scrapes, and bruises. He was groggy from drugs, so he couldn't make out the pattern of the wallpaper. Cecil's face was a blur too, but a welcome blur. The drugs had dried Dave's mouth and made it taste bad. His face was stiff, but he tried for a smile.

"It's all that Camp Fire Girl training," he said.

"Mine," Cecil said, "or yours? You hid pretty good too. No bears going to get you in that mess of brush."

"It was jump or be barbecued," Dave said.

"I didn't know," Cecil said. "Climbed down as far as I could. Muddy, sliding on my ass. No use to it. I couldn't get close. It was too hot. All I could do was stand there and cry and throw up."

"You found a phone. You got help," Dave said.

"Fire department, ambulance," Cecil said. "It was them found you. Then it was laugh and cry. I was on the ground, rolling around, howling. They had to give me a shot to get me sane. But I'm still half crazy. Shut my eyes to try to sleep, there it is down there in the dark and the wet and the trees, burning up, and you're in there."

"I'm not." Dave reached for his hand. Pain stabbed his shoulder, sharp even through the thick numbness of the drugs. Cecil's hand closed over his on the bed. Dave said, "As for the car, I was trying to figure a way to get rid of it without chagrin. So that's one problem solved."

Amanda said, "Shall I order the brown Jaguar?"

He turned in the direction of her voice. He hadn't known she was here. He hadn't known much, for how long he wasn't sure, maybe two days, maybe three. She was a trim little silhouette against a bright window. The tall silhouette beside her was Miles Edwards. Edwards didn't say anything. Amanda said, "Dave, how did it happen? You're a good driver."

"Somebody else was better," Dave said. "And meaner. Ran me off the road."

"Oh, shit," Cecil said. "Highway patrol says it was an accident. Bad curve, one of the worst in that canyon. Specially when it's wet. Talked to me about fresh skid marks, two sets. Somebody trying to pass, they said. And did I

123

know what you were doing there? I didn't say, because I wanted to talk to you first." His voice began to fade. "It was him, wasn't it? Westover? The Rolls?"

Dave shook his head against the pillows and remembered another thing that was wrong with him—concussion. His head hurt, and the movement made him feel sick at his stomach. "The Rolls was up ahead." His own voice sounded faint and far away. "It was a junk car."

"Don't go to sleep," Cecil said. "Who was driving?"

"Couldn't see," Dave said, and went to sleep.

"Sometimes you don't act quite bright," Salazar said. He sat in the neat hospital armchair and watched Dave eat bland food from a steel tray. His nose was red and peeling around the nostrils but his color was good and his eyes were clear. "We try to teach the public to give the man with the gun the money and keep your life. It's only twenty-five thousand dollars, Dave. Is Banner Life Insurance going broke if it has to pay for once? Would that be worth dying for? What is Banner Life Insurance—mother, home, and apple pie?"

"It wasn't me he was trying to kill," Dave said.

"You were the one who was there," Salazar said.

"Unhappily," Dave said. "But it doesn't make sense. I'm the man who can get him that money he's so crazy to lay his hands on. Anyway, he'd gone into hiding days before I showed up." He finished the tasteless vanilla pudding and swung the table away that held the tray. "No, he's scared of somebody else. Scared to death."

"Who's helping him?" Salazar said. "The son?"

"No." Dave explained about Lyle. "There's a skinny blond girl in the picture. Maybe. I can't figure it. A kid in a

124

gas station up the canyon says she drove in, in Westover's Rolls. Sickly-looking, dirty old clothes. But it doesn't add up. Must have been the wrong Rolls."

"Why didn't Westover pick up some hippie to while away the lonely hours?" Salazar said.

"If he did, it wouldn't be a girl," Dave said. "His ex-wife told me that. Obliquely. It didn't register until later. Anyway, no frail little girl could handle that ton of scrap metal the way it was handled. It would take a big, strong man." Suddenly he felt like smiling and he smiled. "Can I have a cigarette, please?"

"What's funny?" Salazar rose and held out his pack. The cigarettes were short and brown. He lit Dave's and his own. He eyed Dave worriedly. "Are you all right?"

"I'm fine. I think I know the answer." He told Salazar all about Gaillard's sudden disappearance.

"But it wasn't a panel truck that hit you."

"Right. And when I tried searching the back roads of that canyon for Westover's Rolls by daylight, I didn't see any panel truck. But I couldn't cover the whole canyon. Not alone. It's too big. And a lot of it is so overgrown, you can't see anything from the road. It would take a house-to-house search."

"I can't field that," Salazar said. "What reason would I give?"

"Two men missing, linked to each other by a twenty-thousand-dollar loan and an old friendship. Say, thank you for finding Howie O'Rourke. That was neat and quick."

"He's the kind who never stays out of prison long. Very bright guy. Don't ask me how he can be so stupid."

Dave said, "And a third man, linked to the first—bumped off the road and nearly killed."

125

"Half wilderness up there," Salazar said, "more than half. A lot of roads not even on the map. It'll be different when the board of supervisors stops squabbling about who pocketed the most payoffs from the land developers and they get their ass in gear and wangle the coastal commission into issuing waivers and permits and the rest of that shit. Civilization up there in no time. Streetlights, sewers. Wish I owned a piece of it, about ten acres. I'd turn in my badge so fast."

"They're distinctive cars," Dave said, "both of them. Easy to spot. But not by just one man alone."

"Look," Salazar said, "why wasn't it like the CHP said— slippery road, bad turn? An accident. You didn't know the car, didn't see the driver."

"It was no accident," Dave said. "It was on purpose. I know. I was there. Don't tell me it was an accident."

"All right, all right." Salazar cringed in the chair, hands up, hamming fear. "It was on purpose." He sobered. "Let me tell you about the latest wrinkle, okay? Kids with nothing to do, dropping chunks of cement on cars off freeway bridges? Driving around at night shooting down strangers on the streets? Pouring gasoline over sleeping skid-row bums and setting them on fire? For laughs, Dave, for the hell of it. We see it all the time, now. Used to be, they'd settle for showing their bare ass out the window of a car, or throwing eggs. No more. They see what happened to you on TV all the time—a guy bumps another guy off the road, and the car rolls down the slope and bursts into flame. It's a movie, right? They don't know the difference."

"Charming," Dave said. "But I don't believe in coincidences. Why wasn't it Gaillard?"

"He'd seen you, remember?" Salazar said. "He knew

126

you were the nice insurance man, maybe with a check in your pocket that would get him back those life savings of his that Howie blew on the horses."

"It was too dark for him to see my face," Dave said. "And he didn't know my car. He was protecting Westover, covering his rear."

"Only you don't know from what," Salazar said.

"Find him and ask him," Dave said. "What do I have to do—get killed before you move?"

"The department might buy that." Salazar sighed, slapped his knees, got to his feet. His topcoat lay over the foot of the bed. He picked it up. "But I wouldn't count on it." He gave a regretful smile. "Get well, all right?" He flapped into the coat and pulled open the door to the hallway. "Keep out of trouble," he said, and left.

Cheeks rosy from the cold, Max Romano waddled in. He held an attaché case flat out in front of him. Fat, beringed finger to his lips, acting conspiratorial and scared, he laid the case on Dave's bed and snapped the catches and opened the lid. The lining of the case was aluminum foil. Out of the case rose steam and wonderful smells. "Lasagna," Max whispered. "I made it myself, the way you always liked it back in the old days." He meant when the restaurant was in West L.A., with stained-glass windows and big, steel-doored pizza ovens in view of the tables, and the menu was simpler, like the rest of life.

"Sweet sausage?" Dave said.

"I didn't forget." From his bulky overcoat Max produced forks, napkins, a bottle of wine, even wineglasses. Plates came from under the lasagna. Max chuckled, setting the swivel table.

Amanda peered in, wide-eyed. She had on a Hans Brinker cap and jacket and kneepants, and a bulky muffler so long it nearly dragged on the floor. "Ready?" she whispered, took a last glance up and down the hallway, and slipped into the room. "Doesn't it smell lovely?"

Max had time for only a token forkful of lasagna—it made him hum, roll his eyes, and show his dimples—then was on his way back to the restaurant. But Amanda stayed to help Dave polish off the food. It was rich, and he hoped it wouldn't make him sick, but it tasted too good for him to worry about that. The wine made him pleasantly drunk. The room was softly lamplit. Cecil had left a big, battery-powered, so-called portable radio that sat on the floor in a corner and played quietly. Piano music. Schubert? When the last morsel of food was gone and the wine bottle was empty, Amanda laid bottle and plates, forks and napkins and glasses in the attaché case, and snapped the case shut.

"I'm going to rattle on my way out," she said.

"Don't hurry off," he said.

She looked at her watch. "I've got a date—sorry."

"Give me a cigarette," he said. "Sit down, and listen to me. It's important."

She frowned, but she got him a cigarette from a pocket of her Rodeo Drive boutique Dutchboy jacket. She lit the cigarette for him, handed it to him. "You always have cigarettes," she said. "Are you trying to quit?"

"Not here, I don't have them. Maybe Cecil is trying to get me to quit. I ask him to bring me cigarettes. He brings me everything else I ask for. Not cigarettes. Please. Sit down. I'm not going to like this, you're not going to like it, but I'll make it quick."

"Won't like what?" She sat on the edge of the chair. "You know I hate being late."

"Who's the date with?" Dave said. "Miles, right?"

"Yes, of course." She was impatient. "Dave, what is this?"

"It's unpleasant news about Miles," Dave said, and told her. She tried to interrupt, but he talked through her interruptions. He finished, "If you'd like to see the pictures, they're in the top drawer of my desk. Help yourself. In fact, I think it would be nice if you were the one to hand them back to him."

"Oh, stop." She stood up. "There are no pictures, and you know it. You made them up, like you made up the rest of it. What in the world is the matter with you? Did you think I don't know Miles? Did you think I'd believe just any wild lies you told me about him? Why?" She gasped a little, shocked laugh. "Good God! You're jealous, aren't you? That's what it is. Jealousy. You want me all to yourself, don't you? Or is it him you want?"

"You don't want to be saying these things," Dave said. "I'm sorry I upset you. It was clumsy, but I couldn't figure out a kinder way to handle it."

She was rigid, trembling with anger. "I've heard about malicious old aunties," she said, "but I never thought you could be like that. Not you, Dave, not you." And she burst into tears and ran from the room. She forgot the attaché case of dirty dishes. He sat waiting a few minutes for her to come back and get it. She didn't come back.

11

She was right. There were no pictures. Not anymore. Edwards had come back and taken the envelope away. Dave shut the desk drawer. He felt bad about it, but not beaten. She had good sense. When she got over her hurt, she would begin to use her brains. And they were better brains than Edwards possessed. He smiled. To smile was easier here, at home again in Horseshoe Canyon, clothed, walking around. The doctor had asked him not to leave the hospital, but he had left anyway, limping, arm in a sling, rib cage tightly bandaged, bruises colorful and tender, cuts and scrapes not yet healed. Pills of several kinds stood in little amber plastic containers on a bathroom shelf. What he needed two hands for, Cecil could help with—Cecil napping right now up in the loft. Dave sat down, picked up the phone, and punched Lovejoy's number at Banner Insurance.

"You came highly recommended," Lovejoy said, "but we didn't have in mind for you to get into it so sincerely as to get yourself killed." Dave could picture him, a sleek, well-

130

fed black, with an easy chuckle and sad, solemn eyes. "I was by to see you, but you weren't conscious."

"Thank you for the flowers," Dave said.

"We'll cover your medical bills, the hospital."

"I appreciate that," Dave said. "Do something else for me, will you?"

"Any way I can help," Lovejoy said.

"Write Westover a letter, please. Make it read as if Banner is all cocked to pay. Say your claims investigator just needs the answers to a few simple, routine questions, so he can authorize payment of the claim. We'll have set up a meeting so he can sign the forms. Include my phone number and address, and spell my name right."

"He tried to kill you," Lovejoy objected.

"He won't, when he knows what I want," Dave said. "I should have thought of the letter as soon as I found out he was picking up his mail. I wasted time."

"You really think he'll come out to meet you? After what happened?"

"He doesn't drive all the way down out of that canyon to his mailbox every night to collect valentines. He wants that money. Don't ask me why. It's only a fraction of what he needs. But he wants it. Desperately."

"We could pay it," Lovejoy said doubtfully. "We always could have. Fifty-fifty chance the girl is dead, I suppose. I just hate not knowing, is all."

Dave told him about his talk with Lucky at Perez.

"Is a month in the ground enough for a body to rot that badly?" Lovejoy said. "In the desert?"

"Not in summer," Dave said. "But it's been winter. The wild flowers are out up there. Never seen so many. Which means there has to have been a lot of rain. Which means a month may have been enough."

"I'm not going to like paying a man that tried to waste my investigator," Lovejoy said.

"He didn't know who I was," Dave said. "Anyway, you're not writing a check. You're only writing a letter. This isn't over yet. Far from it."

"I'll write the letter," Lovejoy said. "No need for you to go following him again."

"I'm not planning on it," Dave said.

He sat on a couch in the front building and ate wheat crackers that he spread with a French herb cheese, soft, white, specked with green. He washed the crackers and cheese down with bouillon from a mug. Lunch had been late. One-armed, he'd been slow in getting it ready. And proud of maneuvering it without Cecil's help. It was fancy, a kind of chicken parmesan. Cecil had liked it. They'd taken their time over it. And afterward, there'd been only just enough time for Cecil to shower and get to work. So Dave wasn't all that hungry now. The expensive stereo equipment Amanda had installed up here played the new Paris Opera recording of *Lulu* with Teresa Stratas. Berg's music made all other music sound anemic. But he disliked the way recordings hurried operas past him. He missed the intermissions. He got off the couch to turn the record over and winced. He ought to have brought the pain-killers with him. He didn't feel like hiking for them to the rear building. Maybe he ought to go back there and get into bed. It was early, but he felt bad, he ached. He stood where he was, unable to make up his mind. Out beyond the shiny black french windows, crickets sang—the pulse slow be-

132

cause of the cold. He switched off the stereo and, moving gingerly, made himself a drink. He returned to the couch with it and, clumsily, one-handed, wrapped up what was left of the cheese in its soft foil. He set the empty bouillon mug on the plate with the knife and the cheese. But he couldn't carry them and the drink too to the cookshack. He twitched a smile. Bad luck. He'd just have to finish the drink here and, when he got to the back building, make another to take up to bed with him. He lit a cigarette and sipped the Scotch, and the telephone rang. He could let the machine answer it. He didn't. He forced himself up and limped to the phone.

"You're looking for Charles Westover," a voice said.

"Where is he?" Dave said.

"It'll cost you." A man's voice. Oddly muffled. Dave didn't recognize it. He said, "How much?"

"Five hundred bucks," the voice said. "Cash."

"Is this Howie O'Rourke?" Dave said. "I thought you were in jail."

There was a pause. "A dude I know went bail for me. That's why I need the five hundred. To pay him back."

"I doubt that," Dave said.

"You want Westover or not?" Another pause. Dave didn't fill it. O'Rourke went on, "Bring the money to the Santa Monica pier. I'll meet you there in an hour."

"Come here," Dave said. "I haven't got a car."

"Find one," O'Rourke said.

"A hundred when we meet," Dave said. "The rest when I've found Westover."

"I need it all up front," O'Rourke said. "You can trust me. Come on, man. I have to have the five."

"Good-bye," Dave said.

133

"No, wait!" O'Rourke yelped. "You've got a deal."

"It's suppertime," Dave said. "There'll be a lot of people on that pier. For the restaurants. How do I find you?"

"Just walk around out there," O'Rourke said. "I'll find you." The receiver hummed in Dave's ear. He laid it in its cradle. Why had Salazar told O'Rourke about Westover's disappearance? Why had Salazar mentioned Dave to O'Rourke? He sat on the couch, picked up the receiver again, and punched Salazar's number.

"I want to go home," Salazar said. "I'm already late."

"Howie O'Rourke just phoned me," Dave said. "He's out on bail. How does he know I'm looking for Westover?"

"He didn't hear it from me," Salazar said. "But it wasn't O'Rourke you were talking to. A man doesn't get out on bail when he's in for breaking parole."

Dave recited the conversation.

"You made a mistake," Salazar said, "giving him a name to use, saying you thought he was in jail. Whole scenario."

"What a shame," Dave said. "First mistake I ever made. But it's interesting, no? Hell of a lot more interesting than if it had been old Howie himself. He isn't truthful."

"My dinner will be interesting," Salazar said, "if I don't have to listen to my wife bitch about how late I was getting home for it."

"I'm stuck up here with no car," Dave said. "Drive me to the pier? You can arrest the man for attempted extortion and impersonating a criminal. Afterward, I'll buy you a big juicy lobster and all the booze you can drink."

"You want the Santa Monica police," Salazar said.

"I don't know anyone on the Santa Monica police. I've only got an hour. It would take that long to explain to a stranger what it's all about. Anyway, Westover's officially a missing person. His son reported it. Westover disappeared from your jurisdiction. Now's your chance to find him."

"Shit." Salazar sighed. "Okay. Where do you live?"

He peered through a grimy window in the hangar-size room where the merry-go-round used to turn, all gilt and crimson, aglitter with mosaics of mirror, the staunch and gaudy horses rising and falling on their tall brass poles in ceaseless dream. Worklights glared tonight where for years there had been only darkness. The horses lay along one side of the room, their paint and gesso stripped, their white carved wood shining softly, like the pieces of unfinished furniture in Don Gaillard's shop. Under the worklights, reaching from ladders, men painted the carousel itself. Someone was restoring it. It was going to turn and glitter again. From its bowels the orgatron would shout and wheeze and bang its drums and cymbals into the popcorn night once more. He was pleased. He had good memories of this merry-go-round. Old, very old, but still good.

He turned away and checked his watch. The man who claimed to be Howie O'Rourke was forty minutes late. Dave glanced back toward where the pier raked up to meet the palisades. Salazar leaned against a lamppost, smoking one of his little brown cigarettes. Dave wanted to go to him, find the car with him, be driven home. He wasn't in pain. He had swallowed pills to keep the pain back. But he was tired. He had walked twice to the end of the pier, along the thick, splintery planks, through pools of yellow light cast by spaced lamps along the pier, to where winches rusted now that used to raise and lower boats before the building of the marina, but where people still fished at night, elbows on chalky wooden railings, eyes on the black water below that lisped around barnacled pilings and gave back wavery reflections of the lamplight. He had been out there twice and back here to the merry-go-round barn. He was fed up. But he didn't want to leave too soon. He would give it another few minutes.

"What happened to your arm?" Lyle Westover said. He was neat, new suit, shiny shoes. A girl almost as frail as he was with him. She stood back a pace and looked shy. Her hair was honey-color. She didn't wear makeup, didn't need it. She was pretty. Poor Trio! "Are you alone? We're going to eat over there. Will you join us?"

"Thanks, but I'm working. Look, don't take anything out of your mailbox addressed to your father, all right?"

"Shall I watch for him, talk to him?"

Dave shook his head. "That would be dangerous."

"I do care about him, you know. Just because I flew off to Nashville, just because I'm going out to dinner—"

"Stop punishing yourself," Dave said. "Who's your friend? What does she play?"

Her name was Jennifer, and she played the cello.

"Dangerous?" Lyle said. "How did you hurt your arm?"

Dave told him. The boy looked ready to weep. He said, "He must be crazy. This isn't him, Mr. Brandstetter. This is not the way he is. Not the way he used to be."

Dave said, "Do you know a young woman, blond, bony, connected with your father? Someone who worked for him, maybe? A secretary?"

"Miss Halvorson was his secretary, but she was sixty. When he closed his offices, she went back to Iowa. That's where her mother lives. Her mother is ninety. I'm sorry about your arm."

"Occupational hazard," Dave said. "Don Gaillard has disappeared too. I think they may be together—up there in Yucca Canyon."

"I left the address book for you," Lyle said.

"There are no Yucca Canyon numbers in it," Dave said. Salazar came up. Dave told him, "This is Lyle Westover. John Salazar, sheriff's office."

Lyle held out his hand and Salazar took it and hung onto it. "Are you the one who phoned?"

Lyle blinked. He said he hadn't phoned anyone. Who did Mr. Salazar mean? But his speech was thick, and Salazar didn't understand. That was clear from the dazed look he threw Dave. He let go Lyle's hand.

"I guess you weren't the one who phoned," he said.

"Good to see you," Dave said. "Have a nice supper."

Lyle mumbled and awkwardly shook Dave's hand. The girl managed a timid little smile. They went off together. Lyle walked like a badly strung marionette. He and the girl entered a shacky, gray board restaurant, where the prices were anything but shacky. Lyle hadn't wanted credit for Nashville, but apparently he'd taken the cash.

"You hustled them off fast," Salazar said. "Did I hurt his feelings? I didn't mean to. I was shocked. What's wrong with his mouth?"

"No one seems to know," Dave said. "It wasn't that. I was afraid one of you might mention O'Rourke. And when that child finds out what happened to the money his father borrowed from Gaillard, he's not going to take it well."

"Where's our man?" Salazar frowned up and down the

137

pier. "You sure there was a man?" He looked closely into Dave's eyes. "What kind of pills are you taking?"

"There was a man, all right." Dave moved off toward the shaky wooden staircase that led by crooked stages down to the parking lot below the pier. "But he never meant to meet me. Not here, not anywhere. He didn't want money. He wanted me out of my house, didn't he? Which means I'd better get back there and find out why."

"You have a blanket or something?" Salazar's suit was thin. He stood in front of the fire he had built in the grate in the back building, but it was still cold in the high, hollow, pine-walled room. Dave sat at his desk, disgustedly sorting through receipts. These had piled up from the remodeling—carpenter's bills, bills from electricians, suppliers of lumber, plaster, conduit, pipe, brick and mortar, shingles, glass, fabric, carpet. Dozens of them. He smiled. Grimly. Here were the ones he needed. Best Audio. Tape deck, cassette deck, turntable, amplifier, receiver. White's. Television sets, video recorder. Bay Office Supply. Typewriter, copying machine, telephone answerer, calculator.

"Take a blanket off the bed, up there," Dave said. "Then if you want to, you can write down these serial numbers for me." Wilshire Camera. Leica, Bausch & Lomb. He kept the receipts for the stolen stuff out, and pushed the rest, flimsy pink, yellow, blue carbon copies, back in the drawer, and shut the drawer. "But they won't turn up, will they? Exercise in futility."

Salazar came to the desk wrapped in a blanket, and made drama out of trying to keep the blanket around him while he dug out a notebook and pencil. Maybe it wasn't acting. He shivered and his nose had started to run. He hooked a foot around a chair leg and moved the chair to the desk and sat down on it. In the band of light from the desk lamp his fingers toiled, copying the numbers off the receipts.

"What you need is booze."

"What I'm going to get"—Salazar jerked his head, sniffing noisily—"is double pneumonia. This son of a bitch must have known you had all this expensive junk. Who could it be? You just remodeled. Somebody who worked here fixing the place up?"

Dave came back from the bar with brandy for Salazar and for himself. "Drink that. If it doesn't make you well, it will make you forget you're sick." He sat down again. The pain-killers were wearing off and he really did want to crawl into bed now. "Maybe you're right. But there were a lot of them, and I didn't stand around admiring what they did as they did it." He pulled the rumpled receipts out of the drawer again. "Here are all the contractors, if you want to check out the personnel."

"Gee, thanks." Salazar closed the notebook. "Okay. That gets the serial numbers of everything stolen." He drank deeply from the brandy. "Hey. You may be right about this." He closed a hand over the receipts and stuffed them into an inside jacket pocket. Blanket huddled around him, he went back to the fireplace and slowly turned in front of it, toasting himself. "Get a lot of robberies up here—housebreakings?"

"I don't know the neighbors well enough to ask," Dave said. The telephone rang. He picked it up. "Brandstetter."

"Is that you this time?" Dave didn't know the voice, not

at first. "Because I don't talk to machines. The stupid country is going to hell. No people anymore, just machines."

"You're at the filling station in Yucca Canyon," Dave said. "What's happened? The Rolls come in again?"

"Not the Rolls," the filling-station boy said, "the girl, the skinny one with the cheap blond hair. Only this time she's driving an old Impala. Right-front fender smashed. The headlight's out."

"Beautiful," Dave said. "Did you get the license number?"

"I thought you'd like that," the boy said. He gave the number. Dave said, "Just a second." And, to Salazar, "You want to write this down for me, please?" He repeated the number. Salazar wrote, the blanket slithering to his feet. The boy said, "Nevada."

"Is that so?" Dave said. And to Salazar, "Nevada."

The boy said, "You see, I didn't lose your card. I tacked it up like you said. This any help?"

"A great help," Dave said. "Thank you very much. Have you seen, by any chance, a gray panel truck, yellow lettering, name Gaillard, 'Fine Furniture' or something like that on the side?"

"Just the Impala. Green and white. Nineteen fifty-eight. The damage was new."

"If you call that damage," Dave said, "you should see the other car."

"What happened? What other car?"

"Mine," Dave said. "Up your canyon, a few nights ago, very late, in the rain, that Impala ran me off the road. I got out, but my TR is ashes."

"Jesus," the boy said. "Was it her driving?"

"I don't think so. But don't cross her, all right?"

"Shit," the boy said. "No way."

He had to be careful not to forget and roll onto his sore shoulder, and being careful of that kept him awake. He piled up pillows and read, and kept falling asleep reading. Finally he switched off the lamp. He woke startled in the dark. The diode-lighted red numerals of the clock said one-colon-two-oh. He turned cautiously to switch the lamp on again and felt something snap under his hip. The light showed him his glasses, one of the lenses popped out. Getting it back into the frame with one hand would be a neat trick. Cecil would do it. He was due. Dave frowned. Overdue. That was what had wakened him. He lit a cigarette and lay propped up in the heavy turtleneck sweater, waiting for the sound of the van jouncing into the bricked yard of the front building. Instead the sound was of the telephone. It was beginning to bore him, the telephone was. But he stubbed out the cigarette and picked up the receiver.

"You are not going to believe this," Cecil said. His voice shook. "I don't hardly believe it myself. But I am under arrest. I am at the central police division. And they are subjecting me to indignities."

Dave sat up fast and swung his feet to the floor. The boards were cold. "What in God's name for?"

"Theft. It seems I crept in and removed from your house your stereo, your TV, typewriter, camera—I don't know what-all. What I do know is that it was all of it right there in the back of my van in the parking lot outside channel three."

141

"I was wondering where it had gone," Dave said.

"I didn't take it," Cecil said. "I hope to Jesus you know I didn't take it."

"I know that," Dave said. He had made a bad miscalculation. He ought to have told Cecil about Miles Edwards—the photographs, the encounter in this bed, the unhappy confrontation with Amanda. "Was Miles Edwards around there tonight? The television studio?"

"He was here. Talked to me for a while at my desk. We had a cup of coffee. Why?"

"That would have been early, right?"

"Six, six-thirty. Who cares? Man, I am in *trouble.*"

"Take it easy," Dave said. "It won't last. They can't hold you if I don't press charges. I can't come, but I'll send my lawyer. He'll have you out in no time."

"How did that shit get in my truck?" Cecil said. "Who told them it was there?"

"Edwards," Dave said. "Was he around there later?"

"Later I was out in a channel-three car. That's how they think I'm guilty. Nobody at the station saw me from seven till ten. Got a call to talk to a man about a story I've been working up. On street gangs."

"Only you couldn't find the man," Dave said.

"You got it. But it sounded so good, I hung around. Then when he didn't show, I went looking for him, places I knew he went. I wasted three hours. Never did find him."

"Had you told Edwards about this street-gang story?" Dave said. "Over your friendly cup of coffee?"

"How did you know?" That was spoken to Dave. His next remark was to someone else. "Keep away from me, man."

"Down there at the glass house," Dave said, "were your keys in your pockets when they told you to empty them?"

"Told me to unlock the van first. Yeah, I had my keys."

"Then Edwards did come back and returned the keys to your jacket pocket, which he'd lifted them from earlier."

"You mean he drove my van up to Horseshoe Canyon and loaded it up with your stuff while I was out chasing around after nobody?"

"He's clever with the telephone," Dave said. "He got me out of here in exactly the same way. Listen, we're wasting time. Let me phone Abe. He'll have you out of there in an hour. Meantime, try not to hit anybody, all right?"

"An hour! I said get away from me, man. This call is my *right*. Leave me *alone!* Can't he make it fifteen minutes? I will never get the stink of this place off me."

"I'll tell him to hurry," Dave said. "And I want you to know how sorry I am. I was the cause of this, and I'm not going to get over it."

"Why would Edwards—?" But something happened to the connection. Dave thumbed the break button on his own instrument and then punched Abe Greenglass's home number.

12

Amanda said, "What in the world is this?" She stood at the door to the rear building blinking in the light that came out. She wore corduroy jeans and two layers of sweaters and a stocking cap. She wore fleece-lined boots. "I thought you'd had a stroke or something."

"Come in." Dave backed into the room and shut the door when she was inside. "I only said it was an emergency. It's an emergency. What do you want, coffee or a drink?"

"I want an explanation," she said. "Dave, it is three o'clock in the morning."

"I know what time it is." Dave went down the room under the high rafter shadows to the bar. He poured whiskey for them both. "Sit down," he called. "I don't know how soon this will be over. You might as well sit." She unwound her muffler and sat on the couch facing the fire. Building the fire, he had hurt the shoulder. The pain had been sharp and he had fainted for a minute. He felt all right now—angry but all right. He handed her a glass and went back for his own. "We are going to keep a vigil, you and I. For Cecil. I want you to be here when he is delivered out of the hands of his enemies."

"What are you talking about?" She was angry too.

Dave told her. Again without permitting her to interrupt, though she tried. He finished like this: "You told Miles what I'd said to you, about the pictures, about his trying to get into bed with me, didn't you?"

"That's how it is between us," she said sharply. "We don't keep secrets from each other. Of course, I told him. It was so ridiculous. So is this. Even more so. What do you know about Cecil?"

"More than you know about Miles," Dave said.

"What?" She laughed. There was no humor in the laugh.

"Did he show you the photographs?"

"How could he? They don't exist."

"Ask Avram, the waiter at Max's," Dave said. "He'll tell you they exist. Miles wasn't with you tonight, was he? So how do you know where he was, what he was up to?"

"I don't, but I'll believe him when he tells me."

"He warned me not to tell you about our little encounter up there"—Dave jerked his head to indicate the loft—"but he didn't say what he'd do if I told you. I might have guessed he'd do something meanspirited. He's reckless, Amanda. Doesn't give a damn for anybody."

"He got Cecil a wonderful job," she cried. "And look how Cecil has repaid that kindness."

"He got Cecil that job to get Cecil out of the way here, so he could take Cecil's place in my bed. Not my affections. He doesn't know anything about affections, he thinks affections are contemptible. Don't marry him, Amanda."

She hurled her glass into the fire. She stood up. "I will marry. Whom. I. Please." Her voice was tight with rage. She turned and marched toward the door. It opened before she reached it. Cecil stood there in his corduroy car coat, looking stunned. "You—!" Amanda shrilled at him, "you—!" And she pushed him. Hard. In the chest. He was a head taller, but she caught him by surprise. He sat down on the bricks. Abe Greenglass was a few paces behind him. Amanda in the dark bumped hard against him, spinning him around, sending his attaché case flying. He was a small, thin man. Amanda stalked away across the courtyard. The black shadow of the old oak swallowed her up.

"Shee-it." Cecil got to his feet, brushing his narrow little butt with his hands. He looked at Dave, big-eyed, aggrieved. " 'Welcome home, baby, I love you.' What's the matter with her?"

"Edwards," Dave said. "Edwards is what is the matter with us all." He went to Cecil, hugged him with his good arm, put a kiss on his mouth. "Welcome home, baby, I love you."

Abe Greenglass picked up his case, and gently cleared his throat. "You want to go after this Edwards character?" His voice was like a whisper of dry leaves.

"Come in, Abe. And thank you. Very much." The lawyer came in. Dave took his homburg and hung it on one of the big brass hooks. He helped him out of his black overcoat with the astrakhan collar, and hung that up too. "We all need a drink." He limped down the room to the bar. His shoulder yelled with pain. His hip felt as if it were grinding in its socket. "Take a seat in front of the fire, there. Get warm."

"I have to be in court early," Greenglass said, but he sat,

leaned toward the blaze, rubbed his fine-boned hands. "What do you want me to do about Edwards?"

"He's vicious, but he's not stupid." In the shadows beneath the loft overhang, Dave fumbled one-handed with whiskey, ice, glasses. "His fingerprints won't be on the evidence, they won't be in the van. He'll have witnesses to account for his whereabouts. He disguised his voice on the phone and I didn't record it, so there's no hope of a voice print. Going after him would be a waste of your time."

"What about the waste of my time," Cecil said, "in that stinking jail?" His voice shook. He headed for the bathroom, yanking out of his coat, slamming it down on the bottom steps. The bathroom light glared. Water splashed. He gargled angrily, spat angrily, angrily blew his nose. "Never get rid of the stink." He stood in the bright doorway, scrubbing his mouth on a towel. "Redneck fools. If I stole stuff, would I steal it from where I live? Would I go to work with it in my car?" He flung the towel away, snapped off the bathroom light, went to Dave. "Here, let me do that." But the drinks were ready. He picked up two of the glasses and went with them to the couch, the fire, Greenglass. "That man wrecked me. Held me up to public ridicule." He handed the lawyer a glass. "Those people I been working with. You think they were going to let this thing go past? They were out there with cameras and microphones so fast. Right on their doorstep, right in their parking lot? No way do I escape getting on the news in the morning."

"I'll stop it," Greenglass said. "What's the channel?"

"Three," Cecil said. "I'll never get a job in television again."

Dave came into the firelight and dropped onto the

couch. "You didn't want a job in television," he said. "Edwards wanted it for you."

"All right, but I didn't want it to end this way."

"Don't worry," Greenglass said gently. "I'll put a lid on it."

"Put a lid on Edwards too," Cecil said. "Put him in the garbage can and put a lid on him. He's a lawyer. He can't do things like this and still be a lawyer, can he? Stealing, framing somebody? Don't lawyers get disbarred for that?"

"Not if it can't be proved," Dave said.

Cecil stood between him and the fire. He stared. "Aren't you even going to try to prove it? You mean he's too smart for you? You never lose. How come you're willing to lose when it comes to this? After what he did to me?"

"I haven't lost." Dave looked up at him. "I've won. We've won. He wanted to separate us. He used the television job to set that in motion. And it worked, didn't it?" He waited. Grudgingly, Cecil mumbled that he guessed it had worked. Dave said, "And then he moved in to try to take your place." He explained how Edwards had done that.

Cecil squinted. "What! Why didn't you tell me?"

"It didn't mean anything. I didn't want you upset."

"Better upset than arrested," Cecil wailed.

"Right. I know that now. Doesn't help, does it? I'm sorry, and if you can't forgive me, I won't blame you. And Edwards will have won, after all."

"Ah, shit." Cecil sat down on the raised hearth. He glowered into his drink. "You couldn't know what he'd do. Wasn't me he wanted to hurt, anyway—it was you."

"I should have been gentler, rejecting him. Maybe it never happened to him before. Unhappily, what he assumed I was willing to do to you and Amanda for the pleasure of his naked company made me lose my temper."

"It wasn't that," Cecil said. "You told Amanda, didn't you? After he warned you not to."

"She was going to marry him," Dave said.

"And she still is, isn't she?" Cecil's smile was grim. "You had her here tonight to show her what an alligator he is, and it didn't work, did it?"

"Nothing seems to be working," Dave said bleakly.

"Speaking of working," Abe Greenglass said, "I want to get the name of channel three's attorney. We should talk right away." He set his glass on the couch arm and went for his coat and hat. "They won't want to show that film when they understand it was all a mistake."

Dave raised his eyebrows at Cecil. "All right?"

"Thank you, Mr. Greenglass." Cecil sighed and got up from the hearth. "But you sure there isn't some way for Edwards to be down in that jail like I was? Just for a few hours? Just to have to breathe that smell? Just to have them treat him like he was nothing, something to step on and smear into the cement?"

"I'll give it serious thought," Greenglass said. He was a ceremonious man. He shook their hands. He waited until he was outside in the cold night and the dark to put on his hat.

They slept the day away. For Cecil it wasn't easy. He kept moaning, waking, shifting position in the wide bed beside Dave. He twitched, kicked, talked. The talk sounded angry though the words were never clear. For a while, he lay sprawled on his back, and when he did that he snored. When the snores got loud enough, they woke him, and he mumbled and shifted position again. About dawn, he

149

shouted and struck out. His flung fist caught Dave in the ribs and reminded him that they were still tender. Dave shook Cecil, woke him, and Cecil clung to him and wept. But when daylight came, exhaustion finally took the boy and, lying on his face, limp as the dead, he slept. Which allowed Dave to sleep.

Dave crept from the bed at two-thirty, showered awkwardly, clutching the hurt arm against himself, trying not to move it, which was tricky without the sling. He got into fresh clothes, which was even trickier. He went to the cookshack and set slowly and carefully about fixing a casserole. When it was in the oven, he poured a mug of coffee and started with it for the back building, meaning to waken Cecil gently, give him a space of time before eating. He was stopped, crossing the bricks under the arbor where the tips of new green leaves were showing on the dry, brown vine, stopped by a loud, painful scrape of metal out on the road. He set the mug on the bench under the live-oak and went to see what had made the sound.

It was the Jaguar from the Beverly Hills showroom. In all the excitement—if that was the right word for it—he had forgotten that delivery had been promised for today. From the hospital he'd had his accountant draw a certified check that Cecil had taken to the dealer. A white-haired black in a crisp brown jumpsuit with the dealer's name stitched across its back bent to unfasten from the rear bumper of the car a three-wheeled motorcycle. He dropped the chain into the carrier of the motorcycle, dropped the lid, and saw Dave. His face lit up as if they'd discovered each other in some hostile alien land after a long, forced separation. Dave had never seen him before. He came forward, pulling a fold of papers from a breast pocket.

"Mr. Brandstetter? Good to see you, sir. Brought your car. Beautiful." He held the papers out for Dave to take, who took them. The man in the jumpsuit said, suddenly very serious, "But you going to have to do something about that driveway, otherwise you going to rip her guts out and that would be a shame."

Clumsily Dave flattened the papers against the doors of Cecil's van. "Do I sign these?" The man in the jumpsuit found a pen and marked an X on the top sheet. "Right there, please. Here, let me hold them for you. Shame about your accident. Pretty little car. Sound like you was lucky. Burned up, Mr. Lowe say." He held the papers while Dave signed them. He put the pen away, handed Dave the white copy of the papers, folded the colored copies into his pocket, and the big loving smile was back as he laid the keys to the Jaguar in Dave's hand. "I hope you have better luck with this one." He stroked the Jaguar's sleek brown-gold finish as he passed it. He straddled the motorcycle, kicked the motor softly to life. It was very quiet, as befitted a motorcycle delivering thirty-thousand-dollar automobiles from Beverly Hills. "Anything you want to know about the car is in the manual. It's in the glove com-part-ment." He separated the syllables carefully. "Have any trouble, just call us."

"Thank you," Dave said. "And don't have bad dreams about the driveway. I'll get it fixed right away."

"This is good." Cecil mopped his plate with french bread. "Wonderful. But you could hurt yourself here. You know where the most accidents happen at home? In the kitchen. And you only have one arm."

"You needed your sleep," Dave said, and drank wine.

151

"Sleep like I had," Cecil said grimly, "nobody needs. I'm sorry about that. Kept you awake, didn't I? Acted like a little child can't wipe his own nose."

"My fault," Dave said. "Don't you apologize. I just hope the nightmares go away soon. None of it would have happened if I'd told you what Edwards was doing. I weighed telling you. I didn't because I thought it would spoil the job for you, and you were liking the job, you were proud of it. I didn't want you thinking you didn't deserve the job."

"I wouldn't think that. Doesn't matter why he did it. I was fine on the job." He looked gloomy. "But I'm not going back there. The way those people acted—black, white, brown, all of them. Nobody is anything to them except a newsbeat. Don't bleed in the barnyard, you know? Other chickens will peck you to death."

"Try not to think about it," Dave said.

Cecil took the empty plates to the sink. "I wish you'd think of how to put that bastard in jail."

"Come on," Dave said, and rose. "I've got something to show you that will cheer you up." He left the cookshack and Cecil came trailing after him, frowning, hands shoved deep in pockets, gait slow and moody and without bounce. But he brightened when he saw the Jaguar. He walked around it, wide-eyed, awed. His mouth shaped a voiceless oh.

"Shee-it!" He grinned at Dave, grinned at the car. "Look at *that!* Whoo-ee!" He opened the door with great gentleness and respect. His hands moved over the seats, the dashboard. "Real wood," he whispered, "real leather." He shut his eyes and breathed in deeply, wrinkling his nose. "And doesn't it smell beautiful." He pulled out of the car, faced Dave, eyes begging. "You can't drive. Not with one arm. Can I drive? Can we go for a ride?"

"I thought you'd never ask," Dave said.

They drove a long way up the canyon and around back streets. It was sunset when they reached the upper end of Horseshoe Trail. The engine of the Jaguar made hardly a sound. Its ride was smooth and easy. Remembering the jouncy little Triumph, Dave smiled contentment.

"Don't you go chasing Westover in this car," Cecil said. "Don't care how comfortable a coffin it would make."

"I'm letting him come to me," Dave said, and told Cecil about Lovejoy and the letter.

"He won't come," Cecil said. "But if he does, you make sure I am with you. Up on the loft, hiding, with a gun pointed at his head."

"What gun? You know I won't have guns around."

"Wasn't a gun almost killed you," Cecil said. "It was a car. I nearly pass out every time I think about it."

"It was a 1958 green-and-white Impala," Dave said, and told him about the gas-station boy's call.

"What is going on with Charles Westover?" Cecil said.

Dave said, "Wait a minute. Slow down. Stop."

Horseshoe Trail had no sidewalks, no curbs, only a shallow cement ditch to carry off rainwater. A brown-and-white sheriff's car, a row of red, yellow, white lights across its roof, was empty and still, with one front wheel in the ditch, beside a mailbox and a driveway that meant that back in the trees and brush a house was concealed. The name on the mailbox was Vosper. Cecil halted the Jaguar, and Dave climbed out of it.

"What's going on?" Cecil said.

153

"I forgot to tell Salazar." Dave limped up the driveway, which was carpeted in pine needles. The house, screened by dark deodars and lop-limbed cedars, was sided in raw shingles, like his own house, but was newer and two-storied. Cecil came running up behind Dave. The little shaggy brown dog came yapping toward him from the house. In the doorway of the house stood Hilda Vosper, talking to a young man in a tan sheriff's uniform. The dog hopped at Dave, happy, ears flapping like fur butterfly wings. Dave bent and ruffled the ears. The dog ran in a circle of delight, barking.

"Why, Mr. Brandstetter," Hilda Vosper called. "We were just talking about you. You had a robbery."

The deputy held out his hand. "Hopkins," he said. Dave shook Hopkins's hand. The little dog was facing Hopkins, barking up at him, and kicking its furry hind paws. Hopkins crouched to play with the dog. He looked up at Dave. "You've got a witness here. Always talk to people with dogs. Have to walk a dog. See what's going on in the neighborhood."

"What was going on?" Dave stared at Hilda Vosper. She wore a checked flannel shirt, black-and-white, and warm-looking gray flannel slacks. "What did you see?"

"I didn't realize what I was seeing." She gave a little apologetic laugh. "A young man, tall and slim." She smiled at Cecil. "I thought it was you. It was your van. The doors were open. Television sets, loudspeakers, all that kind of thing, were stacked up in the yard, and he was loading them into the van."

"It wasn't me," Cecil said.

"Yes, I realize that now. But it was after dark. It must have been seven o'clock. I only saw him against the lighted

154

windows of the house. But you don't have a beard and mustache."

"Also, I am not white," Cecil said.

"But it was your van, wasn't it?" she asked anxiously.

"Stolen," Cecil said. "To get me into trouble."

Hopkins got to his feet. "Description mean anything to you?" he asked Cecil.

Cecil opened his mouth to answer but Dave interrupted. He asked Hilda Vosper, "Do you think you could identify the man if you saw him again?"

"I thought it was this young man just moving some things out of the house," she said. "But yes, I believe I could. I think I'd recognize him. Now that I see you," she said to Cecil, "there isn't much resemblance. You're stronger, your shoulders are broader. I remember thinking that he was wearing very beautiful clothes to be doing heavy work in. Of course"—she gave a little embarrassed laugh—"I didn't stare. I just glanced into the yard and passed right on down the trail. Teddy was off the leash, and he'd run after a gopher or a mole or something. I thought he might have dashed down into your yard."

"You take in a lot at a glance," Hopkins said.

"I paint a little," she said. "It teaches you to see."

Hopkins looked at Cecil. "You know who it was, don't you? You know too, Mr. Brandstetter."

Dave let Cecil tell Hopkins who it was. Cecil would get satisfaction from it. Cecil said, "He's a lawyer. His name is Miles Edwards. But you won't find the stuff he stole when you find him. I've got it back."

Hopkins looked puzzled. "What was it—some kind of practical joke?"

"Do you see me laughing?" Cecil said.

155

13

It came on to rain in the night. In the morning, they inched in Cecil's van along shimmering freeways clogged with cars and trucks. Over the glass towers of downtown Los Angeles, the sky was slate-gray. The rain fell softly but with no hint of ever quitting. They spent the day in noisy offices, jostling corridors, elevators, dark lineup rooms, overheated courtrooms, with assorted police officers, clerks, bailiffs, judges. With Abe Greenglass. With Deputy Hopkins and Hilda Vosper for a little while and, for a little while, with a young woman camera operator who had seen Miles Edwards drop something into Cecil's hanging jacket at the television studio. With Miles, unshaven, pale, sullen. And with Miles's father, a sick and shrunken-looking man who moved like an invalid and was acting as Miles's attorney.

The hours dragged. There was more waiting than anything else. Standing around on marble floors tired Dave and made his bruises and torn ligaments ache. Now and then he studied Cecil, waiting for the boy's exhilaration to wear off, waiting for him to get bored with making Miles suffer. But mostly his thoughts strayed. At first to Amanda, and what learning the truth about Miles was going to do to her. Then to the Westover matter, sorting through all the places he'd been, all the people he'd talked to, all the words they'd said to him. Late in the afternoon, when the courts began emptying out and the plaintiffs and defendants and lawyers with briefcases pushed in herds out the tall doors into the rain and the darkening day, he found a pay phone not in use and rang Salazar.

"The Nevada plates are stolen," Salazar said. "They don't belong to any 1958 Impala. They come off a Toyota pickup in a town called Beatty—Amargosa desert."

"Is that a fact?" Dave said. "Listen, thank you for finding a witness to my burglary."

"Any time," Salazar said. "When do I get that lobster?"

"I'm going to spend a couple of days in bed," Dave said. "The doctor was right. I should have stayed in the hospital. I'm not healing as fast as I used to." Of course he'd get out of bed if Westover came from hiding in response to the letter. "I'll call you next week."

"Take it easy," Salazar said.

Cecil was beside Dave when he hung up the phone. He said, "You want to drop the charges now? Forgive and forget?" He looked a little wan.

"Had your fun?" Dave said.

"It wasn't as much fun as I hoped," Cecil said. "Tell the truth, I'm a little sick about it. A little ashamed."

"I thought you would be," Dave said. "Who do we see?"

"Down here," Abe Greenglass said, and led the way.

Dave sat propped by pillows in the bed on the loft. He had doped himself when they got home from dinner at Max's last night, and had slept from eight until noon. Cecil had brought him breakfast in bed—coffee, fresh orange juice,

157

pancakes, and sausage, the plates covered by foil to keep the heat in and the rain off. The rain whispered on the shingles overhead, but the loft was warm, fire crackling in the grate below.

"While you were fixing breakfast," Dave said, "I tried to telephone Jay's Good Used Cars in Perez. Jay doesn't answer his phone. No one answers for him. On a hunch, having viewed Jay's operation, I tried Lucky's Strike. I thought Jay might be drinking his lunch. He wasn't. Lucky gave me Jay's home number. Jay is not at home."

"You want me to drive down and find him?" Cecil rose with his empty plate and took Dave's. "What do I ask him when I find him?" He started for the stairs and turned back. "If he sold a used green-and-white Impala?"

"To Serenity Westover." Dave nodded. "On the day Akriel shot the deputies and ran. Show him her picture. That car is just the kind old Jay specializes in."

Cecil blinked. His jaw was a little slack. "You mean you think the skinny blond girl the gas-station kid told you about is her? She's alive? She's with her father?"

"Watch the commercials," Dave said. "A girl can have hair any color she likes. A girl can lose weight any time she likes. Just pop a little pill."

"Or live under a lot of stress," Cecil said. "Only what about the Nevada license plates? Stolen in Nevada, didn't you say?"

Dave shrugged and was pleasantly surprised: this morning his shoulder hardly hurt at all. "Maybe she was trying to catch up with Azrael, had some reason to know he'd make for Nevada. That's where his van ended up."

"I know that." Cecil made a face. "But why would she want to catch up with him? I sure as hell wouldn't."

"Why would she stay with him for years? She was at that ranch with him while he murdered six girls—remember?"

Cecil blew out a long breath. He gave his head a shake. He went on down the stairs with the plates. Dave heard him dump another chunk of pine log on the fire and set the screen back, heard him walk down the room to the outside door. Cecil called, "This is weird. This has got to be the weirdest mess on record. No wonder you almost got killed." The door opened to the sound of rain and closed.

When he returned, bearing a fresh mug of hot coffee for Dave, he was frowning to himself. He shrugged into the corduroy car coat and fastened the pegs, put on his leather cap and driving gloves. He bent and kissed Dave, tasting of sweet, creamy coffee. He stood looking down at Dave, forehead creased. "What if Westover comes? I don't like leaving you alone, not all battered-up like you are. How can you defend yourself if he turns mean?"

"All he wants is money," Dave said.

"What if his crazy daughter comes with him? Who knows what she wants?"

"She's supposed to be dead, remember? She won't come. That would spoil their plans." He worked up what he hoped was a reassuring smile. "Stop worrying. Nothing's going to happen to me. Don't forget to take her picture. It's in the top left drawer of the desk. And concentrate on your driving, all right? Don't speed trying to get back here."

Cecil looked doubtful, but he went down the stairs again. Before he left, he called, "I'll phone you, soon as I find old Jay. I'm locking the door."

It didn't stay locked. Cecil hadn't been gone ten minutes when Dave heard footsteps cross the brick courtyard and

159

the tinkle of keys. He reached for his pants. The door opened. With the falling of the rain on the bricks for a background, Amanda called, "Dave?" sounding a little timid.

"Ho," he said. "Warm yourself at the fire. I'll be right there. Help yourself to a drink." Getting the trousers on one-handed took time. He went down the stairs. She stood in front of the fire in knickers, boots, a fur hat, and the long, long muffler. She smiled and held out a glass to him with Scotch in it and ice. Her smile was sheepish. "I'd like you to forgive me, if you can."

"For what? Making a mistake?" He took the glass. "Thank you." He drank from the glass. "Don't brood about it. How were you supposed to know what he was? He didn't tell you—right?"

"I mean for the names I called you," she said, "for the awful things I said to you."

"What's important," he said, "is that you're all right. You're going to be all right, aren't you?"

She looked into her glass. She sat on the couch. She looked at the burning logs. "After while," she said. "Not right away." She looked at Dave. "He admitted it all to me, everything you'd said."

"That's nice. We won't have to ask Avram," Dave said. "I think he'd be a little embarrassed, telling you about those pictures."

"Miles thought if he confessed and said he was sorry, we could go right on." She gave a little humorless laugh, a little shake of her head. "I've just come from him. And, do you know, I was tempted. That's why I came flying to you. I know he's rotten, but he is so damned beautiful, Dave."

"He thinks so," Dave said. "You'll get over it."

She took a sip of her drink, rummaged cigarettes from her shoulder bag, held the pack up to Dave. He took a cigarette, she took one. Dave lit them both. She dropped the long red pack back into the bag and frowned up at Dave through smoke. "Women sometimes make a go of it with—with someone like Miles. Someone sexually like Miles."

"Not someone ethically like Miles," Dave said. "Sure, some women do. So I've read. I've never met one. I've met one lately that didn't make a go of it." He stopped talking. "My God," he said, "how stupid I am." He set his drink on the hearth and went for his jacket. "You're going to have to excuse me. I have to see that woman."

"You got the Jaguar," she said.

"Lock up, will you?" he said, and opened the door.

Rain dripped off the jungle gym whose red paint small hands had worn down in places to the dull steel tubing, rain glazed the yellow-and-blue crawl barrels, splashed in the gaudy little cars of the choochoo that never moved, wept off the steel steps of the slide, slithered down the shiny chute of the slide, and made a deep puddle at the foot of the chute. Rain pooled in the canvas-sling seats of the chain-hung swings. The low end of the gingham-print seesaw drowned in a puddle. It looked sad. But the wide windows of the playschool glowed and were pasted with cutout paper daffodils. Dave worked the latch of the gate in the chain link fence and crossed the yard. Halfway to the door, music met him, noise, the rattle of toy drums and tin xylophones and tambourines, the high-pitched piping of small voices. He looked through the streaming glass of the door. They sat in a circle on their little red chairs and played and sang and kept time by clapping their hands and stamping their feet. If he knocked he wouldn't be heard. He turned the cold, wet knob, pushed the door open, and put his head inside. The air was warm, moist, and smelled of little kids, graham crackers, banana peels, toilet accidents. He stepped inside and closed the door. The kids paid him no attention, nor did the massive moon-faced black woman in the gay patchwork smock, but Anna Westover got up swiftly and came to him, looking alarmed.

"Serenity? Have you found her?"

"It's possible. But not to talk to."

"What do you mean? What's happened?"

"Nothing lately," Dave said. "But about ten years ago something happened, and I'd like you to tell me about it."

The kids were too loud for her to hear him. She lifted her hand to indicate that he was to follow her. They skirted the circle of little red chairs, stepping over spilled toys and storybooks and stuffed animals. She opened a door and waited for him to go through, came in after him, shut the door. It was not a big office, and it was crowded with supplies—construction paper, jars of white paste, bottles of poster paint. Shelves sagged. There were boxes of wax crayons, of chalk, of small scissors, cheap paintbrushes. Cartons were stacked hip-deep—modeling clay, newsprint for painting. The desk was barely visible. She lifted an armload of stuff off a molded plastic chair with spindly steel legs for him to sit on. She sat behind the desk. The door was flimsy, the kids still loud, but it was just possible to talk.

162

"Ten years ago," Dave said, "you caught your husband and Don Gaillard involved in a homosexual act—isn't that so?" He didn't wait for her to answer. "They'd had a long friendship, relationship, and it came to an end suddenly then and there. This was why you told me that there wouldn't be another woman in his life, wasn't it? Because you were the only woman he'd ever been physically interested in. Gaillard had been willing to share him with you, but you weren't having that, were you?"

She had turned white. "Where did you hear this?"

"I pieced it together. You began it. Lyle told me how much he'd liked Gaillard when he was small, how close the friendship was between Gaillard and his father, how puzzled he was when it suddenly stopped."

"Close!" Her mouth twisted in derision.

"Then Gaillard added a few facts. And finally, his mother filled out the rest. She said that her son and your husband had spent every weekend of their lives together, even after you and Charles married. Is that true?"

"What has this got to do with poor Serenity? It's ancient history, past and done with. I forgave Charles. He meant too much to me. He meant everything to me. This thing with Don—delayed adolescence, neurotic nonsense." She snorted. "They weren't boys anymore."

"If you set out to find a man who isn't a boy anymore," Dave said, "you're going to be a long time looking. And you haven't forgotten about it. It's not ancient history to you. Don Gaillard's still the enemy. That's why you never mentioned him to me when I asked you to tell me who your husband might run to when he was in trouble."

"They hadn't spoken in years," she said. "That day when

163

I found them naked in bed together was the last time they ever saw each other."

"They had a place they went to on those weekends, didn't they?" Dave stood up. "And you followed them there. Why? You'd watched them go off together a thousand times."

"To the high Sierras, to the desert, to Baja. Ocean fishing in a hire boat. So they said. Then, one weekend when Chass was busy and Don took the kids, he made a mistake. And Serenity told me all about Uncle Don's little house in the woods, about finding so many of her daddy's things there. What things? Oh, clothes and things." Anna West-over smiled thinly. "Out of the mouths of babes? It was fantastic. All those years I hadn't suspected a thing. And suddenly, at that moment, I knew—I knew and understood it all."

"It was up Yucca Canyon, wasn't it?"

She stared. "Yes. How did you know?"

"And you remembered it when I told you your husband had gone somewhere to hide—when I asked you if you couldn't suggest where that would be. But you kept your mouth shut."

"Because I never in the world would have thought he'd go back there. He promised me." She meant it.

"Doesn't divorce invalidate that kind of promise?" Dave said. "What's the address?"

"Address?" She laughed dryly. "It's wilderness up there. The road's no more than a pair of ruts. I don't think it even has a name. Little box canyon, all overgrown."

Dave stepped to the door. "Can you lead me there?"

She pushed at her hair and laughed helplessly. "You

must be mad. It's been ten years. I don't know how I got there. I simply followed them." Her voice trembled, her eyes swam. "I don't know how I got out. I was blind with outrage and hurt and disappointment and emotions there aren't even any names for." She opened a desk drawer and fumbled tissues out of it to dry her eyes. "No, Mr. Brandstetter—I'm afraid I cannot lead you there." She blew her nose. "It's like a place in a nightmare. Something you wake up from, hoping you'll never sleep again."

"Did they rent it?" Dave asked.

"What?" She blinked, frowning. "Rent it? No. No, they didn't rent it. Didn't I tell you? Don built it. It belonged to Don. He built it so they could have—" But she didn't go on with that. "It belonged to Don," she said again, dully. She shrugged. "Perhaps it still does."

Dave pulled open the door. "Bet on it." The chairs weren't in a circle anymore. They had been pushed against the wall. A game was going on that involved running, squealing, and falling down. Dave said to Anna Westover, "I'll let you know," and walked down the long room, trying not to stumble over children.

"You've hurt yourself." Thelma Gaillard was more noticing than Anna Westover had been. She pushed the screen door and put her head out into the rain to look down the stairs. "You drove here with only one arm?"

"It isn't too hard," Dave said. "There's an automatic shift. May I come in?"

"What's happened?" Looking anxious, she pushed the screen door wider so he could enter. The kitchen was not as tidy as before. Now there were more dirty dishes, not

165

just on the shelf by the sink but on the table. She looked as if she hadn't combed her hair today. She was wearing the same faded jeans and torn sneakers and this time a sweat-top with a hood, dark blue. "Have you found Don?"

"No, but with your help I'm going to."

She shut the door, shut out the cold breath of the rain. "I'm not so sure of that. Don withdrew a lot of money from our savings. Almost all. Twenty thousand dollars." She peered up at him. "Did you know that? Was it to give to Chass?"

Dave nodded. "And Chass promptly lost it. If you were thinking Don used it to travel to some far-off place—he didn't. He's at his cabin in Yucca Canyon."

She had started toward the dim hallway that led to the living room. She turned back. "His cabin? What cabin?"

"How did you happen to learn about the missing money?" Dave asked.

"Well, I phoned the police because you said I should. It was a few days, and then a detective came. He asked a lot of questions. I couldn't tell him much." She smiled wanly. "But you already know that. He said I should check through Don's papers—bills, letters, anything, for clues to where he might have gone or why. Well, I looked but I didn't find anything that meant anything. The detective said check with the bank. At first they wouldn't tell me. Then he went with me." She gave a little unhappy laugh. "I never thought I'd ride in a police car in my life. And they let him see the account record and that's how we found out. But it didn't help find him, did it?"

Dave moved toward the hall. "Where are these papers? In his room?" He found the open door to the room with the neatly made bed. "Is this his room?"

"Yes..." She said it doubtfully. She stood in the door from the kitchen, fingers pressed against her mouth, eyes alarmed. "But I've been through everything. He's so private, Don is. He hates for people to—"

"I think he's with Westover," Dave said. "And Westover may be a dangerous man to be with right now." He laid his hand on the arm in the sling. "If it keeps him from getting hurt, he won't mind a little invasion of his privacy." The room had only one window, and the rain outside made the light from the window dim. Dave groped for a wall switch and turned on a lamp by the bed. He stepped inside, hearing her footsteps come down the hall, and stop in the bedroom doorway, unwilling to come farther. Don Gaillard didn't give an impression of being able to intimidate anyone, but he had intimidated her. "Closet?" Dave asked. "Chest?"

She jerked her chin. "Bottom drawer."

It was a green-metal fishing-tackle box. She got the key. Dave sat on the edge of the bed, the box on his knees where the lamplight would catch it. He unlocked it, lifted the lid, reached for his reading glasses, and remembered that the lens had popped out and he'd forgotten to ask Cecil to put it back. He squinted and sorted through the papers. None related to the cabinetmaking business: these were personal, insurance, property payments, doctor bills, income tax. There was a membership in a so-called health club that was for homosexuals only, though the paper didn't say so. There was a worn, soiled envelope of snapshots—big, barrel-chested Gaillard, slim little Westover. He tucked them back, frowning.

"You see what I mean?" Thelma Gaillard said.

Dave grunted. Here was an envelope marked in large

type "Joint Consolidated Tax Bill." The flap was loose. He pulled a tax bill from the envelope. It wasn't easy for him to read without the glasses, but he made out the address on the bill. Blurrily. It was for this place, shop and living quarters. He worked the bill back into its envelope and picked up another envelope like it and slid the bill out of that one. He held it under the lamp and narrowed his eyes, trying to focus. His heart bumped. Burro Trail, Yucca Canyon. He laid the bill in the green tin box, closed the lid, turned the key, held the box up to her. "You never knew Don had a cabin that he built himself for weekends?"

"Is that where he's gone?" she said. "I never knew."

Dave stood up. "May I use your phone again, please?" He had to let the receiver dangle on its cord, knocking the wall, while he turned the dial. He caught hold of the receiver and held it to his ear. Not expecting Cecil to answer—it would be hours before Cecil got back from Perez. Dave's own voice answered on tape. He waited for the tone, checking his watch. "Three-forty P.M.," he said. "The address is 29934 Burro Trail, Yucca Canyon. I'm going there now."

Thelma Gaillard watched him hang the receiver in its fork, her face creased with worry. She wrung her hands. "You'll find him now, won't you? You'll find Don?"

"I'll find him." Dave gave her a quick smile and hurried out the door and down the stairs in the solemn rain. He didn't feel solemn. He felt elated.

14

The canyon was hung with rags of sooty cloud this afternoon. The rain fell steady and cold. Anything able to turn green had turned green—oaks, pines, chaparral. The grass among the rocks was thick and high. The potholes in the twisting roads were wider today, deeper, but the Jaguar didn't let him feel them. It took the bends, elbows, the steep lifts and falls of the roads without effort. Even so, his good arm grew tired, his hand on the wheel ached.

He stopped on a plank bridge above the tumbling muddy stream and studied again the map he'd picked up at a shiny bookstore in Santa Monica. He had to squint to make out the map. Burro Trail was no more than a thin scribble maybe a quarter-inch long. It was far back in from the roads he'd prowled along the other morning. He hadn't come within miles of it. There'd been no chance that he'd sight the Rolls, the panel truck, the old Impala.

He laid the map on the empty seat beside him and sat flexing his stiff fingers and frowning to himself. He had passed and left far behind the crossroads with the filling station, general store, building yard. Should he drive back there and ring Salazar? Being alone when he found Westover didn't worry him. Gaillard didn't worry him. But what about the girl? If she was Serenity, how sane was she, how stable? Maybe, after all, she had been the one who tried to kill him.

He gave his head a shake. This wasn't like him. This case was humdrum—attempted fraud on an insurance company. He'd handled a hundred of those in his time, more than a hundred. The car smash and his aches and pains were getting to him. And his goddamn age. And the gruesome background of this one. He saw those shacky blue buildings again out there in the desert, the sandy holes where the girls had been buried. He shivered, though the heating system of the car worked well. He wasn't even wearing his jacket. He wished he knew what Cecil had learned at Perez. Had the Impala come from Jay's dusty lot of high-gloss jalopies? Ah, the hell with it. He was acting like an old woman. He started the car and rumbled it off the loose planks of the bridge and went to find Burro Trail.

It climbed a box canyon as Anna Westover said, two ruts that the new spring grass was doing its best to make invisible. The rainy daylight was dying fast, helped by tall trees, pines and pin oaks. He peered past the batting of the windshield wipers, hoping Westover had switched a light on that would lead him to the cabin. But there was only gloom. He didn't want to show headlamps. He wanted to arrive with as little warning as possible. In the TR this would have been unthinkable. It was noisy. The Jaguar's engine purred like the big cat it was named for, powerful, no need for bluster.

Was what he saw now, back among the trees, the straight

line of a roof? He slowed the car, inching it along the bumpy ruts, keeping in his sights that horizontal line until he was sure. He stopped the car, switched off the ignition, set the gears. He stretched awkwardly to paw his jacket off the rear seat, and got out of the car. Under the chill sifting of the rain, he worked his good arm into the jacket sleeve and hiked the left side of the jacket up over his shoulder, over the arm in the sling. He crouched to set the handbrake, straightened up, and quietly closed the door. He stood for half a minute, gazing up the trail. Had Lovejoy sent that letter? Had Westover picked it up? He sure as hell hoped so. He drew a long breath, expelled the breath, and began to climb the trail.

Even in the growing dark, it wasn't hard to see the marks cars had made coming down out of the woods and going back up into the woods. He followed the marks, slipping sometimes in the mud. The house was farther than he had judged. He encountered the Impala first, facing him, front fender crumpled, dripping rust in the rain, the headlamp smashed. Beyond the Impala stood the rain-glossed Rolls. And beyond that, half in some kind of ditch, tilted, Gaillard's panel truck. The light was bad, the paint faded, as Thelma Gaillard had said, but he could make out the yellow lettering, as much of it as showed above the dripping brush: "llard" and, below that "fted furniture." He didn't know why it put him in mind of an abandoned hearse.

The cabin looked deserted. It wasn't. Sounds told him that—the slap of a screen door, the drum of heels on a porch. A rifle went off. The slamming noise it made echoed in the rainy hills. A bullet whined past his ear. Someone shouted, "Hold it right there, mister." Dave stepped behind a tree trunk. The voice called, "You're on private property. You're trespassing. Get off."

"Charles Westover?" Dave called. Could it be Westover? It sounded like a boy's voice. The rifle slammed again, the bullet hit the tree trunk, and knocked loose bark that fell on Dave. He brushed it out of his hair. He shouted, "I'm from Banner Insurance." The rifle went off again. But the bullet didn't sing, and it didn't strike anything. He thought it had been fired into the air, and he couldn't make sense of that. He shouted, "We wrote you a letter. About your claim. Did you get the letter?" The gun went off again. The bullet hit the tree high up. A pinecone rattled down through wet branches and hit the ground with a splash. Dave shouted, "I need your signature on some forms. So we can pay you." Why was he saying these things? Why didn't he just turn around and leave? He turned around to leave, but someone was in his way, someone scrawny. The blond girl, in her raveled sweater, dirty jeans, and dark glasses. The rifle fire had been only cover to let her reach him. A big black machine pistol was in her little hand, and she pushed it into his sore ribs and said, "Not this way, that way. We're going in the house."

"What is Westover so afraid of?" Dave said.

"You think about being afraid," she said. "Don't worry about him. Move. Move." She jabbed him with the gun barrel and pushed him. He wished she sounded nervous. She sounded confident, even bored. He walked ahead of her, watching his step on the rough and muddy ground in the dying light. As if his falling or not falling were a matter of importance. He grinned sourly to himself.

"You're Serenity," he said, "aren't you?"

172

"That doesn't mean it's over," she said. "It's only just beginning. Climb the steps."

"Why aren't you with Azrael?" he said.

She laughed and poked the gun hard into his lower back, right against the spine. "Climb," she said.

He climbed. The stairs were well made. Paint had worn off them but the planks were thick and sturdy, meant to last. He thought about Gaillard, hanging onto this place in the frail hope of getting Westover back here some sweet impossible day. Only it hadn't been impossible, had it? It had just been all wrong. At the top of the stairs, Dave lifted his eyes. The rifleman was scrawny too. He held the rifle under his arm, pointed at Dave. The roof overhang made the porch dark, so there was no way to see his features. He looked as blond-haired as Serenity. And his eyes were so pale they seemed to glow.

He backed through the cabin door, keeping the rifle barrel leveled at Dave. The girl pushed Dave ahead of her across the porch and through the door into a room that was pitch-dark. The door closed. A match was struck, and the flame showed Dave a second man, slight, gray-haired, bending above a kerosene lamp on a table of thick, polished planks. The man touched the flame of the match to the wick of the lamp and the wick took fire softly. The man blew out the match and set a slim, smoky glass chimney over the flame. The top part of the man's right ear was missing. He looked at Dave sadly and slumped down on a spooled maple sofa with faded chintz cushions. He looked thoroughly beaten.

"Are you Lovejoy?" he said.

"I work for him," Dave said. "I'm Brandstetter."

"That's good," the rifleman said. "That means we've got a name to contact at the insurance company. That's very good. Where did you leave your car? Is there anyone in it? You came alone?" His pale eyes were crazy and he smiled. It was a wide smile meaning nothing. He had cut off his holy-man hair and beard. But there was no mistaking him.

"You're Azrael," Dave said.

"Azrael died in the desert on the way to Las Vegas," Azrael said. He sat down at the other end of the sofa, the rifle laid carelessly across his knees. But Dave wasn't going to escape. He could feel the girl's breath on the back of his neck. "His soul is in limbo, waiting to be reborn in a far country, to begin a new life."

"You had Serenity follow you to Nevada," Dave said. "You dumped the van out there in that barranca and doubled back here." He looked at Westover. "It wasn't your idea to apply for her insurance. It was theirs. They wanted the money to escape on."

Westover sighed and nodded glumly.

"You didn't leave your house to avoid creditors," Dave said. "These two brought you here." He glanced over his shoulder at Serenity. "You remembered this place. Uncle Don's cabin in the woods. A good place to hide until the insurance company paid up."

"Too many neighbors down there," she said.

"Where is Gaillard?" Dave said.

Westover made a sound and put his hands over his face.

"You want to see Gaillard?" Dave had thought Azrael's smile was wide before. It stretched wider now. He looked straight into Dave's eyes. The effect was like an electric shock, but less pleasant. Dave tensed to keep from shiver-

174

ing. Azrael jumped up off the couch, laid the rifle on the table, scratched a match on its blue cardboard box, and tilted the chimney of a lantern to set its wick afire. He picked up the lantern by its wire-loop handle. "Come with me." He went down the room, making a sound that might have been a chuckle. It resembled the noise hyenas make around a kill. Serenity's gun nudged Dave and he moved after Azrael.

Dave asked Westover, "Why don't you run away?"

Westover's mouth twisted. "Because if I try, he'll kill Serenity. Oh, he will. Oh, yes. And you, too."

"Move," Serenity said. And Dave moved, through a door Azrael had opened and down a short hallway, half-open doors on either hand, and through a kitchen strewn with empty cans and wrappers and stinking of garbage. The lantern swung in Azrael's hand. At a door that led outside, he turned back to give Dave another look from those insane pale eyes and to make the hyena noise again. He was amused. He pushed out a screen door and the lantern stairstepped downward. Here were more of Gaillard's sturdy steps. They ended in a puddle. The rain fell through the swinging nimbus of the lantern up ahead, sparkling. Dave stumbled on clods and rocks. Brush lashed his trousers, soaking them, chilling his legs. Branches slapped his face. He wiped the wet off his face with his hand. The land sloped off. Azrael had moved faster than they. The lantern stood on the ground and Azrael moved in its glow. For a second, Dave couldn't figure out what he was doing. Then he knew. He had a spade, and he was digging. Dave stopped.

"I don't want to see this," he said.

"You said you wanted to," Serenity said. "Anyway, it doesn't matter what you want. All that matters is what he wants. That's all that matters in this world. You'll learn that. You'll be happy when you learn that." She jabbed him with the gun. "Go on. Go on down there."

Dave shut his eyes. Thelma Gaillard was looking up at him, pleading, wringing her hands. *You'll find him now, won't you? You'll find Don?* He opened his eyes and went on down to where Azrael was throwing heavy clods of mud to one side and making the hyena sound. He grinned at Dave.

"You wanted to see Gaillard?"

He threw the spade aside and dropped to his knees and dug with his hands, scrabbled with his hands like some animal after some other animal in a burrow. The glow of the lantern in the falling rain made it stranger even than it was. In Dave's mind, Cecil said, This is weird. Azrael made a new sound. A long-drawn growl of satisfaction. He turned his sharp small-boy face up to Dave, his mad eyes. With animal quickness his hand caught Dave's and yanked Dave to his knees in the mud. Azrael grabbed the lantern and held it low over the hole he had dug. A face looked up at Dave, a face already eaten at by the things that live in the ground, waiting for such faces, but a face Dave knew, the face of Don Gaillard. A terrible smell rose out of the hole. Dave turned away and vomited.

"You wanted to see him," Azrael said. There was no expression in his voice. He got to his feet, set the lantern down, picked up the spade, and began filling up the hole again. "I wanted you to see him. I want you to believe in me." The wet earth slopped into the hole. "I want you to remember my deeds. By their fruits shall ye know them, all right? I always mean what I say. Mortals say"—he was panting a little with the effort it took to move the sodden earth—"I'll kill you. But they don't mean it. When the angel Azrael says I'll kill you he means it."

Behind and above where Dave hung on hands and knees, trying to make his stomach stop convulsing, Serenity laughed. The spade slapped the wet earth. Dave felt splashes of mud from the grave. The spade rattled when Azrael tossed it aside again. Dave felt arms under his arms. He was lifted to his feet. He couldn't look at them in the lantern light. He kept his face averted as they climbed back to the cabin. In the main room, Charles Westover sat slumped on the couch just as they'd left him. He lifted his beaten eyes to Dave.

"They made me eat his heart," he said.

"He wanted to help you," Dave said. "He loved you."

Westover nodded. "I know." But it didn't appear to matter to him anymore. "He drove into the yard. I saw him from that window. Smiling. He looked so happy." Tears were supposed to break in here. Westover waited for them, or seemed to, but they didn't come. He looked bitterly at Azrael. "He shot him. Over and over again. He didn't even have time to get out of his truck." He looked at Dave again. "You were lucky."

"Is that what you call it?" Dave said.

"Perverts," Azrael said. "Perverts."

"I was glad my son was gone," Westover said. "When they came, I felt like thanking God that Lyle was gone. Is he all right? He didn't kill himself, did he? He said he was going to kill himself. It wasn't true, was it?"

"It wasn't true," Dave said. "He's all right."

Azrael said to Dave, "Sit down. You don't look very well. I don't want you to get sick: I've been waiting for you. I have plans for you. If you carry them out, I won't kill you. I won't even kill the pervert, here. If you don't carry them out, I'll kill him." He sat opposite Dave at the table with the lamp on it. "And if you try to bring anybody else here, I'll kill them too."

Dave felt sick about the message he'd left for Cecil.

Azrael got up, went out of the circle of lamplight, came back dragging a wooden box the size of a milk crate. He shoved it with his foot to the edge of the circular braided rug that was under the table. The lamplight fell on it. With a muddy shoe, Azrael lifted the loose lid. "Ammo," he said. "Between us, Serenity and me—we can kill five hundred people before they kill us." His eyes fixed Dave again. "We can, and we will. Remember that."

"What are these plans of yours?" Dave said.

"You are going to telephone Mr. Lovejoy"—the scrawny boy sat down again—"at Banner Insurance Company, and tell him that you are in the hands of the Angel Azrael."

"I didn't see any phone lines leading up here."

"Serenity will drive you down to the crossroads, and you'll use the pay phone in the booth outside the filling station. You won't try to run away or yell for help. You will deliver the message and come straight back to the car and straight back here. Because I'll be timing you. And if you're late, I'll kill Mr. Westover, the same as I killed Mr. Gaillard. I will put him in the same grave, and the two perverts can rot into each other and be one flesh forever and ever, amen."

Westover gave a soft moan from the couch.

"What's the message I give Lovejoy?" Dave said.

"That the Angel Azrael will kill you and bury you in a muddy hole unless Banner Insurance Company pays him one hundred thousand dollars. In cash. New, unmarked bills. At three o'clock tomorrow afternoon. You will pick up the money yourself. From Mr. Lovejoy himself. He will bring it to the beach—Cormorant Cliffs. Nobody ever goes there. He will come alone. After he has put the money in your hands, he will go back where he came from. And you will bring the money here to me. If you don't, if you are even the least little bit late, I will kill Mr. Westover. If you do, if you come back on time, alone, I won't do anything to him. I won't do anything to you."

"And Serenity?" Dave said.

"Serenity will go away with me forever," Azrael said.

Serenity crooned, "In a great silver bird in the sky." Then she said sharply, "Wait." She ran to the front window. Curtains were drawn across it. She stood with her back against the wall and with a finger made a gap between the edge of the curtain and the window frame. There was the slight rattle of venetian blinds. Azrael had the rifle again. He was standing, pointing the rifle at the door. "Someone's out there in the trees," Serenity said.

Azrael glared at Dave. "Who did you tell?" He didn't wait for an answer. He ran to the other front window, stood beside it as Serenity stood beside hers, edged the curtain away, squinted out into the dark and rain. "I don't see anything. Blow out the lamp."

"I heard a car stop in the road," Serenity said. "I saw somebody move in the trees."

Dave stood. He told Westover, "Go into the kitchen."

Westover simply stared at him. He didn't move.

Azrael said, "Shut your mouth." He gestured with the rifle barrel. "Blow out that fucking lamp."

The lamp was all glass. A lot of kerosene was in the well. Dave picked up the lamp. Steps thumped on the porch. Cecil's voice called, "Dave?" Dave yelled at Westover, "Run!" and Westover's eyes opened wide and he jerked alive. He ran for the hall. The venetian blinds clattered. Serenity had got the machine pistol caught in them. "Dave?" Cecil called outside in the rain. Azrael lunged for the door. "Cecil, hit the deck!" Dave shouted. Azrael tore open the door. With a knee, Dave tipped the table on its side. He slammed the burning lamp down hard into the crate of bullets and threw himself behind the tabletop. The light of the kerosene flared up and made the room bright. Azrael's rifle went off. Then the bullets in the crate began to go off. Crazily. In every direction. Serenity screamed. Crouched behind the table, Dave felt the thick wood jar and jump from the force of the bullets. "Ah!" Azrael said. "Dave?" Cecil said. Something was wrong with his voice. A river of flame shot across the floor. Bullets shredded the curtains, shattered the frail blinds, the window glass. The couch began to burn, the ragged curtains above the couch. The bullets banged and ricocheted. Empty casings tinkled like rain, spent lead rattled down. There was smoke, and a strong smell of gunpowder.

"Westover!" Dave shouted. "Run for help."

If there was an answer, he didn't hear it. He crouched behind the tabletop. Bullets kept slamming into it. He felt them strike, heard the wood splinter. Smoke swirled. He

180

got smoke in his lungs, convulsed with coughing. When he got over that, he glanced behind him. Azrael and Serenity lay sprawled in front of the open door, the boy across the girl, both facedown. Blood had puddled around them. It shone bright red in the firelight. Dave blinked against the smoke, trying to see out the door. Fire climbed the walls. By its light he made out the soles of long shoes at the edge of the porch in line with the door. As if Cecil had been struck just at the top of the steps and had fallen backward down the steps. Ah, Christ.

The explosions of the bullets stopped. But the rafters were burning now, crackling, spitting down a rain of sparks. And it was hot, too hot for him to stay here any longer. He started to straighten up, and more bullets exploded and he crouched again. He crawled, keeping flat as he could, the side of his face rubbing the floor. His head struck the softness of the children's bodies. Their blood wetted his face. He tried to push them ahead of him out the door, but they were heavy and he couldn't get purchase. He lay coughing, bullets whining over him, expecting at any second one of them to drill into him. Then a rafter fell. He didn't see it. It was behind him. But he heard its roar and felt the jar of its weight through the floor under him.

He lunged over the bodies, struck the porch and rolled, screaming at the pain in his shoulder. He scrambled into the shelter of the cabin wall beside the door and hunched there, coughing, panting. His clothes were sweaty, and in the sudden cold he shivered. The bullets stopped exploding. He waited. There might still be more. There didn't seem to be more. Now there was only the crackle and roar of the flames inside the cabin. He crept on knees and one hand and, flinching in the fire heat, dragged Azrael onto the porch and across the porch. Westover stood below the porch, staring.

"Take him down into the trees," Dave said.

Serenity's hair, jeans, and sweater were burning when he dragged her out. He beat out the small flames with his hand. He dragged her to the porch edge. Westover came for her and carried her away. His feet went out from under him and he sat down in the mud, the girl in her scorched and smoking clothes lying across him. He struggled from under her. Even over the noise of the fire, Dave could hear him sob. Somehow, he staggered to his feet with the girl in his arms and bore her away into the rainy darkness. Dave dropped from the porch to the ground. He swayed for a second with the pain in his shoulder. He saw the shadowy Westover lay the girl down and kneel beside her. Dave knelt beside Cecil. The boy was covered with blood. Dave laid fingers on his neck, under the hinge of his jaw. Flames were licking out the front windows of the cabin. He dragged Cecil away from the cabin, then ran skidding down to Westover. Westover looked up at him, face wet from more than just the rain.

"She's dead," he said. He stretched out beside her in the mud, put his arms around her, and laid his head on her breast. "No no," he said, "no no."

Back of them, the cabin roof fell in. It gave a hoarse roar. Sparks and flame reached up into the rain, lighting the tall pines and pin oaks with a nightmare orange glow. Dave stepped around Westover and his dead girl and crouched by Azrael. There was no need to feel for a pulse in this boy's neck. A red ragged hole as big as a fist had opened in his forehead. His strange pale eyes looked straight up into the rain that fell upon them. Dave reached across and shook Westover's shoulder. Westover raised his head. His eyes were open, but he wasn't seeing.

"I'm sorry," Dave said, "but I've burned my one good hand. I don't think I can drive." He climbed to his feet and, hurting the blistered hand, dug into the pocket of his ruined jacket for his keys. He held them out to Westover, who blinked at them for a few seconds as if he didn't know what they were, then wiped his runny nose on his sleeve, took the keys, and got up off the ground. Dave said, "One phone call ought to get fire, paramedics, ambulance, the works."

Westover's face twisted. "But she's dead," he said. "They're both dead."

"Not the black boy," Dave said. "The one who came to the door. He's alive. And I'd like for him to stay that way. My car is the Jaguar, a little way down the road. Can you hurry, please?"

Westover looked at the keys in his hand. He looked at Dave. Something cleared in his eyes. He nodded, and began to run, slipping in the mud, stumbling over roots, down through the trees and the dark rain toward the road.

NIGHTWORK

For Bobker Ben Ali

1

The creekbed was paved with sloping slabs of concrete and walled by standing slabs of concrete to a height of ten feet. Weeds sprouted from the cracks between the slabs, showing that water seeped underneath, but the slabs were bone dry, bone white, and glared in the morning sun. Seeing them, no one not native here would credit that when the rains came, water would rush muddy, deep, and dangerous under this concrete-slab bridge.

Before the construction of these acres of shacky stucco houses in 1946, the creekbed was shallow, cluttered with boulders from the far-off mountains, shaded by live oaks, and clumpy with brush. He remembered it that way from the 1930s. Then, the only house out here was on a rise. He looked for it out the window of the Jaguar now. There it stood among trees, a white Victorian hulk with cupolas, scalloped shingles, long porches bristly with jigsaw work. The Gifford place. Back then, this flat land by the creek was all that remained of the once vast Gifford Ranch.

Los Angeles had expanded even before World War II. One by one, the upland sections of the ranch were sold off and turned into pleasant suburbs. During the Depression, only the well-off could buy land and build on it. But then the aircraft factories and shipyards put everyone to work. Goods became scarce. People saved. Housing couldn't be built during the war. Afterward, contractors couldn't put up houses fast enough. Buyers were waiting. Dave smiled wryly to himself. These places must have gone up in summer, while the creekbed was dry, and been sold in the dry autumn.

With winter came the rains. And the creek flooded, as it always had. And the bright new little houses were up to their windowsills in swirling water. Overnight, mattresses, sofas, armchairs that still smelled fresh from Sears and Montgomery Ward became bloated sponges. The new Philco radios crackled and expired. The new Fords, Chevies, Plymouths everyone had waited years to buy drowned behind the warped doors of garages in the dark. It was a headline scandal. It became a headline scandal winter after winter—until the County at last gouged out the creekbed and lined it with concrete slabs. Much too late.

He swung the Jaguar off the bridge and onto a street that paralleled the creek. The paving was patched and potholed. Cans, bottles, wrappers clogged the dusty gutters. Squat stucco shops lined the street. Many of the signs were old, sun-faded, crackled. A few were new—shallow tin boxes of fluorescent tubes, fronted by crisply lettered white plastic sheets. Stones or bottles had been thrown through some of these—LAUNDROMAT, DISCOUNT APPLIANCES, FRIENDLY LEO'S. Dave couldn't make out what Friendly Leo sold. The unwashed windows were empty.

The high white sign that said LIQUOR was intact. Under it, brown men in ragged clothes sat on the littered sidewalk with their backs against a storefront in whose windows pyramids of soft-drink cans, beer cans, wine bottles sparkled in the sun. The brims of straw hats were pulled low on the foreheads of the brown men to shield their eyes from the sun. They clutched rumpled brown sacks that appeared to hold beer cans or wine bottles. Some of them smoked. Now and then they spoke, but none of them smiled. They looked sad, aimless, and without strength.

Around a corner of the building, on a bumpy dirt parking lot where no cars waited—it was not yet eight in the morning—teenage boys tilted back their heads and poured soft drinks down their throats from bright cans, or jokily pushed each other, or halfheartedly wrestled, or leaned watching beside bicycles against the liquor store wall, which was spray-painted with graffiti. They were Chicanos. Some wore green jackets stenciled GIFFORD GARDENS on the back. Dave halted the Jaguar at a battered stop sign. The boys turned, nudged each other, stared at the car.

Dave drove on, disgusted with himself for bringing the car here. He glumly eyed the Blaupunkt radio in the burled wood of the dashboard. They might not strip a Jaguar here. Where would they fence the parts? But they would almost certainly steal a Blaupunkt. He could afford to replace it—that wasn't the point. He hated the notion of the car being broken into, violated. It would be like splintering an Amati. At another corner with a stop sign, he glanced into the side mirror. Boys in green jackets were following him on bicycles. He waited for a dirty white van marked in red with a plumber's name to turn out of the side street, then drove on. He pressed the accelerator pedal. The speedometer needle climbed. There was no engine roar—just quiet, powerful obedience.

But they continued to follow, patient as a pack of wolves. For maybe ten blocks. Then, suddenly, when he glanced at the mirror, they had vanished. On a corner lot fenced in sagging chainlink, a corrugated iron garage yawned blackly. Old Mustang automobiles clustered in front of it, waiting to be made new. And beside an old-fashioned red ice chest labeled Coca-Cola in scuffed white script, eight or ten black youths, some teenaged, some a little older, lounged, laughing with very white teeth. They sobered when they saw the Jaguar. They looked thoughtful, tilting their heads. They wore black jackets stenciled THE EDGE.

Dave drove on, frowning. Ought he to have brought Cecil Harris? Cecil was a young black who lived with Dave and shared his bed. And his dangers. Cecil was just out of the hospital where, for long, slow months, he had mended from bullet wounds. He was still weak and thin. He tired quickly. This day would be a scorcher. It would wring the boy out. He had begged to come along, but Dave had made him stay behind in the comparative cool of the rambling house in the tree-grown canyon. Dave doubted that Cecil's presence with him in the Jaguar would change attitudes in Gifford Gardens. He drove on, watching the mirrors for signs of The Edge.

He saw none until he reached Lemon Street. On this corner, flat-roofed, concrete-block buildings bracketed a courtyard with a big rubber tree. A sign read THE KIL-GORE SCHOOL. The school was fenced in brick, topped by neat, square-cornered iron bars. Small kids in tanktops and shorts, yellow, green, magenta, clutched books and lunches outside the gate. Anglos. Two or three orientals. No blacks, no browns. Through a glass door at the end of the courtyard, two striped gray cats looked out expectantly. He swung the Jaguar off the creekside street, and here were cramped, lookalike tract houses on narrow lots. Around the corner after him turned a 1973 Mustang that had been sanded down to its body steel and had black holes where its headlights used to be.

4

It parked across from the school, and he forgot about it until, five or six blocks onward, when he stopped at the curb in front of the Myers house, he glimpsed it in the door mirror as he left the Jaguar. The Mustang rolled to a halt a few doors back. He gave it only a glance, reached into the rear seat of the Jaguar for his jacket, put this on. No one got out of the Mustang. The windshield was dirty, but he thought two people were inside. He locked the Jaguar and went up a cracked sidewalk between patches of summer-seared grass where an old heavy wooden skateboard lay like a dead beetle on its back, one set of wheels missing. He climbed two short steps, pressed a door buzzer, and turned to look again at the Mustang. It sat there like a steel coffin.

The house door opened. A young man stood inside, naked except for briefs, hair uncombed, a stubble of dark beard. He winced at the brightness of the morning. His eyes were bleary and bloodshot. He licked cracked, dry lips, and croaked, "Who the hell are you, now?"

"Brandstetter." Dave had a card ready, and poked it at the closed aluminum screen door. "I'm from Pinnacle Insurance. Death-claims division. It's about Paul Myers. I need to see Angela Myers, please."

The young man grunted, snapped a catch on the screen door, pushed it open six inches, took the card and squinted at it. "Something wrong with the insurance?"

"Something wrong with how he died," Dave said. "Is Angela Myers here? Who are you?"

"Gene Molloy. I'm her brother." He turned and shouted into the house, "Angie? Some guy for you from the insurance company." He frowned at Dave through the silvery mesh. "It was an accident. He lost control of his rig. It went off a curve in Torcido Canyon and exploded and burned." He stepped back and shouted, "Angie!" This time, a female voice, high-pitched and short-tempered, shouted back.

Dave couldn't make out the words. Car doors slammed. Two black youths had gotten out of the Mustang, one muscular, the other fat, both in jackets marked THE EDGE. They came ambling up the sidewalk, looking at everything but the Jaguar. Molloy saw them. "What the fuck," he said.

"They followed me," Dave said. "They admire my car."

"Oh, shit." Molloy pushed the screen. "Get in here." He grabbed Dave's arm.

Dave held back. "I don't want them to dismantle it."

"Better it than you," Molloy said. "Get in here."

Dave got in. The room was dim, the air close, smelling of sweaty sleep and stale cigarette smoke. The sofa had been used as a bed. The rumpled sheet looked as if it covered a dead body. Empty beer cans stood on a cheap coffee table by the sofa. So did a fluted pink china ashtray full of butts. On a stack of magazines. *Scientific American?* At the foot of the sofa, on a wheeled tubular cart, a small television set showed blurred images without sound. Dave said, "Where's the telephone?"

"You don't need a telephone, you need a gun." Molloy snicked the lock on the screen door, shut the wooden door, locked it, fastened a chain that looked flimsy. "The cops will take all day getting here. They don't like messing with the gangs. You can get shot that way, knifed—you can get dead. Two of them died already this year."

"It seems a good neighborhood to leave." Dave pried open two of the thin slats on a blind and looked out. The Edge youths were walking slowly around the Jaguar, wagging their heads in admiration. But their hands were still in their pockets. "Why don't you move?"

"Paul and I bought this house." It was that angry female voice again. Dave let the blind go. It rattled loosely. "If we only rented, that would be different. But everybody knows what Gifford Gardens is. Who'd buy? Who'd be stupid enough to move here? We're stuck. I mean—I'm stuck." She turned in the door, calling into the back of the house. "If you two don't get a move on, you'll be late."

Children's voices called, each canceling out the message of the other. Didn't raising your young here amount to criminal child endangerment? They appeared. They looked all right, bright-eyed, rosy-cheeked, carrying books and lunch sacks.

Molloy told them, "Go out the back way. Cut across the vacant lot. Go down Lime Street."

"What's wrong?" Angela Myers stared.

"The Edge is out front," Molloy said. "Two of them. They followed Mister"—Dave's card was crumpled in his fist; he smoothed it and peered at it—"Mister Brandstetter here. He's got a big, fancy foreign car."

"Brian. Ruth Ann." Angela Myers gave her head a sharp tilt. The boy, fair hair in his eyes like a sheepdog's, Dave guessed to be about nine, the dark-haired girl perhaps eleven. They turned and disappeared. A door banged. Small shoes ran away quickly in the morning stillness. The Myers woman said to Molloy, "At least it's not the G-G's."

Dave studied her. She wore a starchy sand-colored outfit with white trim. A starchy little cap was on her head. Her shoes were stubby, with thick crepe soles. Something was wrong with her face—with the shape of it. The light was bad. He tugged a frayed cord on the blinds, and slatted sunshine came in. Her face was swollen as if from a beating. She'd applied thick pancake makeup, so the colors of the bruises didn't show, but he thought they were under there. One eye was still partly closed.

"What happened to you?" he said.

"My husband was killed," she said. "He was just a young

man. He was doing nightwork, trying to earn extra money to help out my parents, and it killed him. A man can't drive all day and all night too. You have to have sleep. I kept telling him. So what happened? He fell asleep at the wheel and drove off the road, and now he's dead. And how is that going to help anybody?"

"Did you bring the check?" Molloy asked Dave.

Glass shattered outside. Dave turned to the window. Through the slats, he saw the fat boy with the skateboard in his hand. He stepped back and watched while the muscular boy reached in through the broken window and opened the door of the Jaguar. "Damn!" Dave said, and lunged for the house door. He twisted the bolt and yanked. The door stopped with a jerk on the end of its short chain.

"Don't go out there." Molloy grabbed him from behind, pinning his arms.

"Listen!" Angela Myers ran to the window.

A siren wailed. Not far off. Dave shook free of Molloy. He pushed the door to, twitched the chain out of its slot, pulled the door wide, was stopped by the screen, scrabbled at its little lock. The Edge youths ran back to the Mustang. The fat one still had the skateboard in his hand. Did the muscular one have the radio? He couldn't. There hadn't been time. They fell inside the Mustang and slammed the doors. Dave stepped outside. The Mustang's engine thrashed to life, its tires screamed. Behind its blind eye sockets, it sped off up the street, swerving wildly. Dave ran down the walk. A Sheriff's car came up the street, gold and white, an amber light flashing on its roof. It rocked to a halt beside the Jaguar.

"They went that way," Dave said.

2

The Sheriff's car did not go that way. A brown man and a black man in suntans and sunglasses stepped out of it. They were young. The black one looked overfed. He eyed the Jaguar and turned his opaque gaze on Dave. He shook his head and smiled sadly. "This yours?" And when Dave nodded, "Not your smartest move. Beverly Hills where this belong." With a careful finger he touched a splinter of glass sticking up in the window frame. "They get anything?"

Dave bent and looked through the hole. The Blaupunkt was still in the dash. "I don't think so. I think they wanted the radio."

The Latino deputy scratched his chest and looked off up the bleak street where now nothing moved. "You take what you can get. You know what the unemployment figures are for teenage blacks around here? Sixty percent. Did you get a look at them? If we catch them, would you be willing to testify in court?"

From her front door, Angela Myers said, "No, he wouldn't. You know how they make life hell for you." She came at a soft-soled run down the walk. "They telephoned all night. They broke our windows, killed our dog, scared the kids so they couldn't go out and play."

The black deputy said, "He don't live around here."

"They'll find him," Angela Myers said. "You know that." She looked at Dave. "Paul, my husband—he testified against Silencio Ruiz. For a supermarket holdup. Other people saw it, but Paul was the only one brave enough to testify."

"Dumb enough." This was Molloy. He had put on faded blue jeans. A cigarette burned at the corner of his mouth and jumped when he spoke. "What did he think was going to happen? The Gifford Gardens gang would give him a medal?"

"He did the right thing," the black deputy said.

"What made you come here?" Dave said.

"Mr. Gifford called us." The Latino pointed. The Gifford mansion shone white in the sun behind its big trees. The windows glittered in the sun. "De Witt Gifford. He lives up there."

The black deputy chuckled. "Ain't much gets past old De Witt. Mind everybody's business. Like he was the King in his High Castle. Watches out that tower with binoculars. Nothing else to do."

Dave looked at the cupola. Maybe he imagined it, but he thought he saw a wink of reflected sunlight sharper than that off the curved window glass. The lenses of Gifford's Bausch & Lombs?

"Told the dispatcher some boys was after your car."

Dave said, "I'll have to go up and thank him."

"You'll have a hard time." The Latino deputy walked around the Sheriff's car to the driver's side. "He's got more chains and locks and burglar alarms than you can count. Guard dogs too. Nobody gets in there." Across the roof of the car where the amber light still winked, he said, "Those boys will be back at the Mustang garage, probably. You

10

want to drive with us, point them out to us?"

"Don't do it," Angela Myers said.

"Don't worry," the black deputy said. "I ain't going in there. No way."

"I'll call for backup." His partner dropped into the Sheriff's car and reached for the dashboard microphone.

"We'll need the marines," the black deputy said.

"It only adds up to a broken window," Dave said. "It's not worth risking life and limb for. I'll let it pass. I have work to do in this town."

"Get yourself another car," the black deputy said. "Look like you could buy a fleet for what this one cost." He stroked the lustrous dark brown finish. "You want one, if they remove certain parts it don't much matter." He grunted when he dropped onto the seat of the Sheriff's car. He closed the door. "I'm serious."

"I take every man who wears a large gun seriously," Dave said. "Thanks for coming. Thanks for your advice."

"Mrs. Myers?" This was the Latino deputy. He bent his head and peered past his partner. "Silencio. Ruiz. He hasn't been bothering you, has he?"

"What do you mean? He's in San Quentin."

"I mean your face. It looks like somebody beat you up. It wasn't him, was it?"

"I had a fall." She touched her swollen eye. "At the restaurant where I work."

"He's out on parole," the deputy said. "A week already. That's why I asked. Your husband—has Ruiz been bothering him?"

"My husband is dead," she said.

"I'm sorry to hear that. If Silencio bothers you, that will constitute breaking the provisions of his parole. Don't let him intimidate you. Call us right away, okay?" He smiled briefly, raised a hand, and the Sheriff's car rolled off down the empty morning street. The amber light was not winking anymore.

"I have to get to work." Angela Myers hurried toward the house. "I can't afford any more days off."

Gene Molloy started across the brown grass toward two narrow strips of cracked cement that were a driveway. "I'll drop you off."

"So you'll have the car to run around to bars all day, wasting gas?" She jerked open the screen door. "Like hell you will." Dave was right behind her. She marched for the rear of the house, and so did he. In a kitchen that smelled of burned toast, and where spoons leaned in cereal bowls on a steel-legged table with a yellow Formica top, she snatched up a soft leather handbag from a yellow Formica counter beside a steel sink, and reached for the back door.

"Please wait," Dave said. She swung around sharply, surprised and annoyed that he was still here. He said, "I have bad news. Call your brother and sit down, all right?" He turned a steel-legged chair with yellow plastic padded back and cushion out from the table. Crumbs strewed the seat. He brushed them off. She didn't move. She glared at him. He said, "Your husband didn't fall asleep. What happened to him was not an accident. Any more than what happened to your face was an accident."

She said, "Look, mister, I don't know who you think—"

Molloy appeared at the back screen door. "What's going on?" He came inside, glanced at angry Angela, scowled at Dave. "Listen, friend, this is my sister."

"Sit down, please." Dave hooked another chair by the leg with his shoe and swung it out from the table. "The Sheriff's lab men have been examining the wreckage of Paul Myers's truck. It's taken a week, but now they're sure. He

12

didn't have an accident. Someone attached an explosive device under the cab, and blew it up."

"No." Angela clutched Molloy's arm, as if her legs wouldn't hold her. She was more than surprised. She was frightened. She looked up into Molloy's unshaven sulky boy face, as if he could change the truth. "They wouldn't do that. Why would they? He was tired. He drove off the road."

Molloy regarded Dave. "You sure about this?"

"The technicians are sure. It was detonated by remote control. Someone followed him and set it off when he reached that particular curve. They meant for it to look like an accident. Trucks have gone off there before."

"Silencio," Molloy said. He helped Angela to a chair She collapsed onto it. She was shivering. Molloy said, "I'm calling the cops." He moved to leave the kitchen.

"Save your dime," Dave told him. "They're on their way. Lieutenant Jaime Salazar, Sheriff's homicide." He checked his watch. "He was supposed to meet me here. Is there any whiskey?"

"Huh?" Molloy gaped. Dave nodded at Angela. Molloy looked at her and understood. "Yeah, sure." He climbed on a chair and from a high cupboard brought down a fifth bottle with a red label, SLIM PRICE. He unscrewed the cap and poured from the bottle into a glass that had held orange juice. He pushed the glass at Angela. "Here. This will make you feel better."

"I can't go to work with liquor on my breath."

"You can't go to work anyway. You have to tell them about Ruiz in the courtroom, what he yelled when the judge sentenced him. He was going to kill Paul. Isn't that what you told Mom? He was going to kill Paul when he got out?"

She leaned back in the chair, sighed, shut her eyes. "They get excited and say crazy things. Mexicans."

"Angie, it had to be him. It happened just after he got out. You heard that deputy." He took her hand, folded the fingers around the glass. "Drink that, will you? You look like you're going to pass out." She opened her eyes, drank, made a face, shuddered. Molloy said to Dave, "Who in hell else could it be? Didn't it have to be him?"

"It was a sophisticated device," Dave said. "I understood Ruiz was a street punk."

"There's training shops in prisons," Molloy said.

Dave sat down. Angela sat with her eyes closed, the whiskey forgotten in her hand. He reached out and gently touched her arm. She opened her eyes.

"Mrs. Myers—who beat you up?"

A corner of her mouth twisted. "Who always beats women up? Husbands. You look old enough to know that."

Dave looked up at Molloy. Molloy seemed surprised. Dave said, "Didn't you do anything about it?"

"Me? I wasn't here. You think he'd let me live here? Forget it. Not for years."

"He wouldn't let you live off him," Angela said dully.

Molloy told Dave, "I came after he got killed. Has to be a man in the house. In Gifford Gardens? You better believe it. Anyway, Angie always wanted me here. It was Paul that hated my guts."

Angela found Molloy's hand and smiled up at him with gentle reproach. "He didn't. He just wanted you to stand on your own feet. As long as you could live here with us, free meals, free rent, pocket money, you never would. He did it for your own good. Just like Daddy and Mama."

"Oh, boy." Molloy gave a sour laugh and asked Dave, "Can you figure that? Just out of high school. Your folks kick you out, your brother-in-law kicks you out. No job, no money, no place to sleep. And they call it love."

14

"They call a lot of things love," Dave said, "and some of the most unlikely ones turn out to be just that."

Molloy snorted. Cigarettes lay on the table. He pulled out a third chair, sat on it, shook a cigarette from the pack, lit it with paper matches whose print urged him to complete his high-school education at home. He blew out the flame with a stream of smoke and asked Dave, "Does it make some difference to the insurance company if he was murdered or died by accident?"

"It could. In either case, I'd be here."

"What for?" Angela said. "I already told the police all I know. I don't know anything. Gene's right. It has to be Silencio, doesn't it? Ruiz?"

"Sometimes," Dave said, "we know things without knowing we know them. Paul Myers went for years without life insurance. Then, suddenly, a month ago, he took out a policy for a hundred thousand dollars." Dave glanced at the shabby kitchen, faded yellow paint, scuffed vinyl tile, crooked cupboard doors. "That's expensive. What happened to make him do that?"

She shrugged. "Ossie Bishop died. It scared Paul. It happened so fast. No warning. He didn't want to leave me and the kids and my folks high and dry."

"Ossie Bishop!" Molloy jumped up, making the movement noisy, scraping the chair legs. He went to the stove. A glass coffeepot stood there, half full, over a low flame. He turned up the flame. Anger was in the sharp twist of his wrist. "He'd have that jig in the house. He wouldn't have me—his wife's own brother."

"Ossie was Paul's best friend," Angela told Dave. "I didn't like having one of them in the house, but he wouldn't hear a word against Ossie. And that wife of his, Louella—big, fat, black thing. Always trying to be friendly, asking me to go to that nigger church with her, wanting our kids to play together. Paul didn't see anything wrong with it, but I don't believe in it. I wasn't raised that way."

"This is a mixed town," Dave said. "Surely, in school—"

"I don't let them go to public school. White kids get mugged and knifed and raped at public school in Gifford Gardens. That's the reason I waitress. So I can pay to send them to the Kilgore School."

"Was Ossie Bishop an independent trucker too?"

She nodded. "It was him who told Paul about the night-work. He was doing it trying to save up enough to buy a second truck so his oldest boy could drive it when he got out of high school."

Molloy banged mugs onto the table among the milky cereal bowls, whose spoons tinkled from the jar. "Jesus, have you told Dad that? That even a nigger thinks of his own flesh and blood first? I'm sure as hell going to tell the old bastard."

"Gene," she said wearily, "that's all past and gone. It's no good eating yourself up inside over something that can't be changed. He's sick, anyway. Leave him alone. You never wanted to be a truck driver."

"I sure as hell never wanted to be a carpenter." Molloy brought the coffee pot and filled the mugs. "Not for free, for Christ sake. He paid his other apprentices. I was his kid—so I didn't get paid. Beautiful." He set the coffeepot back on the stove.

Dave asked Angela, "What happened to Bishop? A road accident?"

"He got sick. He was away from work a couple of days. Then he died. In the middle of the night. He couldn't get his breath. Louella called a doctor, but it was too late. Big healthy man, still young. It scared Paul."

16

Dave tasted the coffee. Hot but weak. He lit a cigarette. "When was Silencio Ruiz locked up?"

Angela wrinkled her forehead. "Two years ago? Eighteen months?" Her laugh was bitter. "The sentence was five years. It didn't mean anything, did it?"

"Not much," Dave said. "Ossie Bishop died a month ago?" He reached across the table for the ashtray. "I don't think Silencio Ruiz killed your husband."

3

Above his raised coffee mug, Molloy squinted at him. "What the hell do you mean? What's Ossie got to do with it?"

"Ossie just got sick," Angela said.

"Maybe somebody made him sick," Dave said.

"What for?" Molloy twisted out his cigarette. "Paul fingered Silencio for that holdup. That's why Silencio killed him. Where does Ossie come in?"

"He got Paul the nightwork." Dave turned to Angela. "What was he doing up in Torcido Canyon at three in the morning? What was he hauling? Who was he working for?"

"He—never told me." The bag fell from her lap with a muffled thud. She snatched it up, rummaged in it, brought out a little mirror. She touched her bruises. "I'm a mess."

"You weren't curious about what he was doing? You said it worried you, how tired he was making himself."

"It paid well. That's all he said. He wanted to help my folks." She glanced at Molloy. "Our folks. Dad had a stroke. He was always strong as a horse, so naturally he didn't have any health insurance. They used up all their savings practically overnight—doctors, hospital bills. He's a carpenter, and you know how much work they've been getting lately. They were running out of money even before he got sick."

18

"What about the union?" Dave said.

Molloy's laugh was dry. "He didn't believe in unions. He wasn't going to shell out dues every month so some fat wop racketeer could sit with his feet up on a desk drinking beer while he earned a living for the son of a bitch."

Dave watched Angela apply fresh lipstick. Her hand trembled. He said, "Every man doesn't feel so responsible for his in-laws."

Molloy made a sound of disgust. "Dad bought Paul his first semi, started him out as an independent. Do you think he did the same for me when I got old enough? Forget it."

"Paul still owed him for the truck?" Dave asked.

"He paid that off long ago." Angela closed the lipstick and dropped it into the bag. "No. Dad was good to him when he needed help. Paul wouldn't forget a thing like that. Dad was in trouble. Paul did all he could."

"He doesn't sound like a wife-beater," Dave said.

"He was tired and strung out. He was taking pills to keep him awake. Amphetamines. Truckers always have them. Pass them around to their buddies at rest stops." The mirror was propped against her coffee mug. She dropped the mirror into the bag now and zipped the bag closed. "He wasn't mean. It was too much pressure for him. He was frantic, and I got him sore, nagging at him to give it up. He was kind and patient before." Her eyes leaked tears. She wiped them away with a finger. "You ask the kids."

"Amphetamines can make a man edgy," Dave said.

"Where the hell is your County friend?" Molloy was reading a five-dollar digital watch. "Silencio will be in Mexico by now. In Argentina." He laid his cigarette in the ashtray, picked up his mug. "What did you say this deputy's name is?"

"Salazar," Dave said.

"Jesus, another spic." Molloy choked on coffee. "Don't

they hire white people anymore? What's a guy named Salazar going to do about a guy named Ruiz?"

"Whatever has to be done," Dave said.

Angela got to her feet, clutching her bag. "I have to get
to work."

"You'd better phone in sick," Dave said.

"I've already been off a week. They'll replace me with
some other girl. I have to have that job." She unzipped the
bag again to dig keys out of it. "I have children to feed and
bills to pay."

"I don't like to sound heartless or anything," Molloy said,
"but you've got a big fat insurance check coming."

"Hah." She looked glumly at Dave. "Have I?"

Dave gave her a little half smile. "Possibly. Tell me
Louella Bishop's address."

"She left town. I don't know." Angela pushed open the
back screen door. "I don't care. I'm glad she's gone."

"Lieutenant Salazar will want to talk to you."

"Paul's dead," she said, "and you say someone killed
him. That's all I know. There's nothing to talk about." The
screen door fell shut behind her. He went to it. The backyard was patchy grass, clotheslines, a twiggy lemon tree.
She hoisted a garage door that creaked. "Tell him I couldn't
wait." She went into the garage, a car door slammed, an
engine started, stalled, started again. The motor raced hard
and loud for a moment. Smoke poured out the garage door.

Dave asked Molloy, "What restaurant is it?"

"Cappuccino's," Molloy said. "They won't like the cops
coming to talk to her there." He made to pass Dave, to go
out and stop her. But the car, a dented, ten-year-old Toyota
station wagon in need of a wash, bucked backward out of
the garage and rolled quickly from sight along the side of
the house. It jounced noisily across the gutter out in front.
Molloy ran barefoot through the house. The front screen

door rattled. Molloy called, "Angie, wait!" But the car went off up the street. Dave heard it.

He began opening drawers in the kitchen. Papers lay in one of the drawers. Supermarket tally tapes, receipts for electricity, water, gas, phone. Canceled checks in bank envelopes, old income-tax forms, property-tax forms, ownership registrations for a 1973 Toyota and an eighteen-wheel rig, and loan papers on the house at 12589 Lemon Street. He pocketed a check and a bankbook. There were no slips of paper with addresses scribbled on them.

Molloy came in. "What the hell are you doing?"

"Looking for Louella Bishop's address. Your sister is too frightened to tell me about Paul's nightwork. Maybe Louella Bishop will tell me."

"Frightened? Come on." Molloy opened a refrigerator door taped with children's watercolor drawings. He brought out a can of beer. The drawings fluttered when he closed the refrigerator door. "You don't ask your old man questions when he keeps putting a fist in your mouth. She doesn't know. Why would she lie to you?"

"You don't think Paul beat her up," Dave said. "It surprised the hell out of you when she said that. You didn't like him, but you know he wasn't a wife-beater."

Molloy pried up the tab opener on the beer can. "Then it had to be Silencio, didn't it?"

Dave shook his head. "She didn't know until this morning that he was out of prison. Anyway, what would be the point?"

Molloy sat at the table and took a long swallow from the beer can. He wiped his mouth with the back of his hand and belched. "He probably came looking for Paul, and when Paul wasn't here, Ruiz beat up Angie just for openers, and she's scared to say so because he's still running around loose." He looked at his watch again. "And the way this friend of yours is moving on the case, he always will be. 'Scuse me. You want a beer?" He half offered to get up.

"It's a little early for me." Dave judged Molloy to be twenty-five. He was already thick through the middle. It wouldn't take many more years of drinking beer all day to turn him to flab. "Where's the telephone?"

Molloy told him. The instrument sat on a spiral-bound leatherette book with lettered leatherette tabs on the page edges. He laid the book open at *B*, but the address for Ossie Bishop was local. He flipped pages ahead, pages following. Nothing. He lifted the phone, slid the book back under it.

He opened a door and saw bunk beds, stuffed animals, toy trucks, a poster of the Dukes of Hazzard. He closed the door, took a few steps, opened another. The bed was unmade. Women's clothes lay around: skirts, blouses, jeans, crushed panty hose. Makeup and crumpled tissues littered a dressing table. He rolled open closet doors. A lone blue polyester suit hung on a wooden hanger. It smelled of drycleaning. Did she mean to bury him in that? There were two tan windbreaker jackets, a corduroy jacket, brown dress slacks, some heavy plaid wool shirts.

"You have to have permission," Molloy said.

Dave didn't answer, didn't turn. He went through the pockets of Myers's clothes and found a small address book. Knuckles rattled the front screen door. The door buzzer sounded. Molloy said, "For Christ sake, now what?" and went away. No new out-of-town address for Bishop was in the small book, but Dave pocketed it anyway and shut the closet. Where had Myers kept business records? Dresser drawers? Nothing but clothes. Drawers were under the closet doors, and he crouched and opened one. Sheets, towels, blankets. He shut that drawer and opened the other. Papers lay there, flimsies, dim carbon copies, pink, blue, green. He grabbed a handful, stuffed them into an inside jacket pocket, closed the drawer with a foot, and went to find Molloy.

Jaime Salazar was saying, "Then there's no need to bother your sister at work. You can tell her." He was slim and dapper in a lightweight blue denim suit, maroon shirt and socks, blue knit tie. Heat had already begun to gather in the small living room, but Salazar looked cool. His skin was smooth, pale brown. He wore a neat mustache and sunglasses. "There you are," he said to Dave.

"What kept you?" Dave said.

"Trying to find an ex-convict called Silencio Ruiz. Paul Myers's testimony got him convicted of armed robbery year before last. He said he'd kill Myers when he got out. He's out two days and pow—Myers is killed."

Molloy grinned at Dave. "What did I tell you?"

"That bomb was no amateur effort," Dave said.

"He could have paid somebody to make it for him."

Dave said, "Why would he bother? Silencio was a street-gang member. Whatever happened to switchblade knives?"

"He's disappeared. He was supposed to see his parole officer yesterday. He only slept at his parents' house his first night. They haven't seen him since. His gang has a hangout at a liquor store down by the creek. They haven't seen him either—not since Myers's so-called accident was on the breakfast news."

"What reason would he have to run," Dave said, "if the whole world believed it was an accident?"

"When we catch him, we'll ask him." Salazar looked out through the open blind. "Did that happen to your car here, this morning?"

"Gifford Gardens doesn't have a red carpet," Dave said.

Molloy said, "Care for a beer, Lieutenant?"

"Orange Crush?" Salazar asked wistfully.

"I'll look. Maybe she keeps some for the kids." Molloy went away whistling, pleased with himself.

Salazar tilted his beautiful head at Dave. "You don't buy it? You think the wife did it for the insurance money?"

"She says he beat her. It wasn't smart to tell me that. It also wasn't true. She's scared of whoever beat her. Since he's dead, that makes no sense. I think whoever beat her also killed him. Why they would do that puzzles me. But if it was to keep her from telling what she knows, it had the desired effect."

"If it wasn't her, what's left for you to do?"

"Life insurance can be tricky," Dave said. "Ever hear of a two-year conditional clause? It lets the company back off if it turns out the insured lied to them. Paul Myers outlined for Pinnacle the kind of cargo he hauled—routine, machine parts, unfinished furniture, clothing. Nothing out of the way. Nothing anybody would want to blow him up for. So maybe he was lying."

"If he was—she won't get anything?"

"Something. Not a hundred thousand."

Molloy came in and held out a frosty purple can. Salazar took a step backward and put his hands behind him. He said in an appalled voice, "Grape?"

"It's all there is," Molloy said.

"No, thanks," Salazar said. "Thank you very much."

"I'd better go," Dave said, and went.

4

Guava Street had no sidewalks. Little enough remained of its paving—bleached, cracked islands of blacktop that stood inches above the dirt level of the street. The Jaguar rocked and rumbled. Weeds edged the street, seedy, sun-dried. There were a few fences, chainlink, picket, grapestake. The houses, on narrow lots, were smaller here, the stucco sometimes broken away, showing chicken wire and tarpaper. Under untrimmed, drooping pepper trees, the composition roofs were losing their green and silver coatings. Rooflines sagged.

Small black children, in paper diapers, rompers, jeans, or nothing at all, tottered and squatted, hopped and hollered in dusty yards of pecking chickens, sunflowers, hollyhocks. Auto bodies rusted in a few yards. A rope holding a tire swung from a tree branch. Scruffy dogs lay in patches of shade, tongues hanging. On stoops, on sunny roofs, cats washed themselves or dozed. Other than the children, he saw only occasional women, young and pregnant in cheap bright cotton prints and hair straighteners, or old and bony, or old and fat. No teenage boys.

Mount Olivet Full Gospel Church might have been a warehouse but for its location in a grove of walnut trees and its stucco steeple. It was built of cinder block. Through a fresh coat of pale yellow paint the ghosts of Spanish graffiti showed. The windows were narrow and sparse. There was no stained glass. Louvers, the pebbled panes amber-colored. A strip of clean concrete lay alongside the church and he followed it in the Jaguar. A typical Gifford Gardens house sat behind the church. He climbed the stoop and pushed a doorbell button. LUTHER PRENTICE, D.D., was on a weather-yellowed business card tacked beneath the bell push.

But it was a reedy, butter-colored woman in an apron who opened the door. Good cooking smells rushed out at Dave through the screen. The woman dried her hands on the apron. Her hair was abundant, soft, and white. She gave him a quizzical smile, blinking, tilting her head a little. "Yes. Good morning." Beyond him she saw the Jaguar and her soft brown gaze rested on it a moment. "How can I help you?" He told her who he was, and offered his card. Like Gene Molloy earlier, she took it gingerly through a narrow opening between screen and doorframe. She read it and said, "I'm afraid we have all the insurance we need."

"I'm not selling it," Dave said. "I'm a death-claims investigator. I'm looking into the death of Paul Myers."

She frowned a little. "Was he a member of this congregation? I don't remember the name."

"He was a friend of a member of this congregation." Beyond her, Dave glimpsed movement in a room dark by contrast to the blazing sunlight outdoors. "Ossie Bishop. I'm told he died recently too. I'd like to talk to his wife, Louella, but I hear she's moved."

A tall, lean old man, very black, bald, with a fringe of springy white hair, appeared beside the woman. He took off horn-rimmed spectacles and peered at Dave. "She and her children left right after the funeral—I'd say it was more than just leaving. I'd call it running away."

"You men talk," the woman said. "I've got chickens and a whole lot of ribs to barbecue." She faded from sight. Her tall, straight old husband pushed open the screen door. He said, "Come in and sit down. Perhaps you'd enjoy to have a little iced tea." As Dave went indoors past him, the man peered, squinting, at the blazing morning. He too saw the Jaguar and was quiet for a moment. He closed the screen door and latched it. "I hope the damage to your car didn't happen here."

"It was my own fault." Dave waited among folding chairs in a room surprisingly large. Walls had been knocked out, hadn't they? This place had to do as parish house as well as rectory. The good cooking smells were strong here. A pair of long, fold-down tables rested against a side wall. He had glimpsed others set out in the walnut grove. There was going to be a picnic today or tonight. Luther Prentice, D.D., closed the wooden house door and said, "There is going to be a church picnic tonight at six." He smiled. "You're welcome to come." He motioned with a long hand whose nails were large and pink and whose palm was pale. "Please sit down. These are not comfortable chairs, but they are what we have, and we are thankful for them."

"I appreciate the invitation to the picnic." Dave sat. The chair was steel, with a thin seat cushion. The metal of the back made a cold band below his shoulder blades where jacket and shirt were sweaty. "But the Sheriff's men advise me not to drive that car here anymore. They cite the high unemployment rate in Gifford Gardens as responsible for the risk to property."

"It is a beautiful car." Prentice's smile was slight as he sat down. He wore dark suit trousers and a neat plaid cotton shirt, buttoned below a large larynx that made his voice deep. "Beauty is so often mankind's undoing. The Sheriff was right. It is too bad he couldn't have warned you before the damage was done."

"Perhaps then I wouldn't have taken him seriously. Reverend Prentice, do you know where Louella Bishop ran away to? It's vital that I talk to her."

"I'll get you the address," Prentice said. "But I don't know that talking to her will be of any use. She is a frightened woman. Her husband's death frightened her. Ah, I'm forgetting the iced tea." He got to his feet, went as stiffly as a man on stilts down the long room, and pushed open a swing door. Dave rose and opened the front door so he could watch the Jaguar. He couldn't be sure who, from inside what house, had seen him driving here. He saw no one now. Off to the west, the curved glass of the towers of the Gifford place sparked sunlight above their treetops. Dave heard Prentice returning. "I'm sorry," he said. "It appears to be lemonade today."

"That's fine." Dave smiled and took the icy glass.

"Here is Louella Bishop's address." Prentice had written it in an old-fashioned angular hand on a slip of paper. Dave glanced at it and pushed it into a pocket. Halcon. A small town in a valley of boulder-strewn hills inland from Escondido. Avocado country, he seemed to remember. Citrus too. Hard blue skies. Prentice said, "A family she used to work for. Please—sit down."

"Thank you." Dave sat. So did the tall old man. "Paul Myers died in a truck crash. His wife says he was a good friend of Ossie Bishop. It was when Bishop died so suddenly that Paul took out life insurance. Did you know Bishop well? You conducted the funeral, am I right?" Prentice nodded. Dave said, "What can you tell me about the reason for his death?"

"Very little. It was sudden—that was all. He was here in church with her on Sunday. By Friday he was dead. Before sunrise. I know he was working hard, because she said so. Working day and night. But he was a robust man. She said it was a heart attack brought on by overwork. It's possible, I suppose."

Frowning thoughtfully, he paused and sipped his lemonade. Dave tried his. Nothing frozen about it. It was what it was supposed to be, and it was not too sweet.

Prentice said, "Sometimes those that look the strongest are really frail. To survive in this world, a black man has to start working early in life, and sometimes they burn out early." He gave his glossy bald head a worried shake. "But she was afraid to talk about what took place that Thursday night. It wasn't like her. She was talkative as a rule, open and easy." He smiled to himself. "Always could find something to laugh about, didn't matter what. She was a great help here at the church, and she lifted all our spirits with her gift of laughter. We already miss her sorely. However, she was normally a slow-moving woman, and she moved as if the Devil himself was after her when it came to leaving Gifford Gardens once Ossie was in the ground. Funeral was Monday morning. She was on her way south with the children and her worldly goods by nightfall."

"That didn't give her much time to sell the house," Dave said. "Or did she only rent? What about his truck?"

"House wouldn't be a problem. People around here dying for a roof to get in under that they can afford." Prentice furrowed his brow. "As to the truck, most likely the boy drove it, the oldest, Melvil. His father hoped for him to be a driver too, once he finished high school. It would be a means of livelihood for the family, wouldn't it, now that the father is gone? The investment in one of those big trucks must be considerable."

"In the neighborhood of a hundred thousand dollars, these days," Dave said.

29

"Speaking of Melvil reminds me." Prentice lifted his glass to take a final swallow from it. "He said something to his mother at the graveside. That she called the wrong doctor. He seemed angry with her, though he spoke low."

"Who would have been the right doctor?"

"Most of us around here go to Dr. Hobart. He is a member of this congregation. Most Christian man I know."

"Did Melvil name the doctor his mother called?"

"He was something to do with the trucking business." Prentice took off his glasses and wiped them with a white, sharply creased handkerchief. "That's all Melvil said. And white. Melvil didn't like that." Prentice looked sorrowful, putting his spectacles on again, pushing away the handkerchief. "I regret it very much when youngsters feel that way, but so many do now. 'A new commandment I give unto you—that ye love one another.' That's what the Lord Jesus told us. That's what I preach, is love. But the young men don't come." He stared forlornly past Dave at the door Dave had left standing open. "Those come that don't need the sermon. But the young men don't come." He sighed. "It's why we're having this barbecue, you know. There won't be any preaching. There'll just be food. They are hungry, most of them." He shook his head. "They take it out in hatred. Enmity between the races—it's brought nothing but grief and sorrow and loss. But they are hating now more than ever. These gangs—black against brown. I don't know where it's going to end. We're located here, where we are sitting now, right in the middle of it. Next block"—he held up a long black thumb—"you won't hear anything but Spanish spoken. They come at night and paint their marks all over the walls. Obscenities too. But that's not the worst." He eyed Dave bleakly. "They are killing each other. Killing. And the innocent too. Children. They drive by and shoot, and it could be anybody gets hit. The police, they try to stop it, but they get killed too. We are in the last days, it appears."

Dave set down his glass. "Who was the undertaker?"

"Wrightwood." Prentice got up when Dave did. "This Paul Myers—why are you investigating his death?"

Dave told him, and the minister's eyes widened. He said, "Then Louella Bishop was frightened. I was right."

"I don't know." Dave started for the sun-bright doorway. "Paul Myers was murdered, so perhaps it's natural that his widow should be frightened. But what frightened Louella Bishop? If her husband died of natural causes, why did she run so far, so fast?" He held out his hand. "Thank you for the address."

"Whatever I can do." Prentice shook Dave's hand. His face changed. He lunged past Dave and flung open the screen door. "Get away from there!" He went down the steps. "You hear me? Drop those things!"

Two black kids raced off down the driveway, hubcaps flashing in their hands. Prentice ran after them at an old man's run. Dave passed him. The car the boys piled into was another Mustang, its rear end smashed in. The bent trunk lid flapped high as the car careened away up Guava Street, a door still hanging open, legs kicking from the open door, laughter shouting from the open door. Dave halted on the grass in front of the church. Prentice came panting up to him.

Dave said, "Where did they get that name—The Edge?"

Prentice wiped his face with the neat handkerchief. "From a song—'Don't push me, 'cause I'm close to the edge, trying not to lose my head.'" He gazed dismally off up the street. He told Dave, "I am so terribly sorry."

"It's not your fault," Dave said.

5

The high wall around the grounds of the Gifford place was almost invisible under matted honeysuckle vine. So were the pillars that held the tall iron gates. It took time to locate an intercom outlet among the leafage. The outlet looked new. It probably had to be replaced fairly often. He pressed a rectangular white plastic button. From here, because the trees were large and shaggy, he couldn't see the cupola where he supposed De Witt Gifford sat. Beyond the gates, the grounds were neglected. Oleanders tall as trees crowded the drive, dropping the last of their blossoms, pink, white. Roses bloomed blowsy on long canes in flowerbeds rank with wild oats and milkweed. Dark ivy covered the ground and climbed the tree trunks. The intercom speaker crackled.

"I'm busy." The voice was an old man's, brittle. "Who are you? What do you want?" Dave told him. The snappishness went out of the voice. "Oh, yes, of course. How very— gentlemanly of you to come. Please wait."

The wait was a long one. Dave spent it in the car. That seemed the best way to guard the car. The sun beat down. He lit a cigarette, but it tasted dry, and he put it out. He wished for a fresh glass of Mrs. Prentice's lemonade. Below him lay the roofs of Gifford Gardens, drab gray, drab green, drab red, under a drab brown sky. He located the big rubber tree that marked the Kilgore School, the walnut grove where the church steeple rose, the pepper trees on Guava Street. Elsewhere in Gifford Gardens, trees were scarce. The developers in 1946 had bulldozed the oaks. Now dogs began to bark—big dogs, by the sound of them. Dave got out of the car.

Down the drive beyond the gates came a motorized invalid's chair. The wire spokes of its wheels glittered in the darts of sunlight through the oleanders. In the wheelchair rode an old party in a tattered picture hat. Across blanketed knees lay a rifle. The picture hat was a woman's, faded purple, decorated with bunches of wax grapes and cloth grape leaves, but the rider in the chair had a long white beard and long white hair.

"Mr. Brandstetter?" He twitched a smile of white dentures through the whiskers. "I'm sorry to have kept you waiting." He stopped the chair, peered fearfully through the gates, up and down the street, then set the rifle aside and began, with a rattle of keys, to undo padlocks that held thick chains in place where the two gates came together. "I have no one to help me right now. The television tells me constantly that unemployment today is a national disaster, yet no one seems to want to work."

"How much do you want to pay?" Dave asked.

"Ah-ha! You've put your finger on it, haven't you?" The last of the chains rattled and hung loose. "They think I'm rich." He scraped a key around on the lockplate of the gates. The hand that held the key was bones under dry, brown-spotted skin, and the hand was not steady. "They want ten dollars an hour, don't they? And if they can't have ten dollars an hour, they'd rather steal, thank you." Gifford cranked the key around in the lock. "I'm talking about the blacks, of course. The Hispanics already have jobs. They know what real hunger is. There are no food stamps in Mexico." Gifford caused the chair to move a couple of feet. His breath came in gasps as he dragged at something inside the gates. A bar. The sound of it said it was thick and heavy. "There, now." Gifford picked up the rifle and backed the chair out of the way. "Just push, please."

Dave pushed. Sirens went off. Bells clamored. The old man in the grape hat grinned and yelled something. Dave couldn't make it out. Gifford pointed a bony finger at the Jaguar. He made a summoning gesture with a skinny arm. Dave ran out to the car, got inside, fumbled to get the key into the ignition. He waited for Gifford to roll to the side of the drive, out of the way, then pulled the Jaguar through the gates. He jumped out of the car and ran to slam the gates shut. The sirens and the bells ceased. Except inside his head. Up at the house, the big dogs raved. Dave closed the padlocks on the chains, and slid the bar across. Gifford wheeled up and turned the key in the lock again.

"I'm not rich," he said. "No way in the world can I pay a servant eighty dollars a day. I'm lucky to have a roof over my head." He pushed his clump of keys into the pocket of a raveled brown cardigan sweater and turned the chair so that he faced Dave. "Mother always warned me I would someday regret my riotous youth. I do regret it—but not in the way she meant. I certainly do not regret the riotousness." The motor of the chair whined. It rolled up the drive toward the house that rose high and white among the trees. "I regret the days when I lacked the imagination to get up to anything riotous." He stopped the chair and half turned it back. "Come along. I'm delighted to have a visitor."

"It was good of you to call the Sheriff for me."

"I couldn't let anything happen to a car like that. My friend Ramon and I favored Jaguars in our time." Gifford's eyes were small and sunken but bright. "Ramon Novarro,

34

you know? Will it shock you if I tell you we were lovers?"
He looked Dave up and down. "That's Brooks Brothers,
isn't it?" He stated it as fact. It was a fact. He nodded. "Yes.
It suits you. You have a beautiful figure. When I saw you
stop on Lemon Street, I thought you were younger. There's
something young about your carriage, isn't there?" He
turned the chair abruptly and wheeled away up the drive
again. "What did you want at the Myers house? A lot of
strangers have been stopping there lately."

"Paul Myers died suddenly." Dave walked alongside the
wheelchair. "That usually brings strangers. I'm from the
company that insured his life. Do you know the names of
everyone in Gifford Gardens?"

"Paul Myers was witness two years ago to a supermarket
holdup." Gifford rolled the chair up the long, easy grade of
a wooden ramp to the spindlework verandah. Dave climbed
the stairs. He wondered about those big dogs barking inside the house. Gifford said, "He was on the television
news. That brought him to my attention." The house doors
were a pair, each with two tall, narrow panes of glass etched
with Pre-Raphaelite lotuses. Gifford pushed open the
doors. The dogs did not come bounding out. The dogs
stopped barking.

Gifford rolled his chair into a hallway spacious and two
stories high, where a broad, carved staircase climbed, to
divide left and right at a landing beneath a stained-glass
window. Dogs clawed, snuffled, growled behind closed
sliding doors. Dave followed the old man in the floppy
grape hat into a passageway beside the stairs. He glimpsed
a large, dim room with furniture under shrouds. Gifford
told him, "I used to entertain a good deal. Especially
when Mother was away in Europe. She didn't take to my
friends." He bumped open a swinging door to a pantry pas-
sage. "Now that she's dead and out of the way, so are they."

He gave a brief hoot of irony. "Oh, my dear. What a joke life is."

He poked a black button in a brass wall plate. A metal door whose white enamel bore long horizontal scratches slid open. "This was once a dumbwaiter. The kitchen is below. I adored riding up and down in it as a little girl." He slid aside a folding metal grille. "When I lost the use of my legs, I had it converted." He gestured with the impatience of an old man irritated by his incapacities. "Get in, get in." Dave stepped into the cramped metal box, and Gifford backed his chair into it and rattled the grille shut. He poked a button, the steel door closed, the elevator jerked, thumped, began to rise. Slowly. Shivering. "That's a handsome young man staying at the Myers house," Gifford said. "I saw you talking to him. Who is he?"

"Mrs. Myers's kid brother," Dave said.

"I love it when they go around without their shirts."

"He's there to protect her," Dave said. "Somebody gave her a beating. She says it was her husband. I don't think so. A day or two before he was killed, did you see anyone stop there, any strangers? When Myers wasn't at home?"

"He was rarely at home." The elevator jerked to a halt and Gifford tugged back the folding grille. He pressed the button that worked the steel door. It slid back, and he rolled out of the elevator. "He was always off somewhere in that enormous truck of his. Often gone for days."

They had reached the attic, wide and high and gloomy. Also hot, though an air conditioner rattled someplace out of sight. With its quiet whine, the wheelchair took Gifford along a crooked aisle between heaps of packing cases, barrels, trunks thick with dust and cobwebs. Dave followed, dodging the corner of an old yellow life raft.

"Mind your head," Gifford said. "I should get rid of that. A young man who lived with me for a time after the war had survived on one of those for days after his ship was sunk in the South Pacific. Once, driving to the beach, he caught sight of that propped outside a surplus store. He got all nostalgic and simply had to have it. I bought it for him. Along with the compressed-air containers to inflate it. Absurd. Still, it made him sleep easier." Gifford sniffed. "Naturally, he left it behind when he decamped."

He rounded a chimney of rosy old brick and crusty mortar, and was in a cleared space that held a four-poster bed with a handsome patchwork spread, a chest of drawers with a cankered mirror, and a television set. On the wall was a blown-up photograph of Ramon Novarro, stripped to the waist and oiled. Off this space opened the tower room— couch, coffee table, wing chair. A pair of large, expensive binoculars stood on a windowsill. Gifford said, "A wife can grow weary of being left alone so much." He leaned the rifle against the chest, tossed the picture hat onto the bed. "No wonder she took a lover."

Dave stared. "Are you talking about Angela Myers?"

"Who else?" Gifford smoothed his uncut hair. He nodded. "Behind that partition"—he meant the one at the head of the bed—"you'll find a kitchen. I do all my living up here now. It's simpler. And cheaper. And the attic was always the most amusing part of the house. I spent much of my wretched childhood up here—the unwretched part. Old books, old magazines, old steamer trunks full of gowns and hats."

"You're sure about the lover?" Dave said. "Who is he?"

"I was trying to say"—Gifford struggled to get out of the frayed cardigan—"that it is hot up here, and a gin and tonic would be welcome, and would you fix it, please?"

"My pleasure." Dave found the kitchen in a sunny gable, everything neat and compact, stove, refrigerator, steel sink, cupboards, floor mopped and waxed. He found glasses. Gin, ice, and quinine water were in the refrigerator. He built the drinks while Gifford talked on.

"Wonderful, awful old books. I read them all, no matter how boring. There were tons of yellowback French novels, terribly naughty by *fin de siècle* standards. With a dictionary, I used them to teach myself French. And when reading palled, and dressing up, there were always these windows to watch out of. We were isolated out here in those days, but hikers came, and sometimes lovers. I saw some charming pastoral tableaux down among the oaks by the creek on warm summer days. At nights, I crept down for a closer look. That was how I learned anatomy and physiology. I was keen on self-education, you see. Naturally, I saw some things I ought never to have seen, and that haunt me still. But that is what little boys who prowl and spy upon others can expect, isn't it?"

"I couldn't locate any mint." Dave found Gifford in the tower room, seated in the wing chair, peering through the binoculars, frail fingers adjusting the focus. When he heard Dave, he set the glasses on the windowsill, sat back, smiled, held out his shaky hand to take the glass. "There is no mint, alas. In the kitchen garden, there used always to be mint. But that was long ago." He rattled the ice in his drink and sipped at it, dribbling bubbles into his beard. "Ah, delicious." He waved at a couch, Empire style, covered by a fringed Spanish shawl almost as threadbare as the upholstery it was meant to hide. "Sit down."

Dave continued to stand. "You know the man's name?"

"I make it a point to learn the names of people who interest me from afar. Bruce Kilgore. He operates a school down there, under the rubber tree." Gifford gestured vaguely. "I believe the generic term for them is white-flight schools."

"Right. How do you know they're lovers? There are no more oaks for them to make love under down by the creek."

38

Dave walked to the windows. They were shiny clean, inside and out. How did Gifford manage that? The view was amazing for distance and breadth. "Can you see her bedroom windows from here? Does she forget to lower the blinds?"

"You ask a good many questions for an insurance salesman," Gifford said, and his sunken eyes, bright and curious as a six-year-old's, fixed Dave from under brushy white brows. "That isn't what you are, really, is it?"

"I'm a death-claims investigator," Dave said. "When it looked as if Myers had an accident, the insurance company wasn't unduly worried. When it emerged that somebody blew his truck up with a bomb, they hired me."

"You didn't come here to thank me," Gifford said. "You came to pump me."

Dave gave him a thin smile. "One of the deputies who came in response to your telephone call about my car said you see everything that goes on in Gifford Gardens. You're obviously civic-minded. I assumed you'd want to help me."

Gifford studied him for what seemed a long time. He cleared his throat. "She didn't forget to pull the blinds. But he came only late at night, when the husband was away"— Gifford drank thirstily again—"and the children were almost certain to be asleep. What would you make of that?"

"And the night Myers was killed?"

A ledger lay on the coffee table, with stacks of magazines and books, a potted fern in supermarket green foil, an ashtray with a cigarette butt in it. Dave saw no cigarette pack on the table, nor on the stand by the bed, which held a lamp, a clock radio, a telephone, and another photograph of Ramon Novarro, this one in a tarnished silver frame. The ink of an inscription had faded. Gifford stretched a hand out for the ledger, laid it on his blanketed knees, turned pages covered with closely written ballpoint script. "Ah-ha. Here we are. Night of the ninth." Gifford smoothed the page. He sat straight. His eyesight must have been childlike too, un-blurred. "On that night, she was away. With the children. All night. Kilgore did not appear. Mrs. Myers reached home with the children about seven-forty-five. Sheriff's officers were waiting to give her the bad news." He closed the ledger and gave Dave a smug little nod. "I keep written records. The memory plays so many tricks."

"Thank you." Dave frowned. "You used the word 'came' about Kilgore. Is it over? Doesn't he come anymore?"

"Not since Myers died." Gifford shrugged. "After all, the beautiful brother is in the way, isn't he? But no, it is not over."

"They meet at Kilgore's, while the brother babysits?"

"Kilgore has living quarters at the school," Gifford said. "Yes, as you say. Twice, anyway. Perhaps more." He twitched a smile inside the frowsty beard. "After all, I am not King Argus of the Hundred Eyes, who never slept." His two creepy, clear child's eyes twinkled at Dave. "It will amuse you to learn that Mrs. Myers went straight to see Kilgore after she left the house this morning in her wait-ress's uniform, while you remained behind with the beauti-ful brother. What did you say his name was?"

"I didn't say. For what it's worth, it's Eugene Molloy." Dave nodded at the ledger. "No one came and beat Mrs. Myers up on the night of the ninth. When did they come? Who were they? Or were you sleeping?"

"It was two nights before." Gifford's hand strayed across the rough gray fabric of the ledger cover, as if to open the book again, but he didn't open it. He said, "I have my own reasons for remembering that night. It was well after dark. A stocky, middle-aged woman came, and two muscular men. She was startlingly well dressed. They, I think, were truck drivers. They arrived in a van without markings. I

40

can't see license numbers at night. They didn't stay long. Five or ten minutes. When they came out, one of the men was rubbing his knuckles. The next day, when I got a glimpse of Mrs. Myers taking in some dry clothes from the backyard, her face was a mass of bruises, and she moved as if in pain."

"Never seen the stocky woman and her goons before?"

Gifford shook his head. "It wasn't her husband who beat her. Why do you suppose she told you that? He didn't come home that night, or all the next day until dusk. I gather he was moonlighting." Gifford laid the ledger back on the table. "Who was that handsome chap who arrived this morning while you were there? Spanish, right? What we might call 'a living doll,' might we not? What did he want?"

Dave told the old man who Jaime Salazar was. "He came to say they have a suspect in the murder of Paul Myers. A recent parolee named Silencio Ruiz." Gifford gasped and stiffened in his chair. Dave said, "Are you all right?"

"I live my life in pain," Gifford snapped. "So will you, when you're seventy-five." His voice was a wheeze, he gulped feebly and pointed. "If you don't mind? The bathroom? Digitalis."

A small bathroom backed the small kitchen. A dozen little amber plastic cylinders held pills in a medicine cabinet that also contained a pressure can of shaving cream and a pack of throwaway razors. Dave put on reading glasses and found the digitalis. He tapped a pill into his palm. A glass stood on the washbasin beside a box of denture cleaner. He filled the glass. In the tower room, trembling, the old man popped the pill into his mouth and gulped the water. He sat with eyes shut, panting. He whispered:

"Thank you. I won't keep you. The keys to the gates are

in my sweater." He fluttered a weak hand toward the bed. "When you've locked up, throw the keys as far up the drive as you can. I'll retrieve them later."

"Shouldn't I call your doctor and wait till he comes?"

"It's nothing. Happens all the time. It will pass. You're very kind." Gifford opened his eyes. They were cold. So was his voice. "Be careful on your way out of the house. My dogs are trained to kill." The coldness left. His smile was saintly. "Thank you for coming to see a boring old cripple. I hope I've been of some help."

"I appreciate it." Dave dug the keys from the ragged sweater, and found his way out. Carefully.

6

Chunky, hairy, tanned, Bruce Kilgore pedaled an Exercycle in one of three rooms at the back of the lot occupied by the Kilgore School. His black, sweaty hair was thinning, he wore blue jogging shorts and running shoes. Sitting straight, look-ma-no-hands style, he spooned yoghurt from a yellow paper cup. Outside an open sliding glass door, the children Dave had seen earlier, waiting by the front gate, kicked a black and white soccer ball around. Their voices were shrill. From the size of the exercise ground, Dave guessed that once there had been a swimming pool in its place. Had the buildings originally housed a motel? The rooms were uniform motel-unit size. The others he had peered into held school desks. This one had a big desk, file cabinets, telephones, bookcases, typewriter, home-size computer, framed certificates on the wall. Except for the Exercycle, it was unmistakably a school office. It was also unmistakably a motel room.

"I'd ride a ten-speed on the streets," Kilgore was saying by way of apology, "but the only ten-speeds you'll see in Gifford Gardens are the green ones that belong to the G-G's." He climbed off the machine and picked up a towel from a chair heaped with workbooks, wrapped reams of pa-.

per, a half-dozen boxed videotapes. "They're our local Chicano gang." He set the yoghurt cup on a corner of his paper-heaped desk, where the cup fell over and spilled its spoon. The spoon rattled on the floor. Kilgore ignored it and dried himself. "They discourage anyone else from riding bicycles. And if they weren't enough, there's our local black gang, The Edge."

"Tell me about it," Dave said. "They've already made a pass at my car radio and stolen my hubcaps." He leaned out the door for a look at the Jaguar at the curb. It was all right. For the moment. "And I've only been in town for a few hours."

"In Edge territory." Kilgore threw the towel over the Exercycle and pulled on sweatpants, having a little trouble with the elastic at the cuffs getting caught on the jogging shoes. "The way they've laid out this community puts political gerrymandering to shame. 'Turf' they call the parts they rule. By terror. You never know where you are—not for long. The boundaries keep shifting. There are continual skirmishes. It's like the Middle East." He went to the door, blew a steel whistle, and called, "Okay. Time's up. Back to class. Don't leave the ball there. Somebody will climb in and steal it." He waited and watched, the whistle dangling its black leather thong from his mouth, while the youngsters funneled back into school. The last to go was Brian Myers, head hanging, with its shock of fair hair. Hands jammed into pockets, he scuffed his feet. Kilgore called, "Brian—you okay?"

The boy halted, turned, gave a wan smile. "I'm okay, Mr. Kilgore." He went on through an open glass sliding door into the school. One of the gray striped cats bumped his legs, looked up at him, meowed. He bent and petted it for a minute. Then he glanced back at Kilgore across the empty yard, stood, and went on out of sight, still dragging his feet.

"Poor kid," Kilgore said mechanically, returning to his desk, sitting down behind it, tossing the whistle into the litter there. "Just lost his dad."

"Paul Myers." Dave glanced at the Jaguar one more time, where it waited beyond the side gate. He came inside the office and walked to the desk. "It's about him that I've come." He laid his card in front of Kilgore. "Mrs. Myers was here earlier. I presume she told you what happened to her husband was no accident. That somebody blew him up with a bomb planted in his truck."

Kilgore stared. His tan turned putty color. "Silencio Ruiz, but how did you—" He half stood up, and sat down again as if he hadn't strength in those muscular brown legs of his. "Who told you she came here?"

"You're close friends," Dave said. "It's no secret. You've been close friends for some time. The kind of close friends who visit one another late at night when the husband is away at work."

Kilgore's color darkened. Veins stood out in his short, thick neck. "It's a lie. Your implication is a lie. Yes, I visit late at night. Look at this." He spread his hands, palms up, above the cluttered desk. "You think I've got help around here? Think again. The last thing I am is principal of a school. I don't know what comes first—janitor, accountant, secretary, fund-raiser, teacher? You decide. When the hell else do I have time to visit but late at night?" He picked up the card, glared at it, glared at Dave. "What business is it of yours, anyway?"

"Maybe none," Dave said. "I don't know yet. If it has something to do with Paul Myers's death, it's important, isn't it? With what happened to him, why it happened, and who was behind it?"

"What do you mean?" Kilgore licked his lips. "Myers appreciated my looking in on his family. He had to be out of town a lot. He was a cross-country trucker. If he was going to earn a living, he had to leave them here, unprotected. And that's not a figure of speech, either. After his testimony put Silencio Ruiz in jail, the G-G's harassed them night and day. Ruiz was their leader."

"Mrs. Myers told me," Dave said. "She didn't tell me it was you who made them stop."

"First I tried the Sheriff." Kilgore dug among the disorder on his desk, found a handball, and began squeezing it. He snorted. "Fat lot of good that did. Even after they smashed the windows, even after they shot the dog, the Sheriff wouldn't put a guard on the house. Didn't have the manpower, they said." He switched the ball to his other hand and squeezed. Muscles showed in his forearm. "Then they started this program to get the gangs off the streets. They enlisted businesses, banks, churches, to start basketball teams, figuring the G-G's and The Edge would get the same kick out of slamdunking as they do out of slaughtering each other with guns and knives and bicycle chains." His laugh was sour. "It didn't work, of course. I mean, you know what we're talking about here—subhumans, primitives, savages. Jungle warfare. It's in their blood, right?"

Dave said wearily, "Is there a point to this?"

"There's a rich old geezer out here," Kilgore said. "Maybe you've seen his house. The old mansion on the hill with all the gingerbread work? De Witt Gifford. And this is the interesting part—he donated the jackets for one of the basketball teams. The Gifford Gardens gang, the Latinos. There's no team anymore, but they still wear the jackets."

"I've seen them. What's interesting about it?"

"It didn't add up. He never contributes anything to this community—not a dime. It's named after his family, but he doesn't give a damn what happens to it or anybody in it.

So why the jackets for the G-G's? I began nosing around, asking questions. About Silencio Ruiz's trial. Now, normally he'd have had a public defender, right? And normally he'd never have made bail. He'd have sat behind bars for months, waiting for his day in court. Well, he didn't. He made bail. And he had an expensive attorney. At first everybody kept their mouths shut. They'd been paid to. That's what I figured. So I shelled out a little money myself. And guess what I found out?"

"Gifford put up the bail and paid the lawyer. You mean you used this to get him to make the G-G's quit harassing the Myerses? Seriously? He worried about it being known? At his age? In his condition?"

"He was scared to death." Kilgore flipped the handball into an empty metal wastebasket across the room. "I only went to him on a hunch. I was surprised as hell when it worked. He panicked. Gave me a five-hundred-dollar check for the school, and made me promise I wouldn't tell anybody about him helping Silencio."

"You're telling me," Dave said.

"All bets are off now," Kilgore said. "Silencio killed Myers. The minute he got out of prison. Gifford didn't prevent that, did he? It was him who told you I was seeing Mrs. Myers late at night, wasn't it? He spies from one of those towers up there. Everybody knows it. He hates me because I won't let Latinos in my school. Crazy old bastard. He wears dresses—did you know that?"

"Mrs. Myers has her brother to guard her now," Dave said, "but you still see each other at night. Only now she comes to you. What about? The children's grades?"

"I don't have to answer your questions." Kilgore got to his feet without trouble this time. "Get out of here."

"Paul Myers doesn't care if you're sleeping with his

wife—not anymore. Neither do I. If that's all you have to hide, why not answer my questions?"

"You care. You're implying collusion between us—me and Angie—Mrs. Myers, I mean."

Dave raised his brows. "Am I?" He went to look out the door at the Jaguar again. No crime in progress. He turned back. "You mean I think you murdered Myers so as to marry his widow and share in the insurance money?" Dave gestured to indicate the school and its burdens. "You're hard up. A hundred thousand dollars would hire a lot of help. No? You could ride your exercise machine all day."

"Silencio Ruiz killed Myers," Kilgore said.

"There are reasons to doubt that," Dave said. "Where were you on the night Myers crashed and burned? You didn't visit Angela Myers that night."

"She was at her parents' house," Kilgore said. "Her mother needed her. The old man was acting up. She took the children and stayed there overnight."

"And where did you stay?"

"Right the hell here," Kilgore said. "And no, I can't prove it." He came from behind the desk, fists bunched. "And I don't have to prove it. Not to you. I know what you're doing. Trying to link Angie to Paul's death so your company doesn't have to pay. And you think you can get to her through our relation—through me. Well, the hell with you, mister. Just leave, all right? I'm warning you."

Dave pointed to the wall. "That certificate says you graduated from the California School of Engineering. Did they teach you how to wire up an explosive device? And detonate it by remote control?"

Kilgore narrowed his eyes. "Do you carry a gun?"

"I'm licensed to carry a gun." Dave smiled. "Why do you ask?"

48

"Because if you haven't got a gun on you," Kilgore said, "I'm going to beat the shit out of you."

"Not bright," Dave said. "It would draw adverse attention to your school. And the Sheriff's department would wonder about your overreaction to a few harmless questions. Also"—he smiled again, and patted his ribs on the left side where a holster would be if he owned a holster, if he owned a gun to put into a holster—"maybe I have a gun. What was Myers hauling in his semi at night up in that canyon?"

Kilgore looked sulky. "How the hell should I know?"

"Angie Myers doesn't know either." Dave lit a cigarette. "Neither of you gave a damn about Paul Myers, did you? You had each other, after all."

"Don't smoke in here," Kilgore said.

Dave said, "I'm leaving in a minute. She was beaten up about the time he was killed. That must have upset you, caring for her as you do. How did it happen? Who did it to her?"

Kilgore went back to his desk but didn't sit down. "She wouldn't say." He picked up a stack of unopened envelopes and sorted through them, frowning. "Why wasn't it Paul? He was nothing but a truck driver, after all."

"You seem ready with your fists, yourself," Dave said.

"And your face doesn't look marked." Kilgore let the envelopes fall. "Which is remarkable, considering the things you say to perfect strangers."

"Nobody's perfect," Dave said.

A voice called across the play area. "Mr. Kilgore?" Kilgore muttered impatiently, rounded the desk, passed Dave. A fragile-looking young woman in big tinted spectacles stood in the open doorway of the complex under the rubber tree. Red paint had splashed the front of her skirt. "I've got a mini-riot." She sounded on the edge of tears. "Can you settle it, please?" Kilgore sighed and jogged across the sunlit space. The two of them vanished into the building.

Dave left the office. He tried the door of the unit next to it. The door opened. At the rear of the room was a kitchenette with a breakfast bar and two stools. At the front stood a chair and a two-seater sofa in tough green and tan plaid. A low table held books, magazines, and two empty coffee mugs, one marked with lipstick. Stereo components occupied modular shelves that also held records. A door stood open to a bathroom. Dave went just far enough into the larger room to see that the bathroom had a door on its other side. This too stood partway open. And beyond it he glimpsed, in a band of sunlight, an unmade bed and the corner of a television set. He stepped outside again, pulled the door shut, and went quietly away.

7

Terence Molloy wore a new bathrobe but food had spilled down it and dried. He stood clutching the shiny bars of a walker, and screwed up his face against the bright hot daylight outside the screen door. His face was twisted anyway, mouth drooping at the left corner, left eyelid drooping. His thick gray hair had been slicked down with water, but his beard was bristly—he'd gone a couple of days without a shave.

He croaked, "Who are you? What do you want?"

Dave gave his name and stated his business. "I'm sorry to bother you, Mr. Molloy. I know you're not well. Is your wife at home?"

The street of clipped hedges and Spanish-style bunga-lows was quiet. Dave heard a toilet flush inside the house, heard footsteps hurrying. Faith Molloy appeared, a dumpy woman in a faded house dress. Molded shoes made her feet look big. Above them, her ankles were swollen. "It says no salesmen or solicitors."

Her husband said, "You don't know what you're talking about. It's about Paul. You always go off half-cocked." He hiked the walker forward and fumbled with a trembling hand at the screen-door latch. "Come in."

"Oh, sure," Faith Molloy said. "I haven't got anything to do but entertain strangers."

"I won't be long." Dave pulled open the screen door and stepped inside. He told the old man, "Thank you."

"Go crazy around here with only her for company," Terence Molloy said. "My glad-hearted colleen. Look at her. Face like a sour apple."

"He's not himself," Faith Molloy said.

"On the night Paul died," Dave said, "did Angela bring the children and stay here with you?"

"I needed her. This one was acting up. Of course, I needed two more children. A sixty-five-year-old one isn't enough." Faith Molloy snatched up scattered sections of the morning *Times*. The furniture was puffy overstuffed covered in a yellow and pink flower print. She kneed the Off button of a television set. A game show quit in the middle. "Sit down. I suppose you'll be wanting coffee?"

"Not if it's any trouble." Dave sat on the sofa.

"I wouldn't know how to handle it, if it wasn't trouble." She went away with the crumpled newspaper.

Dave asked the old man, "Paul was working nights so he could help you out financially. Do you know what he was hauling, who he was working for?"

"He never said." The old man shuffled in his shiny rack to the easychair that faced the television set. "And I wasn't about to pry. None of my business." He threw Dave a warning scowl. "No, don't get up and help me, God damn it. I can manage." He wangled the rack into position and dropped onto the sagging cushions. With his good foot, in a fake leather bedroom slipper, he pushed the rack clumsily aside. "Going to miss Paul. He was a real son to me."

"Where was Gene that night?" Dave said.

"He's over there, isn't he? At Angie's? That's where you come from, I suppose." Terence Molloy looked at the small

52

table beside his chair. The lamp was painted china with a fluted shade. Under it clustered pill containers and medicine bottles. He frowned. Then he began poking with his hand down between the chair arm and the cushion. He came up with a round snuff can, fidgeted it open, tucked snuff into his cheek. He looked anxiously over his shoulder, closed the can, tossed it to Dave. "Hide that. They want you to relax, but anything that would relax you—tobacco, booze—you can't have those."

Dave pushed the can under the sofa cushion. "Where was Gene? Here?"

"I wouldn't let him through that door. Living off some woman, probably. His mother spoiled hell out of him. Angie always had a soft spot in her head for him. You watch, he'll live off her the rest of his useless life."

"She seems to know how to handle him," Dave said.

Terence Molloy snorted. "He's there, isn't he? And Paul not cold in his grave."

"It wouldn't be worth it to him for her wages as a waitress," Dave said. "She'll barely make ends meet that way for herself and the kids."

The old man's attention wasn't on him. He was staring blankly, slack-jawed, at the blank television screen. His nails needed trimming. With them, he was plucking at his beard stubble. Under his breath, he sang, quavery and off-key. Some old Irish song. "'And in all me life I ne'er did see such a foin young girl, upon my soul . . .'" He looked at Dave with sudden sharpness, and said, "It's for the insurance money. That's what you're thinking, isn't it? You said you were from the insurance company."

"It will be a lot of money if it's paid," Dave said. "Would Gene be sure enough of Angie's taking him in to cause Paul to have an accident that would get him out of the way so he, Gene, could live happily ever after on the insurance?"

The old man stared, mouth open. "Are you saying it wasn't an accident?"

Dave told him what it was.

Faith Molloy came in with coffee in a cup and saucer, and bent to set it on a little table at Dave's elbow. "Who would do such a thing?"

"I was wondering if it could be Gene," Dave said.

Still half bent above the table, face close to the lampshade, white as the lampshade, Faith Molloy went still. For a moment her face was expressionless. Dave could see where Gene's good looks came from. She must have been a beauty, forty years ago. At last she found her voice, enough to whisper, "Gene?"

"It would be a fitting end," the old man said. "The hangman's noose."

The woman turned on him in fury. "He never harmed anyone in his life. He's weak, that's all. He'd never hurt anybody." She looked at Dave. "It isn't in him."

"Weak? He's a liar, a thief, a gambler, a drunk, and a lecher. No morals. No scruples. No self-respect. What did you expect, woman?"

"You shut your crazy old mouth." Faith Molloy screamed this. She turned frantically to Dave. "Don't listen to him. He's sick. His mind's gone. Half the time he doesn't know his own name."

"Gene's at your daughter's now," Dave said. "Where was he living before?"

"I've got it written down." She threw a savage look at her husband and left the room, muttering, "You wicked old devil. Your only son. Your flesh and blood. Name of your name."

Terence Molloy picked up a metal crutch from beside his chair, reached out, and with its rubber tip pulled the television button. The game show returned. Gold curtains flew open. A new blue automobile gleamed on a turntable. A young red-haired woman in green jumped up and down with joy and hugged the wrinkled MC, who raised his eyebrows in simulated surprise. Terence Molloy let the crutch fall. "I'd beat her with that," he said, "if I had the strength. I was a strong man once. She wouldn't have dared plague me then as she does now. Now all I can do to her is spill my food and piss in the bed."

"Here it is." Faith Molloy came hurrying back in her clumsy shoes and pushed a scrap of paper into Dave's hand. "Gene has a lot of friends. He'll have been with his friends. He likes to have a good time. They'll have seen him that night. They'll tell you."

"Thank you." Folding the paper, tucking it away, Dave got off the sagging couch. "There's nothing to worry about, then, is there?"

"Oh, my dear man." She shook her head despairingly. "I hope you never know how much there is to worry about."

"If you'd be quiet," the old man said, "I could hear the television. This man doesn't want to know your troubles. People have troubles of their own."

Dave moved toward the open front door, the screen with the sunlight glaring on it. Faith Molloy tagged after him and plucked his sleeve. "You won't stop the insurance coming, will you?"

"Not I," Dave said.

"Paul told us we wouldn't have to worry if anything happened to him. He'd bought a hundred thousand dollars worth of insurance, and we were to get half."

"He sounds like a good man," Dave said.

"Oh, he was. Why is it the awful ones go on and on living?" She turned to glare at her husband. "Why does Our Lord always take the good?"

"Because nobody on earth deserves them," the old man

shouted over the television racket. "No woman—that's for sure."

The building was two-story brown brick, on a Hollywood corner opposite two filling stations and a hamburger shack with a tin sign: BIGGIE'S. Downstairs, the brown brick building housed a bar called Liza's, with caricatures painted on its windows of a young woman with wide eyes, scarlet mouth, long black gloves, champagne glass in one hand, long cigarette holder in the other.

Down the side street, near the back corner of the building, Dave found a door whose beveled glass bore the address that Faith Molloy had given him. He climbed narrow, newly carpeted stairs to a hallway of old closed doors. The air was hot and smelled of room deodorant. At the far end of the hallway, a window showed a slatted iron fire escape. But the inspectors hadn't been here lately; across the window, shelves held trailing philodendrons.

Dave knocked on door number three. Music thumped up from the bar below, but no sound came from beyond the door. He knocked again. A door down the hall opened and a tall, reedy man stepped out. He wore an apron, short shorts, and cowboy boots, and he had a small gold ring in one ear. His hair ought to have been gray but it was strawberry color, upswept, shiny. In one scrawny arm he cradled a brown Mexican pottery bowl. It held yellow batter that he was whipping with a wooden spoon.

He said, "You're too late, darling. The hunk has flown."

"Gene Molloy?" Dave said. "You a friend of his?"

The man shook his head. The strawberry curls quivered. "He didn't have boyfriends; he had girlfriends." The man let go of the spoon, laid the back of a hand against his forehead, sighed. "God knows, I tried. But that old green taffeta just doesn't fool them anymore."

56

Dave grinned. "I thought he lived with somebody."

"*Off* somebody. Liza. You'll find her downstairs. She'll be the one gnashing her teeth. I've warned her it'll play hell with those mail-order dentures, but women are so emotional." He lifted the spoon and critically watched the batter run off it. "Look, I have to get this in the oven. My God, it's hot. I'm dying for a drink. How about you?"

"I'll die a little longer, thanks. Would you know—was he around here on the night of the ninth?"

The man turned his head, watched out of the corners of his eyes. "That was the night he smashed up the bar. But you already knew that, didn't you?"

"Late or early?" Dave said.

"Late—one o'clock. It was just Irish high spirits, but Liza got hysterical and called the cops."

"Did they arrest him, book him, lock him up?"

"All night. But Liza bailed him out next morning."

"He brought the body here in his own car," Cole Wrightwood said. A plump, sleek black, he wore a dark pinstripe suit, a quiet tie, and a large diamond ring. The desktop in front of him was polished to a high gloss. Along its front edge in a planter grew a neat low hedge of marigolds. In corners of the paneled office, tall white baskets held sprays of gladioluses. The cool conditioned air was laden with the damp perfume of flowers. Electronic organ music—Fauré? Widor?—whispered from hidden loudspeakers. "And waited while I filled out the death certificate. As I expect you know"—Wrightwood smiled a grave, apologetic little smile—"the mortician fills in all the data—name, address, that sort of thing. The physician merely has to write in the cause of death and sign the certificate."

"He has to have been the attending physician," Dave said, "for at least twenty days. Otherwise there has to be an autopsy. The word of a man called in just for the emergency isn't enough."

Wrightwood nodded. "The departed's wife, widow—she came along with the doctor. She said he was the family physician."

"Did that seem likely to you? White, isn't he?" A leaded window, diamond panes, churchlike, was at Wrightwood's back. A long, glossy Cadillac hearse slid past the window. "Had you ever seen him before?"

"He was white." Wrightwood's smile was thin. "Most doctors are. I saw no reason to doubt the woman's word. She was in tears, deeply grieved, shocked. In my experience, people don't lie at times like that."

"May I see the death certificate?"

Wrightwood stirred in his tall leather chair, but he didn't rise. "You say Oswald Bishop was insured by this company you represent?" The card Dave had given him lay on the desktop. He blinked at it through large round lenses framed in heavy black plastic. "Pinnacle?"

"I didn't say." Dave took from inside his jacket the leather folder that held his private investigator's license, and held it out across the marigolds for Wrightwood to read. "Pinnacle has asked me to investigate the death of a close friend of Ossie Bishop." He flipped the folder closed and slid it back into his jacket. "Another gypsy trucker. Paul Myers."

Wrightwood's eyebrows rose. "That was on the news. An accident. He drove off the road in some canyon."

"No." Dave told him what the Sheriff's lab had discovered. "Now, Ossie Bishop was doing the same sort of nightwork as Myers. He even got Myers the job. His death coming so close to Myers's disturbs me." Dave smiled. "I'll regard it as a great kindness if you'll let me see Bishop's death certificate."

"What was this nightwork?"

"I don't know. You say Mrs. Bishop was distraught that night. She didn't happen to say—didn't blurt it out in anger or despair, perhaps?"

"You mean you don't know what these two men were doing with their trucks? Not even the one you insured?"

"Myers seems not to have told anyone. That in itself isn't exactly reassuring, is it? Not when you add the fact that he was very well paid." Dave took out Myers's bankbook and held it up. "He was making frequent fat deposits. In cash." He put the bankbook away.

Wrightwood sat for a few seconds longer, moving his chair very slightly from side to side on its swivel base. He shrugged and rose. "It was a heart attack." He rounded the desk, crossed deep purple carpeting, opened one of a pair of tall, carved, double doors. Through the doorway came the quiet chatter of a typewriter. Wrightwood spoke. The typewriter ceased. Branches of firethorn showed outside the window. Small birds were harvesting the berries, their squabbling shrill beyond the panes. Wrightwood returned and handed Dave a manila folder marked BISHOP, OSWALD B., with a date a month old.

Dave put on reading glasses and opened the folder. The shadow of Wrightwood came between him and the window light. The cushion of the big desk chair sighed as Wrightwood's two hundred sleek pounds settled on it. Written after CAUSE OF DEATH was *Massive coronary occlusion*. TIME OF DEATH: 1:50 A.M. ATTENDING PHYSICIAN: Ford T. Kretschmer, M.D. Kretschmer had written down an address and telephone number. Dave took off the glasses, folded them, pushed them into a pocket, closed the file, handed it across the sunny little flowers to Wrightwood. "Thank you." He got to his feet. "I appreciate it."

"It's on file at the Hall of Records."

"You were nearer," Dave said. "I'm sorry for the trouble. Anyway, you've told me things they couldn't at the Hall of Records."

Wrightwood turned his head slightly, wary. "It was a heart attack. Big, heavy man. He'd overworked himself." Wrightwood got to his feet, buttoned his jacket. He didn't appear worried about his own weight. "Hypertension kills a good many of my people. I see men who have gone down in their prime all the time." He had come around the desk again, and now took Dave's arm to walk him to the door. His grip was as gentle and comforting as if Dave had just brought him a dead friend. "You interest me." He didn't let go Dave's arm. With his free hand he gripped the fancily wrought bronze handle of the tall office door, but he didn't move it. "Just what have I told you besides the obvious?"

"That the widow came here." Dave didn't want a cigarette, but he wanted the undertaker's hand off his arm. Nobody was dead around him—he didn't want to be treated as if somebody was. So he reached for a cigarette, found it, found his slim steel lighter, lit the cigarette. "Did the oldest son come too? Melvil?" He put the lighter away.

Wrightwood shook his head. "A woman came. I assumed she was a nurse—perhaps the doctor's receptionist."

"What made you think that?"

Wrightwood turned the handle and opened the door. "She fit the role. You develop an instinct about people in this business. She had that self-assured way about her. They boss their bosses." They were in a quiet reception room now. He gave the slim, pale black, fortyish woman at the desk a grin. "Don't they?"

She looked up at him, wide-eyed, and patted her beautifully set hair. "I can't think what you're talking about." Her laugh was soft and dry.

Dave smiled at her and moved toward the doors that

would take him along a hushed corridor hung with ferns and caged canaries, a corridor that passed rooms where the embalmed dead slept in coffins, rooms where damp-eyed families sat on spindly chairs, and past the chapel. It was the route he had taken to get here. With the door open, he turned back. "Can you describe her for me? Stocky, middle-aged, well-dressed?"

Wrightwood tilted his head. "You know this woman?"

"Not yet," Dave said. "But I'm looking forward to it. Thanks for your help."

8

The place he lived in had, he judged, started life as riding stables. He left the Jaguar beside Cecil's van, walked past the end of the long, shingle-sided front building, crossed the uneven bricks of a courtyard sheltered by an old oak. He unwrapped and laid on plates in the cookshack pastrami sandwiches he'd picked up on Fairfax, built Bloody Marys, and carried these on a bentwood tray across to the long, shingle-sided rear building. The arrangement of the place was awkward, but it amused more than bothered him. The last of his dead father's nine beautiful wives, Amanda, had made the buildings handsome and livable inside. If, during the short winter, getting from one building to another meant being soaked by rain or chilled by wind, novelty was on its side. It was never boring.

The back building was walled in knotty pine. There was a wide fireplace. The inside planking of the pitched roof showed, and the unpainted rafters. Above, Amanda had designed a sleeping loft. Climbing the raw pine steps to it now meant climbing into heat. The smell of sun-baked pine overlaid the old, almost forgotten smell of horse and hay that always ghosted the place. Cecil sat naked, propped black against white pillows, in the wide bed, sheet across

his long, lean legs. He gleamed with sweat. His collarbone
and ribs showed. Dave kept trying to fatten him up. It
didn't seem to be working.

"Hey." Cecil tossed aside the latest *Newsweek* and
smiled. "How was Gifford Gardens?"

"Words fail me." Dave set the tray on the long raw pine
chest of drawers, carried his glass to Cecil, bent and kissed
his mouth. "How are you?"

"I rested, like you told me," Cecil said. "Nearly driving
me crazy." With a wry little smile, he raised his glass.
"Cheers," he said cheerlessly, and drank.

Dave tasted his drink, then brought the sandwiches and
napkins. He sat on the edge of the bed. "It's a little bit
racist out there. Eat that. They also have gangs." He bit
into his sandwich. That was the best delicatessen in L.A.
When he'd washed the bite down with Bloody Mary, he
said, "Can I borrow your van tomorrow?"

"Something happen to the Jag?" Cecil looked alarmed.

Dave told him what had happened to the Jag.

"Aw, no. Shit. It's my fault. I heard the kind of place it
was, when I worked for Channel Three News." Cecil shook
his head slowly in self-disgust. "I should have warned you."

"I wouldn't have taken you seriously." Dave set his plate
on the bed and shed his jacket. "The place is beyond belief.
Next time I'll drive a junk heap."

"Next time, just don't go," Cecil said. "Wonder is you
came back with a car at all. Wonder is you came back alive.
That is a killing ground out there. Grannies, little children,
policemen." Cecil stretched out a long, skinny arm to take
the cigarette pack from Dave's jacket where it lay on the
bed. "I should have been with you."

"You're not supposed to smoke," Dave said. On a deadly
night of rain last winter, in the lost back reaches of Yucca
Canyon, flames leaping high from a burning cabin, bullets

had punctured the boy's lungs. Cecil acted as if he hadn't heard. He lit the cigarette with Dave's lighter, and choked on the smoke. Coughing bent him forward, shook him. "Damn." He wiped away tears with his knuckles. "Damn."

Dave took the cigarette from him, stubbed it out in the bedside ashtray. "That'll larn you," he said.

For a moment, Cecil got the coughing under control. Eyes wet, voice a wheeze, he asked, "Where you going tomorrow? Where you taking my van?"

"San Diego County," Dave said. "And no, you can't go. It's too far. Look, will you please eat?"

Cecil coughed again, fist to mouth. When he finished, he picked up the sandwich. Wearily obedient, he bit into it. With his mouth full, he said, "Seem to me, if you take my van, it's only fair you take me." He gulped Bloody Mary, wiped tomato juice off his chin with the napkin. "Dave, I can't eat this. I'm not hungry." He laid the sandwich on the plate. His eyes begged. "I'm sorry. Maybe later."

"Right." Dave knew his smile was stiff, mechanical, false. He was growing discouraged. And frightened. "I'll wrap it in plastic and put it in the fridge. Don't forget it, now, okay?" Cecil nodded mutely and handed him the plate as if looking at it was more than he could bear. Dave rose and set it on the tray. He turned back. "I'll take you tomorrow, if you promise me something." The rear of the van was lushly carpeted—floor, walls, ceiling—in electric blue to contrast with the flame colors of the custom paint job. Picture window. Built-in bar, refrigerator, drop-leaf table. Electric blue easy chair. Electric blue wraparound couch. "You lie down. All the way."

Cecil made a face. He poked grumpily at the ice cubes in his Bloody Mary with a finger. He licked the finger, tried for a smile, and almost managed it. "Okay. I promise." He livened up a little. "Why are we going?"

"The reasons keep piling up." Dave sat on the bed again, worked on his sandwich and drink, and reviewed the morning's events for Cecil. He finished, "So I went to see Dr. Ford Kretschmer. Only his address is a storage lot for galvanized pipe. And the telephone number is out of service."

Cecil stared. "He wasn't a doctor at all?"

"Maybe not." Sandwich and drink finished, Dave wiped fingers and mouth with his napkin, took Cecil's empty glass and his own with his plate to the tray on the chest. "Whoever he was, the woman with him was no nurse. She was the same one who showed up with goons at the Myers house three weeks later."

"The ones who beat her up?" Cecil said.

"You've got it." Dave picked up his jacket and shrugged into it. "I have to take the Jaguar down to the agency so they can replace that window." He dug from the jacket pocket the crumpled flimsies he had taken from the drawer under Paul Myers's bedroom closet. He hesitated. "You want to rest while I'm gone, or you want to do some work?"

Cecil reached for the papers. "Busy hands," he said, "are happy hands." He began separating the papers, frowning at them. "What are these? What do I do?"

"Telephone those companies. Get hold of whoever is in charge of shipping. Get out of them, if you can, whether Paul Myers was hauling anything except what's listed on those manifests. What did they think of Myers? Did any of them know him? If so, did they know who he was moonlighting for, what he was hauling? Anything, everything."

"Do I pretend I'm you again?" Cecil said.

Dave grinned. "If it's not too much of a strain on your natural femininity."

Cecil threw a pillow at him.

Dave laughed and carried the tray down the stairs.

On sun-scorched lots where weeds grew through the asphalt, and faded plastic pennons fluttered from sagging wires overhead, he looked at battered cars not quite but almost ready for the junkyard. Two or three he test-drove. They bucked and gasped through trash-blown neighborhoods of desolate lumberyards, warehouses, and shacky motels, while salesmen in polyester doubleknit suits breathed mouthwash fumes beside him, lying about mileage, lifetime batteries, and recent overhauls. In the end, he escaped Culver City in a 1969 two-door Valiant. A sideswipe had creased it deeply from front to back. Its crackly plastic upholstery leaked stuffing. But its gears worked, the engine ran smoothly, and the tires still had treads. It was a vague beige color, a hole gaped where its radio had been, and Dave pried loose and handed to the surprised salesman its one remaining hubcap before he drove off. The car labored up the canyon, but it didn't overheat. And when he left it parked on the leaf-strewn bricks of his tree-shady yard where the Jaguar customarily stood, he felt good. No one in Gifford Gardens would give this car a second look.

This time he fixed double martinis in the cookshack. And when he carried them into the rear building, music was in the air—Miles Davis, "Sketches of Spain." The ice in the hefty glasses jingled as he carried them up the stairs. The flimsies in their pale pinks, blues, yellows, lay spread out on the sheet across Cecil's legs. He told the telephone receiver "thank you" and put it back in its cradle. He reached for the martini and gave his beautiful head with its short-cropped hair a rueful shake.

"Not one of these companies shipped anything with Paul Myers but what's listed on these manifests." He patted the papers. "They all liked him. He was reliable, friendly, intelligent." Cecil sipped the martini, hummed, and for a

66

moment shut his eyes in unwordable appreciation. "They are all sorry he's dead, but nobody can guess what he was hauling at night up in that canyon before he crashed." Cecil held the glass up in a salute to Dave, who was shedding his sweaty clothes. "You came back just in time. I was about to die of temperance up here, all alone by the telephone."

"Sorry about that, but when you hear what I've done, you'll be proud of me." Dave sat on the foot of the bed, perched his drink on the loft railing, shed shoes and socks. "I bought a jalopy to drive in Gifford Gardens. A genuine eyesore." He tried his martini. Better than usual. Most things were, now that Cecil was with him. "When you chance to pass it, avert your gaze, all right?"

"I can't promise." Cecil gathered up the flimsies. They crackled and whispered together. "Morbid fascination may be too much for me. How did you force yourself to commit this act of sound common sense?"

"I had the man at the Jaguar showroom in Beverly Hills run me over to the used-car lots on Washington in Culver City. You should have seen his expression. He couldn't believe the place." Dave hiked his butt and shed his trousers. He stood, holding the trousers up to get the creases straight. "The poor man kept repeating that he'd furnish me with a loaner until the window was fixed. I didn't have to do this desperate thing. He was almost in tears." Dave took down a wooden hanger from a wide knotty-pine wardrobe, and hung the pants on it. "But I was firm." He retrieved his jacket from where he'd draped it over the rail, and hung that on the hanger too. "If I made him strand me there, I'd have to buy wheels to get home on, wouldn't I?" He hung the suit in the wardrobe. It was damp with sweat and must go to the cleaners, but that could wait. What would he wear to Gifford Gardens next time? A raveled sweater and an old picture hat? He closed the wardrobe doors. "I knew nothing less would force me into it." He went to get his drink and saw Cecil watching him soberly and big-eyed over the rim of his martini glass. "What's the matter?"

"You saying it's going to get you to San Diego County? You don't need my van, so you don't need me?"

"I'll be stretching my luck if it gets me to Gifford Gardens and back." Dave took off his tie, unbuttoned his shirt, picked up his glass, sat on the bed. He put a hand on Cecil's thigh. Too thin. "No, if you feel up to it at five tomorrow morning, we'll go in the van, the two of us." He smiled. "I know I sound like the witch in the wood, but what will you eat for supper that's fattening?"

Cecil's eyes brimmed with tears. "Man, I am so tired of being sick and weak and no good to you and skinny and ugly and full of scars. I am so tired of that."

"Hey," Dave said. The boy was weeping, and Dave took the glass out of his hand. "If you're going to turn into a maudlin drunk, I'll have to put you on Perrier water. And there are no calories in that." He pulled tissues from a box by the clock and the lamp. He dried Cecil's face and kissed his salty mouth. "Come on, cheer up. You're home. That means you're going to get well. All it needs is time. I'm glad you're home. Aren't you glad you're home? If the answer is yes, smile."

Cecil worked up a forlorn smile. It didn't last. "Burden on you," he said gloomily. "I didn't come back to you for that."

"You didn't come back to me to get shot up, either," Dave said. "How do you suppose I feel about that?"

"Comes with the territory." This time there was some conviction to Cecil's smile. He reached out. "Give me back my strengthening medicine."

Dave put the glass in his hand. "I need a shower. You think you can wait here and not cry anymore?"

Cecil read the big black watch bristly with stops on his skeletal wrist. Miles Davis's thoughtful trumpet had gone silent. "Time for the news." Cecil nodded at the television set on the far side of the bed. "How can I cry, with all the happiness they are going to spread out for me, in all the colors of the rainbow?" He groped around in the bed for the remote switch. The set came on.

The picture was file film—of a charred eighteen-wheeler lying on its top in a canyon among blackened rocks and scorched brush. The big tires of the truck still smoked. Men in yellow hardhats and rubber suits crunched around the wreckage. High above, fire vehicles and a wrecking truck stood at the edge of a cliff road. Sheriff's cars. A television reporter's voice came through the speaker.

". . . but today, Sheriff's investigators revealed that the semi, owned and driven by independent trucker Paul Myers, thirty-six, of Gifford Gardens, exploded before it plunged off the road into Torcido Canyon. Laboratory evidence has uncovered the presence of an explosive device, a bomb, under the cab of the truck. Myers was killed in the explosion and crash. He leaves a wife and two children."

Jaime Salazar stood in dark glasses in glaring sunlight.

"We're talking to Lieutenant Salazar, who is heading up the investigation for the Sheriff's department." The reporter was a chubby-cheeked blond boy. His microphone wore a round red cap to keep the wind out. "Lieutenant, any motive for the killing? The trailer of the truck was empty. Had there been a hijacking?"

"We don't know." The wind blew Salazar's soft, dark hair. He smoothed it with a hand. "It's one of the possibilities we're looking into."

"Before we went on the air here," the reporter said, "you mentioned a suspect you wanted to question."

"A convict named Silencio Ruiz," Salazar said.

"Right." The reporter turned to face the camera. "We'll have a photograph of Ruiz on our five o'clock segment of the Channel Three News. Anyone with knowledge of the young man's whereabouts . . ."

"That's your case." Cecil tried not to sound proud.

Dave grunted, frowned, picked up the flimsies, and sorted through them. On the day before he died, Myers had trucked leather coats from a loft in downtown L.A. to a cut-rate retailer in Covina. Later he'd hauled pet supplies from Glendale to Ventura. The manifests had been dropped into the drawer in order, the latest on top, but there was no manifest for what Myers had hauled up Torcido Canyon after midnight. That one would have burned, wouldn't it, with the truck, with the man himself?

"You going to take the shower before I run out of martini?" Cecil watched the tube. He was a news junkie. "In my diminished state, I could dry up and blow away."

"Give me ten minutes." Dave snatched briefs and jeans from an unpainted pine drawer and started down the stairs. "Meantime, phone Jack Schuyler at Pinnacle Life, will you? Introduce yourself and ask him who referred Paul Myers to them. It should be on his application."

The shower didn't take ten minutes. When Dave got back up to the loft, Cecil held out his empty glass. "It was a friend," he said. "Bruce Kilgore."

"Do tell." Dave took the glass, found his own, and made for the cookshack. He hoped a second martini would work up Cecil's appetite. Then they would leave for Max Romano's. Everything on Max's menu was fattening.

9

The van climbed through a crooked pass where ragged rocks thrust up high and cramped the narrow road. And here was the valley. The hills all around were brown, brushy, strewn with bleached boulders. The valley itself was green with groves and meadows. But the sky was hard as he remembered, a relentless Southwest blue, yellow heat in it, even so early in the morning.

Twice Cecil had come out of the back, bored with lying on the couch, watching the coastline, the stucco roadside motels and eateries, the monotonous blue glitter of the Pacific, bored with the magazines he'd brought, the cassettes. Dave had sent him back. Now he came out again and dropped his lanky self into the passenger seat. Dave glanced at him. He looked all right. When he was tired—like last night by the time they'd finished dinner at Max's—his skin took on a dry, dusty finish. It glowed now, and his eyes were clear.

"Pretty," he said. "Picture postcard." He saw something, bent forward, peered upward through the windshield. "Look at that. Hawk circling."

"*Halcón*," Dave said. "That's the name of the place." He saw the hawk and remembered another time when he'd seen a hawk against a sky like this. From the top of a bare, brown mountain back of Sangre de Cristo, up the coast. He'd parked his car outside a bleak concrete-block building there, a television station where a few minutes later he was to encounter Cecil for the first time. He told Cecil about this now. "Maybe it means good luck."

Cecil smiled. "You know it means good luck."

The road sloped down to the valley floor. The tidy rows of round and glossy orange trees looked as if Grant Wood had painted them. Sprinkler pipes worked among the avocado trees, whose branches drooped and tangled. Beneath them the light was undersea light. On tilting, sunswept pastures, Rainbird sprinklers cast sparkling arcs, strewing the grass with emeralds under the hoofs of stocky black cattle that browsed and did not look up as the van passed.

White letters on a modest green sign read HALCON, and here, in the long morning shadows of old live oaks, buildings clustered—metal filling station, railroad-car diner, bat-and-board tavern with COOR's in red neon in the window. The general store was barn-red shiplap, with a long plank front porch and a neat red, white, and blue enamel sign: U.S. POST OFFICE. Dave wheeled the van onto gravel and parked at the end of the long building. He opened the door and stepped stiffly down, glad for the chance to stretch his legs. And a bullet whined past.

Cecil called, "Look out. They're shooting at us."

Dave lay on the ground, the side of his face stung by gravel and by the sharp, dry, curled little leaves of the oaks. Far off, he heard shots. Four, five? He flinched, waiting for the bullets to strike him, to kick up gravel around him, to bore into the sleek metal of the van, to plunk into the crooked gray boles of the oaks. Nothing like that happened. The distant gunfire ceased. Silence. A meadowlark sang.

Nearer, a rooster crowed. Dave turned his head and called: "Are you all right?"

"I want to go back to the news business," Cecil said.

"Where are you? Your voice sounds funny."

"I am in here with my face in the carpet," Cecil said. "That can mess up your diction worse than a course in Afro-American English."

"Stay there." Dave rose cautiously. Gravel clung to his face, the heels of his hands. He brushed it off. The van door hung open. He brought his eyes to window level and looked out past the oaks. Flat land stretched away, empty in the sun. Chainlink fencing glinted far off. He wished he had De Witt Gifford's binoculars. Did tiny figures move out there against the dry brown background of the mountains? Was that a line of parked automobiles? Yes. Sunshine glanced off a windowpane. A moment later, dust rose and traveled. A car the size of an ant crawled off. A second. A third. The line of dust stretched out along the foot of the hills. When it settled, he saw no parked cars. He drew a deep breath, straightened, and looked into the van. Cecil had done his panicked best to fit his gangly body under the control panel. Dave reached across and touched him.

"All clear," he said.

Cecil looked up, forehead wrinkled. "Who was it?"

"Too far away to tell," Dave said. "Come on."

Their heels drummed hollowly on the planks of the long porch. Past a screen door, across which angled a shiny metal bar printed DRINK DR. PEPPER, was a wooden door with a top panel of glass. Inside the glass hung a sign: *Closed. Sorry We Missed You, Please Call Again.* Dave read his watch. Two minutes past nine. He went on along the porch with Cecil following. Plank steps went down, and so did they.

Behind the store, a frame cottage stood inside a picket-fenced yard. The house was barn-red, like the store. So was the fence. Grass grew in front of the house. In a bare side yard, white hens pecked near a doghouse that bore the name DIGGER. From a cleat beside the doghouse door a rusty chain hung dragging in the dust. Dave reached over the gate to work the latch, when the house door opened and a stocky brown man came out, buttoning a red and black checkered flannel shirt. His hair was cropped close to his scalp. He pulled the door shut, turned, and gave a little jerk of surprise when he saw Dave and Cecil. He was short, but with a big man's chest and shoulders. He came to the gate bandy-legged in cowboy boots.

"What can I do for you?"

"Tell us about the sharpshooters," Dave said.

The man glanced over his shoulder. "They out there again?"

"Bullet just missed us," Cecil said.

"Damn." It was an apology. "I didn't hear them." He unlatched the gate. "Did they quit at nine?"

"And not a moment too soon," Dave said.

"It's the Sheriff's rifle range." The man let the gate fall shut and walked toward the front of the store. Dave and Cecil followed. Above the beat of their footfalls on the planks, the man said, "Been there forty, fifty years. But I don't think rifles fired so far then." He jingled keys, unlocked the door of the store, and with the scuffed, pointed tip of a boot, kicked a brown rubber wedge under the door to keep it open. "No limit to them now. All the way to Moscow."

The store was gloomy and smelled of onions, cheese, new blue jeans. The man followed a crowded aisle of canned goods—soup, baked beans, chili, Spam—on shelves and in cartons on the floor. He passed out of sight around a stack of new bushel baskets. A cash register beeped. Dodging rakes, hoes, brooms hanging from rafters, Dave and Cecil went after him. He stood behind a counter on whose front a faded sign read KEROSENE. Open boxes of candy bars and chewing gum and digestive tablets lay on the counter. On little wire racks hung cellophane packets of beef jerky, yellow envelopes of corn chips. At his back, shelves held bottles—whiskey, rum, gin, vodka. Cigarette packs were pigeonholed. The man dug a wad of currency from a pocket of his Levi's and sorted the bills into compartments in the shallow gray metal drawer of an electronic cash register. "What I think," he said, "is they want me out of here. Fellow got shot right outside here, four months ago. Walked out with two sacks of steer manure to his car and a bullet hit him. He still don't walk right. They killed my dog."

"Isn't there anything you can do?" Dave said.

"This is the main road," Cecil said. "People could get hit in their cars."

"They have to quit at nine now," the man said. "That was all I could get. County supervisors told them they could only use it in the early morning when there's nobody around. Digger wasn't nobody. Just a dog. They didn't give a damn about a dog." He pushed the cash drawer shut angrily, and the machine emitted a stutter of protesting beeps. "People around here tell me go to court, sue." A wry smile twitched his mouth. "I say, 'I'm no Sioux—I'm a Ute.'" He sobered. "How much do I sue for? Money's not going to get me Digger back. He's dead. Anyway, the lawyers would get all the money. And I haven't got time to hang around courthouses. I got a store to run."

"And a post office," Dave said. From a shirt pocket he

took the slip of paper on which Luther Prentice had written Louella Bishop's address. "Can you tell me how to find this place?" He held out the slip.

The man rummaged under the counter for dime-store reading glasses, put them on, took the slip, peered at it. "Oh, sure." He turned the paper over and, with a ballpoint pen from a plastic cup on the counter, drew a map. "There you go." He handed the paper back to Dave, dropped the pen back into the cup, which had a round, yellow 49¢ EACH sign pasted to it. "Nice lady, Mrs. Bishop. Comes in here a lot. Shops for the Hutchings. Funny thing. You're the second ones to come looking for her." He eyed Cecil. "You a relative?"

Cecil shook his head. "Friend," he said.

Dave said, "Let me tell you who the others were who came looking for her. Last evening, was it?"

"I keep open till nine. Folks forget things, and I'm the only store. They'd have to drive clear up through the pass to town if it wasn't for me."

"A stocky woman," Dave said. "Middle-aged. Well dressed. A pair of big men with her. Goons."

"Drove a white unmarked van," the storekeeper said.

"Right." Dave turned away. "Thank you."

"They called her Duchess," the storekeeper said.

"She wanted to buy the truck." Louella Bishop's haunches were vast as she bent to set breakfast-soiled plates, cups, saucers in the white racks of a dishwasher. Her upper arms were thick as a man's thigh and their flesh jiggled. Above the dishwasher, twin stainless steel sinks were set in a surround of flower-painted shiny Mexican tiles. The electric stove was so surrounded, above it a dark copper-lined hood whose ventilator pipe went up among black rafters. The walls of the kitchen were roughly plastered and very white. The floor was waxed squares of terracotta. In planters outside deep-set windows, geraniums grew intensely green and red in the morning sunshine. Louella Bishop rolled the rack back into place, its glassy burden jingling, and closed the dishwasher door. With a wheeze of breath she straightened up. "And she bought it. Nothing more to tell."

"Why did you sell it?" Dave and Cecil sat at a plank table of wood almost as dark as the rafters, built sometime in the 1920s to imitate a refectory table from a California mission. Coffee mugs were in front of them. "I thought your husband's plan was for Melvil to begin driving as soon as he got out of high school."

"His plan was not to cough and choke himself to death at an early age," Louella Bishop said. "To die in convulsions in the middle of the night. And he gone now. And it's me that going to do the planning now. And it is no way in my plans for Melvil to end up like his father."

"The doctor said it was a heart attack. Dr. Kretschmer. The one who came to your house in Gifford Gardens. The one you called. He didn't put anything about convulsions on the death certificate."

"Ossie—he come home one morning, about three o'clock, three-thirty. He was working nights, you know, to get extra money. They put on all these new taxes—license, tires, no end to it. And he was trying to put money by so as to get another truck, like you say, for Melvil when the time came. We wanted him to get his education first. Anyway"— she filled a mug from a pottery urn, brought it to the table, lowered her bulk onto a chair—"Ossie was sick. Stumbled in the door. Looked like death. Couldn't catch his breath. Says he had to get to the bathroom but he couldn't get across the kitchen. Fell to his hands and knees. Soiled himself, like a little child. Oh, I tell you, that man was sick!" She wagged her head gloomily and sipped her coffee. "Doctor come and give him a shot, and that cleared up the trouble with his bowels."

"Dr. Hobart?" Dave asked.

She looked at him sharply. "Ossie say no Dr. Hobart. Say to call this here Dr. Kretschmer. Something to do with the nightwork. Had to be secret. I shouldn't be telling you, now. I'm talking too much."

"Did the Duchess come with him that time?"

She stirred on the chair, shifting from one mighty flank to the other. She drew a deep breath. Her big bosom rose with it. "I think you better go now."

"What's her real name?" Cecil said.

"Seemed like Ossie was going to get better after that," Louella Bishop said. "But it wasn't more than a few days, and he was dead."

Dave said, "Did Paul Myers come to see your husband when he was sick?"

She frowned. "You say they blew him up?"

"Who do you think they were? The Duchess and her strongarm boys?"

She opened her mouth to answer but she caught herself. "Yes, Paul came. He was a true friend. Had this here magazine with him. Something about science. But I don't know what they talked about. That's the truth. Paul closed the door, and they spoke low. When he left, he was pale, and he was angry." She put her hands flat on the table and heaved herself to her feet. "You best go now. I have a whole big house to clean."

"Why?" Cecil said. "You got a lot of money for that truck. Stands to reason. And what about all the money your husband saved, moonlighting?"

"I've got children to raise and send through school. Melvil's going to college. Be something. It's a good place to raise children down here." She rinsed a yellow cellulose sponge at the sink and wiped the handsome tiles. "I worked for the Hutchings before I got married. Says, 'Louella, if ever you want to come back, you come. You a part of this family and you always will be.' And they meant it, too." She glanced at Cecil. "Lord, child, I can't be idle the rest of my days. A person has to work."

Dave rose. "Thank you for your time." He took his coffee mug and Cecil's to the sinks and set them there. "You have no idea who would have wanted to kill Paul Myers? It didn't occur to you that your husband's death wasn't natural? There is no Dr. Kretschmer, you know."

She was wiping the handles of cupboard doors. She frowned at him. "I seen him plain as I see you now."

"He has no address, no telephone number, and no Ford T. Kretschmer is licensed to practice medicine in the state of California." Louella Bishop gave no sign that she was listening. She wiped drawer pulls. Dave said, "The Duchess and her handymen beat up Angela Myers a short time before Paul was killed. These are bad people, Mrs. Bishop. You shouldn't protect them."

"What was your husband hauling for them?" Cecil said.

The massive woman gave him a brief dismissive blink. At the sink she rinsed the sponge again, then took it to the table, bent over the table, began wiping the glossy old planks. She asked Dave, "Did Angela Myers tell you it was them that beat her up?"

"I have a witness. No, she didn't tell me."

"And why not?" Louella Bishop straightened her back and faced Dave, calm, monumental, fists on her hips. "Because she know worse could happen."

Cecil said, "Worse than having her husband killed?"

"She got little children, same as me." Louella Bishop set the chairs neatly at the table. "None of them got any daddy to look out for them now. Nobody but mama." She threw Dave a look of sour reproach. "You think I don't know what kind of people they are?"

"Someone has to stop them," Dave said. "What's her name? She had to sign the check. For the truck."

"Wasn't no check," she said. "She brought cash."

High-school boys in gym trunks collided with each other, dodged and ducked each other, bounced a basketball, threw a basketball, waved their arms, missed the hoop, on sunbaked asphalt beyond a chainlink fence. Their trunks were shiny green. Their skins were shiny with sweat. Up in Los Angeles these days, teenage boys cut their hair short, 1930s-style. Here in the boonies they still wore it long and floppy. Its color ranged from taffy to white, and the skin colors too. But there were two brown-skinned boys and one with black skin.

This was Melvil Bishop. He was thickly built. Basketball wouldn't be his true game, if he had a true game. He looked like a wrestler or a shot putter. He stood by a bench under an old pepper tree and talked to Cecil. Dave watched from the van across the street. Melvil looked sulky. He kept shaking his head. At last, with a bony shrug and a lazy lift of his hand, Cecil came away. He climbed into the cold, conditioned air of the van, looking disgusted.

"Don't help, my being black," he said. "He still would have talked more to you than he did to me. He never saw the Duchess before last night, never saw the phony doctor, never saw the heavies. His father died of a heart attack. He never said what he was hauling in his truck at night, or who he was working for. The old preacher is lying; Melvil never said anything to his mother about any doctor at any grave. Louella Bishop is just plain scared. Melvil—I'd say he was scared with all the extras."

"You want to drive now?" Dave said.

Cecil brightened. "All the way home?"

"Till you get tired," Dave said.

They changed seats and Cecil started the engine. "Why did the Duchess buy that truck?" He released the parking brake, frowned into the side mirror, steered the van down the sleepy morning street past old white frame cottages. A dog ran out and raced beside them, barking and trying to nip the tires. "Jesus." Cecil twisted the steering wheel, left, right. The tires squealed. "That is one ignorant dog. Going to get himself killed." Sweat broke out on Cecil's forehead. He pawed for the buttons that controlled the windows. His window slid down. "Get away, fool. Get away." He tramped on the brakes.

"Take it easy," Dave said. "He'll be all right."

It was the end of the dog's block. He left off barking and chasing, trotted back across the street, and went uphill along a sidewalk strewn with bright children's toys, his plumy tail waving. Cecil leaned his head on the steering wheel. He was trembling. "Shit," he said. He sat up and for a moment stared straight ahead through the windshield. He shivered. Eyes shut, he drew in air deeply, held it, blew it out. It didn't stop his trembling. Dave touched him. He looked at Dave. Tears were in his eyes. "I can't do it. Can't even drive a car anymore."

"You can," Dave said. "Of course you can. Just get your composure back, now. It's all right. Everything's cool. The dog is fine. No harm done."

But Cecil shook his head and lifted his butt up off the dark blue velvet of the driver's seat. Dave swiveled aside, then slid back of him and sat behind the wheel. Cecil sat in the passenger seat, long fingers interlaced hard between his knees. He sat looking down at his hands and said nothing. Dave got the van to Main Street, with its sallow brick and bright signs and dusty pickup trucks and shiny shopping carts. He got the van out of town, brown hills on the right, blue glitter of ocean on the left. He looked at Cecil. His eyes were closed again. Tears ran down his face. Tissues were in a dark blue box on the control panel. Dave pulled two out and nudged Cecil with the hand that held the tissues. Cecil opened his eyes, mutely accepted the tissues, wiped his face, dropped the wet tissues into the blue trash receptacle, clasped his hands between his knees again, slumped in the seat, chin on his chest.

"We can stop for a drink," Dave said. "Will that help?"

Cecil said, "You don't understand, do you?"

"I'd like to," Dave said. "Why don't you make me?"

Cecil managed a damp, crooked smile. "I'll make you later. Now, I'll explain." He looked somber. "You know what is going to happen to me if a bullet ever comes at me again? I am going to die. I don't mean if it hits me. If it hits me or not, I am going to die. Rifle range? Shit!"

"You held up fine all morning," Dave said.

"What kind of dog do you think Digger was? They killed my dog,' the man said." Cecil swiveled the seat, stared straight ahead again, fingers of both hands pressed flat against his mouth, tears running again. At last he dropped his hands. He drew a long, shuddering breath. "When he said that, I could feel the bullet going in. I don't want to kill anybody's dog."

"Right," Dave said, and handed him more tissues.

Cecil dried his eyes and blew his nose. He dropped the used tissues into the blue bin. "Why did the Duchess buy that truck?" he said. "Why now? Why not before? This a long way to come."

"Since she got here before nine," Dave said, "she must have left L.A. about the time of the afternoon news. When they said the Sheriff didn't think it was an accident anymore, what happened to Paul Myers."

"So what happened to Ossie Bishop wasn't an accident, either? And the truck has got evidence in it of that?"

Dave smiled. "You have a future in this business."

"If I can keep away from bullets," Cecil said. "If I can keep away from dogs."

10

Dave swung the van in at the Myers driveway, those two narrow strips of cracked cement leading past the side of the house to the garage, whose overhead door gaped, slumping in the middle. Dave slid the van into the garage and stopped it. "Come on," he said. "On the double." He jumped down out of the van and so did Cecil. Outside, Dave reached and caught a frayed rope end and dragged the garage door down. "If nobody's watching, it will be safe for a few minutes."

Cecil glanced around. "I don't like the odds."

"We're not staying." Dave crossed grass so dry it crackled underfoot. At the back door, he rapped the frame of the screen with his knuckles. No one stirred inside the house. He peered, holding hands at his eyes as blinkers. The sun was far to the west and low, but it still glared against the smoggy sky. He could make out nothing indoors. Cecil climbed on a bricked square meant for a planter, in which nothing grew but a few dry weeds. He peered through a window. "Looks like nobody's home," he said.

"That's all right. I didn't come to talk to anyone." Dave slipped a thin steel pick from his wallet and worked the screen-door lock. The lock of the wooden door, with its glass pane, was even easier. That required only the insertion of a credit card between lock and frame. When the door opened, the children's artwork fastened to the refrigerator fluttered. Empty beer cans stood on the kitchen table, a full ashtray. Dirty dishes were piled in the sink. The smell this time was of peanut butter. Dave left the kitchen for the hall.

The door to the children's room was open. Inside, a portable radio whispered rock music. Nothing in Angela Myers's bedroom was different from before except that possibly more underclothes were strewn around. Dave went straight to the closet, straight to the drawer with the shipping manifests. He knelt, pulled it open, and released breath he hadn't even known he was holding. He'd feared Salazar might have beaten him to it. Or the Duchess. This time he took them all. Half the stack he handed up to Cecil.

"Stash those on you, out of sight," he said. The other half he folded and pushed into the inner pocket of his jacket. He closed the drawer and rose. "Let's go."

They were rolling backward out the narrow driveway when someone shouted. Dave braked the van. Weighed down by bulging white plastic supermarket sacks, Gene Molloy halted on the front sidewalk. The children were with him. Each of them carried a sack. Molloy set his down and jogged to the van. "I want to talk to you," he said. "I want to show you something. Better not leave this out where the jigs can see it." He meant the van. In the sun glare he hadn't noticed Cecil. Or maybe he had and didn't care. "Put it in the garage and close the door," he said. "I'll let you in the back way." He let them in the back way, frowning. "I know damn well I locked these doors."

"This is my associate, Cecil Harris," Dave said. "Gene

Molloy." Molloy shook Cecil's hand, but his Irish eyes were not smiling. Cecil muttered something polite. Dave said, "Did you ever hear your brother-in-law mention someone called the Duchess?"

Brian, the Myers boy with the white sheepdog hair, took cans out of the slithery white sacks that lay bulging on the kitchen chairs. He climbed a short aluminum ladder to stow the cans on cupboard shelves. He set boxes—cereal, crackers, tea bags—on the shelves. Stretching, he put plastic-wrapped chicken legs and hamburger into the freezer. A deep tin drawer rattled when he opened it to drop in lettuce, tomatoes. carrots.

"I told you," Molloy said, "I wasn't around here that much. A Duchess? What kind of sense does that make?"

"A nickname. Someone he worked for. Possibly the one he was working for nights."

Cecil helped the child by arranging boxes of frozen vegetables along a freezer-door shelf. He said, "Possibly the one who killed him."

Molloy glared at him. "Watch your mouth."

Cecil touched the boy's shoulder. "I'm sorry."

"It's not your fault," the boy said. He looked at Molloy. "I did my half. It's Ruth Ann's turn."

"Go get her," Molloy said. And to Dave, "It wasn't any Duchess. I know who it was. I've got proof. Come on. I'll show you." He left the kitchen for the living room. Up the hall, the rock music was loud now. And louder still were the voices of Brian and Ruth Ann. Quarreling. Molloy turned back, pushed past Dave and Cecil, went to the door of the children's bedroom, and put his head inside. "Knock it off. Right now. Ruth Ann, God damn it." He disappeared into the room. The music broke off. "Get out to that kitchen and put the rest of those groceries away, and when you finish with that, wash the dishes. By yourself."

"See, stupid," Brian's voice said.

"I'll stupid you," Ruth Ann's voice said.

She came out of the room with Molloy behind her, his hands on her shoulders. When he had deposited her in the kitchen he came into the living room, where Dave and Cecil stood waiting. "Look at these," he said, and dug under the cushions of the sofa and brought out crumpled sheets of paper. He pushed them at Dave, who took them, frowned, reached for his reading glasses, turned the pages around, studied them. Cecil peered over his shoulder. Molloy lit a cigarette and smiled grimly. "You know what those are?"

"This is Kilgore School stationery," Dave said. "Is this Brian's work, Ruth Ann's? They look like diagrams."

"I don't think any kids drew those," Cecil said.

"I'm ashamed to have to say it," Molloy said, "but Bruce Kilgore has been sleeping with my sister."

"So I've heard," Dave said.

"What do you think his reason was?" A crash sounded from the kitchen. Molloy grimaced and left the room. Ruth Ann wailed. Molloy shouted. Dave frowned at the copies of *Scientific American* on the coffee table. He picked up the top one and leafed through it. Silence reigned in the kitchen. Molloy returned with cans of beer. He handed one to Dave, one to Cecil, and popped the opener tab on one for himself. "Maybe you think it was love," he said.

"Possibly loneliness," Dave said. He held up the magazine. "I'd like to borrow this, if I may."

Molloy shrugged. "Be my guest. I can't read the God damn things. No, there's lots of lonely housewives. Why Angie? She's sure as hell no *Playboy* centerfold."

"What are you trying to say?" Dave rattled the papers. "What have these got to do with it?"

"Look." Molloy sat on the couch and balanced his beer

can on the arm. A large, thick book lay on the coffee table with the magazines. Molloy sat forward, spread the book open, leafed over glossy pages, some of them smeared and thumb-printed. It was a truck-repair manual. When Molloy found the page he wanted, he slapped it and reached up for the Kilgore School papers. Dave handed them to him. Molloy swiveled the book so it faced Dave, and laid the pages beside it. "Check this out."

Dave bent above the book, hands on knees, the glasses slipping down his nose. The diagram in the book covered two pages. It detailed the air-brake system of an eighteen-wheel truck and trailer. The Kilgore School pages broke the diagram into three parts, but each part had plainly been copied from this book or another book of the same sort. Dave pushed the glasses up his nose, and straightened. He said, "You think Bruce Kilgore drew these?"

"I found them in the dumpster back of the school. I knew what they were right away. When Paul did let me live here, he made me help him do maintenance on the truck. I don't think Kilgore ever did maintenance on a truck. He had to copy the diagram because he doesn't know it by heart the way any trucker would."

Cecil tilted his head. "You think Kilgore wanted to kill your brother-in-law by rigging the brakes on his truck? But that wasn't how it happened."

"It was just his first idea," Molloy said. "I don't know why he changed his mind. But he could make a bomb easy. He's a trained engineer."

"What would be the point?" Dave took off the glasses, folded them, pushed them away. "To marry your sister, and use the insurance money to bail out his school?"

Molloy frowned. "You been thinking that too?"

"What does Salazar think?" Dave said.

Molloy laid the pages in the big book and shut it with a thud. Mouth a tight line, he twisted out his cigarette in the fluted pink china ashtray. "He hasn't got time to see me." Molloy slumped back on the couch, gulped beer. "That's why I'm glad you showed up today. He's your buddy. If you tell him about Kilgore, maybe he'll tear himself away from that moron street-gang shootup for five minutes."

"Where was that? When?"

"Yesterday. Sundown." Molloy fingered another cigarette from the pocket of his sweaty T-shirt, faded red with STUD POWER lettered across the chest. "Silencio Ruiz and his hot tamales." Molloy scratched a paper match and lit the cigarette. "Raided a barbecue at the nig—" He darted a glance at Cecil and changed the word. "At the black church on Guava Street. Mount Olivet? Free food, so guess what? The Edge showed up to eat it, didn't they? You should have seen it." He waved his beer can at the gray-faced portable television by the couch. "Blood and barbecue sauce all over the place."

"We'd better go." Dave set his beer can on the table. It was still full. Cecil set his beside it and followed Dave, who took long strides toward the kitchen. Molloy jumped up. "You tell Salazar for me, okay? About Kilgore? All he can think about now is Ruiz."

Dave stopped in the doorway from hall to kitchen. "Did they catch him? Is he locked up?"

"It happened too fast. They came through those walnut trees screaming and shooting and in a minute, ninety seconds, it was all over. They were gone. They rounded up most of them later. But not Silencio. He got away."

Ruth Ann stood on the aluminum ladder stool and fitted a roll of paper towels on a rack beside the window over the kitchen sink. The dishes in the sink floated in sudsy water.

So did the plastic wrapper from the paper towels. Dave and Cecil went to the outside kitchen door.

"Goodbye," Ruth Ann said.

"Wait a second," Molloy said. He held the edge of the wooden door. "Did Mr. Smithers contact you?"

"I've been out of town," Dave said. "Who is Smithers?"

"Oh, shit," Molloy said. "You don't know him? He was here last night, suppertime. Said it was about Paul's insurance. Wanted to talk to Angie. Asked the same questions you did. I told him you'd already been here. He said it was a communications mixup, and apologized and left. Tall guy, thin, bald." Molloy studied Dave. "Must be big bucks in checking insurance claims. He drove a Mercedes."

"Did it leave here on its wheels?" Cecil said.

"The gangs were busy at the church," Molloy said.

Dave said, "Have you got Smithers's card?"

"He didn't give me one. I showed him yours. I think he put it in his pocket. What's it all about?"

Dave tugged at the doorknob. Molloy let the door go. Dave swung it open, pushed the screen door, stepped out and down. "I'll tell you when I have a chance to look into it. It's probably as he says." Dave watched Cecil lope to the garage and raise the warped door. "Just a mixup. I was hired from outside. He's probably from inside." Dave lifted a hand, started to turn away.

"Maybe." Molloy stood holding the screen door open, beer can in his hand. "But there's one funny thing. Angie told me. Smithers went to the restaurant, Cappuccino's, right? Where she works? He ordered dinner, but he didn't eat it. All he did was ask her questions."

11

He stopped the van behind the cinder-block church through whose thin yellow paint the shadowy street-gang *placa* showed. An old gray Ford LTD sedan waited back here. It was beautifully kept, not a dent in it, the paint glossy as new. Dave switched off the engine of the van and sat for a moment beside Cecil, looking at the walnut grove. Under the trees, the long picnic tables lay on their sides. Steel folding chairs had been overturned. Among the branches, lights had been strung. Many of the sockets showed splintered stumps of bulb. One string had come down and trailed on the ground among paper plates and plastic utensils that glinted in the dying daylight. Raw wood shone through the torn bark of trees, pale white. The leaves of trees hung tattered. Round green walnut husks strewed the ground.

"Machine guns?" Cecil said.

"God knows." Dave climbed down from the van. In the evening hush, music came from the church—piano, voices. Cecil stood listening. Dave pressed the bell push beside the rectory door, over the weathered business card of Luther Prentice, D.D. But it was Mrs. Prentice who came to the door. She didn't look so tall now. Maybe it was the black dress. She looked old and weary. "I came," Dave said, "to tell you that I'm shocked and sorry this happened. Can I help in any way?" He glanced toward the trees. "I might have been here, you know. Reverend Prentice invited me."

She made a grim sound. "It's as well you weren't."

Still standing beside the van, his face turned toward the music, Cecil sang softly to himself, "'Amazing grace, how—'"

"They are rehearsing," Mrs. Prentice said, and came out to stand on the step. "For the funeral. It will be a communal funeral. Five dead, you know. One minute eating, laughing, having a fine time. Next minute, dead on the ground in their own blood."

"The boys from The Edge?"

A bitter smile moved her mouth. "It was supposed to be them. That was what they came for. But it was only two of them got hit at all." She looked quickly at Dave. "I mean that's terrible enough. But they will be all right. The ones who died—they were just in the way."

"That's where your husband is?" Dave said. "With the families?"

She nodded. "A mother dead, not thirty years old, three little children left behind. A boy fourteen, could play any instrument you put in his hands. A wonderful, talented boy with such a marvelous future ahead of him in this world. We need all the beauty we can get, it seems to me." A black handbag was in her hand. She dug in it for a handkerchief and touched her wet eyes. "I know I wasn't meant to understand Our Father, but sometimes I wish He would let me understand. An old man going, like Mr. Jackson, that's not so hard. But that fine young boy, and the others in the sunshine of their days. We needed them here."

"What was the reason for the raid?" Dave said.

"Reason?" Her laugh was bleak. "The Edge boys were bound to be here, weren't they, and they wouldn't be expecting a fight, wouldn't be ready for it. Hatred's the only reason I can give you. But it seems as though hatred is enough." She looked at the watch on her thin wrist. "You must excuse me now. I have a good many visits to make at the hospital." She pulled the house door shut. Her eyes begged Dave for an answer. "Where did they get guns like that, that fire so fast, so many bullets it seemed like rain?"

"Guns are big business these days," Dave said. "Did you see Silencio Ruiz? Do you know him when you see him?"

"Oh, yes." She stepped past Dave and unlocked the gray car. "They are saying on the news that he led the raid." She bent to get into the car, then straightened and rolled down the window of the open door. "They are saying no such things happened while he was away in prison." She took the handkerchief from her bag again, and stooped a little, and waved the handkerchief inside the car, as if to stir the air that had baked itself in there. "They are saying he must have got them the guns—something he learned in prison."

Dave stared. "And you don't think so?"

"He was trying to stop them" She got into the car, behind the steering wheel, and stretched across to roll down the window on the passenger side. Sweat broke out on her face, and she wiped it with the handkerchief. "Car gets so hot. I don't remember when we ever had weather like this."

Dave frowned down at her, his hands on the window ledge of the car door. "Why would he try to stop them? He was their leader."

"Used to be, I know." She dug keys from the handbag in her lap, set the handbag beside her on the seat, fitted the key into the ignition lock. "But, you see, he didn't come with them." She turned the key. The engine started. It ran so quietly it sounded new. She looked up at Dave. "He came from the street. He ran in amongst the tables. Now I don't understand but a little bit of Spanish, but the way he was waving his arms at them and shouting and the expression on his face—it was plain to me he wanted them to stop. Wonder is he wasn't killed himself."

"Did you report this to Lieutenant Salazar?"

She managed a wan smile. "He said I was mistaken." The parking brake made a clunk when she released it with her foot. Her hand came out to take the inside door latch. Dave let go of the door and stepped back. "I was not mistaken. I was here. And I know what I saw." She pulled the door shut. "I was right there, at the corner of the house, with a fresh platter of barbecued wings. I wasn't in the line of fire. I didn't have to crouch down under the tables like the rest. I saw. I saw it all. And he was trying to stop them." She gave her head a sorry shake. "But it seems I was the only one who did, and one old black woman's word is not enough." She glanced at her watch again. "Oh, dear. I am very late. I must go. Excuse me."

"Just one more minute." Dave put on his glasses, drew a leather folder from his jacket, leaned on the hot hood of the car, and wrote a check. He tore it from the pad and handed it to her. She blinked in surprise. Putting away the folder, he said, "I've made it out to the church. You see that whoever needs it gets it, all right?"

She read the check and her eyes widened. "But this is a great deal of money." She stared at him, openmouthed.

He smiled. "Money isn't what it used to be."

She laughed. "Truly. When I was a little girl in Georgia, my whole family could have lived for a year on this." She folded the check and tucked it into her purse. She looked at him solemnly. "Bless you," she said.

Cecil said, "Excuse me, but the Edge boys, the wounded ones, will they be in that hospital too?"

"Mrs. Prentice," Dave said, "this is my associate, Cecil Harris."

She nodded. "Yes. And if it's like last night and this morning, the others will be there too, the ones that weren't hurt, and some that didn't come to the picnic at all. They'll be in the rooms, in the halls, guarding their friends, seeing that nothing more happen to them. The authorities don't like it, but they're afraid to order them out."

"Oh, yes, I saw it." De Witt Gifford had painted his face. Rouge was thick on the wrinkled cheekbones above his beard. In the murky light of the attic it looked black. So did the slash of red that was his mouth. He had shaved off his eyebrows and drawn them thin and high and arched. Blue paint was above his curious eyes. Out in the daylight, he had looked like the bearded lady left behind by some circus that had pulled up stakes and departed town fifty years ago. His hat, this time, was a high-crowned blue-black straw, entangled in netting. He pulled it off and tossed it on the bed as his motor-chair whined past. Its wheels bumped him into the tower. "From here there's quite a good view. Of course, the walnut trees interfered. I couldn't see it all. But I saw enough. It was horrible."

"It was the gang you sponsored," Dave said. "You bought them those green jackets."

"Don't throw my follies up to me," Gifford said. "I can't change the past. Good God. The only philanthropic gesture in my selfish life, and look what it gets me." He picked the big binoculars up off the windowsill and peered through them out the clean, curved glass. "Obloquy. Well, I assure you, I am not to blame for that raid. I am sickened by it. Absolutely revolted."

"The jackets weren't your only philanthropic gesture," Dave said. "There was another. You bailed Silencio Ruiz out of jail after his arrest for holding up that supermarket. You hired a high-priced defense attorney for him."

Gifford sat motionless in slim, ragged silhouette against the dying light of the hot day. He seemed not to breathe. Then he breathed, but he did not turn. "No wonder you can afford the clothes you wear and the cars you drive. You are very good at your work. Did they tell you these things downtown? Or was it Bruce Kilgore?"

"He figures his vow of silence isn't sacred anymore. In his estimation, you didn't keep your end of the bargain. You see, he thinks Silencio blew up Paul Myers's truck. And he's not alone. The Sheriff thinks so too."

Gifford set the binoculars down and turned. The backlight of the windows made a scarecrow halo of his white hair and beard. "And you? I really don't give a hoot what Kilgore thinks. He's a clod. The police are"—he shrugged bony shoulders under a moth-eaten afghan—"we all know what the police are. What do *you* think? That I would find interesting."

Dave smiled. "I think I'd like a drink. You?"

Gifford's laugh was a crackle of dead leaves. "Of course. When wouldn't I? You know where the bottles are, I believe?"

Dave switched on lights in the tidy kitchen. Two plates drained in the rubber rack beside the small sink. Two forks lay there also, and two spoons. Two blue pottery bowls drained upside down. In the sink, with water standing in them, were aluminum-foil trays that had held, at a guess, frozen enchiladas. The water was chili red. Dave found glasses, ice cubes, Scotch, switched off the light, returned to the tower with the drinks. He put one in Gifford's claw, and with his own drink sat on the Empire couch with its threadbare Spanish shawl. The cushioning of the couch made dry sounds under him like very brittle straw.

"Lieutenant Salazar reasons this way," he said. "No sooner is Silencio out of prison than Paul Myers is murdered. And where is Silencio? Nobody knows. He sees his parents only once, fails to report to his parole officer, sees nothing of his gang. He vanishes. That is suspicious."

"Thank you for the drink." Gifford held it to his mouth and sipped from it, small sips, one every few seconds. He was gazing out the window. "It was not quite, I think, the most shocking thing I ever saw. No, it wouldn't be, would it? Nothing can shock us as things do in childhood. I told you how I used to creep down by the creek at night. Interesting things went on down there under the oaks and in the brush close to the water. I remember it had rained for days. Then the storm passed and we had a glorious day. That night, the stars were bright, the moon was very full. It shone on me and woke me, and I crept out. The house was asleep. The ground, of course, was still wet. So I thought no one would be out there, making love as they liked to do. There'd be nothing interesting to watch. Nothing educational.

"But there was. A young woman—a girl, really, as I see her now—probably fifteen, sixteen. I was perhaps ten or eleven. And something seemed to be wrong with her. I was vastly ignorant. She was all alone, half hidden in the undergrowth, writhing on the ground, moaning, whimpering to herself. In Spanish. Prayers. I won't go on with the details. She was giving birth. I can't tell you how dumbfounded I was when this wet, struggling thing came from her in the moonlight. The scream she gave is still in my ears. I understood and didn't understand. I turned my face away. I'm afraid I threw up.

"And when I looked again, she was on her feet, clutching the baby. It was gasping, crying. Like a sick cat. And she ran down to the creek with it. And without a sound, without a moment's pause, she threw it into the rushing water. I heard a scream and looked around to see who it was, but of course it was me, wasn't it? It frightened the girl. She ran away, slipping, sliding, falling.

"I rushed down to the creek, stumbled in up to my waist. The current was very strong. I wanted to save the baby. I couldn't see it. I called and called. As if a newborn child would know it was being called to. I knelt in the rocks and splashed around for it with my hands. But I didn't find it. It was gone. The creek had it."

"Sounds like a dream," Dave said. "You sure it wasn't a dream?"

"I hoped so, next morning. But my clothes were still wet. And they found the baby. Miles downstream. The story was in the newspaper. I clipped it out and kept it. I suppose I still have it somewhere. They never found the girl. My God, she's an old woman by now. Or dead. At my time of life, you look around, and everyone you ever knew is dead. My glass is empty."

Dave rose and took the glass. "Silencio's gang killed five people. Not one of them was a member of The Edge."

"It's not Silencio's gang," Gifford said sharply.

"He was there. The minister's wife says so. You saw it too. Wasn't he there?"

"If I were Silencio," Gifford said, "I should be hiding somewhere. He must know they believe he killed Paul

Myers. He's such an obvious suspect. He'd be a fool to add to his troubles by leading that raid."

"Mrs. Prentice says he was trying to stop it. The Sheriff won't believe her. She needs a backup. Silencio needs a backup. You sure you didn't see what she saw?"

"I told you." Gifford motioned at the window. "The tree-tops. I only got glimpses. But Silencio didn't lead that raid. He was through with gangs. Prison cured him of that. He came to see me, briefly, the day he returned from San Quentin. He told me, and I believed him. Now could I have my drink?"

Dave fetched it. "Last night at six, a tall, bald man in a Mercedes stopped at Myers's. You notice fine cars. Did you see it? Did you happen to get the license number?"

Gifford drank from his glass. "I was watching the church, the walnut grove."

Going out through the shadows of the garret, Dave jerked his head aside to avoid the pale canvas corner of the old life raft. The elevator creaked him down to the deserted pantry. He stood frowning while the elevator door slid shut. He listened. No dogs whined or snuffled behind closed doors. The looming old house stood hollow, silent, empty of life. He walked out into the hallway beside the great, gloomy staircase, thinking his footfalls might rouse the dogs. No such thing.

He opened doors and peered into shrouded rooms that breathed dust, mildew, neglect at him. He went back the way he had come and into the gaunt, disused kitchen. It smelled of dogs. He crossed scuffed linoleum, pulled open a door, and found himself on a screened porch where an old oaken icebox lurked, and an old Maytag washer with gray, crumbling wringers. A strong latch was on the screen door. A pair of bolts of bright new metal. But not fastened. He pushed the door open. Wooden steps, frail with age, went down to what must once have been the kitchen garden Gifford had mentioned—where there was always fresh mint. It was weeds and creepers now, matted, brittle.

Beyond it, a hurricane fence crossed, barbwire-topped. And a few yards farther off, an old stable building reared up, jigsaw work along its eaves, slats broken out of its cupola. The stable door stood open. The glare of the setting sun was in Dave's eyes, but he thought he saw movement inside the stable. He waited, squinting, straining his ears. But the building was too far off. He started to take a step down, then thought better of it. It looked to him as if the gate in the fence was ajar. The stable and the yard were probably where the dogs stayed when not on duty. He didn't want to meet the dogs. He stepped back onto the porch and was just letting the screen door fall shut when he heard a dog bark.

A man yelped, "Lady, no! Damn it, come back here."

Out the stable door, dragging a large, heavy, green paper sack, came a big, lean Doberman. The man appeared. He was slender, brown-skinned, curly-haired. He lunged for the sack, grabbed it, tugged, and the sack split open. Kibbled dog food rattled on the hard ground. The young man took a laughing swing at the dog, who dodged away. The young man hung for a moment on hands and knees, wagging his head in amused despair over the spilled food, the torn sack—then jumped to his feet and went back into the stable. He spoke the dog's name, but she didn't respond. She stood at the fence, staring through at Dave.

Dave let the porch door close softly and went back through the dark house and let himself out through the front doors, with their etched-glass panels.

It wasn't far to the hospital, but by the time he reached

it, all light had gone from the sky. He left the van in the parking lot slot of some doctor he hoped had gone home for the day or wouldn't arrive too soon. The parking lot was otherwise filled, unbroken rows of cars—a number of them Mustangs in various stages of repair—among the long strips of ivy geranium and the decorative palms. The long, curved fronds of the palms blew in a southeast wind that had risen with the coming of night. The wind was cool and Dave turned up his jacket collar, making his way toward the lighted glass side doors of the hospital. He looked up bleakly at the ten stories of shining windows, and lowered his eyes. He didn't want to think about the misery behind the glass. His horror of hospitals had been sharpened by Cecil's recent ordeal. But it had originated when Rod Fleming died slowly in a hospital a dozen years ago—of a kind of cancer they were now learning how to cure. There was no humor in the irony of that. He had lived with Rod for twenty-two years. He would never stop missing him.

But his spirits lightened when he found Cecil in a big, lamplit room of couches and easy chairs, where the sick and the well made ready to leave this place. Cecil sat talking with Luther Prentice, whose glasses and bald head gleamed. Cecil saw Dave coming, making his way through a clutter of empty wheelchairs, and smiled and waved. Dave smiled back. He shook Prentice's long, kindly hand. The preacher said, "My wife tells me you have made a generous donation to the victims of the shooting. Please accept my gratitude. It was a terrible thing to happen. I don't know what I was thinking of, bringing all those people there, putting them in danger of their lives." Behind the shiny lenses, his eyes misted. "I have asked the Lord to forgive me for my foolishness, and I expect He has, but I don't know that I will ever be able to forgive myself."

"You only wanted to feed people," Cecil said.

"You couldn't know what would happen," Dave said.

"Someone more worldly-wise than I am"—Prentice shook his head sorrowfully—"would have realized that with their leader back out of prison, that gang would get up to something evil again."

"Your wife doesn't think it was Silencio's doing," Dave said. "She thinks he was trying to stop it."

Prentice's smile was gently tolerant. "She is even less worldly-wise than I am." He sighed. "No, I'm afraid this is only the beginning of the shootings, ambushes, deaths. The Edge will want revenge. And then—" He straightened. "Ah, here comes Mrs. Prentice now." He looked at an old silver watch on a bony wrist. "She is behind time. Prayer meeting begins at seven."

She came and spoke in her soft, musical voice to Dave and Cecil, her gentle brown eyes reflecting the suffering she had just been witness to, even while she smiled politely at these two strangers. Then she and her stilt-tall husband excused themselves and went away into the night. Luther Prentice's voice drifted back as he pushed open the heavy glass door for her. "We'll be late."

"The Lord will wait," she said. "He always has."

Dave said to Cecil, "Is he right? Are there going to be more ambushes, more deaths?"

"It's a good thing all the G-G's are in jail," Cecil said. "If The Edge ever gets hold of any of them, they won't live through it."

"Shall we go?" Dave said, and moved back toward the wheelchairs, toward the parking-lot doors beyond the wheelchairs. Cecil came along behind.

He said, "I'll be glad to get out of here. I've had enough of hospitals to last me the rest of my life." Dave pushed the door open. Wind gusted in. "Whoo! That is cold." The door closed behind them. Cecil put his head down and hugged himself. They trotted toward the van. "Spooky wind, too. Can't make up its mind where it's coming from." They climbed into the van and slammed the doors. "Hot today, too." Cecil shivered and rubbed his arms.

"Looks like the end of summer," Dave said. He started the engine. "You talked to The Edge. Which ones?"

"Rollo Poore. He's the head honcho. He's got a bullet in his thigh. Must have been some bullet. I would judge him to be made of some very tough alloy. I tried to talk to the ones leaning around looking mean in the hallways, but Rollo—he the spokesman. Nobody else gave me squat. All they did was point at this particular room and say, 'Talk to Rollo Poore.'"

Dave backed the van, changed gears, joined the red and yellow lights of traffic heading away from Gifford Gardens toward the freeway. "And what did Rollo say?"

"You should have seen that room. Like something out of an old Edward G. Robinson movie, only all black, of course. The heavy standing outside the door. The heavy leaning against the wall by the window. Sulky. Watching me like he was thinking up ways to take me apart and put me back together again all wrong. Mrs. Prentice—I saw her before I saw Rollo. She said the authorities won't let The Edge carry weapons. No weapons in the hospital, she said. But I swear, the one in the room had a gun stuck in his pants. His jacket covered it, but it was there."

"I'm sorry," Dave said. "I ought to have gone."

"You're the wrong color. He'd never have talked to you." Cecil had stopped shivering. "It's a good heating system in this van. Rollo said, when he gets out of bed, he and the rest of them are going to find Silencio Ruiz and kill him. How was your crazy old peeper today?"

"Makeup an inch thick," Dave said. "He denied it before, but he has a man around the house. I wondered who smoked the cigarettes, who washed the windows, kept the kitchen and the bathroom spic and span. I wondered who looked after the dogs. I saw him today."

"Hired hand?" Cecil asked.

"They take their meals together," Dave said. "I don't know what else they do together. What does Silencio Ruiz look like? Did you see his picture on the news last night? Well built, six feet, curly hair? Ramon Novarro?"

"I don't know who that might be," Cecil said, "but if you mean is he pretty, you got it."

"He was feeding the dogs," Dave said. "It figures. Gifford's been looking out for him for a long time."

"That was why he paid off Bruce Kilgore not to leak it about the bail and the expensive lawyer. To keep Silencio's gang from suspecting what was between him and Gifford. It wouldn't fit the macho image."

"That's the explanation that makes sense," Dave said.

"And when Silencio learned about Paul Myers's death, he ran to Gifford's enchanted castle to hide out, right? Lucky old Gifford." They sloped onto the freeway. "What are you going to do?"

"Tell Salazar." Rain began to spatter the windshield. "Get Silencio into jail with the rest of the G-G's. To keep The Edge from killing him." Dave switched on the wipers. "And that silly old man."

12

I t was a lazy rain, the warm, tropical sort that now and then drifts up from Mexico. It fell all night on the shingles above the loft and made sleeping good. It was still coming down from ragged, gray-black clouds when they went their separate ways next morning. Cecil took his van. Dave took the sideswiped car. Rain had leaked into it, probably because the rubber around the doors was rotten. The floor was puddled. The rubber of the wiper blades was also shot. He stopped at a filling station for new ones, then wheeled onto the first of three freeways that would take him out east of Pasadena to a plant called Tech-Rite. That name, and the names Chemiseal and Agroplex on the new batch of waybills taken from Paul Myers's closet drawer, had interested Dave.

Tech-Rite occupied long buildings far off across empty land backed by rain-shrouded mountains. The buildings were flat-roofed, windowless, featureless. Big white storage tanks loomed behind them. To a security guard in a black rubber hat and poncho, Dave showed his license and explained his business. The guard made a phone call from inside his white stucco booth. Light flickered off his rain-slick poncho from a small black-and-white television set in the booth. He hung up the phone and came down out of the booth and leaned to the car window. A gnarled hand pushed something shiny at Dave, a card enfolded in clear plastic, printed with the name TECH-RITE, the word VISI-TOR, and some blank lines.

"Write your name on there, will you?" the guard said. "Truth is, I'm supposed to, but I can't hold a pen too good anymore." He appeared past retirement age. The raindrops on his drooping, hound-dog face looked like tears. "When your name is on it, pin it to your jacket and I'll open the gates and you can drive on in."

Dave did as he was told. The guard continued to lean at the window, watching but probably not seeing. Dave pricked a finger pushing the pin through his lapel. He sucked the finger. "That do it?"

"Fine, thanks." The guard stepped creakily up into the booth again and shut the door. The wide, high, chainlink gates swung open. Dave drove the rattly car through, and headed it up a two-lane strip of blacktop that glistened in the rain. He passed parking lots filled with cars parked on the bias in neat, shiny rows. He drove on. A sign read EXECUTIVE PARKING LOT. He slowed and almost swung in at the arrow painted on the paving, then saw ahead through the rain another sign—VISITORS. He left the battered Valiant there, among new Audis, Cutlasses, BMWs, and hurried, head down, toward double glass doors that glowed with light in the bleak, unbroken plane of the building front.

He waited an hour for Lorin Shields, in the reception room of offices marked PUBLIC RELATIONS. He was not neglected. He was served tea from a Worcester pot in a Worcester cup and saucer. At a guess, English breakfast tea. There were English muffins. There was English marmalade. The young woman who served them on a Japanese lacquer tray was oriental herself. She apologized smoothly and smilingly for Shields's tardiness at first. He was rarely late. It must be the rain. He had a long way to come. But as time dragged on, she became embarrassed. Little lines appeared between her beautiful brows when she glanced up from the whispering electronic typewriter at her desk, saw Dave, saw the clock.

Dave, trying to make sense of a trade journal article on the molecular structure of a new breed of plastics, gave her a smile. "It's all right. I have no other appointments. I don't mind waiting."

"I can't think why he hasn't telephoned."

In the end, a blond, rosy-cheeked, chubby lad named Jochim led him into an office that did not have a name on its door, and that was some little walk from Shields's door, which not only had Shields's name on it, but SENIOR VICE-PRESIDENT as well. Jochim probably wasn't even a junior vice-president. But he was friendly and welcoming. For a while, at least. At the word "murder," his smile faded. He watched worriedly as Dave brought out a rumpled cargo manifest from his jacket, unfolded it, held it out.

Jochim read it, frowned. "But this was weeks ago."

"He didn't have a waybill for what he was hauling that night. Did it come from here? Could you check your files? Night of the ninth?"

"Why?" Jochim gave back the paper. "Why Tech-Rite?"

"It's someplace to start. The records, Mr. Jochim?"

"We've nothing to hide." Jochim touched an intercom button. "Shipping records for the ninth of this month." He tilted his head at Dave. "But surely this man hauled all sorts of cargoes, from all sorts of businesses."

"Not a lot that was dangerous," Dave said.

"Dangerous?" Jochim's voice squeaked like a high-school boy's. "What are you implying? We observe the strictest standards of safety in all our manufacturing processes. We have to. Most of our contracts come from the U.S. government. You've no idea of the restrictions they impose."

"That suggests that some of the materials that go into Tech-Rite products aren't exactly harmless."

Jochim drew breath to answer, and the door opened. The young oriental woman looked in. "I'm sorry, Mr. Jochim, but files from around that time are missing. No one in Shipping or Order has them. Shall we keep looking?"

Jochim raised pale brows at Dave. Dave shook his head. Jochim said, "That's all right, Frances. Forget it. Thank you." When the door closed behind her, Jochim said to Dave with a thin smile, "The environmentalists really make very little sense. Why would Tech-Rite or any of us manufacture products that would harm the very people we want to serve and serve again? Think about that."

"There was the asbestos business," Dave said. "And the coal-mining business. Not to mention the lead business. But okay. Even if what you make is harmless—poisons, pollutants, carcinogens come out of the manufacturing process, don't they? It's in the papers all the time. What does Tech-Rite do with its toxic wastes?"

"Just a damn minute." Jochim's face was red. "Are you holding Tech-Rite responsible for this trucker's death?"

Dave looked blank. "Why would you think that?"

"Then I don't understand your line of questioning," Jochim said. "And I don't like it."

"Let me explain," Dave said. He outlined the story of Paul Myers's lucrative, secretive, late-night hauling operations, the beating of Paul Myers's wife, the earlier recruitment of Myers by Ossie Bishop, the curious circumstances of Ossie Bishop's death. "I went down to Halcon to talk to his wife about it. She won't talk. She's frightened. But that I expected. What I didn't expect was that Ossie's truck was sold. For cash. In a great hurry."

"Yes?" Jochim asked warily. "To whom?"

"To a woman known as the Duchess. Ever hear of her?"

"Sounds like a cheap television show," Jochim said.

"Doesn't it? Unhappily, it's real. Why did she want that truck to disappear just when it was discovered that Paul Myers's death was no accident?"

"We farm out shipments to many independent truckers," Jochim said impatiently. "We really have no control over their activities, outside of their work for us. As for this missing truck—"

"I can't help thinking the Duchess wanted it out of the way because it contained evidence that would link Myers's death to that of Ossie Bishop. And I wondered what sort of evidence that would be. The truck was empty. Like Myers's. But law-enforcement laboratories don't regard 'empty' as the rest of us do. The Duchess must have been afraid traces of whatever Bishop was hauling at midnight in that truck were still there for electron microscopes to find."

"Are you suggesting that Tech-Rite—?" Jochim began.

"I read a disturbing article last night," Dave said. "In *Scientific American*. It describes the reactions of people who have handled toxic wastes carelessly. Violent diarrhea, vomiting, coughing, lung congestion, paralysis of the diaphragm—the same symptoms Ossie Bishop showed before he died."

"I see." Jochim gave a short nod and stood up. "Let me show you something. Can you spare me"—he looked at his wristwatch—"half an hour, forty-five minutes?" He didn't wait for an answer. He opened a closet, took out a pale raincoat, a rumpled rainhat. "I'm sure I can clear away all your doubts and dark suspicions." He smiled and opened his office door.

Dave smiled back. "Best offer I've had all day," he said, and followed Jochim out of the building. It was still raining in those fat, lazy drops, out of the sort of sky water-colorists like best, smudgy grays and whites. Beyond the hulking curves of the storage tanks, the mountains had already begun to show a tinge of green on their tawny summer hides. Dave walked beside Jochim into the executive parking lot. Coming out of the lot, hurrying in a clear plastic raincoat that rustled, a tall man nearly collided with them. Rain dripped from the brim of his rough Irish tweed hat as he glared at Jochim. The tall man was Lorin Shields.

"This is Mr. Brandstetter," Jochim told him. Dave wondered why the name seemed to startle Shields. Or was he imagining things? Jochim said, "He's an investigator for insurance companies. He's interested in our system of disposing of hazardous wastes. I thought I'd just show him."

"Good idea." Shields gave a brisk, executive nod, twitched a smile and tugged the brim of his hat to Dave, and loped off toward the bright doors of Tech-Rite.

Dave got into Jochim's Cimarron. "Your Mr. Shields looks like a man under a lot of strain."

"Lost his wife recently." Jochim drove down the long wet tarmac strip toward the gates. "Very suddenly. It was a shock. She was young. Beautiful. He worshipped her, built her a glorious new house. Married in April. Dead in September. Lorin hasn't collected himself. This place used to mean everything to him. Now he doesn't even come in, half the time."

The kitchen help, in rumpled, food-stained white jackets and pants, were eating when Dave stepped into Max Romano's through the back door. Steamy heat embraced him. The smells were overpowering—of garlic, cheese, fish, onions, basil, oregano. Alex, the skinny head chef with caved-in, acne-scarred cheeks, looked up from his plate of Alfredo and gave Dave his graveyard smile. The other men in puffed white hats—fish, soup, salad, dessert chefs—murmured welcomes. Dave pushed out a zinc-covered swing door into the quiet dining room. Max—short, fatter than ever, his few remaining curly locks combed glossily over his pate—was counting lunchtime checks by a tiny bright lamp at the cash register. Cocking an eyebrow at Dave, he turned back a snowy cuff fastened by a big diamond stud to read his watch, and shook his head in mock-fatherly reproach.

"You late again," he said. "Keep everybody waiting."

Dave laid a hand on his shoulder, then moved between white, empty tables to the corner table where Cecil sat. He gave him a kiss and sat down. "Sorry. I was treated to a demonstration of how scrupulous Tech-Rite is about dumping its toxic wastes." He laughed. "Or what was meant to be that." A little green bottle stood beside Cecil's wineglass. Perrier water bubbled in the glass. "You're not drinking?"

"I didn't know how long you'd be," Cecil said. "Didn't want for you to have to carry me out over your shoulder." He glanced through the shadows, looking for Max, but Max was already in the little bar. The restaurant was so quiet they could hear the clink of bottles, glasses, ice, that told them he was fixing their drinks. Cecil said, "What was it instead?"

"A farce." Dave told him the morning's events. "So we drove for twenty minutes to a place beyond beyond, with high fences and warning signs—a square mile of carefully labeled barrels of dangerous chemicals. And guess what? A picket line. All these men, women, adolescents, little kids, in jeans and parkas and slickers and stocking caps, carrying signs in the rain. Tech-Rite and the rest are poisoning the ground and water for miles around and dooming the people and their children for ages to come."

"Oh, wow! What did Jochim say?"

"He'd been lecturing me all the way how this was a government-approved dump. No danger of seepage, leakage, pollution. Tech-Rite and the others had gotten an order two years ago to clean it up and make it safe. It cost them millions—oh, grief, oh, sorrow. But now it was totally harmless." Max brought the drinks and set them down. Dave laughed again. "When Jochim saw those pickets, he stopped the car so fast it stalled. Then he dented the rear bumper, turning around to get the hell out of there."

"Was television covering it?"

"Men with cameras on their shoulders. Pretty girls of both sexes with microphones. Another reason Jochim stood not upon the order of his going." Dave grinned and picked up a chunky glass in which ice chilled Glenlivet. "Thank you, Max. What's left for lunch?"

"No leftovers." Max wagged disapproving jowls. "You tell me what you want, I fix with my own hands."

They told him, and he waddled away, singing to himself. Dave drank. "How did you fare at Chemiseal?"

"And Agroplex. I interviewed two merchants of death while you messed with one." Cecil pretended to preen. He drank, shrugged, made a wry face. "Guess that's what they mean by haste make waste. I didn't get anywhere."

"No one knew the Duchess?" Dave lit a cigarette.

Watching him wistfully, Cecil shook his head. "They let me see the shipping records. Paul Myers didn't haul for them the night he died." Cecil reached for Dave's cigarette pack on the white cloth, and drew his hand back empty. "They used Ossie Bishop, time to time. But when I raised the subject of toxic-waste disposal, the interviews were over. I sure as hell didn't get an all-expenses-paid, luxury vacation trip to the dump."

"Don't feel bad," Dave said. "Maybe they haven't got a dump."

112

13

The Valiant started reluctantly in the rain, but once all the cylinders began igniting in order, it followed the van without trouble back to Horseshoe Canyon. Dave had stretched lunch out, glad for the chance to rest, and it was ten past four when the van tilted ahead of him down the sharp drop from the trail into the bricked yard, and he jounced down after it. Rain still fell, dripping from shrubs, trees, eaves, and darkness was coming early. A four-wheel-drive sports wagon stood reflected in the front building's row of French doors. The vehicle was high on its wheels, well kept, three or four years old, with simulated wood paneling—and it looked empty in the rain.

But when Cecil rolled the van up beside it, Dave the jalopy, and the engines stopped and they got out, someone stirred in the wagon. A broad, black young face under a Padres cap looked out the driver's window. The door opened, Melvil Bishop got out. Three more faces appeared at the rear windows. Young boys' faces, somber. "Man, I was scared you'd never get here," Melvil said. "We been waiting for hours." He glanced at the small boys in the car. "They peed in your bushes. I'm sorry, but you know little kids. Always have to pee when it's no place for it."

"What are you doing here?" Cecil said.

"Where's your mother?" Dave said.

"Escondido," Melvil said. Rain was darkening the satiny fabric of the baseball cap. He moved away from the car, jerking his head to indicate that they should follow him. Out of earshot of the children, he said in a low voice, "Mercy Hospital. Critical condition." He glanced back at the car. All three faces were lined up at the rear window. Melvil said, "They don't know. They think she took sick. It wasn't that. She was shot."

Cecil sucked air through his teeth.

Melvil's eyes smoldered at Dave. "I knew something bad would happen when she told me she talked to you. We weren't supposed to talk."

"You mean the Duchess's goons shot her?"

"Sheriff say it was an accident." Melvil's tone was contemptuous. "First she talked to you. In the morning. Later on to Smithers." Melvil looked sharply at Dave. "Claim he work with you. It's a lie, isn't it?"

"It's a lie," Dave said. "I don't know him."

Cecil said, "Shot her at Hutchings's?"

Melvil shook his head. "You know the store in Halcon? General store? Post office? Indian dude run it?"

Dave stared. "The rifle range? A bullet from the rifle range?" He glanced at Cecil.

Cecil looked sick. "That almost happened to us."

"No 'almost' about this." Melvil's fists bunched in the pockets of his Padres windbreaker. His feet, in worn jogging shoes, nudged wet leaves on the bricks. He watched them. His voice wobbled. "She could die."

"I'll phone the hospital." Dave turned up his jacket collar and started off. "Collect your brothers and come inside." He took a few steps, then turned back. "Better get your car out of sight. Cecil, drive it up to Hilda Vosper's, will you?"

114

She was a neat little gray-haired widow who lived up the road with a feisty little ragbag dog, and had helped Cecil out of trouble once. "She only uses half her garage. She loves you—she'll let you hide it there." Cecil saluted, and Dave hunched his shoulders and hurried around the end of the front building, across the uneven bricks of the courtyard under the old oak, and into the rear building.

His desk waited at the far end of the long, high, plank-walled room. He sat at the desk and used the phone for a jokey, neighborly call to Hilda Vosper. Then he got to the process of connecting with the hospital down the coast. Before he managed it, Melvil came in, shepherding the small boys, two of them skinny, one stocky, a miniature Melvil. The room was gloomy, so their teeth and eye whites shone. They rolled their eyes. Plainly, they had never seen a place quite like this one. Come to that, neither had Dave.

"Cecil manage your car all right?" Dave called.

"Say he be back in a minute." Melvil shut the door. "Then he going to cook. These babies don't only always have to pee, they always hungry. He going to fix food for these here babies." Melvil gave the little boys quick, rough, affectionate shoves. "Don't push me, man," they said in small, high voices. "Look out who you messing with," the stocky one said. "I got me a big brother can beat the shine out of you."

"Where? Bring him on. I ready." Melvil scowled around him in mock truculence, and jabbed the air with blocky fists. The two skinny boys jumped on him from behind, clutching his shoulders, circling his neck, dragging him to the floor, where they piled on him and pummeled him.

At the Escondido end of the telephone line, a nurse, deceived by Dave's fast talk about insurance into believing he had a right to know, told him that Louella Bishop was in stable condition after surgery, though she was still unconcious. Dave thanked the nurse and hung up. Melvil had heard his voice, and now sat up on the floor, brushing the giggling little boys off him, his eyes anxious. Dave rose, went to the broad fireplace, crouched there, and, with the aid of a gas jet, set kindling crackling and smoking under logs in the grate. Melvil came to him.

Dave got to his feet. "She's holding her own."

Melvil said darkly, "Why won't they sneak in and kill her in the hospital?"

"Intensive-care wards are busy places, filled with doctors and nurses," Dave said. "She'll be all right."

"I wanted to stay and guard her," Melvil said, "but they'd only kill me too. They know I know."

"If it's like that, why didn't you tell the Sheriff?"

"If Mama got shot for talking to you and Mr. Smithers, what do you think would happen, they see me talking to the Sheriff? Deputy phoned me at school, told me Mama had this accident, and could they come and get me, take me to the hospital? I say okay, but I didn't wait. I had the car. Mama used one of the Hutchingses' cars when she had errands. And I drove to the grade school and scooped up the babies and we came here."

"That's all right." Dave switched on lamps at either end of the long, corduroy-cushioned couch that faced the fireplace. "But I don't know why."

"Because Mama trust you. I yelled at her for talking to you. She say it's all right. You a fine man." He dug into his windbreaker pocket. "Gave me your card. Say if there was ever trouble, I was to get you." He showed the card. "I didn't know where else to go."

Dave looked at the little boys, who were playing tag up and down the pine stairs to the loft. He said to Melvil, "Why don't you take them to the cookshack? Then come back here and tell me what it is they know you know."

"All I want is to hide," Melvil said.

"That won't work forever," Dave said. "Maybe if you had talked to Cecil yesterday, your mother wouldn't be in the hospital now. Maybe the sooner you tell what you know, the sooner you can stop hiding, the safer you'll be, and your little brothers and everybody else."

Melvil eyed him skeptically. "Insurance? What do you think you can do?"

Dave shrugged, smiled. "I sometimes surprise myself."

Melvil didn't look persuaded, but he rounded up the little boys and herded them, jumping and skittering, out into the rainy dusk. Dave made himself a drink and stood at the desk, listening to messages on his answering machine. Gene Molloy's voice, excited, exasperated. Salazar's voice, bored, exasperated. The voice of Amanda, his very young stepmother, widowed a few years back when Carl Brandstetter's heart stopped in his Bentley on a freeway. Amanda was cheery. She'd just got a new interior-decorating job and wanted to celebrate by taking Dave and Cecil to dinner. No more voices came from the machine. Dave reset it, lit a cigarette, picked up the drink, started for the couch, and the telephone rang. He sighed, sat down at the desk, picked up the receiver.

"You ought to stay home more," Salazar said. "Gene Molloy showed me those sketches of the brake system of a tractor-trailer rig that Kilgore drew. Kilgore doesn't look it, but he's weak. In ten minutes I had him in tears. And now I've got him in jail."

Dave raised eyebrows at the phone. "You mean he admitted blowing up Paul Myers? For Angela's half of the insurance money?"

"Not yet, but he will. He was read his rights, but he

babbled. He admitted he was planning it."

"Planning it is one thing," Dave said, "doing it is another." He took a quick gulp of whiskey. "What about Silencio Ruiz? Did you pick him up?"

Salazar's laugh was short, sharp, humorless. "That crazy old Gifford! You didn't tell me he's got a fortress out there. Electrified fence on top of the wall. Iron gates. Dogs that will tear your throat out."

Dave frowned. "Your men out there knew that."

"Yes, well, I didn't know it, did I? And Silencio is important to me. I got a warrant and went myself. And I blew it. No way was he going to let me in there. And no way was I going to risk ramming those gates. Those were little machine guns Silencio's boys took to the church barbecue. He could spray us with bullets from that tower."

"Right. So you staked the place out?"

"It's too big for that. We patrolled the walls. I did flyovers in the helicopter. It's got a spotlight on it to rake the ground, you know? Only with all those trees and bushes in there, what could we see? There's a loudspeaker. I kept telling Ruiz to come out, surrender. All it did was keep the old freak awake."

"He never sleeps much," Dave said.

"He complained anyway. This morning. When he came down in his wheelchair. To let us in. Holding up a pink Japanese parasol to keep off the rain. It was paper. It came to pieces while we watched."

"Did he have his rifle?"

"No rifle. You don't understand. He was a welcoming committee. I don't know what the hell he thought he was wearing. It looked like a glass bead curtain. 'Come in, come in,' he says. 'By all means, search the house and grounds. Freely. Take all the time you want. No need to worry about the dogs. I wouldn't let them out in the rain.'" Salazar snorted. "Sons of bitches were out in the rain all night, jumping at the walls, barking, snarling."

"Silencio got away," Dave said. "I hope when he went over those walls, The Edge wasn't watching."

"They were hanging around," Salazar said. "A crowd gathered when they saw all those County cars, all those spotlights, guns, uniforms. The noise of the chopper brought more. I saw Edge jackets."

Dave said, "Maybe he's still inside."

"No way," Salazar said. "We practically tore up the floorboards. The place is a museum, did you know that? No, he escaped in the dark. I'd feel worse if it was the first stupid mistake I ever made. I'd feel better if it was the last. It was a great tipoff, Dave. Sorry."

"He didn't blow up Paul Myers," Dave said. "I don't think he led the raid on the barbecue. I believe the minister's wife. I think he tried to stop it."

"No way. Everybody was hysterical. I don't blame them. But witnesses are unreliable enough under normal circumstances. What am I saying? This is getting to be normal. Backyard terrorism. An American pastime."

"Bigger than divorce." Dave twisted out his cigarette and drank again. "No, I believe her because of something Gifford said—that prison changed Silencio. Gifford must have seen the G-G's from his tower, heading for the barbecue with their new guns, and told Silencio, and Silencio ran to try and stop them, and got there too late."

Salazar said, "Dave, Silencio Ruiz is human garbage."

"Probably literally, by now," Dave said. "The trash collectors will find him in a dumpster soon. That was why I wanted you to jail him."

"You don't think he killed Myers. You don't think Kilgore killed Myers. Who do you think it was?"

"I haven't got names," Dave said. "Only suspicions. Give

119

me a little more time, and I'll lay it on your desk."

"You always say that," Salazar said, "then you try to do it all by yourself. You can get killed that way."

Salazar had it backward. Dave never acted on his own, except when Salazar or Ken Barker of LAPD couldn't or wouldn't help. He didn't remind Salazar of this. He only said, "Tell me about it."

And Melvil came through the door, out of the rain.

14

He was eating a hamburger. Cecil made hamburgers with lots of mayonnaise, catsup, sweet pickle relish. The paper napkin in which Melvil's was wrapped was soaked with all these, and the juices of rare ground beef, tomato slices, onion slices. He came down the room through the circles of soft lamplight, the soft flicker of firelight, and laid another hamburger, swaddled in a napkin, on the desk in front of Dave, who nodded and watched it begin to ooze through the napkin while he wound up his talk with Salazar.

"Was Angela Myers in on Kilgore's plans for Paul?"

"Sorry to disappoint you," Salazar said. "That would lose her the insurance, wouldn't it—whether they actually killed him or not? Conspiracy to defraud? I questioned her. In my opinion, she didn't know Kilgore was using her. She's sick about it. She'll never speak to him again." At Salazar's end of the line, someone shouted his name in the background. "Listen, my wife's on the other line. I'll talk to you later. Don't do anything crazy, all right?"

Dave said he wouldn't, and cradled the phone. He regarded the hamburger on the desk and pushed it toward Melvil, who was standing, chewing, wiping mouth and fingers on his ruined napkin. Dave told him, "You have that one too. I finished a big lunch only an hour ago."

Melvil wrinkled his forehead. "You sure?" Dave nodded. Melvil tossed the crushed napkin side-arm down the room into the fireplace, where flames were lapping around the logs now. He picked up the second hamburger and lovingly peeled back half the wrapper. "That Cecil," he said, "make the best burger I ever tasted. Something about my people—what they cook taste better."

Dave grinned. "I taught him everything he knows. Bring that chair over and sit down." It was a wicker barrel chair. Melvil's stocky body fitted it exactly. "Who is the Duchess?" Dave said.

"I don't know her real name," Melvil said. "Don't guess nobody know that. She a broker. Work for factories that wants to get rid of poisons the cheap way. Hire truckers to take it off and dump it wherever they can. No questions asked."

"Did your Dad tell you this?"

Melvil looked ashamed. "I wanted to know what he was doing nights. We used to have good times together. Basketball games, Dodgers, boxing. All that stopped. Says with the new taxes and all that, he had to get more work. I don't know." Melvil shrugged, took a large bite from the hamburger. A scrap of lettuce pulled loose and hung at the corner of his mouth. He poked it inside. He spoke with his mouth full. "Was I mad at him, or jealous, or curious? Little of each, maybe. I wanted to be with him. He wouldn't take me. Course not." Melvil swallowed. "He knew how dangerous it was. Most truckers that did it—they knew. Acids to burn you, poisons to make you sick, fumes to make your eyes itch so you nearly blind, give you cancer, make your wife's babies come out deformed."

"And yet they do it?" Dave sipped his drink.

"The Duchess pay big bucks, man," Melvil said.

"He wouldn't take you. How did you learn?"

"Sneaked in the cab. They a big space behind the seat. Sometimes, some rigs, it living quarters, a bunk, all that. Hid myself back there. Saw it and heard it all. Scared me half to death. Dad never knew. I never said a word. I also never went with him again."

Dave lit a cigarette. "Where does this happen?"

"I'll show you, if you want to go there."

"A truck stop, rest area? Will the Duchess be there?"

"Sooner or later. This would be a good night. Raining. Not all that much traffic out late."

"If I were you, I'd be afraid," Dave said.

Melvil shrugged and munched his hamburger. A ring of raw onion tumbled down his front. He bent to pick it up off the floor. He carried it to the fireplace. "If it killed your father, you'd want to do something about it if you could, wouldn't you?"

Dave's drink was only ice now, no Scotch. He rose and went into the shadows where the bar was, and built a new drink. "A few minutes ago, you didn't think I could be of much help."

"Cecil told me about your track record." The firelight flickered orange-red behind Melvil. "You a real, live private eye. I didn't know they had those. You don't look it, you don't act it. You famous, too." He poked a last bite of hamburger into his mouth, wiped his mouth with the destroyed napkin, wiped his fingers, tossed the napkin into the flames. "Guess I should have known." He came back to the desk. The straw chair creaked under his weight.

"Did your mother know what your dad was doing?" Dave sat in his desk chair, high-backed, leather, swivel. "The Duchess seems to think so."

"I don't know what Mama knew. I got it together when

Paul Myers came over when Dad was sick and had that magazine article about the symptoms you get from handling toxic wastes, pollutants, all that jive."

"You overheard their talk?"

"I plain listened. Something those drivers said at the truck stop came back to me. I wasn't sure what it meant at the time. Then, when Paul talked about what was in that magazine, I understood."

"Your mother said Paul left the house angry."

"He was going to expose the Duchess and the whole rotten operation. That what he say." Melvil laughed wryly to himself and shook his head on its thick neck. "Folks talk big and bad, times like that. It the mob back of the Duchess, ain't it? Organized crime? What's some nobody truck driver going to do against organized crime?"

Dave said, "I think he meant it. I think he tried. He loved your father, you know. I read that magazine article. It must have been obvious to Paul from that, that your father was going to die."

"Tried how?" Melvil peered into the darkness behind Dave. "There water back there?"

"And glasses," Dave said, "and ice. Help yourself. There's a refrigerator under the bar, if you want a cola."

"Water be fine." Melvil pushed up out of the chair. "Cola rot you teeth and make you jumpy." He went into the darkness, silent on his soft-soled shoes. "Those babies—you think they grasshoppers now?" Ice clacked into a glass. Water drummed in a small steel sink. "Used to be they was into cola. Whoo. They was nonstop, eighteen hours a day." Melvil came back with the glass and sat down again. "What make you say he tried?"

"The Duchess brought her boys and beat up Paul's wife."

Melvil frowned, cocked his head. "Her? Not him? I thought they broke you legs."

"You can't drive a truck with broken legs," Dave said. "The Duchess preferred to have things both ways. Paul frightened into silence and still working for her. She managed that by abusing and threatening his family."

Melvil was staring gloomily at the fire. "Yeah. It wasn't herself Mama was scared for, taking off for Halcon that way right after the funeral. It was for us. Told me ten times a day, never say nothin' to nobody about what happened to Dad. None of it." His laugh was brief and bitter. "I wasn't about to. I knew more than she did, and what I knew scared me so I was afraid to go to sleep nights for fear I'd say something in a nightmare." He shook his head sorrowfully. "Turned out, she the one who talked. And look at her now."

Dave frowned. "It doesn't add up. The Duchess came for the truck. She got the truck. She went off with it. The night before Cecil and I talked to your mother."

"Then who fired at you from the rifle range?"

"Accidents have happened there," Dave said. "The storekeeper's dog was killed. That had to be a stray bullet. A customer was wounded, carrying sacks out to his car."

"The dog and the customer weren't trailing the Duchess," Melvil said. "Asking Paul Myers's widow questions. Drinking coffee with Ossie Bishop's widow."

"There's Smithers," Dave said. "Tall, bald, drives a Mercedes?" Melvil looked at him curiously and nodded. Dave added, "Did your mother tell you what Smithers wanted?"

"Pretty much what you wanted," Melvil said. "What was Paul carrying up in Torcido Canyon the night he got killed? Exactly where did he take it? Stuff like that." Melvil got out of the chair, went to stand looking at the fire. The flames had died down. There was a lot of smoke. He shifted the screen aside, found the poker, jabbed at the logs. Sparks flew up the chimney. "Oh, and about Ossie. He wanted to know did Ossie ever go up that canyon. See, he knew Ossie got Paul the nightwork."

"He learned that from Angela Myers," Dave said.

"What are you worrying about Smithers for?" Flames worked on the logs again. Melvil rattled the poker back into its glinting brass rack and hauled the screen once more across the rough brick hearth. "You think it was him shot at you, shot my Mama?"

"A man who goes around passing himself off as someone he isn't just naturally worries me. I know what the Duchess's stake is in all this. Where does Smithers fit?" Dave drank, scowled, chewed his lip. "How did he locate your mother? Angela didn't tell him—she doesn't know. Did he follow Cecil and me to Halcon?" On that long drive, had Dave been too concerned about Cecil to notice a conspicuous car trailing them, mile after mile? Shouldn't reflex have alerted him, a lifetime's experience? The years were catching up to him: he was losing sharpness. Annoyance at himself was in his voice when he said to Melvil, "What does Smithers want? Who is he?"

"Maybe he after the Duchess too." Melvil came back to the desk. He watched Dave light a cigarette. "You shouldn't do that. Ruin you lungs." Dave picked up his glass. "Alcohol too. Make you old before you time."

"It is my time," Dave said, and drank. "All right. To hell with Smithers. We'll go after the Duchess." He examined the boy's square, solemn face. "You really want to show me that truck stop? She's a deadly lady."

"You going to try to take her?" Melvil sounded awed.

"I'd prefer to leave it to the Sheriff. He has troops. I have a feeling troops are going to be needed. But you don't want anything to do with the Sheriff."

"If Mama die," Melvil said, "who going to look after those babies except me?" He laid a hand on the telephone.

126

"Do you think, if I was to get on here now and tell the Sheriff what I know, I'd still be alive to testify when they put the Duchess on trial?" He withdrew his hand, sat down. His look at Dave was grave. "If it was a matter of troops, Mr. Bannister, how come she never been on trial yet? This been going on since before I was born. They never going to catch her. Nobody know who she is."

"Maybe we can find out." Dave rolled open a deep drawer of the desk, meant to hold files but holding cameras, binoculars, tape recorders. Elaborate and expensive equipment. None of which he had ever found a use for. "It will help to have a picture of her, won't it?" He lifted out a camera by the long strap on its case. "Something for me to show to Lieutenant Salazar, to accompany my description of the Duchess at work and play. Mine and Cecil's." He looked at Melvil. "Not yours. We'll keep you a secret." Beside the camera on the desk, Dave laid a camera-shop sack filled with little boxes. "How far away is this place? When should we start?"

Melvil peered into the sack. "You can't use these. Flash one bulb, everybody leave."

"Not those—this." Dave probed the sack and brought out a box of film and held it up. "Infrared-sensitive. For taking pictures in the dark." He unsnapped the camera case. "When do they meet at this truck stop?"

"Late. Midnight." Melvil watched Dave turn the camera over in his hands, frowning. Melvil said, "You don't even know how to get the film in there, do you?"

Dave held it out to him. The stocky boy put his hands behind him, shaking his head. "Don't ask me." He laughed. "This going to be some evidence-gathering expedition."

Dave set the camera down. "Cecil will know," he said.

The door flew open, and the small boys hurtled in. Two of them. The third, the chunky one, was riding on Cecil's back. Cecil rolled his eyes. "Will somebody please take these monkeys off my hands?" The two skinny ones rattled up and down the stairs again, raindrops sparkling in their hair.

"Cool it!" Melvil shouted.

They came to a halt and stared at him. The chunky one slipped silently down off Cecil's back. They stood chastened. Melvil looked at Dave. "What we going to do with them? Do you know any baby sitters?"

"Amanda," Dave said, and reached for the phone.

Amanda said, "But I don't know anything about children."

"We were all children once," Dave said. "Some of us still are."

"Ah-ha!" she said. "I'll bring electronic games."-

15

It was a lonely place, a long way from anywhere. Miles before they reached it, they saw the glow it made above the dark, rolling hills of the endless valley. When they did reach it, Dave drove on past. It was a black-topped acre or two, where the boxy hulks of tractor-trailer rigs loomed up against the lights of a filling station, a cinder-block motel, a glaring, glass-walled eatery. On the roof of the eatery, red neon spelled GOOD BUDDY. Plumes of smoke rose from the tall, plated exhaust pipes of some of the rigs. The rain laid a shine on the trucks, the paving, the jackets of men climbing down out of cabs, moving among fuel pumps, heading for or coming from the café. But the shine did nothing to change the bleakness of the place.

"There her van," Melvil said. "She here."

In the rear seat, the camera burred and clicked. Cecil had spent the evening hunched at Dave's desk, studying the instruction manual. He had fitted the camera with a night telephoto lens. At the time he bought the cameras, Dave had let the clerk sell him every sort of gadget and attachment. The motor traveled the film in the camera. Cecil clicked the shutter again. "Do you see her?" he said.

"No, but she there." Melvil twisted on the seat to peer back through the rain. "You want her license number."

Dave stretched across him, opened the glove compartment, took out pad and pen, dropped them in Melvil's lap. The boy held the pad close to his eyes and traced the numbers large and slow. "Look it up," he said, "find it belong to somebody dead, most likely."

Dave squinted past the batting wiper blades. "You picked the right night," he said, "but won't the weather keep her indoors? Won't she make her contacts in the café?"

"She work in the dark." Melvil stowed pad and pen in the glove compartment. "She don't trust but a few." The little door clapped shut feebly. "Where we going?"

"To find a side road," Dave said.

"Where would a side road go out here?" Cecil said.

"Maybe noplace," Dave said, "but we sure as hell are not going to drive into that truck stop and announce ourselves, now, are we?"

"She don't know this car," Melvil said. "Ain't that why we brought this car? Figure she know Ossie's car. Maybe she know Cecil's van. She don't know this car."

"She knows *you*," Dave said.

A truck lumbered out of the rest stop and onto the road. Its headlight beams glared in Dave's rearview mirror. He winced and moved the Valiant along faster. But very soon the diesel finished clashing its gears and roared up behind them. Dave looked for a wide, flat shoulder he could pull off onto. The headlights didn't show one. The diesel gave a blast of its air horn. Dave pulled onto a narrow, tilted shoulder and felt the rear wheels slide. The truck howled past, red lights glaring off its towering rear. The red lights dimmed and disappeared in the darkness and the rain. The Valiant stalled. It coughed when Dave tried to start it. But at last it started. He shifted into drive, and the rear wheels spun, whining.

"Oh-oh," Melvil said, and got out into the rain.

Cecil got out the back door. "Yuck," he said, "mud."

Dave stretched across the seat and looked out. He had turned off the headlights. Cecil and Melvil were almost invisible, a tall shape, a bulky shape in the blackness. Melvil lifted one foot, then the other. They came away with a sucking sound. "What do we do now, coach?"

"Should have brought Amanda's car," Cecil said. "Too light to get stuck." He didn't have a hat. He pulled his jacket up over his head.

"Too small," Dave said. It was an Alfa-Romeo two-seater. No room for his knees. Certainly no room for Cecil's knees. "There are three of us, remember?"

Cecil moved. "That's why we are all right." His voice came from farther off. "Two of us to"—he grunted—"push!"

"Not you." Dave got out of the car quickly and lunged for the rear, skidding in the mud, almost falling. The two leaned their weight against the trunk. Dave caught Cecil's arm. "You drive. You're in no condition for hard labor."

"Ah, listen, I'm okay," Cecil said.

"You want to go back to the hospital?" Dave said.

Cecil sighed and, with slumped shoulders, went and got into the car, behind the steering wheel. The whirling rear tires plastered Dave and Melvil with mud. But they got the old car onto the paving. And they found that side road. The trouble with it was that as it climbed into the hills, it veered away from the lights of the truck stop. Slithering and sliding, they backtracked.

"This is the closest point," Dave said. "Stop here."

"It quit raining," Melvil said. "That's nice."

Snagging themselves on barbwire fences, sometimes up to their ankles in mud, they slogged across farmland, uphill, toward the glow in the sky. Cecil's legs were longest and he led, camera case, equipment case, binocular case swinging from their shoulder straps, banging his lean hips. Breathing hard, muscles aching from the bad footing, they topped a ridge. Below lay the truck stop.

Dave unsnapped the binocular case. The view was good. A stout woman in a dark raincoat, a dark slouch hat shadowing her face, stood beside the high tractor of an eighteen-wheeler, out near the edge of the shiny blacktop, where the light from the buildings was poor. A hulking man held a clear plastic umbrella over her, though the rain had stopped. In his other arm he cradled a stack of big brown envelopes wrapped in clear plastic. The long door of the truck cab opened and the driver climbed down, in a cowboy hat and dirty leather jacket. The woman passed him one of the envelopes. The binoculars were 7 x 50s with night lenses. Dave could see the driver's beard stubble, the pores under the woman's thick makeup. He handed Melvil the glasses.

"Is that the Duchess?"

"Where?" Melvil had trouble finding in the lenses that brought her close a figure that a moment before had been tiny. "Oh, yeah, that's her. See the big ugly with the stupid umbrella? He always with her."

"Probably the one who beat Angela Myers," Dave said.

From the darkness, Cecil said, "Damn," to himself. The camera churned and snapped. Again. Again. "Wish she'd take off that hat. Can't get her face. Now she's going to another truck. If she'd just once look up—"

"Don't worry about that," Melvil said. "Focus on the driver, man. Get pictures of what he going to do." Melvil nudged Dave's arm with the glasses. "Watch."

Dave watched. The man in the cowboy hat peeled the Saran Wrap off the envelope, dropped the wrap into an oily rain puddle at his cowboy-booted feet, tore open the flap of the envelope. He peered inside for a moment, reached inside, drew out thick white plastic sheets with raised red lettering. He reached up, slammed the door of the cab, hiked himself up, and flattened one of the sheets against the door: ACME WASTE DISPOSAL.

Melvil said, "Mama say you told her there ain't no Dr. Ford Kretschmer. Not in the phone book. Noplace. Well, ain't no Acme Waste Disposal, either. 'Peerless Sanitation' going to drive out of here tonight, too. Another one called 'Certified.' Names you might believe, if you didn't know the Duchess only made them up."

"Look at that." Cecil kept snapping the camera shutter. "Now it's a pirate ship."

Dave focused on the cowboy driver. He was slapping skull-and-crossbones warning placards on the trailer of his truck: HAZARDOUS CARGO. Dave lowered the glasses and frowned at Melvil. "I don't follow. You camouflage yourself as exactly what you are?"

"This only half of it," Melvil said. "He still got a lot of goodies in that envelope. You want to see how the last part work? We'll have to follow him."

"We can try," Dave said.

It was a grimy corner of L.A. At two-forty-five in the morning, the wet streets were empty. A freeway arched past, its trees and shrubs an unearthly green in the blaze of lights. Beyond the freeway, the glass towers of downtown glowed tall against the dark sky. Down here, there was a lot of shadow. The streets edged between old buildings, half of them blinded by plywood or rusty corrugated sheet iron. Dave held the Valiant back two blocks behind the giant semi, which bulked ahead of them almost as wide as the street. Red braking lights flared now on its rear. Its air brakes brought it to a hissing, clattering halt outside a brick wall where metal signs read MILLEX CORP.

Dave swung down a side street, then into an alley, to park between walls where graffiti was dense and as intricate as lace. Rain-soaked trash overflowed dented dumpsters and squished under the tires. The eyes of cats shone in the headlight beams and vanished. Dave switched off lights and engine. "That's a high wall," he said, and wearily pushed the door handle and climbed out. He left the alley and went back up the side street. The truck was inching through open gates into the Millex yard, which was now brightly lighted. Dave studied the street, then returned to the car and leaned at Cecil's window. "May I have the keys, please?"

Cecil pulled the keys out of the dashboard and handed them to him. Their little jingle was loud in the silence. Dave unlocked the trunk of the Valiant. The light was poor. He shone the sharp, thin little beam of a penlight into the trunk. A tire iron lay on the frayed carpet. He closed fingers around it and brought it out and slammed down the lid of the trunk. He pocketed the keys and started deeper into the alley. "Come on," he said, and heard them open car doors, scramble out, come hurrying after him. He played the little light along dank walls. The windows were high up and barred with iron. In sunken doorways, trash had accumulated against doors sheeted in metal, padlocked. He touched one or two of these padlocks, studied the slits of Yale locks, went on.

In the next block he found the kind of door he wanted. It was wooden. The hasp that held its padlock was rusty and hung a little loose off its screws. He wedged the tire iron under it, pushed. The screws came out and rattled in the litter underfoot. He didn't worry with the spring locks. He jammed the tire iron between door and frame and leaned his weight on it. Wood cracked and splintered. The tire iron slipped. Dave fell against the door. It gave, and he pitched into blackness. He fell, bruising elbows and knees on gritty concrete. The penlight skipped away. He dug out his cigarette lighter and flicked up a flame. The tube of the penlight glittered. Melvil picked it up and handed it back to him. Cecil helped Dave to his feet. "Stairs," Dave said.

They found a corner room on the third floor, empty, dusty, plaster fallen from the ceiling, where the view was good of the Millex yard. The window glass was dirty, and the lock on the window was corroded. Melvil hammered at it with the tire iron.

"Don't break the glass," Dave said.

"Hurry," Cecil said. "They're loading now." He had his face pressed against the next window. He rubbed at the grime on it with a hand, and shifted anxiously from foot to foot, and made small sounds of frustration while the camera, on its neck strap, jogged against his chest.

"Let me try," Dave said, and took the tire iron. He tapped it in under the window lock and pried. With a squawk, the lock came loose and flew in the air. Dave dropped the tire iron and pushed up the window sash. Cold, wet air came in. Cecil bumped against him and leaned far out the window. He began snapping the camera shutter again. Dave got the binoculars from the case on his hip.

Steel drums were stacked along a loading dock. Not many of them were new. A few had a little shine left to their finish, red, yellow, black. Most were mottled, pitted, streaked, colors no one could name. Wearing gauntlets and black rubber aprons, three men—two dockers and the driver—rolled the drums on dollies from the lighted platform into the dark trailer of the truck. A few drums bore faded company stickers, warning stickers. Not many.

"This a sleaze operation," Melvil said. "They don't care about nothing. Place Dad went did everything up neat, labeled what the chemicals were in the barrels, all that. Tech-Rite. They just as evil, but they make it look nice."

The loading took forty minutes. Then the driver shut down the door at the back of the truck, shoved the lock bolts to, and shed gloves and apron. A squat, paunchy docker dug under his apron and brought out folded papers. The driver unfolded these, read the top one, taking his time. He walked to a crate beside a door that gaped wide on a dim, empty storeroom, picked up his cowboy hat and put it on, laid the papers on the crate and signed them. The squat man took the papers back, separated the copies, handed a couple to the driver, folded the others and tucked them back under his apron. The other docker, a gaunt Latino with rounded shoulders, came out of the warehouse, carrying Styrofoam cups.

"Oh, no," Cecil groaned, and pulled himself back into the empty office. "They aren't going to drink coffee now." He peered at the elaborate black watch that made his wrist look fragile. "Don't we ever get to sleep?"

Dave heard his exhaustion. "Let's go," he said.

"Wait." Melvil took the binoculars. "It's not all over yet." He leaned out the wondow. "He ain't got time for coffee. Wherever he going to dump that stuff, it's a long way from here. He got to do it before daylight."

Dave touched Cecil's drawn face and returned to the window. The driver jumped down from the loading dock. He carried papers and coffee to the truck cab and climbed in. The big engine roared into life. Smoke poured out the high exhaust pipe. The brakes hissed, the gears ground. Jerkily, snorting, the truck nosed out the gates and lurched on big tires into the street. The space was narrow, so it took backing and filling, but at last the entire length of the rig was once more in the street. Headed back the way it had come. The yard gates swung to. A moment later, the yard went dark. The truck came on toward the building where Dave, Cecil, and Melvil waited. It stopped almost under their window. The driver climbed down, peeled the white magnetic signs off the doors, the skull-and-crossbones placards from the trailer.

"See?" Melvil whispered. "Now he nobody again."

The man climbed back into the cab. The angle from up here was steep, but Dave could see the man's hands sliding the signs back into the Duchess's brown envelope. He folded the posters and pushed them into the envelope too. He stuffed in the manifests given him by the Millex docker and drew out another set, green ones. These he stowed above his head, where Dave couldn't see. He dropped the brown envelope behind the seat and reached for the gear stick.

"Now he got cargo manifests he can show," Melvil said, "in case the CHP stop him or they a roadblock or something."

The brakes hissed. The big rig growled slowly off.

"Prepared by the Duchess," Dave said.

"Anything," Melvil said. "Stuffed toy animals."

"Paper hats for your end-of-the-world party," Cecil said, and began laughing and couldn't seem to stop.

Dave lifted the cases off him and draped them on himself. Cecil staggered with laughter. Dave took his arm and, by the gleam of the penlight, steered him toward the hall. "You're hysterical. Let's get you home to bed."

Melvil followed them, plaster crunching under his shoes. "Don't you want to see him dump it?"

"Not tonight, thanks." Dave's voice echoed in the stairwell. "Not unless it's up Torcido Canyon. Where Paul Myers went. That I want to see."

"Why didn't you say so?" Melvil said. "Torcido Canyon where Dad went that night I stowed away with him."

16

Cecil slept, slumped across the back seat, hands open in his lap, camera in its case in his hands. Melvil slept in the passenger seat, head over against the window, rolling against the glass with the movement of the car. The glass was wet. Rain had begun falling again about the time they reached Horseshoe Canyon. It was five o'clock but still dark. Dave ached from all the driving. He swung the Valiant gratefully down into the bricked yard and stepped on the brakes. The headlights shone on a patrol car, black and white, PROTECT AND SERVE on the door. Uniformed officers climbed out of the car, shining flashlights. One stood back, hand on the butt of a big revolver on his hip. The other came forward cautiously. He was young, blond, and looked sleepy.

"See some identification, please?"

"I live here." Dave dug the leather folder from his inside jacket pocket, flapped it open, held it out where the officer could shine a light on it. Plastic covered his badged cap. Rain beaded on his leather jacket. He squinted at Dave's private investigator's license. Dave said, "This is my house. What's the trouble?"

"You can put that away, thanks." The officer bent and shone his light inside. On Cecil. On Melvil. "Who are they?" He swung the light so it shone in Dave's eyes. "Are you all right? What's the situation here?"

"You mean," Dave said, "they're black and I'm white, they're young and I'm old, so something must automatically be wrong?" He pushed the door handle and moved to get out. The officer didn't step back. Dave jerked his head to indicate Cecil. "And he is surrounded by rich men's toys?"

"This car is no rich man's toy." The flashlight played over the dented thin-gauge steel. "Guess I'm a little confused."

Cecil stirred, lifted his arms to stretch, stopped and sat up straight. "What's going on?"

"Just keep your seat, please," the officer said.

"The car is a cover," Dave said. "For stakeouts. That young man is Cecil Harris, my associate. He lives here. This is Melvil Bishop. I'm looking into the death of his father. He's helping me. He's my houseguest."

Melvil opened his eyes. "Oh-oh," he said.

Dave asked the officer, "What are you doing here?"

"Mrs. Brandstetter called us. Prowler with a gun. Tried to make her let him in. When she refused, he sat out here in his car." The young man smiled slightly. "Rich man's toy. A new Mercedes. By the time we got here, he was gone. Smithers. You know a Smithers?"

"Nobody knows Smithers." Dave pushed the door a little farther open. "Not by that name. Excuse me—I'd like to get out of the car now." The officer took two steps back. Over beside the black-and-white, where a radio dispatcher's voice crackled quietly, the other officer kept his hand on his gun. Dave got out into the gentle rain. "Smithers is involved somehow in a case I'm working on for Pinnacle Life. That's all I know."

"Your wife," the officer said, "seems to think he came to kill you."

"Is she all right?" Dave said.

Melvil leaned across the seat. "What about the babies?"

"She's worried for you," the officer said. He frowned at Melvil. "She didn't mention any babies."

Melvil scrambled out of the car. The officer by the patrol car drew his gun. "My little brothers," Melvil said, turned, and took steps across the wet bricks.

"Hold it right there," the officer with the gun said.

And Amanda came through the headlight beams, small and trim, cinching the belt of a red raincoat. Her dark eyes were wide with worry. "Thank God you're back," she said, and put her arms around Dave and laid her neat head against his chest for a moment. She looked up into his face. She was pale. "Are you all right?"

"Fine," he said. "I'm worried about you."

"I'm unscathed," she said. "Just scared witless."

"What about my brothers?" Melvil said.

"Asleep." Amanda gave him a weary smile. "And if they sleep as hard as they play Donkey Kong, they'll stay asleep for a while."

"You right about that." Melvil laughed relief.

"You know Bishop here?" the officer asked Amanda. "Harris, in the car there?"

"Yes, they're friends." Amanda nodded.

"And this *is* your husband?"

Amanda blinked at Dave, mischief in her eyes. She was about to complicate things. Dave wanted to sleep. He shook his head at her pleadingly. She sighed, looked at the officer, and said, "Yes, of course. Thank you for staying. I'll be all right now."

"You're welcome." The officer touched his cap. He

looked at Dave. "Two other patrol cars searched the area. No sign of Smithers. We ought to locate him. Forty to fifty years of age? Tall—six three or four? Slender—hundred sixty-five pounds?"

"Bald?" Dave said.

"He was wearing a hat," Amanda said.

The officer asked Dave, "Sure you can't help us?"

"If I learn anything," Dave said, "I'll call you."

Tapping woke Dave, the sharp rap of a finger ring against glass, one of the square panes of the door from the courtyard into the front building. He didn't make a lot of use of the front building, though Amanda had made it handsome. He entertained in it. It had the best sound system, so he sometimes did his listening here. Otherwise he rarely entered the place.

But last night Amanda had put the little Bishops in the bed on the loft in the back building—the only bed in the place. So Melvil had slept on the one couch in the back building. And Dave and Cecil had slept on couches up here.

Daylight, gray and rainy, but daylight, came into the big, raftered place through clerestory windows above a curtained row of French doors. Dave turned on the couch, stiff, aching, fumbled on the floor for his watch, and squinted groggily at the time. Not yet ten o'clock. Clutching the blanket around him, he sat up and peered.

A big-shouldered man was doing the rapping. Not a tall, thin man. Dave shrugged off the blanket and, shivering in briefs and T-shirt, kicked into trousers and pushed as creakily as old Reverend Prentice up off the couch. He crossed deep carpet, climbed a level, unchained and unbolted the door, opened the door to cold dampness.

142

"Ken," he said. "What is this?"

"Sorry to wake you." Rain dripped from the crumpled canvas hat of Captain Ken Barker, homicide division, LAPD. He had a broken nose, and eyes the same dark gray as the clouds that hung low over the canyon this morning. "But I understand a man came by last night to murder you. It awakened my protective instincts."

"Come in," Dave said. He rubbed his forehead. There was an ache there. Barker stepped in, dripping, and Dave shut the door. It closed with a stutter against the sill; the rains had swollen it. "Let me take your coat and hat." Amanda had stationed a coat rack by the door. Dave hung Barker's mac on it, hat stuffed in the pocket. "I didn't get to bed until six." Dave moved down into the room. "What else did you hear?"

"Westside went to work on Smithers." Barker followed, lighting a cigarette, watching Dave, who sat on the couch again, picked up socks, found them damp and muddy, didn't put them on. Barker said, "No Smithers owns any Mercedes—not in California. Why didn't your lady get the license number?"

With slow, mindless motions, Dave folded the blanket. "Because, when it rains too much, the landscape lights in front short out. I keep forgetting to get them fixed."

From down the room came Cecil's voice: "Oh, man, do you know what time it is?" His head appeared above the back of the couch. He looked as cranky as he sounded. "We just got to sleep. Why do you want to start so early?" He saw Barker. "Oh, sorry."

"Who are you?" Barker said.

"You got older," Dave said, "and they made you a captain and gave you more help. I got older, but I had to round up my own help." Cecil came from the couch, yawning, shuffling, wrapped in his blanket. Dave introduced them. They shook hands. Cecil's blanket slipped off his shoulders. The scars showed on his ribcage. Barker recognized them for what they were and frowned.

"Where did you get those?" he said.

Cecil pulled up the blanket. "Line of duty," he said. "You going to find Smithers?"

"He never registered that gun," Barker said.

"It's not his real name," Dave said. "The case we're working on is full of phony names—individuals, companies." A coffeemaker was behind the bar. He loaded it and set it to work. Then he started the signal going on an intercom he had never used. Barker blinked. "We need dry clothes," Dave explained.

"Out in the rain all night," Cecil said.

"What kind of case?" Barker said.

Dave told him about the Myers case—omitting the parts involving Ossie Bishop and family. "Smithers appeared after the newscasts about the bomb. He didn't realize I'd already been to see Angela Myers, and he tried to pass himself off as an investigator for Pinnacle Life."

The beeper stopped. Melvil's voice came from the intercom, cottony with sleep. "I'm sorry. I couldn't find it. Looked high and low. How come you hide it?" Dave remembered only now that he had cleared the intercom in the back building off the desk as superfluous weeks ago and stowed it on a bookshelf. "Woke the babies up too."

"They've had their sleep," Dave said.

"That's just the trouble." The voices of the little boys were shrill in the background. "They got cartoons on up there. Use your bed for a trampoline."

"We'll feed them," Dave said, "just as soon as you bring over dry clothes for Cecil and me."

144

"I didn't hear the phone ring," Melvil said. "So they ain't no news about Mama?"

Dave read his watch again. "Amanda should be at the hospital by now, unless the traffic was bad. She'll be calling soon."

"Hope so. Those babies going to miss Mama pretty quick now. They all start crying together, you never heard nothing like it." Melvil sighed. "All right—I'll bring you clothes." The intercom went silent.

Dave found mugs under the bar. He said to Barker, "Mrs. Myers was at work." He peered into the mugs. Dusty. He rinsed them at the little bar sink. "But her brother was at home. All muscle and gut. Bright enough to guess Smithers was lying, but dumb enough to show off how smart he was by flashing my card."

"And letting Smithers walk off with it," Cecil said.

"Pinnacle never heard of him?" Barker said.

"You should be a detective." Dave dried the mugs with a starchy little towel and set them on the bar. They looked good—hand-thrown, with a drizzly brown glaze. Expensive. Of course. Amanda had chosen them. "We'll have some coffee here shortly."

"Good." Barker leaned on the bar. "Is your lady sure he came to kill you? Or did she jump at that when she saw his gun?"

"Let me tell you how it went." Dave took the cigarette pack from the breast pocket of Barker's whipcord jacket. "I've got a client staying here." Lighting a cigarette, Dave nodded at the intercom. "The boy whose voice you just heard. Also his three little brothers."

"Name of Bishop," Barker said, taking back his cigarette pack, tucking it away. "I read the report."

"Then you know Amanda was babysitting while Cecil and

I took Melvil with us on this stakeout."

"I want to hear about the stakeout next."

Dave shook his head. "No, you don't. It's not your worry. It connects to the Myers matter, and that's County, not City. I promised to lay it on Jaime Salazar's desk. I'm going to do that this morning—for what it's worth."

"Smithers came here." Barker stubbed out his cigarette in a brown pottery ashtray on the bar. "This is City."

"Amanda had tucked the kids in." Dave tilted his head. "You've been here. You know the layout."

Barker nodded. "Loft in the rear building."

"And she thought she'd like to relax with television," Dave said, "and she didn't want the kids to wake up again, so she turned down the lamps back there, put on her raincoat, and started for this building."

"And she saw a guy skulking around with a revolver," Barker said, "and she was closer to this building by then, so she ran for it."

"And he saw her," Cecil said, "and chased her."

"He didn't shoot at her," Barker said.

"It was me he wanted to shoot." Dave took the pot and filled the mugs. "Amanda and I don't look alike—not even in the dark." He set the pot back in place.

"She locked and bolted the door there." Barker's somber eyes measured the door, unhappy at all those glass panes, thick though they were, and even though the old wood that clinched them was heavy and strong. "And she very sensibly did not turn on the lights."

Dave slid one of the mugs at him. "She started for the phone over there. To summon your people."

"But he banged on the door." Cecil came to the bar, still wrapped in his blanket. "And gave his name—if that is his name." He was tall enough to bend far over the bar and peer beneath it. "Sugar?" he asked Dave. "Cream?"

146

From the little refrigerator Dave brought a brown pottery sugar bowl, a cold spoon leaning in it. "Afraid you'll have to rough it." He showed Cecil a blue pint carton. "This cream is dated two months ago."

Making a face, Cecil spooned sugar into his coffee.

Barker said to Dave, "So he yelled through the door that he had to see you. It was urgent. He knew you were here because your car was here. He meant the van out there with the flames painted on it." Barker gave the semblance of a laugh. "He doesn't know you very well."

"It's Cecil's van." Dave tried his coffee and it made him feel better right away. "I drive a brown Jaguar these days. It's in the repair shop for the moment."

"She insisted you weren't here and told him to go away and he went away," Barker said, "but only out to his car, to wait for you to show up. That's what bothers me. He had to know she'd call the police."

"He wasn't here when they got here," Cecil said.

Barker nodded, frowned, worked on his coffee. "But it's as if he meant to be. At first. Then changed his mind. That's puzzling." With a thick finger, Barker dug out his cigarettes again, extended the pack to Dave, to Cecil. Dave's cigarette still burned. Cecil wanly shook his head. Barker's lighter was an old Zippo, embellished with a small police badge in worn gold and silver. He lit his cigarette and put pack and lighter away. He lifted his coffee mug and frowned at Dave over it. "Has it occurred to you that Smithers might be an investigator? Federal, state? Even County? The grand jury's investigating the illegal dumping of toxic wastes."

"If the grand jury wants me," Dave said, "sending a prowler with a gun in the middle of the night seems an odd way to go about it."

"And that isn't all," Cecil said. "That same man—"

147

Dave reached to clap a hand over Cecil's mouth, when the door opened and Melvil came in with an armload of clothes wrapped in dry-cleaning-shop plastic. "I didn't know what you needed, so I brought everything I could think of." Melvil looked around the big, comfortable, multilevel room. "Where shall I put them?"

"Thank you," Dave said. "On that couch is fine."

Barker turned to watch Melvil carry the clothes to the couch and lay them down. Behind Barker's muscular back, Dave frowned at Cecil and put a finger to his lips. Cecil showed bewilderment, but he gave a shrug of acceptance. The blanket slipped off his shoulders again. He pulled it up.

"This plastic wet," Melvil said, and began to unwrap the clothes. "Listen, those babies want breakfast. Be all right with you, if I was to—?" The telephone rang. It sat on a table at the end of the couch. Melvil didn't wait for Dave. He stepped to the phone and picked it up. He started to say "Hutchings," but caught himself and said, "Bannister residence," instead. Then he listened. It was quiet in the room. The rain pattered on the roof, splashed on the bricks outside, pinged on the parked cars. Melvil's face lit up. He put a hand over the mouthpiece and said, "She all right. My mama going to be all right." He said into the phone, "Mama? How you doing? No, they fine. We all fine. Mr. Bannister looking after us. I will. I'll thank him. I want to see you too. Soon as it safe. Won't be too long now. You take it easy, hear me? I be calling you." He put the phone into Dave's hand.

"Amanda?" Dave said.

"She saw the man who shot her," Amanda said. "He stepped from behind the store. It was Smithers."

17

After he had delivered the film to Salazar, along with his clumsily typed report of last night's watch—bearing his own fingerprints in bacon grease because he had been too hungry to forgo breakfast, and in too much of a rush not to work while he ate—after he had delivered these, he didn't wait around. The Jaguar was ready. The agency had telephoned just as he was going out the door of the back building in Horseshoe Canyon—or trying to go out the door, hobbled by Melvil's giggling little brothers clinging to his legs. From the Sheriff's, he drove out the Santa Monica Freeway to Beverly Hills, the junkyard car developing croup as the wet miles passed. He left the snooty dealership the embarrassment of returning the Valiant to his house, and himself drove the Jaguar to a gun shop.

It stood on a quiet street in West L.A., in a row of shops climbed on by vines that gave them a cozy look. Knitting yarn should have been sold in this one, or dolls. The place was hushed by carpeting. The paneling looked almost real. Gentility seemed to be the aim. The salesman wore a quiet, high-priced, three-piece suit, a handsome white mustache, an English accent. His coloring harked back to that old rhyme about the good roast beef of England. He was affable and ready to chuckle. He was selling death.

Dave let him place on top of a glass showcase several brands of death—Colt, Smith & Wesson, Browning—snubnosed .38 Detective Specials, the .45s favored by television cops. Dave hefted them by turn, let them nestle cold in his hand. The man found good and bad to say about each one, his bloodshot blue eyes watching Dave closely, sensitive to the slightest signal of acceptance or rejection. To relax the man, Dave said the gun should be simple and reliable, and be able to shoot many times without reloading. The cost didn't matter.

He walked out onto the dripping, tree-lined street with a Sig Sauer nine-millimeter automatic, pride of the Swiss army, able to fire eight thousand rounds in the field without a hitch. It held thirteen rounds in the clip, one in the chamber, cost five hundred fifty dollars, and rode snugly in a Bianchi holster against his left ribs. He would never be comfortable with it. He had never wanted a gun. For decades he had managed without one. But times had changed. The game he loved had turned lethal. People kept trying to kill him and his.

As he unlocked the Jaguar, folded himself into its comfort, started the quiet, powerful engine, listened to it purr, the notion came to him again that had surprised him often lately—that he ought to quit. That would be sensible. He wasn't getting any younger. He didn't need the money; his father had left him a great many shares of Medallion stock. But sensible was boring. What the hell would he do with his days and nights? He grimaced, read his watch, looked in the side mirror for a break in traffic, swung the Jaguar in a fast U-turn, and headed back to Horseshoe Canyon to pick up Melvil.

The spur of Torcido Canyon to which Melvil pointed him would have been easy to miss. Its road was a narrow strip of blacktop that the rain had damaged. It followed a crooked creek along the bottom of a canyon whose walls went up

150

steeply, covered in dry brush showing new tips of green, with occasional clumps of live oak and outcrops of rock. The ridges were high above. The creek ran rough and swollen among boulders and twisted white sycamores hung with scraps of yellow leaf.

"Hard to imagine a semi negotiating this road," Dave said. "How much farther is this dump?"

"Dad, he took it real slow, change gears a lot." Melvil frowned ahead through the afternoon rain. "Not too far now. Look a little different in the daytime."

"You sure you can find it?"

"I think so. Yeah. There. See that turnoff?"

The Jaguar scraped bottom, following ruts carved by the giant tires of tractor-trailer rigs. Oaks grew large and close here, very old. The wheels of the Jaguar slurred in mud and wet grasses. And here was the dump, in a declivity circled by dead ferns. Filled with steel drums like those they had watched trucked out of Millex last night—this morning. Tumbled there, labels peeling, rusting in the rain.

"Smell it?" Melvil put a hand over his nose and mouth. "Make you sick, you breathe that for long." His eyes clouded. He turned his face away. "Worse than sick. Kill you." He whispered. "Killed my daddy."

"I need the camera," Dave said, and got out of the car. The smell was strong, caught in his throat, stung his eyes. Melvil pulled the camera from the glove compartment, lay across the seat, handed it out to Dave. "Thanks. I'll make it quick." He fiddled with the camera, uncertain, hoping he was making the correct adjustments for the poor light. He took twenty shots, got back into the car, passed the camera to Melvil. He slammed the door, started the engine. "What a nightmare," he said. He pressed the throttle, and the rear wheels spun.

Melvil sighed. "One more time," he said, and got out into the rain to have a look.

Dave got out too. "I'm a slow learner," he said.

"Be all right," Melvil said, and looked around him. "If we can find something to put under the wheels." He made a face. "Don't like touching nothing here." He rubbed his hands on his pantlegs. "How about this?" He took a few steps, slipping a little in the mud, then bent and heaved up from among the brittle, rust-brown ferns the end of a four-by-four, six feet long. He wrestled it loose from creepers that had gripped it. They were dead and dry too. The end of the timber came loose with a ripping sound.

A signboard was bolted to that end. Melvil wrestled the four-by-four toward the car. "'No dumping,'" he said. "How about that?" With a disgusted laugh, he let the post drop behind the car. Dave went to help him. Muddy-handed, they wedged the four-by-four under the rear wheels. Halfway back to the road, the rear of the car slewed and the wheels mired again. They hiked back for the post. In small print across the bottom of the sign were numerals from a County ordinance book. And below that, TORCIDO CANYON HOMEOWNERS ASSN.

Back in the car, inching it warily along the muddy ruts, Dave said, "No homeowners in this part of the canyon."

"Up there." Melvil sat forward on the seat, peering upward through the glass. "One. Look new to me."

It hung two hundred feet above them on the brushy canyon wall, all alone, raw cedar and tall glass, sharp roof angles, decks thrusting out like bony wings. Tall pin oaks grew around the house. It looked beautiful in the sifting rain—a picture for an architecture magazine. But there was something desolate about it.

Dave checked his watch. No time to go up there. Salazar expected him at four. He'd be late as it was. The Jaguar lurched heavily onto the potholed blacktop of the trail. He drove it as fast as he dared, the tires spraying water at places where the creek overflowed onto the paving. He skidded at the boulevard stop where the spur canyon opened on Torcido Canyon road. The spur canyon had a name—Concho.

Darkness was coming early again. The shift was changing. Men were leaving the squad room in dry raincoats. Men in damp raincoats were coming on duty. They brought whiffs with them of the moist air of the streets, the smell of rain on sidewalks. Phones rang. Voices spoke, laughed, swore. Typewriters rattled. From outside, above the steady growl of home-going traffic, sirens wailed and faded.

"Who led you into this?" Salazar looked and sounded pained. His hand slapped a stack of papers in front of him. "Do you realize how big this is? And how nasty?" Dave blinked at him. Salazar said, "What took you in? And I don't mean the Myers matter."

"An informant." Dave hung his raincoat on a hook by the door of the glass box that was Salazar's office, off the squad room. "On the understanding that I wouldn't disclose his name or whereabouts." He sat down facing Salazar across the desk. "The pictures came out, then?"

"The pictures are lousy. You can't take telephoto pictures without a tripod. Handheld is too jittery." Sourly, Salazar passed the pictures across. They looked as if they had been taken at night in the rain. "But he got one that wasn't too bad. Even with the hat."

"Of the Duchess." Dave studied it.

"We got responses on that from all over the state, all over the country. Clara Blodgett, née Leopardi. In twenty-five years, eleven arrests, no convictions."

Dave handed back the pictures. "Why? Her operation depends on a great many people she can't really know well enough to trust."

"She doesn't trust them. She scares them."

"She ever blow anybody up before?" Dave said.

"Maybe." Salazar thumbed through the papers. "Your license number didn't lead us anywhere. Belongs to a car junked years ago. Owner, no connection."

Dave laughed wryly. "My witness thought the owner would be dead."

Salazar said, "Sounds like he knows her. Don't feel bad. Even if we located her and took her to trial, nobody would testify against her. They got a witness once in—where? Florida? Texas? I forget." He scowled at the papers, sat back, gave his head a dismissive shake. "Doesn't matter. They registered him under a false name in a motel. Officers around the clock, eating with him, sleeping with him. They didn't go to the bathroom with him. Somebody shot him through the bathroom window. But mostly, by the time law enforcement gets a line on a witness, the poor bastard is already dead—accident, suicide. You know."

Dave reached across and touched the papers. "In all of that, did you run across an associate of hers, a hitman maybe, named Smithers? Using that name, that alias?"

"I spent the whole day with this file." Salazar found a flat box on his desk, lit a thin brown cigarette. "I'd have noticed that." He pushed the papers around for a minute, regarded Dave through blue smoke. "Smithers? Smith? That's a dumb alias."

Dave lit a cigarette of his own. "So you're saying I wasted a night and risked pneumonia for nothing? She can't be touched?"

"You get this witness of yours to drive a truck there, get an assignment from the Duchess, the signs, the warning stickers, the phony documents, the trailer full of chemicals, and bring them all to us, and—"

"She already wants him dead," Dave said. "His mother's been shot. I sent Amanda down there. The woman told her it was Smithers. San Diego County's got deputies in the hospital now, guarding her."

Salazar went straight on: "And even then, we'd haul fat Clara in, she'd have a high-powered lawyer with her, be out on the street in an hour, and when it came to trial in a couple of years, there'd be ten witnesses that she wasn't even there. Nobody at the truck stop would talk. Who wants to end his life wrapped up in razor wire? As for the company that shipped the stuff—maybe they'd get fined a few thousand bucks for illegal dumping. And they'd be right back at it the next week."

"My witness heard Paul Myers say he was going to expose the Duchess." Dave stretched to use the ashtray. "You know what happened. Myers's wife was beaten up, and when that didn't work, Myers was killed."

Salazar swiveled in his chair to gaze at the rain running down his window. "The witness, Dave."

"Give me back my report." Dave rose wearily. "And the pictures. I'll turn them over to the grand jury. I'll testify to the grand jury."

Salazar swiveled around and gazed up at Dave with pity. "They'll jail you for refusing to divulge your source. And if you get out of jail alive, you'll turn the ignition key to start your car, and blam! Instant cremation. No waiting." He slipped the envelope of photographs from the stack of papers, along with Dave's typed pages fastened with a paperclip. "Here you go." He passed them over. "But don't do it. It's not worth it."

"It might save some lives," Dave said. "This is going on all over the country, been going on for decades. They make more and more laws against it, federal, state, local. Talk about it, write about it, but it just gets worse." He went for his coat. "The air is poisoned, ponds, rivers, lakes, whole oceans. The water under the land. The land itself. Farms, the animals on the farms. People. Whole towns have to be abandoned.

Somebody has to stop it." He shrugged into the coat.

Salazar came to take down his own coat. "Did you see that picket line out at the Foothill Springs dump? They had it on TV." He put his coat on.

"I saw it in person." Dave folded the useless photos and report and jammed them into a pocket.

"Yes, well," Salazar said. "It will be them that stop it, Dave. Not you. Not the grand jury. The grand jury has been promising a report for months. It never comes." Salazar opened his door. The noises of the large room—telephones, typewriters, voices—were suddenly loud again. He led the way between busy desks. "Why don't you forget it, and do something you can do? Sign the papers on the Myers case and get the widow her check." He opened another door, and they were in a bright hallway. "Whoever killed him—the Duchess or Silencio or Kilgore—he's just as dead. And she can use the money. She's got kids."

"Also a sick old father," Dave said. "Damn it, I wish the man hadn't been hauling dangerous cargo. On that two-year conditional clause, Pinnacle won't pay her a dime."

"The truck was empty." Salazar pushed a wall button to bring an elevator. "Why isn't that enough for them? You don't have to tell them everything you know." The elevator doors opened. Two uniformed women stepped out. Salazar stepped in, waited for Dave, pushed a button. The doors slid shut. The elevator moved. "You don't really know much, the way I see it. Not that you can prove."

Dave smiled bleakly. "I've made a lot of trouble for a lot of people. It would be pretty sad if it all added up to nothing."

"You're not going to quit. Right?" Salazar said.

"I guess I don't know how," Dave said.

18

The little Bishops slept in the big bed in the loft again. Cecil had stuffed them with lasagne Bolognese until they nodded. "They liked it better than Spaghetti-O's," Melvil said. Melvil was in the back building with them. Cecil had lent him a big portable radio and cassette player. Wearing headphones, and wrapped in blankets because it was another cold, wet night, Melvil lay on the long corduroy couch in front of the fireplace where logs flamed low, and listened to Blondie. He could watch the door from the couch. It was bolted and chained, but he was afraid, just the same. Of Smithers.

In the front building, Dave sat relaxed with a drink on another couch, facing another fire. Cecil lay stretched out on the couch, his head in Dave's lap. The sing-along recording that Glenn Gould had made of the Goldberg variations just before his death was on the turntable. No light was in the room except that from the fireplace. The gain was low on the stereo equipment. Dave wanted to be able to hear cars on the trail. Passing, he hoped. Of course, if Smithers came back, his headlights would swing across the clerestory windows. But only if he left his lights on. He might not do that.

The Sig Sauer automatic lay on Cecil's belly. Its bronze metal gleamed in the firelight. His hands rested on it. He grumbled, stirred, laid the gun on the floor, out of sight. "You want me to say it's a beautiful piece of machinery?" Dave didn't answer. Cecil was quiet for a long time, touching whiskey to his mouth from a squat glass in which ice trapped the color of the flames. "Ought to be," he said. "Cost enough." Dave made a noncommittal sound and absently traced a fingertip over the intricacies of one of Cecil's tight little ears. "Man who trained me with the targets at LAPD," Cecil said, "told me that in this country law enforcement says a .45 stops a man best. But in Europe it's the nine-millimeter. Don't you love thinking about the kind of research that went into forming conclusions like that?" He touched the glass to his mouth. "They could have used me—if I'd just been a little deader."

Dave laid fingers on his mouth. "Please," he said.

"I don't want to shoot anybody," Cecil said.

The telephone rang. It was at Dave's elbow. He picked it up, grateful he'd remembered to unplug the two instruments in the rear building. The little Bishops would sleep on. "Brandstetter," he said.

"They're breaking in here." The voice was hoarse, quiet, shaky, distorted because the mouth was too close to the instrument. "They've cut off the electricity. The alarms aren't working, the electrified fence."

"Gifford?" Dave frowned at the phone. "What are you talking about? Who's breaking in?"

"The Edge, of course," Gifford snapped. "That black gang. I don't know what's happened to the dogs. They raved and raved, and now it's silent out there."

"What does The Edge want with you?" Dave didn't need to ask. "It's not you. It's Silencio, isn't it? Ruiz. He's there with you."

"Of course. You know that. You knew it all along. You've protected him as much as I have. We had an understanding,

158

didn't we? No need for words—not between us. You'll help me now. I know you'll help me now." Something crashed in the background. "No, wait! Silencio!" A voice spoke, but too far off for Dave to make out what it said. Gifford had the phone to his mouth again. "They are on the porch. They're breaking down the doors."

"Phone the Sheriff," Dave said.

"How can you say that? You know what the Sheriff will do to Silencio. Are you coming to help me or not?"

"I'll be there," Dave said. He hung up. "Got to go," he said, and lifted Cecil's head. "Get hold of the Sheriff substation in Gifford Gardens—or whichever one is nearest Gifford Gardens." Dave went down the long, shadowy room for his raincoat. "Send them to De Witt Gifford's. Someone's trying to break in." Dave flapped into his coat and unbolted the door. "He thinks it's The Edge. Since he's got Silencio with him, I wouldn't be surprised." Cecil came to him, holding out the Sig Sauer. Dave shook his head. "I won't need that. You keep it handy." He dragged open the door on rain and cold and darkness. "Melvil may be right. Smithers may be back."

The tall iron gates with their chain draperies stood open. Spotlights from brown-and-gold County cars shone on them. The cars stood in the street outside the high, vine-grown walls, whose leafage sparkled and dripped. More cars were at the far end of the drive, by the tall, jigsaw-work porch. They were hidden by the overgrown shrubs and untrimmed trees, but lights said they were there. Dave left the Jaguar, crossed the street, showed a Japanese deputy his ID, and started to explain his presence.

The deputy said, "Lieutenant Salazar is expecting you."

He sat in his patrol car and used a dashboard microphone. His thumb came away from the microphone switch. A loud-speaker crackled, staticky, in the car. Dave couldn't make out the words, but the deputy told the microphone, "Ten-four," and hung it up. He leaned out of the car into the rain and called to another deputy in rain gear beside the gate, "Let this man through."

Men moved around the grounds with flashlights. Sometimes the light streaked a yellow slicker. Voices called through the darkness. Someplace off in the night, a siren wailed. The elegant etched glass of the front double doors was smashed out. Both doors stood open. Salazar waited in the doorway. Dave climbed the high, gaunt porch steps to him. Salazar looked disgusted.

"He got away again," he said.

"Is Gifford all right?" Dave said.

Salazar snorted and turned aside. "He tried to shoot that .30-30 of his. The rifle? It blew up. I don't think it had been cleaned in twenty years. Wonder is"—Salazar followed the beam of a flashlight toward the staircase—"it fired at all. Blew half his head off."

"Dear God," Dave said.

"He was trying to save lover boy." Salazar located a staircase on the second floor and went up it, Dave following. "And maybe he did."

"What about The Edge? Your people get here in time?"

"We can't hold them for much." Salazar moved along a hallway to a door that stood open on stairs leading to the attic. "Breaking and entering." Salazar climbed the stairs. "Carrying concealed weapons. Killing the dogs."

"Beautiful animals." Dave climbed after Salazar. "Not savage enough. Not against *Homo sapiens*." They reached the attic. Dave stopped to catch his breath. He ought to quit smoking. He asked Salazar, "How did you get here before me?"

"I live about ten miles closer." Salazar shone his light over the heaped trunks, cartons, packing cases. "I left word at the

160

substation out here to phone me at home if anything went down around the Gifford place. You said maybe Silencio was still here. I kept thinking about that. Look at this mess! You could hide King Kong up here." Shaking his head, he moved down the crooked, narrow aisle between the walls of dusty junk that were De Witt Gifford's legacy to an uncaring world. Dave followed. Salazar stopped. "Coroner hasn't come yet," he said.

The old man, what was left of him, still sat in the motor wheelchair. Salazar brushed him for only a second with the flashlight's glare and swung it away. Blood had spattered the portrait of naked Ramon Novarro, forever young, on the wall above the bed. Were he and Gifford together now? Dave didn't believe it, but he figured Gifford would have appreciated the thought.

Shoes clumped on the stairs below. Voices spoke. Someone laughed. The doorway at the end of the aisle of junk glowed with moving lights. Men's silhouettes filled the door. Someone called, "Body up here?"

"Over this way." Salazar shone his light along the aisle again, then backed to make way for the men to pass. They were big men, young. One of them carried a collapsed gurney, whose metal fittings clinked. To get himself out of their way, Dave stepped past the grisly old man and found himself in the tower room, where the tall, curved window panes were murky yellow from the lights of the patrol cars far below. Like a big dead white bird, the ledger lay open on the coffee table.

Dave pulled the reading glasses from his jacket pocket, also the penlight. He sat on the crackly old Empire couch and bent above the book, moving the thin beam of the penlight along the lines of Gifford's fussy, old-maidish writing, checking dates and times. He frowned and turned back a page. And almost spoke aloud. Gifford had lied to him about the Mercedes. He read the entry twice, closed the book, pushed glasses and penlight back into their pocket, and got up from the couch, smiling grimly.

In the attic, Salazar holding the light, the hulking youths had got the frail old body onto the gurney. They began steering it on wheels back along the aisle. Dave's foot encountered something soft, huddled on the floor. He bent for it and picked it up. Salazar shone his light on it. A woman's cerise velvet hat, turban-style, a crumpled satin bow at the back. 1920? Sometime around there. Dave took three steps and dropped the hat over the stooped back of the coroner's man, onto Gifford's body under its cover.

"You're kidding," the coroner's man said.

"He wasn't," Dave said, and watched as the gurney was half wheeled, half hoisted down the aisle. Salazar's flashlight played on the stacked trunks, crates, barrels again. Dave frowned, turned back, took the flashlight from Salazar, and carefully probed the cobwebs with it. "Good God," he said, and put the light back into Salazar's hand.

"What did you see?"

"It's what I don't see. There was a World War II life raft up here. It's gone. Which suggests that the place you'll find Silencio Ruiz is downstream."

"The creek? Have you seen how that creek is running?"

"People raft it for fun all the time," Dave said. "Why wouldn't he try it to escape being killed?"

"It's only a different way to be killed," Salazar said. "We've had four drownings in this storm alone. Teenagers, grown men. People are crazy, Dave."

"I wonder what makes them that way," Dave said. "Can you run a check on a license number for me, please?"

"A forty-year-old life raft?" Salazar said. "Laying up here all that time? It would be rotten."

"Probably," Dave said. "I need this number."

"In the morning," Salazar said.

19

The rain stopped in the night. The early-morning sky was clear of clouds and very blue above the chilly spur canyon called Concho. The water of the creek still ran hard and deep beside the crooked road, but the dips in the blacktop no longer held overflow. In a few hours the stream would be a trickle, the rocks and sycamore trunks dry again.

He stopped the Jaguar at the place where trucks left the road at night. He got out and stood gazing along the ruts between the oak tree trunks to the place of rusty barrels and dead ferns. Except for the rush and rattle of the creek, the canyon was dead quiet. Birds sang on a morning after rain. Not here. A breeze pushed at his hair. The breeze brought the bad smell from the dump.

He turned away and, wincing against the brightness of the sky, looked up at the house hanging off the canyon wall high above. No sign of life. Maybe whoever lived there was asleep. He had come early so as to catch them before they left for the day. To work? From a house like that? In a setting like this? Why not? It had to be paid for. Everything had to be paid for.

He got back into the Jaguar and drove on, looking for a road up. But all he found were bridges where the creek bent and the road found better footing on the other side. The road petered out after a couple of miles, where the canyon narrowed and a waterfall came splashing down among rocks and ferns to start the creek. He drove back the way he had come. The street map book showed no road along the ridge of Concho canyon, but he explored for it because it had to be there. It took a quarter of an hour.

The road on the ridge was no more than a driveway, one car wide, the asphalt almost new. It ended where a six-foot-high cedar plank fence ended. Dave parked beside the fence and got out into silence. The noise of the creek far below hardly reached here. Quietly he shut the Jaguar's heavy door, and he walked quietly to where a double gate of cedar planks was closed and padlocked. He peered through the slot. A Winnebago camper stood alone in a two-car port. It looked brand-new, meant to go everywhere, never been anywhere. Maybe this was wilderness enough for it. Another gate opened farther along the fence. A leather thong hung down beside it. He pulled this and sleigh bells rang.

But no one came. "Hello!" he called. "Anybody home?" His voice echoed in the canyon hush. No other voice spoke. He waited. He jangled the bells again. He called again. Then he took out his wallet, slid a shiny pick from it, and gently worked the spring lock that was a round shine of brass in the rough cedar. The gate opened on a narrow deck on whose rails stood potted creepers and succulents. Some of the succulents bore very small, bright orange flowers. Below the deck, the roofs of the house made sharp angles. He swung the gate to close it behind him, and its lower edge scraped envelopes. There was a mail slot in the gate. He gathered up the envelopes and closed the gate.

A prefab black iron spiral staircase went down from the

164

deck. He took it. Even his soft shoes made it gong. If the inhabitants were asleep, maybe that would wake them. The deck down here was wider, and trees in wooden tubs stood in its corners. The wall of the house that faced it was panels of sliding glass—closed, curtains drawn. Dave stood regarding it, absently straightening the edges of the pack of envelopes in his hands. He wandered down the deck, looking for a door. It was a double door, when he found it. Locked. He didn't know this type of lock.

An elaborate system of cedar-plank staircases and decks surrounded the house. Someplace there might be an open window or a door with an easier lock. He went from level to level, downward, where the shadows of the tall trees made the morning chill again. The room he got into without trouble was functional, wooden-walled, at one end a workbench under a neatly ordered rack of tools, at the other end a bare desk, a home computer, a file cabinet. A row of windows looked out into trees, the canyon slope falling off steeply below. He looked down. The road beside the stream was visible from here, though the tops of the oaks obscured the dump. Had the raw-throated roar of the big diesels in the silence of the canyon night ever wakened the people who lived here? Were they the ones who had agitated for the fallen signboard? He guessed he wasn't going to find out. Not today.

The desk seemed the right place to leave the mail. He laid it there, turned away, turned back. He dug his reading glasses from his jacket, put them on, blinked at the name typed on the top envelope. *Mr. Lorin Shields.* He frowned. Didn't he know that name? He sorted through the other envelopes. *Mr & Mrs. Lorin Shields. Jennifer & Lorin Shields. Lorin Shields.* He let the envelopes fall to the desktop. Hell, yes. Lorin Shields was the senior vice-president he'd waited for the other morning at Tech-Rite, met

165

for a moment as the man had hurried on long legs out of the executive parking lot. Tall, thin, intense.

But Tech-Rite was thirty, forty miles from here. He stared at the envelopes. And inside his head, Shields's sleek oriental secretary said again, *He's rarely late. It must be the rain. He has a long way to come.* What had been the apple-cheeked lad's name out there? Jochim. The one so flummoxed by the picket line at Foothill Springs. He'd said something about Shields's wife. *He built her a glorious new house.* Dave saw in his mind's eye Shields's face again, under the dripping brim of an Irish tweed hat—drawn, tormented, pain in his eyes. And something else. Startlement, maybe even fear, when Jochim told him Dave's name. Dave had wondered then if he'd imagined it. What kind of sense did it make?

He climbed glossy inner staircases past stretches of polished plank flooring scarcely broken by isolated arrangements of furniture—never more than three or four pieces. He was reminded of those big, unused rooms at old De Witt Gifford's. Except that life had left those. Here, it looked as if life hadn't really had time to get started. The beautiful tall shafts reaching for light, the high sheets of glass framing the trees, the floating lofts and quiet wooden bays of the empty house didn't breathe or speak of a past or a future. Nor even of a present. In a bedroom that gave the effect of resting lightly in the tops of trees, only half of the wide bed had been slept in, sheets and blankets thrown back, one pillow dented. A lonely sight. In the house entryway, Dave took down from one of a row of thick wooden pegs an Irish tweed hat.

Somewhere a telephone rang, the jangle echoing in hollow, wooden vacancy. He stood holding the hat, listening, counting the rings. Did they mean that someone was commonly here at—he checked his watch—eight-thirty in the

166

morning? If so, would whoever that was return soon? It wouldn't be Shields, would it? This was a workday. To reach Tech-Rite from here and keep business hours, he'd have left long ago. His wife? The Jennifer of the envelopes? No. *Lost his wife recently,* Jochim had said. *Very suddenly. It was a shock. She was young.* Dave hung the hat back on its peg. The telephone stopped on the tenth ring.

Down in the workroom again, he pulled open the top drawer of the file cabinet. Like the desk, the cabinet was handsome dark Danish teak. But like the house around it, it hadn't had much use. The few manila folders in the drawer did not stand up. They lay on their backs in a loose stack, as if hastily dropped in and forgotten. He put the reading glasses on again, lifted the files out. TECH-RITE. *Shipping Dept. Do not remove.*

He sat down at the desk and leafed over the papers, yellow flimsy carbon copies of waybills. Two bore Paul Myers's signature. Dave couldn't puzzle out, from the strings of numbers and letters typed on the waybills, what he had carried. He hadn't trucked for Tech-Rite on the ninth, when he was killed. But one date did interest Dave. It was the date on the latest of the waybills in these folders—and it was the date on which the news broke that Myers's truck had not simply crashed but had been bombed. That was when Lorin Shields had brought these files home.

Dave took off the reading glasses and gazed down the room at the workbench. He folded the bows of the reading glasses, pushed them into their pocket, rose, dropped the files back into their drawer, rolled the drawer shut. He walked down the long room and crouched to look under the workbench. There hadn't been time for junk to accumulate there, not much, a few small empty cartons. And a shoe box—not empty. He lifted it, set it on the bench, took off its lid. Inside was a snarl of thin wires of many colors,

167

switches, gadgets he couldn't name. But under these, each trim flat oblong wrapped separately in cellophane, was something he could name—soft, corpse-gray, and sticky. Plastique.

"Stand very still," a voice said. A man stood in the doorway to stairs that led up to the kitchen. Lorin Shields. Tall, thin. And bald. Checked sports shirt open at the throat, hopsack trousers, corduroy jacket, crepe-soled shoes. A revolver in his hand. Forty-five. The sort that U.S. law enforcement believes stops a man best. "Brandstetter," Shields said. "I suppose I knew it would be. I've read about you in the magazines."

"They exaggerate," Dave said. "They get things wrong."

"One thing they didn't get wrong," Shields said. "You never quit."

"If you'd kept out of it," Dave said, "I'd never have connected you."

"I was sure someone knew where Paul Myers had been that night. And why. This house is so near. I had to find them and stop their mouths."

"What had Myers done to you? Besides littering up your landscape?"

"Killed my wife," Shields said. "A lovely young girl. Do you know what she wanted from life? Everything gentle and beautiful. A house in the woods. Quiet. Solitude. Nature. Away from the world."

"You gave her that," Dave said.

"She went walking, didn't she?" Shields said bitterly.

"And stumbled on that dump," Dave said. "And died of uncontrollable diarrhea, coughing, paralysis of the diaphragm. The way Ossie Bishop died."

Shields's mouth spasmed at one corner. "Who knew who Smithers was? Not even you. He came to your house to kill you. Your wife saw him. Even after that, you didn't know. Who told you?"

"A sick old man you never even heard of," Dave said. "Crippled. In a wheelchair. You worried about the wrong thing, Shields. Do you know how H. L. Mencken defined *conscience*? 'The still, small voice that tells us someone is watching.'"

"Not now," Shields said. "No one is watching now."

Dave said, "But your conscience hasn't worked for a long while, has it? Your man Jochim told me that factory out there, Tech-Rite, meant everything to you." Dave looked around at the handsome room, the lovely setting outside the long row of windows. "It paid you well, didn't it? Bought you everything a man could wish for. Beautiful house, expensive cars, lovely wife. It didn't matter to you that it was poisoning people. Not till it poisoned her."

"We're going to take a walk," Shields said.

"And then," Dave said, "you didn't have the guts to plant your bomb at Tech-Rite, did you? Instead, you blew up some man whose name you didn't even know. You didn't know Myers. Wait a minute, maybe you did. You brought those cargo manifests home to hide them."

"I knew we were using gypsy truckers to get rid of certain chemical wastes we weren't authorized to dump at Foothill Springs. You don't understand how impossible all those government regulations make doing business."

"And the horrible thought suddenly struck you that maybe Myers had brought his load that night from Tech-Rite, so you snatched the papers. But you were mistaken. He didn't dump waste from Tech-Rite in your front yard."

"Not that night—no. But earlier someone had, Myers or Bishop or someone. I recognized the barrels. Our codes stenciled on the lids." He gave his head an impatient shake.

"It wasn't Myers. It was what he was doing. It was what he and his kind had done to Jennifer." His eyes were wet. He blinked them hard. He jerked the gun barrel. "Come on." He stepped up backward into the doorway. "And be very careful."

"A walk?" Dave said. "Where? Down to the dump?"

"It kills everything that touches it," Shields said.

He began climbing the narrow steps backward, the gun leveled at Dave's head. After the brightness of the workroom, the stairway seemed dark. Dave watched his step. It wouldn't do to stumble. A noise from the kitchen above made him raise his head. He knew that noise. He had made it often lately. It was the rasp of the slide, backward, forward, on the Sig Sauer automatic, the move made to get a bullet from the clip into the chamber.

Cecil stood at the top of the stairs in sunlight, gripping the gun in rigidly outstretched hands. His eyes were wide. His skin looked dusty. Shields heard the noise when Dave heard it. Shields tried to turn. Too quickly. He lost his footing. His gun went off. The Sig Sauer went off. The bullet thudded into Shields's chest and tore out through his back. Shields's blood spattered Dave's face. He tasted the salt of Shields's blood. Shields fell backward on him, and his dead weight was too much to hold up. Dave folded under it. He ended on his back on the workroom floor, struggling to free his legs. He wanted to get to Cecil. Because, up in the kitchen, Cecil was crying. It was the saddest sound Dave had ever heard.

Romano's was quiet in its candlelight. The white tables with their shimmering glassware and silver had been vacated long ago. Shadowy figures drank in the little bar where Max polished glasses. At the corner table, Dave sat back, smoking a cigarette, holding brandy in a snifter, turning it gently, watching Cecil. Cecil was telling Amanda how it had come to happen. He had already told the story several times today. Dave was hoping that telling it enough would free him of guilt and grief. He doubted, but he hoped.

"So then Lieutenant Salazar phoned. He had the information on this license number Dave had asked him for. From De Witt Gifford's record book. Smithers's Mercedes, right? And I wrote it down. It was at the desk, you know, in the back building. Those little Bishops hopping around."

"I love them," Amanda said, "but they do hop a lot."

Dave looked at his watch. "They should be sound asleep at the Hutchings house in Halcon by now. And Melvil too. I don't think he's had much sleep lately."

"That Duchess made a good substitute for nightmares," Cecil said. "So Melvil heard me say the address, as I was writing it down. And when I hung up, he came and read what I'd written on the pad. Concho Canyon. And he said Concho Canyon was where he took Dave. To show him the dump. Off Torcido Canyon. Where Dave went this morning. To talk to whoever it was that lived up there in that house."

"Shields," Amanda said, "who called himself Smithers."

"Turns out it was his wife's maiden name," Dave said. "Salazar was right. Who would hide behind an alias like Smithers?"

"So I tried to call Salazar back," Cecil said, "tell him to get up there right away. Only by then he'd already left the office. On his way to the beach. The LAPD found Silencio Ruiz's body. It washed clear down to the ocean. But I didn't learn that till later. All I knew now was that Dave was walking into Shields and he wouldn't be ready."

"I thought I was going to talk to people who might be able to tell me something about the dumping up there that

I didn't know. Something that might help me get to the Duchess. They had a marvelous vantage point, perched up there on the side of the canyon."

"Salazar had given me Shields's phone number too," Cecil said, "and I tried that. Don't know what I thought. What good was that going to do?"

"It would have done a lot of good," Dave said, "but I couldn't answer it, could I?"

"You didn't," Cecil said. He told Amanda, "Didn't leave me any options, did it? He didn't even have the gun. Left the gun with me, in case Smithers came around."

"He liked shooting in the early morning," Dave said. "Remember? He was shooting Louella Bishop while I waited for him at Tech-Rite."

"So I drove up there," Cecil said. "And, oh-oh, the Mercedes was there. And it was quiet. So quiet." He gazed at Dave across the candle flame, eyes round and ready to weep again. "And I thought, 'He's dead. Shields shot him.' But this time I had the sense not to make any noise. Last time—remember?—I went up to the door of that cabin and told everybody inside I was there, and they shot me full of holes. Not this time."

"And a good thing, too," Amanda said mildly.

"I climbed the fence. And tried a bathroom window. That's the one everybody forgets to lock. And inside the house, I heard them talking. And." He set down his brandy globe, pushed back the black velvet barrel chair, stood. "Can we go home now, please?" he said to Dave.

"Poor child," Amanda said. "You must be exhausted."

"I'm going back to television news," Cecil said. "There, whatever happens, it happens to somebody else."

JOSEPH HANSEN was born in 1923 in Aberdeen, South Dakota. He is best known for his mysteries that feature Dave Brandstetter, a homosexual insurance investigator, although he has also written many non-mystery novels and collections of short stories, including *Living Upstairs* (1993) and *Jack of Hearts* (1995). In the 1960s he published several novels using the pseudonym "James Colton." He lives in southern California.